Many years ago, **Cynthia Cooke** lived a quiet, idyllic life caring for her beautiful eighteen-month-old daughter. Then peace gave way to chaos with the birth of her boy/girl twins. She kept her sanity by reading romance novels and dreaming of someday writing one. With the help of Romance Writers of America and wonderfully supportive friends, she fulfilled her dreams. Now, many moons later, Cynthia is an award-winning author who has published books with Harlequin, Silhouette and Steeple Hill Books.

Cynthia Cooke
and

USA TODAY Bestselling Author

Vivi Anna

LYING WITH WOLVES
and
SEDUCING THE HUNTER

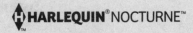

H HARLEQUIN® NOCTURNE™

Recycling programs
for this product may
not exist in your area.

ISBN-13: 978-0-373-60980-2

Lying with Wolves and Seducing the Hunter

Copyright © 2014 by Harlequin Books S.A.

The publisher acknowledges the copyright holders of the individual works as follows:

Lying with Wolves
Copyright © 2014 by Cynthia D. Cooke

Seducing the Hunter
Copyright © 2014 by Vivi Anna

This edition published by arrangement with Harlequin Books S.A.

For questions and comments about the quality of this book, please contact us at CustomerService@Harlequin.com.

® and TM are trademarks of the publisher. Trademarks indicated with ® are registered in the United States Patent and Trademark Office, the Canadian Intellectual Property Office and in other countries.

Printed in U.S.A.

CONTENTS

LYING WITH WOLVES
Cynthia Cooke

I'd like to dedicate this book to my husband, Dale, who has taken this crazy journey with me, loving and laughing all the way.

Chapter 1

As the first streaks of dawn lit the horizon, she ran. Her paws scraped along the fine red dust of the desert floor as she dashed through creosote bushes, snakeweed and prickly pear cacti, her nose filling with the honey scent of graythorn.

She paused, catching a different scent—the tangy musk of fear. Her sharp eyes scanned the area in the lingering darkness as she searched the desert floor for shadows, for movement, for something to chase. And there it was, frozen next to a sage bush, impossibly large ears twitching, its round eyes wide with fear. A jackrabbit.

She gave chase—the rabbit's scent filling her nose, the rapid pounding of its small heart thumping in her ears. The rabbit jumped, launching itself at least ten feet, its long legs propelling it at impossibly fast speeds as it zigzagged through yucca and agave.

Exaltation urged Celia faster. She chased the little creature while the sun, cresting beyond the stark canyons, lit the sky in an explosion of color. Power pulsed through her body, with each step rejoicing in her freedom as she raced through the morning air. She wished she could run like this all day but knew it would be too risky here in the Arizona desert, where people rose with the sun.

Then she heard the sound she'd been so afraid would come.

Just a murmur at first, far in the distance, but then the sound grew louder. Closer.

Humans.

Warily she paused, letting the rabbit get away. Early-morning campers were up ahead in the canyon. She spun, racing away. Too late. Someone yelled a warning to the others. A commotion sounded. The parking lot was just ahead. Her legs, pumping hard, carried her quickly to her car. In the lightening sky, she deftly changed back to her human form, standing naked in the cool morning air until she could reach her clothes inside.

A wolf living among humans was a bad idea. And this was only one of the reasons why. Striking out on her own, leaving the safety of the Colony, was not going to be easy. But for her, freedom from the Colony was worth the price.

Freedom from seeing Malcolm every day, from hearing his voice or sensing him in the forest when she ran, knowing he'd be sleeping with *her* every night—a woman who would give him the control he so desperately craved. Freedom from that was worth any price she had to pay.

Even if she had to live each and every moment hiding her true self from humans and from the demons who were determined to hunt her down and kill her.

Celia Lawson's nerves bunched as she gazed out the large picture window at the red rock mountains. It had been almost two weeks since she was able to transform, to stretch her legs and run. To feel the sweet night air against her face, to chase rabbits and run free. She was trapped in this shop of soaps, lotions and scented candles. Transforming here put her at risk of discovery. Humans were a concern, but the bigger threat were the *Gauliacho*. The demons in shadow form had hunted the shifters for a millennium. They wouldn't overlook her.

She ran her finger across the large red crystal in front of her. The only protection she had from the demons were the crystals composed of dark energy that negated the shifter's energy signature, effectively hiding them from the *Gauliacho* and the lost humans they possessed—the *Abatu*.

The irony wasn't lost on Celia that even though she was free of the Colony, from Malcolm, by leaving the safety of the Colony's borders, she was now trapped in a prison of the shop's four walls, hiding behind the energy of the crystals. Energy only she as the Keeper of the crystals had the power to rejuvenate.

She looked longingly at the mountains one last time.

She couldn't take the chance, even if her skin felt as if it were on fire. She bounced up and down on her feet, anxiety growing within her by the minute. She had never gone this long without making the change to her natural state. Was it the need to run free that had her so wound up or something else?

Something coming.

Abatu? A lost human soul with no will of his own, who didn't have the strength of character to keep the *Gauliacho* from latching on and hitching a ride. *Abatu* were rudderless and easily manipulated and gave the *Gauliacho* a physical form to track the shifters. To search them out and destroy them one by one. There were more of them around lately, almost as if they had her scent but couldn't quite find her.

But as frightening as the *Abatu* could be, it was the *Gauliacho* themselves in their shadow form that struck terror into Celia's heart. She'd dreamed about them as a child, their insidious whispering, the way they'd get inside her mind and stop her cold, turning her muscles to water.

Throngs of people crowded the busy Sedona Street. She should open the door and welcome them into Desert Winds. Thanks to her cousin's recipes of organic soaps and lotions, they were doing a quick and steady business. And she would invite the shoppers in. She just needed…a minute. Pressure built inside her chest, squeezed her lungs and made it difficult to breathe. She needed to run, to escape the walls of the shop, if only for an hour.

Tonight, she promised herself, when the moon was

high in the sky, she would drive deep into the desert where only the coyotes dared roam. She stretched her arms high above her head and turned her shoulders, left, then right until the bones in her back popped. It was times like this that she missed the redwood forests of home, the wide-open meadows and majestic peaks of the jagged, soaring mountains. But when she thought of home, a deep ache settled within her, a longing that twisted and pulled with a sharpness that shredded her insides. Longing for what should have been, and pain for what wasn't.

Pain caused by Malcolm.

Malcolm. His name whispered across her mind, conjured eyes of forest-green and a smile that could melt the coldest ice-covered peaks that surrounded her home at the Colony. She pushed his image away. She would not think of him. She deserved better. Here in this red desert so far from the lush green forests of home was her chance to start over.

The tinkling of the Kokopelli chimes rang as her twin cousins, Ruby and Jade James, burst into the shop. Celia had come to Sedona specifically to find them. She'd grown up hearing about her crazy aunt who'd left the Colony to find adventure and had fallen in love with a human. Together they'd had twin baby girls. She wondered for years what her human cousins were like and if they would they make the change, too.

"You like them?" Ruby asked, pointing to the peacock feathers in her hair. "I loved your eagle feather so much I had to get a feather for myself. Not too many eagle feathers lying around on the ground here, though. But I thought this was real pretty."

Celia smiled and ran her fingertips along the smooth feather twined in her hair. "My mother said this feather would be perfect for me, since I've always wanted to fly away from home and be free."

Ruby laughed. "Really? I can't imagine why. How beautiful your home in the mountains must be. You have to take me there sometime to see it. Plus, I'm dying to meet my aunt Jaya."

"Absolutely," Celia enthused, but she knew she wouldn't. Humans were not allowed into the Colony. Not even if they were married to a shifter, or were a shifter's offspring. Unless those offspring made the change. But with half-breeds, no one ever knew if they would or even when. Ruby and Jade hadn't, and because their mother had died when they were so young, they were completely unaware that the possibility for them to transform into shifters even existed. Which, she supposed, was for the best.

But the reminder of her mother sent a pang of homesickness echoing through her. Celia wished she could see her again or even talk to her. But her mother refused to use modern contraptions, referring to them as the downfall of humanity. Celia sighed. Malcolm believed the exact opposite and filled the village with as many computers and telephones and televisions as he could.

"You are going to love this new concoction we came up with for our lotions," Ruby said, dropping her natural hemp bag on a nearby table with a loud thud. "Not only does it feel incredible, but we've added sandalwood oil, a natural aphrodisiac. Now not only will the wearer feel silky smooth—"

"And relaxed," Jade interceded.

"But it will make them in the mood for love," Ruby said in a singsong voice while holding the lotion under Celia's nose. "Smell."

Celia took a whiff and smiled. "It does smell good." She pulled away. "But since love is not something I'm looking for, I don't think I'll put any on."

"Smart move," Jade said. "Especially after the incantation she put on it."

Celia smiled. She didn't doubt it. She might be able to wield the energy in the crystals, but her cousins could work magic with herbs, oils and spells.

Jade opened a box and handed the bottles to her sister, who strategically arranged them in the window. "Ruby was up half the night practicing—"

Celia flinched as Ruby picked up the dark red crystal Celia had placed in the center of the windowsill facing due north, and moved toward the counter.

Celia lurched forward to stop her. "That can't be moved," she said, and snatched the crystal out of her hand.

Ruby looked up at her, startled. "Why not?" she asked, sounding surprised and a touch confused. She took a step back from the crystal, rubbing her hands across her jeans.

Celia cringed at her too-sharp tone. "I'm sorry." She smiled and tried to soften her words. "I have four of them placed at each compass point of the room for protection. They can't be moved."

"Protection from what?" Jade asked, her icicle-blue eyes narrowing as she studied her.

From the Gauliacho, who want to kill me. But Celia couldn't tell them that. She could never reveal the truth of who and what she was. Not even to them. It was better they didn't know the horrific details of how their mother died, or how easily she could just disappear one day. Even though her aunt, like Celia and her mother, had been a Keeper, the crystals' power hadn't been able to protect her from the demons.

As Keepers, they alone had the gift to rejuvenate the dark energy of the stones and keep the protective force field strong. But as her mother had warned, she couldn't stay away from the Colony for too long. Keeper or not, she would be safe only in the Colony. Aunt Sue's death had been proof of that.

"I'm sorry. Old Native American folklore." Celia forced a smile and spun to place the crystal back in the window.

"No problem," Ruby said, continuing to rub her hands across her jeans. She began rearranging her bottles again. But the happy mood had been broken.

Celia glanced out the window again as an uncomfortable skittering raced once more along her nerves.

Something was definitely coming. *Something or someone.*

Malcolm Daniels sped along the winding desert road through mountains unlike any he'd seen before. And completely unlike the towering ragged granite peaks he'd left behind at the Colony. The deep red of the rocks of the Arizona desert were stunning against the backdrop of blue sky, but the sparse trees and wide-openness of the land left little room for cover against prying eyes. Here there was nowhere to run without being seen. No way to hide.

How could Celia stand it?

He was getting closer to her now. He could feel her—a wave of warmth in the pit of his stomach that spread out to encompass him. Their connection was strong. She might think she could run away from him, but there was no running from the bond they shared. He would find her and he'd make her come back to the Colony. She had to return to rejuvenate the boundary stones. If she didn't, if he couldn't bring her back to the Colony in time, the shifters would die.

He would find her.

Even if she hated him for it.

He touched the string of stones on his wrist, running his finger over the black-and-red crystals that offered protection for three days. Day three was here, and if he didn't find Celia soon, his presence would become known to every demon out there. In physical form and in shadow.

He slowed his truck as he turned the bend on 89A and the town came into view. Small eclectic shops and restaurants lined either side of the highway displaying woodcarvings, paintings, crystals, beads and palm readings in this metaphysical mecca.

He crawled past several stores, each quaint and unique with outdoor tables and pots overflowing with bright flowers. His gaze shot to a storefront displaying an abundance of beauty products. Copper vortexes spun outside the large picture window, but his eyes fixated on the large red crystal sitting on the sill.

A crystal from the Colony.

This was it. *Finally!*

A quarter mile down the street, he found a parking place and pulled into it. His heart was pounding. He rubbed his damp palm on his jeans. He'd wanted to see her. Had thought of nothing else during his three-day journey, but now that he'd found her… How was he going to tell her what had happened to Jaya?

He walked slowly toward the shop, trying to think of words that should never have to be said or heard. What was the best way to break someone's heart?

"I'm sorry…I don't know where to start," he said, practicing, not paying attention when a large man stepped out of a restaurant directly in front of him. Almost plowing into him, Malcolm sidestepped the man, stiffening, his eyes widening. Malevolence, thick and rancid, rolled off the man. An *Abatu*.

Dammit! Malcolm kept his head down and kept going, adrenaline surging through him, kicking up his heartbeat. The *Abatu* hesitated on the curb. Malcolm continued forward, hoping there was still enough energy in the stones on his wrist to keep him shielded.

Through the reflection in the restaurant's large picture window, Malcolm saw the *Abatu* turn toward him, confusion tightening his face for a long moment before he finally spun around and walked away. Malcolm let out a relieved breath. He got by him. *This time*.

If he was going to find Celia and get his crystals regenerated, he'd better do it soon.

Chapter 2

The pressure in Celia's chest was unbearable. Malcolm was here. She could feel him. *Close.* The shop's walls closed in on her as she circled the room. She couldn't face him. Not yet. Damn, why was he here?

Concern widened Jade's all-seeing blue eyes as she watched her pacing from behind the counter. "What is it?" she asked.

"I—" Celia didn't know what to say. How she could explain? *The man who broke my heart into a million pieces is here, and I'm too much of a coward to face him?* Yep, that would sit well. Hell, she wasn't a baby; it was high time she stopped acting like one.

And then she saw him through the window, and her heart leaped into her throat and strangled her.

Jade followed her gaze, then turned back to her, a smile twisting her lips. "Is that *Malcolm?*"

Malcolm. The one Celia could barely think about, let alone talk about. The man who had carelessly ripped out her heart and fed it to the buzzards. How could he still affect her so deeply? She backed away from the window. "Tell him I'm not here."

"What?" Jade blurted, astonished.

"I know, I'm the biggest kind of coward. And I will deal with him. Just…not…yet. Tell him I'm gone. Anywhere. The store. The moon. Please."

"But, Celia, he came all this way. Don't you at least want to know why?"

"No. Not really." Whatever it was, it couldn't be good. Not for her. She shook her head as she backed through the door at the rear of the shop that led into a storage room.

"You can't keep running," Jade said, her voice annoyingly maternal. "One of these days you're going to have to face—" Her words broke off as the bells chimed above the door.

Maybe, but not today. Celia shrank back into the darkness behind the door.

"Hi," Malcolm said to Jade, the warm timbre of his voice reaching inside Celia, twisting and turning, and slicing her heart to shreds.

What was wrong with her? Why was she hiding in the closet like a coward after everything he'd done to her? She'd given him her heart, given him everything she'd had, and he'd tossed it away to marry another woman in his pursuit of power and greed. An arranged marriage in name only, he'd said. As if she'd be okay with that? As if she'd be his "plaything" on the side after all their years together? Anger fueled her once more, reminding her why she fled, why it had been so important to rebuild her life in Sedona. So she could discover who she was, alone, without him, without the influence of the other shifters.

She should go out there. Face him.

"She's hiking," Jade said to him. "In the canyon. She goes there to collect wild herbs for our products. Would you like to try—"

"Are you sure?" he asked. "I could have sworn—"

Celia took a step forward, her hand on the knob ready to pull it open.

"Positive! Really. Here—" Jade picked up the notepad and quickly wrote something down. "Here's a map to where she likes to hike, but I'll be happy to tell her you stopped by. Are you sure you wouldn't like to try—"

"Yes, I'm sure." Impatience rang thick in his voice. "Tell her it's Malcolm and tell her it's important. Critical, in fact. Now, if you could give me directions to this canyon…?"

Celia opened the door enough to peer through and sucked in her breath. How could just the sight of him, his thick dark hair, his muscular frame, that tight butt, still do things to her? It wasn't fair. The universe was testing her, that was all. Jade pointed out the window toward the canyons in the distance and Celia pushed out a relieved breath. He was leaving.

The canyons should keep him busy for at least a few

hours. She leaned her head against the doorjamb. She had only a few hours to pull herself together before he came back. And he would come back. The crystals' dark energy in his bracelet was no longer forming a protective field around him.

Heat seeped into Malcolm's skin and red dirt filled his nose. He'd been walking around this dry dust bowl for more than an hour and had seen no sign of Celia, nor had he felt her anywhere. The longer he looked, the more miserable he'd become. He hated the scruffy bushes and sparse trees of the desert. The mountains, if you could call them that, looked more like deformed fingers pushing up through the earth than actual mountains.

How could Celia stand it here? This dry, barren land couldn't compare to the lushness of their forests back home. Towering cedars and redwoods laced the air with the scent of pinecones and the richness of evergreen. Here all he could smell was dry, dusty dirt.

Perhaps it wouldn't be so hard to convince her to come home after all. Once he found her. If only he could transform and run free. He'd be able to use his wolf senses and cover more ground. But there was nowhere to hide in this large expanse of open land void of thick bushes or large trees. Out here in the open, he could be seen by anyone passing by.

He continued walking down the trail, searching the canyon for another twenty minutes, but still no sign of her. He stared down at the crudely drawn map the girl from the shop had made him. He was where he was supposed to be. Celia wasn't here.

As he looked at the barren land around him, he realized she probably never had been here. He'd been duped. Anger tightened his fists, crumpling the paper clutched in his hand. Time was running out for the shifters at the Colony, and for him. The crystals protecting the Colony needed to be rejuvenated, and she was the only one who could do it. He didn't have time for lies and games. He spun round and stormed back down the path toward his truck. They couldn't waste time like this. He had to get her back to the Colony. He started to run, down one path after another, skirting around a large boulder. He almost plowed into another *Abatu*.

Damn. They were everywhere.

He hurried past, aware of the black shadows surrounding the man's head and what was moving within them. A beefy hand clamped down on his shoulder. Malcolm's eyes squeezed shut. He didn't have time for this. He had to find Celia. He had to tell her the truth about her mother, and about what was happening back home. If he didn't, none of them stood a chance. He jerked out of the man's grasp, turned and crouched down just as the man swung at him. And missed. The second swing didn't. Malcolm felt the blow to his head, like a hammer pounding against a nail. The *ping* echoed through his brain, sending a spray of white dots behind his eyes.

Malcolm wasn't a big man, but he was agile and quick on his feet. He managed to avert the third blow and the fourth, jumping to one side and then the next.

The man swung again, this time landing the blow, knocking Malcolm flat on his back.

The *Abatu* fell on top of Malcolm, pushing the air from his chest in a painful whoosh. He hit him again, a series of blows, pummeling his face. A burning pain stitched his face as his eyebrow split and blood poured into his eyes. He had to get away. He reached forward blindly, searching for the man's eyes, hoping if he could just grab hold, push his fingers deep enough, he could get the beast off him.

The pressure on his chest from the man's knees was becoming unbearable. He felt a rib snap as the man pushed down, leaning forward, using his bulk, his weight, as a weapon. Pain screaming through his system, Malcolm jerked up, snapping his head forward, smacking it into the man's cheekbone and nose with a dull, squishy thud.

The sound of crunching bone was immensely satisfying. He rolled quickly, jumped to his feet, then attacked the *Abatu* viciously with his feet, kicking him over and over until finally he had the upper hand. The demon lay on the ground, groaning in pain and clutching his middle. Knowing he wouldn't be down for long, Malcolm turned and ran back down the hill and toward his truck. He glanced over his shoulder and couldn't believe the *Abatu* was back on his feet, chasing after him. What the hell?

Malcolm reached his truck and unlocked the door, the *Abatu* almost on him. He could practically feel the big man's hot breath rushing down his neck. Without looking, Malcolm jumped inside his truck, slammed and locked the door and turned over the engine. The *Abatu* slapped a meaty hand against the side of the truck with a loud *thunk* as Malcolm peeled off down the road.

He'd made it maybe a mile when he caught sight of his wrist. Staring in disbelief, he hit the brakes and the truck screeched to a stop. The string of crystals, his protection against the *Gauliacho,* was gone. Should he go back and try to find it? Would the *Abatu* still be there? Could he make it all the way home without it? *No!* Every *Abatu* for miles around would be coming for him, and if they didn't get him, the *Gauliacho* would.

He would have to go back.

Like a bug trapped in a jar, Celia paced the small shop. She had to run. But where? This was her home. Her shop. *Her new life.* She wasn't going to let Malcolm chase her out of it. Besides, she couldn't disappear without rejuvenating his crystals. If she did…well, that was more than she wanted to be responsible for. She didn't want anything to happen to him. She just wanted never to have to see him again. Why couldn't he have just stayed where he was?

"It's going to be all right," Ruby said, patting Celia's back.

"I know," she whispered. But she didn't know.

"You want us to stay?" Jade asked.

Celia shook her head, though part of her wanted to say yes. To have them as a buffer. But she had to face Malcolm on her own. They couldn't hear that conversation. "No, thanks." Celia watched her cousins walk out the door and was sorely tempted to call them back.

But she didn't. Instead she squared her shoulders, lifted her chin and sat back down behind the counter to wait for Malcolm to arrive.

By the time Malcolm pulled to a stop in front of the shop, he was furious and hurt everywhere. He was still bleeding, and worse, he'd never found the stones. He was working on borrowed time. Time he couldn't afford to lose. He jumped out of the truck, wincing at the arc of pain slicing through his ribs, and hurried toward the shop.

He pulled open the door, cringing as the bells pierced his throbbing brain. "Celia!" he bellowed.

Silence greeted him. He was about to call her again when the door to the back room opened and she stepped into the doorway. His breath caught in this throat, strangling the yell that had been perched on his tongue.

"Hello, Malcolm," she said, her warm, brandy-laced voice washing over him. She walked into the room. As if nothing had happened. As if he weren't covered in red dirt and blood.

"Celia," he said, not trusting himself to say more.

She walked forward, her long, gorgeous legs hidden beneath a gauzy dark blue skirt. Graceful. Elegant. And yet, as her chocolate-brown eyes caught his, they were filled with wariness. He'd done that to her. Her eyes used to be wide-open and filled with joy. Now they were guarded and hard.

"It's good to see you," he said. She looked beautiful, her copper hair a wild mane bouncing around her shoulders. How he'd missed that hair tickling his skin. How he missed her.

"What are you doing here, Malcolm?" A note of coldness entered her voice, and she clasped her hands tightly in front of her.

"I needed to see you—"

"That's not a good enough reason to intrude on my life. I don't want to see you. To have anything to do with you. Not now. Not ever." Fire flashed amber in her dark eyes as they took in the cut on his brow, the blood on his face. "I would have thought your little field trip into the canyons had made that clear."

Anger fired like a .22 bullet ricocheting off his insides, bouncing within him. "You sent me there on purpose?"

"Of course."

What had happened to her? The Celia he knew never… "You could have got me killed," he said evenly.

"Oh, please, men like you don't die, Malcolm. They live on to make everyone else suffer."

Her sharp words cut him deep. "My protection is gone. I lost the bracelet of crystals in the canyon when I was attacked by an *Abatu*."

"Then you're in a helluva lot of trouble, aren't you?"

He sucked in a quick breath, disbelief thick in his throat. "What are you saying?"

"Get out, Malcolm. And don't ever come back."

He stared at the hard, cold fury in her eyes and wondered what had happened to the soft, caring woman he loved.

He was what happened. He'd made her like this.

"Do you really hate me that much?" he asked, his voice breaking over the words.

"Yes," she said without missing a beat.

He didn't believe it. He couldn't. She was being absurd. Childish. "I made some mistakes…some misjudgments—"

"Don't kid yourself, Malcolm. You are a coldhearted, self-absorbed, power-hungry ass, and as far as I'm concerned, I don't ever want to see you again. So I'll tell you what. I will find your bracelet. I will rejuvenate your crystals. I will do whatever it takes to get you out of here. To go back to the Colony and never return. Is that clear?"

He took in the stiffness in her spine, the hardness in her jaw, the white knuckles of her clenched fingers, and knew there would be nothing he could say or do that would get through to her. And right then, he wished he could leave. Wished he could turn around and not have to face her, not have to break her heart any further. But he couldn't. The Colony needed her. And they needed him to bring her to them.

"I'm sorry, Celia, but I can't leave without you." He took a step toward her, his hand outstretched.

She backed away. "Stay away from me," she warned. "I will hurt you."

"I know that I deserve your anger. I would leave you here in peace, if I could, but I can't."

Uncertainty and fear flashed through her eyes.

"I have to take you back to the Colony."

"Why?" she asked, her voice rising in pitch. She could tell something was wrong; he could see it in the fear creeping into her face. But she didn't want to face it. Didn't want to know. And he wished like hell he didn't have to tell her.

"The Colony needs you," he said, his voice not much louder than a whisper.

She shook her head. "I won't go back. I can't," she insisted, and turned away from him.

He took a deep steadying breath, steeling himself. "You have to, Celia. And not just for me, but for everyone. The stones surrounding the Colony need to be rejuvenated. There isn't much time...."

She was still shaking her head. Her anger and bravado were gone now, replaced by something desperate. Something afraid. "Why can't my mother—" She stopped midsentence as her eyes widened with a whisper of understanding.

He reached into his pocket and pulled out Jaya's necklace, the long purple crystal hanging from a silver chain, and held it out to her. Guilt and shame burned through him. How would he say the words that would shatter her world? How could he confess the ugly truth of what he'd done?

He didn't have to. He knew it was written all over his face.

Her head started swinging violently back and forth as a low keening wail broke free from somewhere deep inside her. The sound exploded into the air, filling the room. "Tell me!" she insisted, her hot, shimmering gaze glued to the purple stone dangling from his hand. "What happened to my mother?"

"I'm so sorry," he whispered, stepping toward her. "She's…she's dead, Celia."

Her loud cry ripped his soul apart. Her knees buckled and she collapsed, slowly falling to the floor. He caught her in his arms and together they fell as she cried heart-wrenching sobs, her hands clutching his shirt as she tried desperately to hang on even as her grief overwhelmed her, pulling her under.

He had done this to her. To her mother, Jaya. To them all.

None of this should have happened. He'd still be Pack leader. Jason would still be his best friend and right-hand man. Jaya would still be alive and regenerating the Colony's crystals and Celia would still be in his house. In his bed. He wouldn't be sitting in a heap on the floor far from home holding the woman he loved while she broke into a million pieces, shattering in his arms. Knowing he'd broken her, and there was no way he'd be able to put it all back to together again. No matter how he wished he could.

Some mistakes could never be fixed.

Chapter 3

Celia's sobs racked her chest, making each breath a painful gulp, as if she were trapped deep under the ocean, drowning on her tears. Wave after wave of debilitating pain crashed over her then, like the tide, rolling out, allowing denial to roll in.

This wasn't right. Couldn't be right. Her mother couldn't be dead.

Awareness hit her and she found herself on the floor, clutching Malcolm, her face pressed against his chest, his shirt clutched in her fists, his scent in her nose. Furious, she tried to push him away, but he held her even tighter as she beat against his chest.

"Get out!" she blurted, and tried to stand, to put as much distance between him and herself as she could. "Get away from me."

"Celia—"

She didn't want to see him, didn't want him to see her like this. He released her and she pushed away from him, quickly getting to her feet. "Don't start. Just leave. Now."

"I can't. I won't leave you. Not like this."

"I don't believe anything you're saying. You're lying. Trying to manipulate me. Trying once more to maneuver everyone around you. I'm not falling for it, Malcolm. I'm over you."

His dark eyes widened with shock. "Do you really think I'd lie about something like this? How could you think that about me? After all we've been through?" He took a step toward her, his hands outstretched.

She backed away from him, brushing up against the counter as her mind finally came to accept what her heart already knew to be true. A fresh wave of pain washed over her. She wrapped her hands around her middle, grasping for something, anything that could explain the unexplainable.

That could make sense of the nonsensical.

"How?" she asked.

"Accident," he murmured. "In the woods."

She heard his words but couldn't fathom them. Couldn't wrap her mind around the possibility. "What am I supposed to do now?" Her kind, their kind, lived a long time. They didn't have accidents. They didn't just die.

Unless the demons…

But that wasn't possible. The *Gauliacho* couldn't get into the Colony; they couldn't get past the crystals.

She started walking around the shop, pacing, moving faster and faster. "I have to get out of here." She swept her hands through her hair. Moving round and round. Back and forth. Muttering to herself.

"We need to go back to the Colony," Malcolm said, his voice calm. Authoritative.

"No. I won't."

"The crystals need to be rejuvenated. It's already been four days since… We need you."

She stopped pacing and looked at him, her eyes narrowing. "Go without me. I will be there when I can. I can't just up and leave right now."

"Celia. You can't send me away."

"Really? You mean like you did to me?"

He stilled, distress crumpling his face.

"Why can't I?" she demanded, not wanting to hear his excuses, his denials.

"I told you. I lost my bracelet in the canyon when an *Abatu* attacked me." He touched the wound on his head. "They've already got my scent. I'm afraid I led them right to you. There will be more coming soon. Coming *here*. We need to leave now or we'll be trapped in this store." He gestured toward the crystals, their protective force field shielding their presence the only thing keeping them safe at the moment.

What he said was true. Soon the *Abatu* would be congregating right outside the door, walking up and down the street, knowing they were close but not knowing where.

"You did this to me," she said, her voice low and

deadly. "They didn't know I was here. They wouldn't have known had you not come."

He hesitated a brief moment as guilt flashed through his eyes. "How could I have not come? I wanted to be the one—"

"The one to break my heart all over again? You like seeing me in pain, Malcolm?" She heard the shrill tone to her voice and knew she was being unreasonable and impossibly unfair, but she didn't care. Hot fury was burning a large path swiftly through her, and he made such a damned good target.

"I love you," he whispered. "I wanted to be here for you."

Her eyes narrowed at his audacity. "You don't know what love is. You're not capable of feeling love."

He took a step back as if she'd physically hit him. "Fine. I guess I deserve that. But you're wrong about me. I only hope one day I can prove it to you."

She looked at him then, really looked at him. At the sincerity in his eyes and the heartbreak and desperation in his voice. Something inside her softened, cooling the anger that had been burning for so long. She turned away. "I can't do this right now."

"I get that. But we have to. We have no choice. You need to come back to the Colony and we need to go together. Now."

There was no use fighting it. She couldn't let everyone back home die at the hands of the *Gauliacho* just because she couldn't stand the idea of spending the next three days trapped in a truck with the man. She looked around the shop that she'd worked so hard to create, that she was so damned proud of, and fresh tears filled her eyes.

"Don't you see, Malcolm? I finally got away. I made my escape from the Colony. This shop—" she gestured wide "—you're standing in is my new life. For the first time ever I'm on my own, discovering who I am, without you. Without the other shifters. Without my—"

She paused as the finality of her words set in. *Without my mother.*

Now she was forced to find her way alone. Without her guidance, no matter how overwhelming it had sometimes been. Fresh pain seared her insides.

"I like it here, Malcolm," she said, pushing through the words. "No, I love it here. And here you've come, riding back into my life, trying to take it all away from me."

"I don't want to take anything from you. I wish I didn't have to. But you don't belong here in this dry desert. You belong at home." *With me.*

He didn't say the final words, but she heard them anyway. She knew him well enough to know what he was thinking. What he was feeling.

"I know I hurt you," he said. "I made you doubt who you are and drove you away. But it's time to come home. I'm sorry about so many things, more than you'll ever know. I just hope I will have the chance to make it up to you. To show you I've changed."

"Malcolm, I don't care if you've changed." Finally her shoulders slumped and she exhaled a breath tasting of defeat and sorrow. As much as she hated to accept it, she would have to go. After a few minutes of silence, she turned back to him.

"I want to know what happened to my mother."

He stilled.

"What kind of accident? We don't have accidents."

He just stood there, his face losing its color.

"Malcolm, what aren't you telling me?"

She could see his pain visibly racking his face. It scared her. "What?"

"Your mom was shot."

His words reverberated around the room.

"Shot? How? Who?"

"Scott. We think. We don't know for sure."

She faltered, leaning against the counter.

"It was an accident."

"How do you accidently shoot someone? I didn't even think... Why would he even have a gun?"

"He was aiming for someone else and missed."

"Who? This is crazy."

"I know."

She looked up at him. "Who could he have wanted to kill so badly, Malcolm?"

And then she thought she knew. It was him. It had to be him. That was why he looked so damned guilty.

"Shay."

She looked up sharply. "Who the hell is Shay?"

"Dean Mallory's daughter."

"You mean your wife?" she said. The caustic taste of her words burned her throat. He actually had the audacity to look confused. His stupidity enraged her all over again. "The woman you threw our lives away for? The woman you'd never met but insisted you must marry? The woman who was supposed to solidify your leadership of the Pack and to hell with everyone else?" She pushed her lips together, refusing to rehash the devastation he'd reaped on her life.

"I'm not married to her."

The softly spoken words ricocheted through her mind. She stared at him as fury hardened her eyes and trapped her tongue.

"She fell in love with Jason before she ever got to the Colony. They're probably married by now and leading the Pack together."

Disbelief overcame her bitterness and broke something loose within her. "But you sacrificed everything, threw everything we had away, just so you could marry this woman and maintain your position of power leading the Pack. And you lost it all anyway?"

"I was an idiot. I know that." His eyes locked on hers. "I am so full of regret and remorse, I doubt I'll ever recover."

"And my mother died because of this woman?"

"Your mother died because Scott or someone in his group wanted Shay dead. They fired, they missed. And now we're all going to pay the price. But you're right, I sent Jason to get Shay, I brought her to the Colony. My plans, my scheming set all this in motion. Help me make amends to you, and to the people of the Colony. Come home, Celia."

She shook her head in disbelief. After all she'd been through, after all he'd put her through, now she had to go back and help *him* make amends. Every fiber within her rebelled bitterly at the thought. More than anything, she wanted to throw him out, to throw him to the *Abatu,* but she couldn't. The other shifters needed her. If she didn't go, if she didn't rejuvenate the crystals around the Colony's perimeter, then within days everyone she knew would be dead.

She couldn't let that happen. She had to go back.

Even if she had to go back with *him.*

Malcolm's stomach folded in on itself as he watched Celia fall apart and desperately try to pull herself back together again. He longed to reach out and hold her, to comfort her and somehow make it all better again. But there was no way he could do that.

No way he could fix this.

He was a man who got things done, who made things happen. Standing on the sidelines helpless was not something he knew how to do. All he did know was that she was the best thing that had ever happened to him, and he'd been lost without her. She grounded him and kept him sane. Kept the shadows at bay. And he'd screwed that up, too. But he'd learned his lesson. Somehow he had to make her see that. And then maybe she just might be able to love him again.

A passerby stopped in front of the large picture window, looked in at them and then hesitated.

An *Abatu.*

"Celia, we really need to go. Now."

Her gaze followed his. She saw the man, and then looked around the shop, her eyes desperately flitting this way and that. "I can't just pick up and leave without notice. I have a business here. I have partners. My cousins."

"You have to. There's already one out there."

"They can't see us beyond the crystals."

"Maybe not. But they know we're around here somewhere. I was still bleeding when I got here. They can smell my blood. Soon there will be more. Then what will we do? Never leave again? Stay in this shop for the next year?"

"I still have my bracelet."

He stared at her, then sat in a corner chair. "You're right. You can leave. This isn't your problem. I'll move in until you're ready to go. Do you have somewhere for me to sleep?"

Her gaze hardened. "Fine. I'll call the twins."

He smiled. "I thought you'd come around to my way of thinking."

"Don't kid yourself, Malcolm. I'm not doing this for you. I couldn't care less what happens to you. I'm doing this for the others. And I will come back one way or another. My life is here."

Was here. He'd make her see that, because if there was one thing Malcolm was good at, it was getting people to come around to his way of thinking.

Celia climbed the stairs to her bedroom above the shop. Unfortunately Malcolm was right on her heels.

"There is no reason for you to come up here," she called behind her.

"Call it curiosity," Malcolm said, suddenly too close for comfort.

"We both know what that did to the cat."

He smiled at her. That wide, charming smile of his that had made her fall in love with him in the first place. She took a deeply annoyed breath and stepped into her small one-bedroom apartment.

"Wait here," she muttered, and went into her bedroom and pulled down an overnight bag from the top of her closet.

"Nice place," he called from the front room.

It wasn't nice; it wasn't not nice. It was convenient.

She stepped into the bathroom, collecting her makeup and toothbrush. When she walked back into the living room, Malcolm was standing by the window, his smile replaced with worry.

"There are three more."

"Surely not hovering in front of the shop."

"No. Walking up and down the street. They know I'm here, they just don't know where."

"It's the blood on your clothes. Here, take that shirt off."

"What will I wear?"

She hurried back into her closet and pulled his T-shirt down off the shelf.

"You kept one of my shirts?" he asked, surprise lifting his voice.

"It was an accident. Don't read anything into it," she said drily.

But he wasn't buying it. A huge smile filled his face as he took the shirt. He stripped out of the dirty one and she couldn't help staring. She'd always loved his chest, sculptured and bronzed. She knew every plane, every soft spot, *intimately.*

And dammit if a part of her didn't still long to reach out and touch him once again. To run her fingers over the hard ridges of his muscles and feel them flex beneath her touch. He might be an ass, but he was a damned good lover. And they had been real good together.

She looked up and his eyes caught and held hers. He knew what she'd been thinking. He knew her *that* well. Too well. She might be a fool where Malcolm was concerned, but she wasn't a pushover. "Just because things didn't work out for you with that woman doesn't mean you can come running back to me and I'll take you back."

"Never thought you would," he said, then broke into that easy smile. "Though a man can hope."

"Are you ready?" she asked, losing her patience.

"Baby, I was born ready."

"Then let's go."

With his dirty shirt in her hand, they went back down the stairs and into the shop. Even more men were in the street. Malcolm hovered by the window. "Any chance you have another bracelet?"

"Nope. There weren't a lot of them to begin with. Besides, honestly, with that many out there, I'm not sure how well the bracelet will work."

"What are you saying?"

"We're going to have to make the change. They can't smell us in our true form. We can run out the back, down the road to the hills beyond."

"But it's only dusk and there are people everywhere. We will be seen."

"What choice do we have? If we wait any longer, as soon as we walk out the door they'll pounce."

"Have you changed here before?" he asked.

"No."

"Have you hiked up into those hills? Are they very secluded?"

"No, and I don't know."

"Well, we can't very well run all the way back to the Colony."

"I'll have Jade meet us in the canyon with your truck."

"What about your car?"

"I'll leave it here. I'm coming back, Malcolm. This is my life now. This is where I belong, and you and the others are just going to have to accept that."

He nodded, but she could see in the stubborn glint in his eyes that he wasn't accepting anything. She picked up the phone and called Jade, telling her what she needed her to do.

"Does she know about us?" Malcolm asked.

"No."

"Then how are you going to explain this?"

"I have no idea. We'll need to put our clothes in a bag on the counter next to your keys and my overnight bag. She'll take them and drive your truck into the canyon and leave it there for us. Her sister, Ruby, will follow her and bring her back."

"What if they hang around and wait for us? What if they see us?"

"We'll just have to make sure that doesn't happen."

He glanced once more out the window at the growing number of *Abatu* walking up and down the street. "You realize there are a million ways this can go wrong."

"Yep. But we only need one way for it to go right."

"Here, give me the shirt," Malcolm said, and dumped the trash out of the metal trash can onto the floor. Celia threw the shirt inside the can and then he doused it with the oil from her oil lamp on a nearby table and set the shirt ablaze.

"Make sure you don't burn my shop down," she said.

"You just get undressed and leave this to me."

"Fine," Celia said, but she wasn't fine. She didn't want to do this. She didn't want to leave and she certainly didn't want to strip in front of him. It was stupid, she knew that. She'd undressed in front of Malcolm a hundred times before, and yet this time it was so much harder.

She tried to be nonchalant, to act as if it were nothing as her fingers fumbled over that first button of her shirt. But it wasn't. Without looking at him, she pulled her shirt off, folded it and placed it in the bag. Next came her skirt. This was no big deal, she told herself, even though she knew it was a lie.

Malcolm's eyes were on her. She could feel his gaze boring into her skin as he watched her every movement. "Do you mind?" Her eyes narrowed with annoyance.

"You're a beautiful woman, Celia. You can't blame a man for wishing."

"Turn around," she snapped.

"Fine."

He did, and within seconds her clothes were in the paper sack, and her purse and keys were lying on the counter next to her overnight bag. They were lined up and ready for the twins, who should be here within a matter of minutes.

She unlocked the back door, opened it a crack and hoped, not only for herself and Malcolm, but for the whole Pack that her plan would work. She began walking around the room, concentrating on the feel of her steps, the wood beneath her feet, her breath deep and steady, the pattering of her heartbeat, the pulsing of her blood. Each part of her, changing, *transforming.*

Her vision sharpened in the semidarkness until she could see clearly into each dark corner. She smelled the subtle differences in the hundreds of delicate scents used in the products they sold—the candles, the incense, the lotions and oils.

And the *Abatu* outside.

She dropped down onto all fours. Malcolm was beside her, his powerful energy filling her. It had been a long time since they'd run together, since she'd felt the tenuous strings connecting them. As they drew her to him, to his power and strength, she felt compelled to lean into him. To let him guide her. She fought the pull. She wouldn't fall for it again.

With her nose, she nudged open the back door and left the shop, walking onto the narrow street behind it. Malcolm was close on her heels. They moved slowly at first, getting a feel for their surroundings, the scents and sounds around them. The location of every *Abatu* and each human. There were so many.

They moved steadily down the alley behind the shops, sticking to the shadows, their nails clicking against the asphalt. They passed cautiously by a large Dumpster behind a busy restaurant halfway down the alley. A man reeking of alcohol and body sweat was sprawled next to it. His eyes opened as they passed, saw them and started to scream.

Spotted. Celia cringed. Back doors opened. Blinds lifted, curtains moved. *Abatu* were everywhere. Moving toward them, trying to capture their scent. They ran down the alley toward the hills and safety.

People were pointing. Staring. Some with amazement. Some with disbelief. Some with horror. They moved quickly, not wanting to burst out into a full run in front of everyone, but the time for not drawing attention to themselves was over.

A police cruiser turned down the alley, a mounted spotlight capturing them in its hundred-watt halogen glow. This was it. Their only chance. They took off running, fast and hard. Sounds of people screaming as they scampered away filled the air, boots slapping against pavement behind them, the squeal of tires, the burning smell of rubber.

Finally they reached the end of the street and tore up the side of the hill, bolting up the embankment. Running hard. Running fast. There were a million ways for this to go wrong. They'd only just begun, and Celia wasn't sure they were going to be able to make it.

Below them on the highway, people stopped their

cars and stared at them, two wolves racing up the hill, chased by the police. Their shouts filled the night air, some with excitement, others of fear. Soon there would be a party of men with guns searching for them, not because of what they'd done, but because of what people were afraid they would do.

When they crested the top of the hill, Celia stopped and turned back, taking one last look at the cop car parked at the bottom of the hill, the cops on their radios calling for backup, the rear door of her shop swinging wide-open as *Abatu* filed inside, tracking their scent.

She hoped and prayed they wouldn't touch Ruby when she arrived to pick up the keys to Malcolm's truck and their clothes. If only she could warn her somehow. But then she saw a cop go into the shop, and she hoped he'd take care of them and lock up behind him. Though that was probably too much to hope for.

She heard a bark behind her, turned and saw Malcolm waiting impatiently for her at the top of the ridge. He was right; they still had a long way to go before reaching the rendezvous point. Reluctantly she pulled her gaze away from the shop. It wouldn't be the last time she saw it, she promised herself, then tore off after Malcolm into the night.

They crested the next hill and disappeared into the mountains, running fast and free. Sand shifted beneath her feet as she bolted up the mountainside. Small animals froze in fear or scurried from their path. They ran through the canyons, around, up and over mountains, following the moon as it rose higher and higher in the sky. Finally she was running free, stretching her muscles, breathing deep the sweet desert air. And all she wished was that she was back in her shop, not having to face the horrors to come. The thought that she could be trapped in the Colony; the fact that her mother was dead.

She pushed the thoughts from her mind as they dropped down into a dry riverbed traveling its meandering path up to the red rock canyon, where hopefully by now Ruby had already left Malcolm's truck and was long gone.

Malcolm.

She didn't have to look to see if he was there; she could feel him next to her. His emotions were wide-open and easy to read in a way they hadn't been in a long time. Their connection was stronger than ever. She tried to block it. She didn't want to feel him, even if he had changed. Even if he really was sincere about wanting to make amends.

Even if he really did love her.

So what? It didn't matter if he loved her or not. Some love wasn't worth having. It was too late for them. There was too much damage between them. Too much to forget or forgive. What she needed to focus on now was her future, and how she could save the Colony without becoming trapped there.

Chapter 4

"Did you see that?"

Ruby's eyes popped open as her sister, Jade, pushed on her shoulder. It was the middle of the night and a chill had seeped into the air and under her skin. They'd dropped off the truck as their cousin Celia had asked but then parked out of sight down the road and walked back up the hill to keep an eye on the truck. Something was wrong with their cousin, and Ruby knew Celia wouldn't let them help her. She was hiding something from them, something big.

Ruby shook herself fully awake and yawned. "What?" she asked.

"I saw something," Jade whispered.

She stared into the darkness and repositioned against the boulder, trying to find a smooth spot. "Where?"

"There." Jade pointed.

Ruby peered into the darkness lit only by the blue glow of a full moon. "Are those wolves?"

"Or very big dogs."

"Shit." Ruby rubbed her arms. "We've been out here a long time. Who knows what kinds of animals roam the desert at night? What is taking Celia so long?"

"Who knows?" Jade said. "She was too cryptic on the phone. I hope she's okay."

"Me, too. She's in some kind of trouble, I just know it," Ruby said. "My scalp has been prickling all day, and you know that only happens when something bad is about to happen."

"I know, I know," Jade said. "But after that huge mess at the shop, why do we have to be so sneaky? Someone broke in and trashed the place, and her apartment upstairs, too. Add that to her phone call to bring her a vehicle and clothes in the desert, well, it would be very logical for us to stay and tell her about the shop and demand some answers."

"True," Ruby agreed, and sighed. "But if she wanted us to know about it, she would have told us already."

"Maybe we should respect that and wait for her to tell us what she's hiding instead of spying on her."

"I would, if it wasn't for what happened at the shop," Ruby whispered. "That and the fact that my scalp is dancing all over my head. As long as she doesn't find out we're spying, no harm, no foul, right?"

"I suppose. She's definitely been hiding something. Even I could tell that, and my scalp doesn't dance."

"Look!" Ruby gestured into the dark ahead.

Celia and the man they had seen in the shop earlier walked out from behind a large outcropping of rocks. *Naked!*

"Well, would you look at that?" Jade whispered, amazement ringing in her voice.

"They don't even have a blanket or anything," Ruby added.

"That is weird."

"Doubly weird."

Celia opened the back door of the truck, took out the sack of clothes and quickly dressed, glancing around her as she did.

"What in the world is going on?" Ruby whispered. "How did they get here? They aren't even wearing shoes."

"And it's not as if they look all that…friendly to me. If you know what I mean," Jade said, her eyebrows raised in that knowing look.

"I know," Ruby agreed. "I thought she couldn't stand that guy. She didn't even want to see him. Hmm. Something weird is definitely going on."

Celia and her man friend climbed into the truck and drove away.

"Is that it?" Ruby asked as they hurried back down the road toward their car.

"Well, what did you expect?"

"I don't know. An answer or something. We've been here for hours."

"But they never even saw us."

"True," Ruby agreed, and sighed. "Now what? Did

we spend all night out in the desert for nothing? What do we do now?"

"Now we follow them."

"What?"

"Obviously something is going on here, something wrong. Celia's in trouble," Jade said. "If we don't help her, who will?"

"You're right. Let's do it."

Several hours later, Celia woke to Malcolm's hand softly stroking hers. In the haze of half sleep a feeling of warm contentment spread through her at the feel of his touch. She started to reach for him, but then the haze cleared and the memory of why he was there surfaced, bringing with it the shadows of regret and pain.

She opened her eyes and the wide expanse of freeway greeted her as she stared out the windshield. They were barreling through the desert, heading north toward home.

"How are you feeling?" he asked, the warm tendrils of his voice reaching deep within her.

"Tired," she admitted, though she didn't know how that was possible considering all she'd done was sleep since she climbed inside his truck the night before. "Where are we?"

"California. You've been out for seven hours. You hungry?"

"A little," she admitted.

"I was hoping you'd say that." He smiled and, for a second, it was hard not to want to smile with him. To just let go of the anger and the darkness growing within her. To succumb to the comfort she knew he could offer. But she wouldn't. She had to be strong. If she let him in, even for a second, he'd only hurt her again. All she had to do was get back to the Colony without letting him back under her skin. Two days. Three at the most. She could do this.

And then what? The stones surrounding the Colony had to be rejuvenated every two weeks. If they didn't find someone else who could do it, she would be stuck there. *Always*.

"There's a truck stop a few miles up ahead."

"Sounds good." She grabbed a book out of her bag, hoping the story would absorb her and draw her attention away from him. As long as he didn't talk to her. Look at her. *Touch* her. She would be fine. A few minutes later, she threw the book back in her bag. It was no use. She could smell him. His rich, spicy scent reached inside her and settled in. She could feel him, his warmth, his strong presence even from across the cab. It made her want to touch him. Obviously she was a lost cause. Pathetic. Hopeless. And when it came to Malcolm Daniels, she always had been.

"Things are going to be a little different when we get back home," he said, thankfully breaking into her thoughts.

"Why's that?"

"Jason is the Pack leader now. Losing you wasn't the only mistake I made. Things got a little out of hand. I made some really bad—"

"I'm sorry to hear that," she said, interrupting him. She was curious and tempted to let him finish, to sit there and let him ramble on about his mistakes and how sorry he was. To find out what he'd done. But did she really want to know? All that mattered was Scott had shot her mother and she would make sure he paid for it. She needed to focus on that and finding another Keeper, so she could get back to her new home. And that meant not getting embroiled in Malcolm's life again. So instead of letting him finish, she pointed at the diner up ahead. "Is that it?"

"Yes," he said, obviously confused and a touch… what? She looked at the sadness on his face. Disappointed? Yeah, she knew that feeling well.

"Good, I'm starving."

A few minutes later, Malcolm watched Celia from across the small laminated table, trying valiantly to ignore him. She was determined not to make eye contact or even to speak. He could see how much pain she was in, and it was killing him. He brought this on her with his stupidity and greed. And he'd lost everything because of it. Somehow he had to make things right. He could live without being Pack leader, but he couldn't live without her. He wouldn't. But how could he get her back?

"So tell me about Sedona?" he asked, breaking the painful silence growing between them.

She glanced up at him, her eyes filled with indifference. "It's beautiful."

"Sparse."

"And yet incredible with the red rock mountains and

canyons. I never knew a place like that existed. So different from home, and yet so beautiful in its own way."

Their food arrived—two plates heaping with thick slices of bacon, fluffy eggs and fried potatoes that were actually quite good. Silence grew once more between them as they ate. A wide chasm he didn't know how to cross.

As he finished his food, fatigue fell over him, pulling him down. He wanted to tell her about the Colony, about his role in what had happened to her mother. He should be the one to tell her. But she wasn't making it easy on him. And he supposed he shouldn't start a conversation like that now. Not when he hadn't slept for almost twenty-four hours. For that he'd need all his wits about him. But he also knew that as soon as she stepped foot inside the Colony's borders, someone would tell her. He sighed and his eyes drifted closed.

"So how did Jason become Pack leader?" she asked, her tone hesitant.

His eyes popped open. He groaned inwardly and took a deep slug off his coffee. "I've made more than a few mistakes," he began. "Starting with wanting to marry Shay."

"It was a stupid plan," she interrupted. "And one I still haven't forgiven you for. But I'm glad it happened."

"You are?" he asked, stunned. "Why?"

"Because it pushed me out of my comfort zone and out of the Colony. I love Sedona. I love my new life and I'm not going to give it up. I'll rejuvenate the stones, but you are going to have to find another Keeper. I'm not staying there. Make no mistake."

A chill filled him at her words. "There is no one else. You know that."

"There could be. We will need to test everyone now, just to be certain."

He watched her as he finished his coffee. She was so sure, so determined, and he knew that even as a Keeper she couldn't survive outside the Colony on her own. Not for long. It wasn't just the crystals that protected them; it was something with the magnetic pull of the mountains surrounding them. There was nowhere else like it.

He scraped his hand across his face. "I want you to be happy, Celia, I really do. But I'm concerned about your safety. You can't stay—"

"I can make it work."

Steely determination filled her eyes. He decided not to push it. Not now. Instead he placed his hand over his mouth as he yawned. "Honestly, I'm not sure how things got so off track."

"Oh, really?" she said drily.

"Everything was going so well…but then you left, and it all just snowballed after that. I wish…" He couldn't say how he wished everything could go back to the way it was before he screwed it all up. "I just don't know how it all went so wrong," he said finally.

She stared at him, her gaze hard. "I do. Scott started making noises—criticisms and complaints—and as his number of followers grew you got scared and made some really stupid decisions."

He looked at her, his eyebrows raised.

"Hard to imagine, I know. But you're not infallible, Malcolm. You're not perfect."

Frustration surged through his veins. "Why couldn't Scott and the others see that bringing technology to the Colony—computers, telephone, TVs, the internet, all these fabulous changes the rest of the world takes for granted—has helped everyone? The economy in the Colony is thriving. People have opened online businesses—we know more now about the outside world than we ever have before. We had become stagnated and inflexible, but with my changes, my vision, all that has changed. Look how much we've grown in just the past year."

"True, Malcolm. But the downside is people can now see what it's like on the outside. They know what they're missing—places they will never be able to visit, jobs they will never be able to have. What once was a sanctuary now feels like a prison. Our window to the outside world, the internet, the television, did that to us."

"I've heard that before, but I don't get it." He pushed out a clipped breath. "I've been out here and I can't wait to get back home. It's dirty. There are people everywhere, and frankly, they're rude with no respect for their surroundings or each other. How could you stand living with them? Living on the outside for so long?"

Finally she brightened. A sparkle entered her eyes and his insides twisted at the sight of it. "It was unbelievable, Malcolm. I loved it. The freedom. The energy. The artistic expression through everything from clothes to food. I saw things I'd never seen before, hell, never even imagined before. Movie theaters! They're amazing and breathtaking. Giant TV screens with sound so loud it moves right through you.

"Foods like you've never dreamed of. And you should see some of the houses, boats and cars. Unbelievable. The excitement, innovation and enthusiasm are intoxicating. People can cut loose and let their guard down and do things they might not usually do when they're at home because they can actually go out to a restaurant or nightclub and not see a single person they know. Can you imagine how freeing that is? To be able to go out to dinner with a friend and not have everyone in town know who that person was and what you were talking about."

"No," he said, and couldn't help the bitterness in his voice. That was the one thing he hated about the Colony—the total and complete lack of privacy. Not only did everyone in town know who he was with and what he was doing, but hell, they were certain they knew what he was thinking. "I can't imagine."

"I really love it and I will go back. That, I can assure you."

At that moment, he believed she would. And it scared the hell out of him. "But wasn't it hard? Always hiding who you are? Never having anyone to run with, to talk to about…things with?"

She hesitated a moment, then looked him square in the eye. "Not at all."

She was lying. He knew her well enough to see that. A yawn overtook him once more. His lack of sleep was finally catching up to him. "We should get going," he said. "We're going to need to drive in shifts so we can get back as soon as possible."

"No problem."

He handed her the keys and paid the bill. They left the restaurant. As they approached his truck, he climbed into the back and stretched out on the seat. "Wake me up in six hours," he said as sleep reached for him. Had she really loved the outside world that much? Would she risk her life to stay out here? Jaya had warned her. He'd warned her. And if anything happened to her because he'd driven her away...

He shook off the thought. The Colony was not a prison. And it didn't feel that way. Her words echoed through his fuzzy mind. *Our window to the outside world, the internet, the television, did that to us. You did that to us.* The words she did not say but meant. He honestly thought what he'd been doing for the Colony had been the best for all of them. Was it possible he'd been that wrong?

He thought of Jaya begging him not to bring the internet into the Colony. The people of the Colony, and especially Jaya, didn't understand or appreciate that he'd done it all for them.

Only now Jaya was dead because of his feud with Scott—the man who had tried to boot him out and take over the leadership of the Pack for himself. They'd both gone too far and made mistakes that could never be undone.

Jade and Ruby dipped farther into the booth behind Celia, listening to their conversation, waiting until they both got up to go.

"Did you hear that?" Ruby asked.

"She is going to kill us," Jade added.

"It was as though she knew we were here or something. It was creepy."

"Don't be ridiculous. She didn't know. We should have announced ourselves."

"What? And pop up like a demented jack-in-the-box stalker and say, 'Surprise! We've been following you, spying on you, listening to you talk about how much you like going into restaurants and not seeing a single soul you know.'" Ruby covered her face with her hands.

"Okay, so now what?"

"Now we should go home. Leave them alone. You heard her. She's going to come back to us."

"Yeah, as soon as they find a Keeper, whatever the hell that is. We don't even know where they're going. What if she never comes back? How will we find her?"

Ruby sighed. "I don't know. She never really said where 'home' was, did she?"

"The mountains."

"Well, that narrows it down," Ruby said, not bothering to hide her sarcasm.

"Okay, so again, what now?"

"Let's just follow them a little farther. Just until we're sure."

"Sure of what?"

"I don't know, but we've come so far already, and I still can't shake the feeling that something's wrong."

Jade sighed. "All right. But let's run into the gas station next door, use the facilities and grab some doughnuts."

"Doughnuts?" Ruby said with a crinkled nose.

"Fine, you grab a whole-grain muffin. I'm grabbing doughnuts. I'm starving."

"One day all that sugar is going to catch up with you and then you'll be sorry."

"Ha! Fine, I'll deal with it then, but look how much enjoyment I'm getting in the meantime."

Ten minutes later they were back in the car, loaded up with food, drinks, extra T-shirts, ball caps—everything they needed to keep an eye on their cousin. They tore out of the parking lot and down the highway looking for that old pickup truck. But before they could find it, Ruby's phone rang.

"Ruby, where are you?"

Ruby turned to Jade, placing her hand over the receiver. "It's Mark," she whispered, her stomach doing a massive flip-flop.

"What does he want?" Jade demanded under her breath.

Ruby shrugged. "Jade and I are taking a little vacation," she said, forcing lightness into her voice. "Why?"

"Someone broke into your shop last night," Mark said. "I'm afraid there is quite a bit of damage."

"Oh, no," she said, feigning shock.

"It doesn't look as if anything was taken, but there is stuff everywhere."

"All right. Thanks, Mark, for letting me know."

"When will you be back?"

Ruby looked at Jade. "Oh, I don't know. We're taking a much-needed break."

"I think you should come back now. You need to file a report. Where are you?"

"Honestly, Mark, we're in Vegas. Just for a few days. We'll be back as soon as we can. Can you lock up for me and keep an eye on the place?"

He hesitated. "Sure."

"Thanks, Mark. I really appreciate it. Thanks for calling." She disconnected the line.

"Vegas?" Jade asked.

"A girl can dream, can't she? Besides, that should keep him from calling me for at least a day or two."

"You are way too nice to that guy," Jade said. "You should have given him the old heave-ho a long time ago."

"I've tried. You know that. He just doesn't take a hint."

"Perhaps a two-by-four?"

Ruby smiled. "I would, but he's a cop. He can and does invent any reason to come by and see me. All the time."

"I'm just worried about you. That guy is freaky."

"I know," Ruby admitted as anxiety skittered along her nerves. "But no matter how distant I am, even rude sometimes, he just won't go away. I've turned down his past three dinner invitations, and yet he still keeps coming around."

"All right. Once we get back we'll have to work on that. No more being nice."

Ruby nodded. "I know, and you're right. Sometimes guys like that do need a two-by-four."

One of the best investments Mark Goodwin had made was the GPS tracker he'd installed under the dash of Ruby's car. For the past three months, he had known everywhere she had gone, and how long she'd stayed there. And right now, by accessing the web through his phone, he'd tracked their location all the way into California.

He smiled as he pulled up behind the sisters on the freeway. He watched Ruby as she talked to him on the phone, as she lied to him. Rage lit a fuse inside him. What, did she think he was stupid? A lovesick puppy panting at her feet? Vegas! She was up to something, and it looked as though he was finally going to be able to prove what he'd always suspected about her.

Last night when the call had come in about the wolves behind the complex her shop was in, he'd known this was the chance he'd been waiting for. But by the time he'd got to the shop, he only caught a glimpse of the wolves high up on the hill with the Wildlife and Animal Control officers pursuing them through the canyons.

The back door of Ruby's shop had been wide-open. The place had been trashed, but the cash register hadn't been touched. Obviously someone had been after something. More secrets. He'd finished his shift and gone after her. He had done everything he could to insinuate himself into her life, knowing Ruby wouldn't be able to keep her mouth shut for long, and here she was lying to him. Anger tightened his knuckles around the steering wheel. But he knew it wasn't her fault, knew Ruby would be so much more manageable if it wasn't for that overbearing and controlling sister of hers. He had to do something about that.

Chapter 5

For hours Celia drove down the long freeway, trying to pretend she was alone. That she wasn't going home to bury her mother. That her life hadn't got so terribly off course. Every now and then her gaze would move to the rearview mirror and she'd catch a glimpse of Malcolm sleeping. Was he truly sorry? Maybe he had changed. He seemed to be different somehow. Not so on edge and more relaxed and comfortable with himself. Was it possible that no longer being Pack leader had freed him?

He'd always taken his responsibilities too seriously. People thought he was an egomaniac, but the truth was, he cared too much. He had grandiose ideas for the Colony and moved heaven and earth to implement them, no matter who he hurt. But now that he was no longer in charge, perhaps he could use his ambitions to contribute instead of letting them destroy his life.

She shook her head and focused back on the road. There was a rest stop a mile ahead. She would stop. Get a soda. Stretch her legs and take a break. She had to stop thinking this way. She was on a slippery slope and falling fast. He was the enemy. He'd turned his back on her and threw away their life together for a woman he'd never met. For his zealous need to be in control. The moment she started excusing what he'd done would be the second she let him back into her heart and the instant when she'd be lost. Once more, she'd be living for Malcolm and what Malcolm wanted, putting her own dreams for a family on a back burner. Losing what she wanted and who she was in her desire to make him happy. She wouldn't fall into that trap again.

She parked the truck and walked into the bathrooms. She was stiff and sore, and they still had a long way to go. When she came back out, a car was parked next to them. Two men were circling Malcolm's truck, peering into the windows at Malcolm sleeping in the backseat. She froze.

Abatus.

"Blazes," she whispered under her breath. She looked around the parking lot. There was a large semitruck, the driver nowhere in sight. A station wagon filled with kids, and a couple of young girls sitting on the grass playing with a puppy. All of them oblivious of the men pulling on the truck's door handles and knocking on the windows.

Malcolm sat up in the backseat rubbing his eyes,

shock filling his face as he realized where he was and what was happening. He climbed into the front seat and got behind the wheel, fumbling for the keys in the ignition. But they weren't there. They were in her pocket. His troubled gaze met hers through the windshield.

He was worried. He might try to hide it, but she could read it as plain as day. She walked purposefully toward the men. "Excuse me," she said loudly, hoping to draw as much attention as she could. "Can I help you?"

Surprised, the men turned to her, gave her the once-over and then dismissed her, turning back to the truck. They tried once more to get in, pulling on the doors, pushing on the cracked windows. "Like a dog with a bone," she called out. "Would you mind stepping away from my truck?"

After being ignored once more, she bolted forward, knowing with her bracelet they would not see her as a threat or a target. She used that to her advantage as she scooted right up to the first guy, the smallest guy, with an unkempt beard and long unruly gray hair, and kicked him hard in his oversize gut.

He doubled over with a loud grunt. Celia kicked him again, using all her force to knock him to the ground, hoping the truck blocked what she was doing to him from the eyes of the young girls on the grass. The second man came running around the front of the truck toward her. Malcolm opened the door, jumped out and joined the fight.

He took a swing at the much-bigger second man, but suddenly the first man was up and back in the game. He was strong, and even though she got in the first kick, the *Abatu* soon had the upper hand. Malcolm was doing his best, but soon they were both taking a beating. Celia hit the ground, landing hard on her butt, when out of nowhere Ruby was there, baseball bat in her hand and Jade right behind her.

Ruby swung the bat, hitting the *Abatu* hard across the shoulders, giving Celia the leverage she needed to volley a new attack. With the help of the twins, soon both men were lying on the ground, groaning.

"Are you okay?" Ruby asked, out of breath, her face flushed with her exertion.

Celia threw her arms around her cousin. She was never so thankful to see anyone in her life. "Where did you come from?" she asked, astonished that they were even there.

"From right over there," Ruby said, and pointed to her old maroon sedan on the other side of the parking lot.

Celia laughed. "I see that, but what are you doing here?"

"We were worried about you," Jade said, stepping forward and wiping her hands on her jeans. "And with good cause, too, from the looks of things. What are you doing way out here? And why were these men attacking you?"

Celia's gaze slid away. "I don't know. But I have to go home. My mom…" She couldn't finish. Couldn't say the awful truth. She glanced over at Malcolm, who was watching the two men on the ground, waiting for them to get back up and go at them again. "She died."

"Oh, no! Celia, why didn't you tell us?" Ruby enveloped her in a big hug. Her embrace and concern had Celia's tears threatening to fall all over again.

"I don't know," Celia admitted. "Everything just happened so fast. I…I just can't believe you are here."

"Us, either," Ruby said. "But it's a good thing we were. What was with these thugs? Why would they attack you out the blue like that?"

"I have no idea," Celia lied, with an uneven breath.

"Maybe we should call the police," Jade suggested.

"No," Ruby and Celia both said in unison.

Surprised, Celia turned to Ruby. Her eyebrows rose questioningly.

"I don't want Mark to hear about it," Ruby admitted on a deep breath.

"Your stalker cop?" Celia didn't like the sound of that. "Is that guy still causing you trouble?"

Jade nodded. "He just called a little while ago. There is something seriously wrong with that man."

"That may be true. Okay, that *is* true," Ruby corrected after noticing the look Jade was giving her, "but he called to tell us that someone broke into the shop. Messed it up quite a bit. So it's actually a good thing he called. For once. He locked it up for us. I'm sorry to dump more bad news on you, Celia."

Celia sighed, not in the least surprised. She'd seen the *Abatu* enter through the back door and just hoped they hadn't caused too much damage. "I supposed you'd better get back, then."

"No way. We're coming with you. Obviously you need us." Ruby looked pointedly at the two men on the ground.

Celia glanced at the troubled look on Malcolm's face and knew he had cause to be concerned. No matter how much she might welcome her cousins' company right then, humans were not welcomed in the Colony. They couldn't be. The Colony couldn't take the chance that anyone would discover their secret, and a whole town full of wolves was a big secret to keep.

"I really appreciate that," Celia said honestly. "But I don't know how long I'll be. There's a…a lot to do. If you could just get the shop back in shape and opened for when I get back, that would be awesome."

Ruby opened her mouth to protest, but Jade stepped forward and placed a hand on her sister's arm. "We totally understand. You can count on us."

Celia sagged with relief. "Thanks, guys. I really appreciate it."

"But what about these two?" Ruby asked. "Who are they? Why would they attack you, and why would someone break into our shop to begin with?"

"I have no idea, and I really can't think about that now." Celia gave them each a big hug, holding on a little tighter and a little longer than she should. "I've really got to get going."

"All right, if you're sure," Ruby said, hesitation ringing loud in her voice.

"I'm sure. I'll see you soon." Celia kissed them both on the cheek, then handed Malcolm the keys. They got into the truck and Celia waved goodbye as they drove out of the parking lot and hoped with all her might that it wouldn't be the last time she saw her cousins.

"You think they'll go back to Sedona?" Malcolm asked, his voice sounding doubtful.

"Why wouldn't they?" Celia said, watching them until they were out of sight.

"Because obviously they followed us here from the canyon."

Celia felt her eyes widen as the implications of his words set in. "You think they saw us?" she asked at length.

"I think they saw something or they wouldn't be here now."

"Blazes!" Celia thought about her and Malcolm walking out of the canyon without a stitch on. How was she going to explain that?

"I must admit, though," Malcolm said with a grin. "I sure am glad they were here."

"Me, too. Truthfully, I wish they could come back with us," she said, her chin lifting. "They're my family. They mean a lot to me, and I hate lying to them."

"You know that could never happen," he said evenly.

"Why not?" she shot back, her temper flaring. "Their mother was my aunt. They have just as much right to be there as any of the rest of us. They have shifter blood in them. They could change at any time. And then what? Who would be there to protect them from the *Gauliacho?*"

"I understand your argument. But we can't have humans in the Colony. If word got out… If people knew… There'd be no place for us. You know that."

She flinched and went stony-faced, then turned toward the window. She did know. And she understood.

But that didn't mean she had to like it. "They're the only family I have left now, Malcolm."

"Come here," he said softly.

"What?"

He patted his shoulder. "Lean on me. You always can no matter how much you hate me. We've been friends forever and I'll always be there for you. I may not be blood, but I am your family."

Against her better judgment, she rested her head on his shoulder. And he was right, she did feel better. And no matter how much they hurt each other, they had loved each other since they were kids. They always would be family.

But sometimes even that wasn't enough.

From his vantage point in the rest-stop parking lot, Mark watched Ruby's cousin drive away and Ruby and Jade follow not long after. Why were they following her? And way the hell out here? He hadn't had the chance to meet Celia, but from what he'd observed, there was something off with her from the start. He drove past the shop several times during his shifts, and the woman never seemed to leave the place. Over and over, he would see her standing at the window, staring out at the canyons. She was creepy.

The two men picked themselves up off the ground and got back into their car. Mark had to admit watching Ruby slam that guy with the baseball bat was pretty impressive. He didn't know she had it in her. He pulled his car behind the two men's vehicle, effectively blocking them in. He flipped open his badge and approached the driver's side of the car. He knocked on the window with two knuckles.

"You mind telling me what all that was about?"

They didn't answer. Didn't move. Just stared straight ahead.

He knocked again. Harder. Finally the window came down an inch. Again, no answer.

"I asked you a question," Mark said through gritted teeth, trying to contain his annoyance.

The driver turned to him, his black eyes suddenly clearing to a bright blue. What the hell? Mark took a quick step back. A shiver tore through him, raising the small hairs on his arms and neck.

"Can I help you, sir?" the driver asked.

"I…uh…" Mark gathered his resolve and stepped back up to the car. "I asked what in the hell was going on here?" He flashed his badge once again, then quickly stuck it back on his belt. No reason to point out he wasn't a cop in this state and had absolutely no authority here.

"I don't know what you mean," the man said, looking very confused.

"You attacked those people."

"What people?"

Mark stared at him. He hadn't really said that. "The man and the woman in the truck. I saw you, both of you." His eyes flickered to the man in the passenger's seat, whose mouth was hanging open in shock. "Yes. Both of you. I should haul you both in for assault right now."

"What people?" the man in the passenger seat echoed

with disbelief thick in his voice. He glanced furtively around the parking lot, searching.

Their audacity was annoying the shit out of Mark, but the unbelievable part was that they actually seemed sincere. He talked to a lot of people, some good, some bad, some just out-and-out stupid, and his liar meter was top-notch. And these guys weren't tripping it in the least bit.

"What about the cuts and bruises on your face and hands?" he demanded.

The driver held his hands out in front of him as if seeing them for the first time. "I don't know, Officer. Really, I don't. We just stopped for a bathroom break. Honest."

Mark didn't have time for this shit. "For both your sakes, I'd better not see either of you again."

"Yes, sir," the driver said.

"Yes, thank you," his partner echoed, his relief thick in his voice.

Disgusted, Mark turned, got into his car and drove away. They were acting just like that one guy he'd managed to catch leaving Ruby's shop the other night. Denied having been in there, denied having touched a thing.

What in the hell was going on around there?

Malcolm drove the next shift while Celia slept. In his mind, he kept running over and over what had happened at the rest stop. Together, he and Celia should have been able to take two *Abatu*. But they hadn't. He was getting weaker and so was she. Other than last night, it had been too long since he'd changed. As he tried to recall the last time he'd run through the forest, he realized he couldn't. A few sporadic changes here and there in so many months were not enough to maintain his strength. He knew that, and yet he'd let himself grow weak.

He'd been too caught up with the problems of the Pack, fighting with Scott and Jason. Working his schemes, setting traps, being a complete all-around idiot. Now he was paying the price in more ways than one. Without transforming, his body was losing power and he had started to age again, the process resuming where it had cut off the first time he'd changed as a young adult. He was becoming more human and losing the magic of the wolf. He only hoped Celia hadn't been as foolish.

She looked like an angel as she slept, her face soft and worry-free. He used to love to watch her sleep. It had been the only time her defenses were down and her watchful all-seeing eyes weren't upon him. She knew him so well, his passions and strengths, but now she couldn't see past his flaws.

If only he'd married her long ago when she still loved him, when she still saw the best in him. But that chance had long since passed him by. He'd managed to destroy her trust and all that had been good between them. He remembered when they'd been teenagers. She'd stolen his breath, sapping it up with her energy and excitement. She'd had a wild streak that burned bright in her eyes and kept him chasing after her from one end of the Colony to the other. He'd tried to tire her out, to see how far she could really go. She'd not only kept up with him but pushed him even harder.

She'd been amazing. They'd made their transformation together and had been connected physically and spiritually ever since. Back then, they'd burned so hot, he was surprised they hadn't self-combusted. But then suddenly he hadn't been enough for her. She'd broken his heart and moved on without him.

He'd hardened after that, wrapping a shell around himself and never letting her or anyone else get that close to him again. They'd grown up. Life went on. And somehow they'd found their way back to each other. Lessons were learned and lost the hard way, but through it all they'd never stopped having that connection to each other.

Until she'd gone away to Sedona.

Not feeling her or sensing her near after all these years was something he didn't know he'd miss. Now he understood what his heart had always known, what he'd been so certain of way back when. She was the one for him. The one he couldn't live without. The only thing that mattered in his life.

Only once again, she wouldn't have anything to do with him. She didn't feel the same as he did; she didn't mind being away from him. From all of them. In fact, she preferred it. Tension squeezed his insides. She wanted to live without him, and now that she'd walked out of his life for good, he had no one.

The thought was sobering and hard to admit, but the truth was he'd pushed her away. He'd make it up to her. He'd make it up to everyone for all his scheming, for the ridiculous plot and warring with Scott that had got Jaya killed and put the Pack in danger. He scraped a hand across his face as he realized none of it would matter if they didn't make it back to regenerate the crystals. The fate of all the shifters rested on them, and they still had so far to go.

Celia sat up in the backseat, her hair a mess and her eyes droopy with sleep, and still she'd never looked more beautiful.

"How are you doing?" he asked.

"All right, I suppose," she said, and stretched. "Stiff."

"You've been asleep for a long time."

She looked around her. "It's good to see all the trees."

He grinned. "We've been pretty much alone on this highway for a while now, and I was thinking once the moon rose higher in the sky…"

"Yeah?" she asked, interest gleaming in her beautiful dark eyes.

"That maybe you'd like to go for a run with me."

She looked around her, weighing his words. "You think it's safe?"

"There is no one around. And the truth is, it's been a long time since I've changed. Since I've run. I think that's why the *Abatu* got the better of me today. We can't take that chance again. We have to strengthen ourselves."

She gave him a wry smile. "I could tell."

He turned to her, his eyes locking on hers. "Yeah?"

"You're going gray."

"I am not." He leaned forward and peered into the rearview mirror. But she was right. There were thin streaks of gray at his temples. How long had he been aging? How much time had he lost?

"Run with me," he said as desperation tore at him. "Last night was the first time I've changed since…" *Since the night Jaya died.* "Since I don't know when."

"Why not?"

"I don't know where my head was," he said quietly, but it wasn't true. He knew too well.

"Hmm, I don't know, Malcolm, but taking a guess, I'd say headstrong, unrelenting ambition got in your way. You could have been a great Pack leader."

He smiled. That wide, charming smile that he wore like a protective shield. "Tell me what you really think, babe."

"Harsh, I know, but you need to hear it."

"Trust me, it's not anything I haven't heard before, but that doesn't matter to me now. Being Pack leader doesn't matter to me now."

Her face filled with surprise. "Then what does?"

"Rebuilding my life in the Colony with you."

Chapter 6

As the moon rose high in the sky above them, Celia wanted out of the truck. She wanted to run, to process what Malcolm had just said to her. Could it be true? Was his obsession with leading the Pack finally over? She hoped so, for both their sakes, but couldn't allow herself to care. Not then. Right then she just wanted to run free. Her body was practically humming with anticipation to be back in high woods again with the soaring trees and a blanket of ferns covering the forest floor.

She rolled down the window and took a deep breath of the cool pine-scented air. Home. It smelled like home; bittersweet longing blossomed in her chest. Malcolm pulled over off the side of the road onto what looked like an abandoned logging road. As soon as he parked and turned off the ignition, she was stripping out of her clothes, no longer caring that he might see her. She wanted to feel the mountain beneath her paws, to stretch her legs and fly.

Without waiting for him, she was out of the truck and running, first on two legs, then on four as the wolf within her fought to be free. She tore off through the woods, not even bothering to look back for Malcolm. She ran forward, her nose high in the air smelling the sweet scent of cedar and pine and the headiness of animals surrounding her—deer, rabbits, raccoons and possums. Water from a nearby river roared in the distance, and wherever there was water there would be wildlife.

Expectation burst within her. She tore off at an even greater clip and soon felt Malcolm flying up behind her at lightning speed. She could hear his heart thundering in his chest, hear his breathing accelerating as excitement pushed him ahead of her.

She wouldn't let that happen. He'd always been the bigger one, the stronger one, but she was faster. She chased after him, giving him a small nip as she passed, just to make sure he felt her beating him as she flew over small bushes, bounding through the water, the moisture tickling her nose. Squirrels and rabbits burst out of their hiding places, scampering out of sight, fear almost stopping their thudding hearts.

And then she smelled the gamey scent of deer nearby. Deer were her favorite. There were always more than one and they knew how to give her a good chase. She took off after the scent, leaving Malcolm behind her as she bolted in another direction. Sensing her pursuit, the deer ran, breaking through the brush. There had to be six of them, maybe even seven. They were fast and knew the terrain. She followed them, racing even harder, her legs pumping steadily as she focused on her prize. It had been so long.

Listening to their blood thundering in their bodies, following the thick, heady scent of their fear, she ran deeper and deeper into the darkness. And then one was in her sight.

It was smaller than the rest, younger...slower. She was gaining on it. Faster and faster she ran, so close she could almost feel the animal's hindquarters in her mouth, could almost taste its sweet flesh as they shot through the trees. She lunged forward, extending her neck, her jaws opening wide and snapping down on... nothing.

Blazes! She burst up a small path and hit pavement with a bone-jarring thud. The bright lights of an on-coming car caught her in its glare. She froze, blinded. Rubber squealed against asphalt, the high-pitched sound stopping her heart. She tried to move but couldn't see which way to go. The light was everywhere. The blare of a horn split the night air, echoing in her ears. Brakes screeched raucously. The car fishtailed across the high-way, coming straight toward her before pitching into a ditch.

She crouched down, whimpering. Before she could move, a man burst out the door, cursing, banging his fists on the car's roof. Hidden behind the bright lights, Celia could only make out his hulking outline. He hesitated as he saw her, then reached beneath his jacket.

Then Malcolm was next to her, growling, bumping

her cheek, biting her scruff and pulling her out of the hypnotic stupor she'd fallen into. She turned, following him off the road, running fast. A shot rang out, ricocheting off a nearby tree. Then another.

Fear slammed into her chest.

"Come back here!" the man yelled. "I know what you are! I know!"

Adrenaline pulsed through her blood, pushing her away from the road after Malcolm, deeper into the woods and out of the sight of the man and his gun. Would he come after them? Into the dark? Alone?

She couldn't guess, but their fun was over. They had to get to the truck and away from this lunatic as soon as possible. They never should have stopped. They must get to the safety of the Colony as soon as they could.

The safety of the Colony.

The place she'd been running away from was the only place she could be truly safe. The irony of the thought wasn't lost on her. She caught up to Malcolm as he slowed, stopping by the river.

What was he doing? *They couldn't stop.* And then the metallic scent of blood filled her nose and seeped dread into her heart.

Blood.

Malcolm's blood.

Malcolm didn't know what was happening. Something was wrong. He played it over and over in his mind. He'd been chasing after Celia but couldn't keep up. Annoyance coiled inside him. She was being too reckless. This wasn't their forest. They weren't free to run as they pleased here. He'd heard the squealing of tires. He'd seen her standing in the middle of the road, bathed in the light from the car's high beams. He'd braced for the thump, his insides tightening with terror. His vision wavered as pain radiated from his shoulder. Wet heat dripped down his leg.

He stopped beside the rushing water and took a deep drink, letting the cool liquid sluice down his ravaged throat. His head was swimming. They had to keep moving, to get back to the truck, but his knees buckled and he collapsed beside the river. He would rest just for a moment, just until the chill coursing through him ebbed.

Celia nudged him, whining as she licked his wound. She wanted him to rise. To move. He raised his head and tried to stand, but his legs collapsed under him and he fell back to the ground. Celia whimpered and lay down next to him. He felt her warmth seeping into his coldness, and it felt good. Just a few more minutes and he'd be fine. He'd be able to stand and make it back to the truck. He closed his burning eyes, searching for relief, and fell into darkness.

Mark knew with a certainty deep in his gut that those were the same wolves he'd seen behind Ruby's place in Sedona. They had to be Ruby and her sister. He ran back to his car and pulled his flashlight out of his glove box. He would find them, and then he'd prove to everyone he wasn't Crazy Mark, and he never had been.

He could still hear the taunts of his father and older brother ringing down the hallway from the kitchen of their small house. *Crazy Mark. Crazy Mark. Crazy*

Mark. In hindsight, he should never have told them what he'd seen. They hadn't believed him, and had used his knowledge like a weapon to bludgeon him.

But what he'd seen was true. There were were-wolves in the James family. First the mother and now the daughters, and he was finally going to be able to prove it. He ran into the woods, following the small path, the bright beam of his flashlight floating through the darkness.

He slowed, trying to soften his steps and quiet his breath. No reason to let them know he was coming. He moved deeper into the woods. The tall trees and their thick canopy of branches blotted out even the slightest flicker of moonlight. The dark was so thick it could smother a man. And he had to admit he was finding it hard to breathe.

He moved slowly, swinging his flashlight back and forth across the trail, when his light moved across something wet. Something red.

Blood.

He'd hit one of them. Yes! He'd thought he had. Exaltation pushed him forward. He was so close now. Soon everyone who'd called him Crazy Mark, everyone who'd taunted him with their cruel laughter, would have to eat their words like yesterday's spaghetti, and, boy, would it taste good!

So many times they'd told him he'd been wrong, but he knew what he'd seen that night. He'd been camping with his Scouts. He'd hated camping, almost as much as he'd hated the Scouts. He'd had to take a whiz, so he'd headed off by himself when out of nowhere he'd seen the woman. He'd had no idea where she'd come from, but when she'd started to take off her clothes he hadn't believed his luck and had quickly hid behind a large rock.

With bulging eyeballs he'd watched that woman strip naked. He'd been fourteen at the time, and hers were the first real big kaboombas he'd ever seen up front and in person. And they weren't at all like seeing them in a magazine or on the internet. He sat there in the middle of the desert behind that big boulder, his need to find biological relief forgotten as he watched her strip way too fast.

Too fast for him to go back and get his best friend to watch with him. The woman's boobs were huge and shiny in the light of the moon. She lifted up her face to the sky, as if smelling the air, and then she started to run, barefoot and naked, across the desert floor. The woman must be crazy. One of those loons you sometimes hear about who run naked through the night and he was just lucky enough to have to take a whiz right at that moment, but then she dropped onto all fours and within the blink of an eye, she wasn't a woman anymore.

She was a wolf, running fast and furious, and then she was gone.

He'd scurried out from around the rock he'd been hiding behind and walked out into the clearing where she'd left her pile of clothes. He knew what he'd just seen, knew he wasn't mistaken, but how could it be possible? People didn't just change into wolves. Unless... unless they were werewolves! But where had she gone?

He picked up her wallet and opened it, reading the Arizona driver's license. Sue James.

A lonely howl splitting the night air pricked the hairs on the back of his neck. He shoved the wallet into his back pocket and hurried up the nearest embankment. If he could get on the other side, he could get a better view when she came back. He didn't care if he had to wait there all night; he wanted to see her again. She had to come back for her clothes, didn't she?

He heard the howl again and followed a path at the top of the hill toward the lonely sound. And then he saw her—a beautiful wolf covered in snow-white fur, the light from the moon almost turning it an incandescent blue. She whined, dropping her head to her paws as something was attacking her. Some kind of bat or something. Mark gasped, squinting, trying to see what it was.

Dark shadows flew at her, ramming against her back, her head, her side. She whined, a high-pitched pitiful sound that made him want to help her. To chase the bat-like creatures away. But as he started forward, the ground rumbled beneath his feet. A loud noise crackled through the air, splitting the night around him with electricity that made his hair stand on end. Before he could take another step, a long crack fissured the ground beneath her.

He yelled a warning just as the earth opened its jaws wide and swallowed her whole. Amazed and horrified, Mark saw her fall into the crack and disappear. He ran toward her, toward the place he saw her fall, but then the ground sealed itself back up again and just like that she was gone. As if she'd never been there. As if he'd imagined the whole thing.

Which, of course, was what everyone told him. Except he still had her wallet in his back pocket. And her necklace lying on the ground in the very spot she'd disappeared. His dad was a cop, so he knew better than to remove evidence, but he did anyway. He picked up that necklace, replacing it with a distinctive rock so he could find the spot again when he showed his dad where it had happened.

As he walked slowly back toward the camp, he took out her wallet and looked again at her picture and photos of her daughters. Twins just a couple of years younger than himself. Daughters who would spend the next six months making flyers, hanging them all over town looking for their missing mother. But he knew the truth of what she was. What they all were. And he'd seen how the earth had swallowed her whole.

But no one had believed him. Worse, they'd taunted and tormented him and accused him of lying. But they would believe him now. As soon as he found and captured that wounded wolf, he'd show everyone exactly how crazy he wasn't.

He only wondered if it was Ruby or Jade he hit. He hoped it was Ruby. He really did. If it was, then he might just keep her to himself. Just for a little while.

Celia lay next to Malcolm for a few moments, listening to his deep, even breathing. She couldn't tell how bad his wound was. Why had that man shot him? They were running away. Thoughts, denials and fear raced through her mind, crowding out what she wouldn't let herself think about. Malcolm had been shot. And it could be bad. If only her mother were there to heal him. Though Celia had tried, she'd never been able to grasp that particular gift with the crystals.

Perhaps if she'd tried harder. Tears misted her eyes, and a fist of pressure clenched her heart. It didn't matter. She couldn't do it and her mother wasn't there, and she never would be again. To help and guide her, to tell her that everything would be all right. That Malcolm would be fine.

The snap of a twig and the rustling of leaves stole into her thoughts. Something was coming. *Something or someone*. She lifted her head, her senses on high alert. The sound of footsteps, clumsy and heavy, breaking through the brush filled the night air. The man with the gun? She looked at Malcolm and nudged him once more with her nose. *Wake up, Malcolm. Please!*

He didn't budge. She had to do something or that man would find them. But why would he come after them? It made no sense, but whatever the reason, it couldn't be good. She had to lead him away from Malcolm. She got to her feet and raced toward the approaching noise. Gathering speed, she ran as fast as she dared, heading back toward the path the deer were following, back toward the road.

And then she saw him, the clumsy human, breaking branches, scaring the animals, not even bothering to conceal his presence. Without slowing, she ran right at him. Not even making sure the gun wasn't still in his hand. All she saw was his dark eyes widening with fear. *Mark*. The cop obsessed with Ruby.

She knew what kind of man Mark was. She had watched him from the window when he'd come by to pick up Ruby. Watched the way he looked at her, the possessive way he kept his hand on her back. After one cup of coffee, Ruby had known there was something off with the guy and had tried to break it off, to let him down gently while still making it clear that she wasn't interested. And yet he still came around. Still called. Now he was here.

And he'd shot Malcolm.

Cold seeped through her, freezing her fear, leaving her feeling nothing but razor-sharp determination as she bolted toward him. He raised the gun, pointing it straight toward her. It wobbled in his hand. She launched herself on him, knocking him to the ground. A shot boomed through the forest, breaking the night air. Pain ripped through her leg. She bit down on his neck, feeling his soft flesh tear easily, shredding beneath her sharp teeth.

She tasted the salty warmth of his blood. She was tempted to bite down harder, to give her head a violent shake and rip open the artery that fed his life. It was nothing less than he deserved. But she didn't. She held back, restraining herself, and then when she didn't think she could hold back a moment longer, she released him and disappeared into the thicket.

She was back across the other side of the road when she realized she'd been hit. The bullet had only grazed her skin, but she was bleeding, leaving a trail for Mark to follow. Hopefully he'd be too concerned with bandaging his neck to come after her.

She kept running along the other side of the road for an hour, maybe more, leading him as far away from Malcolm as she could until she just couldn't go any farther. Tired and out of breath, she collapsed under a massive redwood, her nose buried in the thick moss surrounding the base of the tree. She closed her eyes and rested for a moment, all the while keeping her senses on edge, listening for the approach of the stupid man and his gun.

This never would have happened in the Colony. They should have waited to run until they got home. *Home.* The word reverberated in her mind. The one place she hadn't wanted to be, and now she couldn't wait to get there. As she lay there, the night deepening, quieting, her heart stilling in her chest, she heard something far off. Something she'd never heard in the woods before.

It wasn't the clumsy human or even a forest animal or bird. No, this was something else. She lifted her head, listening, the hair rising on the nape of her neck—a feather's touch scraping along her nerves. She stood, instantly at attention, waiting. A whisper drifted through the trees, filling the air, growing louder as it came closer.

Fear slammed into her, rooting her to the spot as tendrils of whispers, floating like smoke on the breeze, surrounded her, filling her. With a crackling surge of adrenaline, she jumped to her feet and ran, ignoring the pain in her leg where the man's bullet had grazed her skin, burning it and leaving it raw.

She ran as fast as she could back across the road and toward Malcolm even as the whispers surrounded her, filling her head, growing louder and louder until suddenly she could understand the words spoken within the hushed tones, the one word chanted over and over—*abomination*.

Cold seeped through her body, stealing her strength, liquefying her muscles until all she could do was collapse into a quivering heap at Malcolm's side.

Abomination.

Abomination.

The *Gauliacho* were here.

They'd found them.

Chapter 7

Malcolm woke to Celia standing over him, pulling on him. Shaking him.

"Malcolm, wake up!" she said, her voice a strangled whisper.

She was naked and beautiful, smiling down at him with laughter dancing in her eyes. And for just a second, it was the way it used to be when they were young and deeply in love and just by looking at her he felt as if he could conquer the world.

"Malcolm!"

She shook him again and he realized she wasn't smiling. Her face was drawn and hard. And they were no longer kids. He wanted to close his eyes and forget why they were there. To go back to his dreams.

"The *Gauliacho* are here. They've found us," she said breathlessly. "We have to go. Now!"

The *Gauliacho?* Surely she must be wrong. He gave his head a soft shake, trying to clear it, trying to come back to the here and now. But something kept pulling him back. The sweet darkness where pain didn't linger, where he was still madly in love with a girl who thought he hung the moon. The kind of young love where the valve to your heart was wide-open, letting everything out, and everything in. The good, the bad and the, oh, so painful.

"Can you walk?" She shook him again. "Malcolm, wake up!"

He opened his eyes once more. Focusing on her brilliant and intense gaze.

"Please tell me you can walk, because I don't think I can lift you."

Pain shot through him as she pulled at him. He whimpered loudly and she fell back. But she'd had the desired effect that he was definitely awake. The scent of fear filled the air as she quickly glanced over her shoulder. She was terrified. Was she right? Had she seen something? Were the *Gauliacho* really there? How could they have found them already?

His blood.

It was always the blood.

The night was deep, and the air was heavy with moisture and a stillness that only the early morning before dawn can bring. He stood, getting shakily to his feet. He walked beside Celia, following the river back toward the truck. He longed to take a drink from the water, to soothe his parched throat, but knew there was no time to stop.

Celia, beside him once more in wolf form, picked up the pace and started running faster and faster. Her feverish panic pushing him forward, the acrid scent of her fear rolling off her in thick sluggish waves. And then he heard them, heard what had her so terrified. The whispering.

The sounds reached inside his mind, echoing within, scratching his nerves until he thought he might collapse beneath the weight of them. Even with his spilled blood, how had they found them so fast? And what of the man who had shot them? Where was he? Malcolm felt the wound in his shoulder straining under the exertion of their flight and knew he should stay in wolf form until he could heal further, but Celia didn't know the way back to the Colony from here.

This was the only time she'd ever been out of the Colony's boundaries, and this would be the time the *Gauliacho* attacked. She was terrified of them. Her fear, ingrained from childhood, almost bordered on irrational. Somehow she'd always been able to sense them, to hear them, even though they were never near. As far as he knew. Maybe all this time they had been.

He had to get her to safety. They reached the truck and he quickly changed back. As he made the transition from wolf to man, pain ripped into his shoulder and the bleeding started again. Celia was in the cab next to him, pulling on her shirt, slipping into her skirt and looking nervously around her. She took a T-shirt out of her overnight bag and pressed it to his wound. "Drive."

He nodded, and as he backed down the old logging road, heading toward the highway, a wave of light-headedness fell over him. He pushed it away. He couldn't let her down.

"There's a motel about thirty miles up ahead. If we could get to it, get into a room…" He took another deep breath and fought to hold on as his head started to spin.

"Then I could set up the crystals around the perimeter to protect us."

"At least until I can heal a little more." His eyes drifted closed as nausea swept through him. He stepped on the brakes, stopping the truck, not bothering to pull over.

"I'd better drive," she said, climbing over him.

"It's not far. Up on the left," he muttered as his world went black.

The *Gauliacho*'s whispers filled Celia's head. Growing ever louder, distracting her from her driving, from worrying about Malcolm. She held her crystal in her lap and ran her fingers over it, back and forth, focusing on its smooth coolness. Doing everything she could to keep out the noise.

But the crystals could not protect her fully, not here in the truck, not while she was moving. Not while they were both still bleeding. She knew their best bet would be to get to the hotel and set up a crystal perimeter in the room. Like clawing tendrils, the whispers poked at her, creeping inside her mind. Echoing. Repeating. The same word, over and over. *Abomination. Abomination. Abomination.*

Round and round, until she thought she would go mad. She wanted to pull over, crawl up into a ball and clutch her head until the whispers went away. But she knew they wouldn't go away. That it was only the beginning. She looked over at Malcolm, dead asleep on the seat next to her.

Come back to us.

Celia. Celia. Celia.

The urge to stop the truck and flee into the forest overwhelmed her. She wanted to run far and fast, even if that was what they wanted her to do. Hoped she'd do. Tears filled her eyes and spilled onto her cheeks. She couldn't let them get to her. She had to stay strong.

She took Malcolm's hand in her own and clutched it. Focusing on the warm and familiar feel of his skin. She listened to his breathing and concentrated on their connection, weak but still there. It had once been so strong that whenever they were together his essence had drowned out everything else. Even the whispers.

How had they gotten so lost from each other?

She reached for him now, searching for that long-lost thread. Fresh tears filled her eyes. Not tears of anger or frustration, or even fear. No, these were tears of heartache, because in his sleep, in his most unguarded moment, she could feel his fear. His overwhelming guilt. His deep regret. And most of all, his love for her.

She squeezed his hand, concentrating on him—his touch, his pain. Until all she saw, all she felt, was him. The neon red lights of the motel flashed up ahead. She sucked in a relieved breath. She didn't know if it was her focus on Malcolm or if somehow they'd managed to lose the *Gauliacho,* but she no longer heard them or felt their scratching beneath her skin.

She parked the truck, placed her crystal in her pocket, ran into the office and booked a room. With the key in hand, she got back into the truck and drove to the far end of the long one-story strip of units and pulled up in front of the last one.

"Come on, Malcolm, we're here," she said, giving him a gentle shake. He groaned, and she shook him again until he stirred and opened his bloodshot eyes. *Thank goodness.* She hurried around to his side of the truck, grabbed her bag with the rest of the crystals tucked inside and helped Malcolm out of his seat. She took most of his weight onto her shoulders as she helped him toward the rooms.

She unlocked the door and led him inside the small dingy room. Immediately he collapsed onto the bed while she shut and locked the door. She placed each of the four crystals at the compass points around the room, then sat in front of each and said the words, chanting the sounds that would vitalize the dark energy within the stones and protect them, shielding their wolf energy signatures from the *Gauliacho.*

It was the most she could hope for.

Once there had been many crystal Keepers in the Colony. No one knew who would be born with the gift or why. Most times it was passed down from mother to daughter, but not always. But as the years passed, their numbers had dwindled until now, it appeared, there was only one. *Her.*

She shuddered to think what would happen to the

Pack if something had happened to her tonight, if she'd been fatally shot or if the *Gauliacho* had gotten to her. Once she returned to the Colony, the Council would never allow her to leave. How could they? Not only that, but the pressure for her to mate and have a child of her own who could regenerate the crystals would be even stronger than it had been before.

She rubbed the chill off her arms, then tended to her wound, putting a bandage over the bleeding, which had mostly stopped. She checked on Malcolm and applied a clean compress from the first-aid kit in the truck over his wound. It was bad. He was still bleeding, though not as heavily as before. She double-checked the locks on the door and windows, then closed the curtains tight, stripped once again and slipped into the large bed next to Malcolm. Comforted by his steady, even breathing, she closed her eyes and fell instantly asleep.

Celia dreamed of the shadows again. It was the same dream she'd been having since she was a little girl. It never changed. She wandered aimlessly, lost in the woods, trying to follow the dim light from the moon. Her throat ached, strained from calling for her mother, who'd never come.

"Mommy!" she called, running, tripping over roots and bushes, fumbling over rocks. She fell, landing hard, and hurt her knee as she struggled to find her way. Blood trickled down her leg, stinging her. The darkness—so thick and tangible—smothered her, stealing her breath. Everywhere she looked, darkness was all she could see. Even the light from the moon, broken by the hard angles of the trees, fell to the ground and was absorbed by inky blackness.

Dark clouds thickened overhead, swelling into a monstrous form as she walked round and round. Her hands were outstretched as she felt her way. Tears streamed down her face, fear hammered her chest. She was lost and all alone with no one to help her. And then she heard the sounds. Low at first, a soft whispering, calling her name.

She stopped, her small hand reaching forward. "Mommy?"

The whispering grew louder and louder, an insidious noise expanding around her until it felt as if it were inside her, pulsing against the inside of her head. As if it were alive, trapped, clawing to get out. She collapsed to her knees in the damp earth, pushing her palms against her ears as tears, hot and fast, rolled down her cheeks.

"Mommeeee," she cried, but could barely hear her own voice over the one word echoing in her mind, growing louder and louder, stealing her thoughts, her strength until she *was* the word.

Abomination.

Abomination.

Abomination.

Yes.

"No!" Celia sat upright in bed. Her heart hammering, her breath coming fast and deep.

"What is it?" Malcolm asked, his eyes squinting open.

"Just a bad dream. Go back to sleep," she murmured.

He sat up, wincing. "The same dream?"

She nodded. He knew her too well.

"I'm not sure they're dreams anymore," she admitted, voicing her biggest fear. "They shouldn't have found us out there tonight. I fear they have some kind of connection to me. Some kind of…I don't know, tether." She started to shake as the implication of her words hit home. A slow tremble that grew into full-blown shudders.

"It's just a dream, Lia," Malcolm said softly, moving next to her so he could pull her closer to him.

She shouldn't let him. She knew that. But she did. His warmth, seeping into her skin and melting the chill that had stolen in and buried itself deep within her, was too much to give up. She burrowed closer to him, breathing deep his scent, woodsy and earthy and Malcolm. The scent, warm and familiar, drew her to him with a strength she didn't want to think about.

"It's the same dream, Malcolm. The same one I've always had. I heard the same whispers in the woods tonight. They get into your head, and once they do—"

"Shh. Nothing's going to happen to you. I won't let it."

"How do you know that? You don't know the future any more than I do. You could have been killed tonight. Then what?"

"But I wasn't and I'm not going to be. I'll be fine. And I'll get you home. Safe. I promise." He wrapped his arms around her and she snuggled closer. "I've always had your back, Lia. I know I've let you down, but not with this. Never with this."

"I know," she whispered, but she couldn't shake the

chill that had worked its way through her, turning her blood to ice. She burrowed closer to him, absorbing his heat, his strength.

"How's your wound?" she asked, reluctant to lift the blood-soaked dressing.

"It's better. I'll be fine."

She shivered again as she thought of the dream full of whispers that called for her death. She'd known since she was a child that the shadows would get her one day. That they were waiting for just the right time. Malcolm's heat seeped into her body, warming her, thawing the ice that had hardened in her veins. She felt every inch of him pressed against her. And soon his warmth offered more than just comfort. His heat moved through her, sparking her nerve endings, giving her something to think about to focus on other than the fear.

She ran the tips of her fingers up his arms, around the bulge in his biceps, strong and hard. Up to his shoulders. She felt his breath quicken, sparking expectant energy to swirl around them. She turned her head toward his and tentatively pressed her lips against his. They were soft, and warm, and willing. And exactly what she needed. A shiver of anticipation tore through her, chasing away the fear. The darkness. And replacing it with an expectant, pulsing need coiling deep within her.

"Celia," he rasped, pulling away from her.

"What?" she murmured, wrapping her arms around him and pulling him back to her. She knew what he was going to say, what he was thinking. And he was right. She hadn't forgiven him. This changed nothing between them. Except right now she needed to escape the darkness and warm the chill that had taken root deep inside her before it spread any further. And no one else could chase her shadows away better than Malcolm.

"We can't," he said softly. "I want to. Believe me. But not like this."

"We can," she whispered against his lips. But, surprisingly, he didn't respond.

"There's so much we need to talk about."

Inwardly, she groaned. "Tonight I just want to forget everything and feel." She could sense his hesitation. She kissed him again, stroking his lips with the tip of her tongue, coaxing a response from him, reminding him how very good they were together. It wouldn't take much for him to see that once they were wrapped in each other's arms, nothing else would matter.

"Malcolm, I need you to hold me, to love me and make me forget." She kissed him again.

"There is so much that I have done. If you knew…"

She could only imagine. But she didn't know, and right now she didn't *want* to know.

"If you knew, you wouldn't want—"

"Shh, Malcolm." She put a finger to his lips. She didn't want to hear about all his mistakes, about his plans to marry that other woman. She didn't want to be reminded of why she'd left the Colony in the first place. Not now, when she needed him so much. Needed to pretend that everything was back the way it was before. Back the way it should be.

She rolled on top of him, nuzzling his neck, drawing his sweet skin into her mouth and sucking on the pulse point she knew would set his heart racing. She slipped her hand down his stomach and inside his boxers to find his heat. No matter how much he denied it, he wanted her. That much he couldn't hide.

He groaned, and all protestations died on his lips. Smiling, she pressed her lips against his mouth, once more quieting him, kissing him until he was breathless and his concerns were lost.

Chapter 8

Malcolm closed his eyes as the sensations rocked over him. Her touch was the accelerant lighting the flame and awakening a need in him so fierce it could not be ignored. She tasted sweet, and he'd do anything for her, give her anything she wanted, if she'd just continue kissing and touching him like that.

He moved his mouth over hers, drinking in more of her, trying to satiate a need that could not be quenched. She wrenched away from him, pulling off her shirt. He drank in her beauty—her small, firm breasts, pert and high, her nipples tight, dark buds. He longed to reach out and touch one, to feel her breast filling his hand, to rub the nub between his fingers. To relish the tremor moving through her at his touch.

But he wouldn't. He pulled back and rolled off the

bed. He needed to break contact and regain enough self-control to push away from her. He took a quick step back from the bed, wishing he had some way to cover his burgeoning desire that was so plain to see.

"Where are you going?" she asked, her voice husky and raw. "Come back to bed."

"I...I can't," he said, his own voice coming out as a harsh, desperate whisper.

"Why not?"

How could he explain? He couldn't take advantage of her. He couldn't do what he wanted to do and make love to her all night without her knowing the truth about his involvement in her mother's death. He'd been such a fool. He'd been furious and desperate enough to think his plan had been flawless, but he hadn't planned on Jason getting hurt. Hadn't expected Shay to love Jason so much, and still he'd forced her to marry him. Minutes after, Scott had arrived and all hell had broken loose. Jaya and Shay had both been leaning over Jason, trying to stop his bleeding, when Scott had pointed his gun and shot.

Only the bullet meant for Shay killed Jaya. And it was all his fault. If he hadn't dropped Jason in that pit. If Jason hadn't got hurt. If Shay hadn't found Jaya and enlisted her help to save him... The list went on and on. With Jaya dead, there was no witness to his marriage to Shay, and the Council members refused to recognize it—the only good that had come out of that horrible plan. Now Shay was free to marry Jason, and hopefully she could put that whole terrible day out of her mind.

But once Celia found out, she'd never forgive him. And if they made love now, she'd hate him all the more.

"I just can't." He had to tell her. Get it over with. Now. He sat on the edge of the bed and clutched his hands to keep from reaching for her, from touching her. "I've made so many mistakes, Lia. Done so many things I'm ashamed of…."

"Shh." She put her hand on his arm. "I know that, Malcolm. But I don't want to hear about them. Not now."

"But you must. It isn't fair to either of us. If you knew the truth…"

"I don't want to think about my mother. About what happened at the Colony. I just want to forget about my mother's death, about the *Gauliacho*. About what's waiting for us back home. Can you do that? Can you give me some peace of mind for a little while? Because I know this might be the last chance either of us has it for a very long time."

She leaned forward and gently pressed her lips to his and then he was lost, lost in her taste, her touch. He'd wanted to hold her for so long now, to hang on tight and never let go. But he knew he'd have to, and that this was most likely the last chance he'd ever have to show her how deeply he cared about her. How much he loved her.

He ran his hand over her body, remembering every line and contour. It had been so long since he'd touched her, since he'd really felt her. How was it possible that after all this time, her touch, ever so fleeting, still sent shock waves running down his skin? She put him in such a vulnerable place that part of him wanted to protect himself from her, to not let her too close, but he knew better. Knew that if he put up a wall now, she would feel it and he'd lose any chance he had with her.

He took a deep breath, took the plunge and hoped she wouldn't tear him apart. "I love you, Lia," he whispered, but she didn't respond. He didn't expect her to. Instead he showed her exactly how much she meant to him with his hands and his lips, moving over every part of her.

She tasted sweet. His tongue followed the groove where her neck met her collarbone, following the path to heaven. He pulled from her the sweet sounds that made up a symphony of their lovemaking. Sounds so rich with longing and need they were healing music to his ears.

He knew what she wanted and why she wanted it. She wanted to escape the dreams that had stolen her peace of mind and replaced it with a fear so deep and inescapable she had nowhere to turn and no one to run to except for him. He knew just where to take her to chase away the fear and keep the shadows at bay. Knew just where to touch.

And he did. Moving his hands down the sweeping curve of her belly, to her hot core between her legs. She pushed against his hand and her warmth filled his palm. He nipped and sucked her tight nipple, nibbling until the dusky peak beaded in his mouth and a gasp escaped her lips.

He slid his hand over her backside, stroking and loving, moving back toward her heat, relishing the soft sounds of pleasure she made, the mewling moans and sharp intakes as he teased her with his fingers.

His body stirred, his thick hardness straining as it

reached for her heat. As he fondled and played with her, his fingers sweeping inside her warmth, she pushed herself closer to him. Wanting more, impatient with her need.

She took the length of his fingers within her tight grasp. He moved them fast and hard over her sensitive flesh. He knew she was working him, hoping to push him into giving her what she wanted—himself buried deep within her. But she'd have to wait. He wasn't ready. He didn't want it to end that quickly. He gave her one last thrust, then pulled his fingers out of her velvety softness. He guided her onto her back and positioned himself over her, taking first one breast, then the other into his mouth, tasting, nipping. She arched her back and moaned in satisfaction.

He continued licking and kissing the soft skin down to her belly, where he nibbled on her belly button before giving her what she really wanted. Before making his way to the curls at the junction between her legs. His face buried within their softness, he drew her tender nub into his mouth.

She writhed against him, her back lifting off the bed, her hands threading through the thick hair on his head. He licked and kissed and sucked until the nub swelled in his mouth and she was gasping for breath. He enjoyed watching the ecstasy playing across her face and felt his arousal nearing the breaking point.

Her breathing quickened, her heartbeat accelerating, as the honeyed musk of her passion filled the room. She gulped a moan and then cried out as wave after wave rocked through her. After a moment, he moved up her body, slowly pulling her to him as the aftermath of her passion ebbed.

He kissed her nipple softly. Slowly. Then moved his lips up to her mouth. "Are you ready for more?" he murmured against her lips.

"Mmm," she breathed, and entwined her arms around his neck. "Bring it on."

Celia straddled his hard body, then leaned down and kissed Malcolm deeply after he rolled onto his back and pulled her on top of him. He slid his hands under the smooth skin of her bottom and lifted gently. She felt him probing against her, and she opened to him, sliding down his thick, rigid shaft until he was rooted deep inside her.

She stilled for a moment, letting her body absorb his breadth. He was so large and so hot and, after a few seconds, she felt herself melting around him. Felt the exquisite burn that left her breathless and wanting more. She moved forward, bucking her hips slightly, and felt him push against that hidden place inside her.

That place that when pleased would be her undoing. She moved again, then again. He grabbed her hips, his palms cradling her as he drove deep within her, pushing her harder, faster. His hands swept up her body to hold her breasts and send pleasure shooting through her core.

Her temperature spiked, and she sucked in a deep breath as sweet ecstasy built within her, rising to the breaking point. She wanted it to end, felt that it had to end. She would reach that point soon where she lost herself, falling, tumbling over the edge into sweet exultation. But she still wasn't there.

Harder and harder he pushed until she felt as if she'd burst, exploding from within. She opened her eyes and saw Malcolm watching her, his forest-green eyes turning amber as the animal within him pushed him closer and closer to his point of no return. His eyes locked on hers, and she felt his heart. She felt enveloped in a cocoon of warmth, of love. In that moment, she knew she could trust him. That he alone was her...*everything*.

Her muscles tightened, stiffening. She gasped a lungful of air as her body soared, sending her over the edge and into a happy oblivion.

As the sun rose in the sky, Celia rolled over in the bed and felt Malcolm next to her. Her hand immediately went to his back in a loving caress before she stopped herself and pulled back. Images from the night before flitted through her mind. She'd let her guard down and she'd made love to him, letting him back into her body and her heart. She sat up, pulling the covers to her. She'd been a fool.

He stirred, automatically reaching for her. She slipped from the bed as his hand moved into the space where she'd been. She grabbed her pack and hurried into the bathroom, turning on the hot water in the shower and stepping inside. *Coward,* she thought to herself. And she was, because as angry and hurt as she still was toward him, that connection between them, that love was still there. And she supposed it always had been, and always would be.

She'd felt his true heart last night while they'd made love. But true or not, it wouldn't matter if he couldn't put her first. Before the Pack. Before his ambitions. And he'd proved time and time again that he couldn't. The sad truth was, she needed more from him than he'd ever be able to give her.

She picked up the bar of soap and scrubbed her body, wincing when she rubbed too hard across the wound on her arm. She'd been lucky last night. First the man with his gun and then the shadows. They were there. The shadows from her dreams. The *Gauliacho*. And in her fear, in a moment of weakness, she'd turned to Malcolm. She rubbed her hands down her arms, remembering how wonderful it had been. How poignant and special.

They'd been lost to each other for so long and had finally found each other again. Not the shell he showed the rest of the world, but the real Malcolm, the vulnerable Malcolm. And the real Celia. She sighed as tears of regret and sorrow filled her eyes, mingling with the hot water on her cheeks.

But it could never happen again.

With Malcolm it was so easy to get caught up in him, in his world, and to lose sight of her needs, her wants. And how she'd wanted him. All of him. To be there for her. To be her husband, the father of her children. But for him, his power, his ego came first. And as long as he was obsessed with running the Pack, of being in charge, the one always in control, there was no room for her. For so long she'd just been an extension of Malcolm, but not anymore. Now she needed to take care of herself.

She washed and conditioned her hair, then quickly finished bathing and dressed in a fresh pair of jeans and a Sedona T-shirt to remind her where she'd been and where she wanted to return. A life all of her own. They should be home by tonight, and then she'd be able to sleep in her own bed and put what had happened here with Malcolm behind her.

He was sitting on the edge of the bed, waiting for her. Her eyes met his, and something lurched in her chest. Why was it he could still take her breath away?

"Good morning," she said tentatively, trying not to notice that errant adorable lock of hair that fell into his eyes. The one she was always brushing away.

Blazes, she was pathetic.

He smiled, his eyes searching her face. She knew what he wanted. He wanted her to walk into his arms, hold him and tell him that everything was okay. That after last night *they* were okay. But she couldn't do that. It would be stupid. Idiotic.

"How's your wound?" she asked, her gaze moving over the bloody bandage covering his shoulder.

"Better." He stood.

She took a quick step back, her shoulder blades hitting the wall behind her. "Great. You think we'll get there by dark?" she asked, her pitch a little too high as nervousness rolled through her.

"Easily."

He stopped before her as he reached the doorway leading into the bathroom and looked down at her, his nearness making her heart thunder in her chest. He ran a finger along her chin, his soft touch spreading warmth along her skin. She closed her eyes, not wanting him to see inside her heart. To see how much he could move her with one small touch.

"I've got your back, Lia. I always have."

He left her standing there and went into the bathroom, and it was all she could do to stop the tears from leaking onto her cheeks and rushing in after him. She heard the water turn on and then began to repack her stuff, picking up her clothes from the night before.

Annoyance rushed through her. What was wrong with her? How could she even consider letting him back into her heart? After everything he'd done. All the pain…the tears…the sleepless nights. She sighed. Maybe it was time to let it all go. Her mother was dead. The life she had yesterday was not the same life she had today. Today he was all she had to hold on to. And right now he was what she needed.

But what about tomorrow? Would it be fair to lean on him when she knew it wouldn't last? She had to be strong. She couldn't send mixed messages. She had to keep her distance until they got back to the Colony and she could get some breathing room and perspective. He stepped out of the bathroom, shirtless and beautiful, and made her doubt everything she'd just promised herself.

"Would you mind redressing my wound?" he asked, moving toward her.

"Not at all," she answered, and picked up the first-aid kit. She could do this. It was just one more day of being close to him, and then they'd be back home. Back in the Colony.

Where she'd be trapped.

* * *

"Ruby, wake up."

"What?" Ruby said, stretching as Jade pushed on her shoulder.

"They're leaving. Wake up. It's time to go."

"Great," Ruby muttered. "Why couldn't we have slept in a nice bed in the hotel?"

"Because then we would have missed them. Now stop whining." She turned the key in the ignition.

"Wait. I have to pee," Ruby demanded.

"Sorry. Can't now. They've already pulled out of the parking lot, and after all we've been through, I don't want to lose them now."

"Seriously, Jade! I've got to pee."

"Fine." Jade stopped the car. "But hurry."

Ruby looked around her. "We're in the middle of the parking lot. Where am I supposed to go?"

"Over there in the bushes."

Ruby quickly stepped out of the car and disappeared into the woods. She didn't have to go far. The trees and bushes were incredibly thick. And spooky. She was having the worst nightmares, and she was freaking hungry. All the time. She got back into the car and slammed the door. "What do we have for breakfast?"

"Day-old doughnuts," Jade said, and tore out of the parking lot and onto the two-lane road.

"Joy." Ruby dug in the bag, then turned on her phone to check for messages.

"Anything?"

"Nope."

"Well, you'd better turn it back off. We don't have the

charger with us." After a few minutes of following an empty road, Jade smacked the steering wheel. "I hope we catch up with the truck soon. We couldn't have come all this way only to lose them now."

"They can't continue like this for very much longer," Ruby grumbled. "Where in the hell does she live anyway?"

"I don't know. I can't believe we're still following her."

"I know, but, Jade, something is really wrong. There is a dark energy hanging over both of them. I can sense it, and frankly it's making my skin crawl. She needs us because whatever is after them, it's dangerous."

"Then why didn't you tell her back at the rest stop?"

"If she was going to spill her secrets and let us in on whatever is happening, she would have done it already."

Jade sighed. "I hate to admit it, but you're probably right."

"I know I'm right," Ruby said. "The tingling has been growing stronger and stronger."

"Well, I'm thinking the next time they stop we should confront her. Let her know we're still here, tell her about what you're sensing and demand to know what in the hell is going on."

"All right. But she's not going to be happy."

"I'm not happy," Jade grumbled. "We've followed her across three states. It was never supposed to take this long."

"How were we supposed to know she would go so far?"

"What do you really think is going on?" Jade asked.

"Because last night was just plain weird. They took off into the woods for hours only to end up at a hotel a few minutes down the road. What in the hell were they doing out there?"

"I don't have a clue." Ruby took a bite of the stale donut. "Let's just hope they stop soon. I'm sick of trees and doughnuts and am more than ready to go home."

Mark opened groggy eyes to afternoon sunshine beating at him through the thick windshield. He tried to move but ached everywhere. He opened the door and forced himself to get out of the car and stretch. He was stiff from too many hours sleeping in the front seat and his neck hurt. He moved his fingers tentatively over the wound and felt tender, flayed skin. And then he saw the blood. On his shirt, his hand, even the car seat was covered with it.

So much blood.

He was lucky to still be alive. He didn't know how he got back to the car, could barely remember stumbling through the darkness trying to find his way. And now he had to change the front tire and try to get this car out of the ditch on the side of the road where he'd swerved to miss that wolf. He should have just hit her. He opened up the trunk to remove the jack. Once he had the tire changed and the car back on the road, he pulled off to the side, exhausted, and turned on his cell phone.

Service was weak, but he managed to get a signal for the phone, but no internet service. They were too far into the boonies. He sighed and placed a call to the GPS tracking company; within minutes he had a location on the sisters. They were about sixty miles ahead of him. Damn.

He sped along the lonely highway, hoping he'd find a gas station with food before he caught up to them. He needed to refortify. It wouldn't be too long now. He was closing in on them. He could feel it. He wasn't the only one wounded. He'd hit one of them. He'd seen the blood. And now that she-bitch had a taste of his.

He ran his fingertips over the gun in his lap and wondered how bad her wound was. He hoped it was bad. He hoped she was suffering. His phone rang, startling him out of his thoughts. He glanced down at the small screen. It was his brother again. He'd been calling nonstop, wanting to know where he was and why he hadn't shown up to work. This time, he decided to answer.

"This is Mark," he said.

"Where the hell are you?" his brother bellowed. "The captain wants to know why you're not here and when you're coming in. I can't cover for you anymore."

"I just need some personal time, Louis."

"Don't we all?" his brother groaned. "Just what the hell do you expect me to tell everyone? That my pansy-ass brother needs some alone time?"

"Tell them whatever you want," Mark grumbled.

"Does this have anything to do with that blond shop-girl? I know her place was broken into, and then there were the…wolves."

Mark cringed. It would only be a matter of time before his brother figured out that Ruby was the daughter of the missing woman he'd claimed was a werewolf. Oh, yeah, then the taunting and teasing would start up all over again and his life would totally suck. He would get the truth and prove to Louis and his dad that he wasn't crazy, that there were werewolves. And they were living right there in Sedona.

"I just need a couple more days," Mark insisted. "Can you do that for me? Can you trust me, just this once?"

Mark switched off his phone and threw it into the passenger's seat before giving Louis a chance to reply. He knew what Louis's answer would be. You can't trust a crazy man.

Mark shook his head. He no longer cared about his job at the department, or the fact that his life seemed to be falling apart around him. All he cared about was finding those wolves.

Chapter 9

Malcolm watched Celia out of the corner of his eye as he drove down the lonely winding highway. She hadn't said a word, hadn't moved an inch, just sat there with her head tilted against the window. After what had happened between them, he needed to know how she felt about him. It had been so good to hold her again, to lie with her in his arms. He hadn't felt that close to her in years, and she'd felt it, too. She'd had to. And if there was a chance, even a small one, that she could forgive him, he needed to hear it from her lips. To know he still had something to fight for.

"Can we talk about what happened last night?" He cringed at the expectant note in his words. At his hope sounding so clear between them.

She didn't move. Didn't say a word.

"Celia?" he pushed.

"I don't think so, Malcolm. Nothing happened. Not really," she said, not even bothering to look at him.

Frustration surged through his veins. "What?" His voice was low as incredulity filled him. "What happened was beautiful. Wonderful." He wouldn't let her negate that. She was still shutting him out, still running even after everything they still obviously meant to each other. "We haven't shared a connection like that—"

"What happened was sex," she said, cutting him off. "Plain and simple, hot and heavy sex. We fulfilled a momentary physical need. Don't read more into it than was actually there, Malcolm. I haven't."

Her words, wicked and sharp, sliced through him. His eyes narrowed as anger clouded his reason, raging past the boiling point. He couldn't admit to her how badly she'd hurt him. But she had, and the worst part was he still wanted her. More than he'd ever wanted anything.

"What happened to you, Celia? You're so…cold."

She sat forward, pivoting toward him. "You happened, Malcolm. You threw us away and planned to marry some other wolf just to guarantee your leadership of the Pack. Do you really think I could ever forgive you for that?"

He flinched, knowing she was right. She would never forgive him for that. And after his stupid feud with Scott cost him his position and got her mother killed, hell, he didn't think he'd be able to forgive himself.

"So what is she like?" she snapped.

Confused, he looked at her, then realized what she

wanted to know. What had her so angry. "Shay? Madly in love with Jason. Committed to him. And he's committed to her."

"Right." She blinked, processing, and then she started to laugh. Loud, long and hard until tears were leaking out the corners of her eyes.

"She looks at him the way you used to look at me," he added, his bitter regret obvious.

"Yeah, well, there was a time when I stupidly thought we could have it all."

"There was a time when we did have it all."

Her eyes were two glittering stones of fury. "No, Malcolm. We were never even close."

They fell into blessed silence, not speaking again as the sky grew dark. It was late as they approached the tall iron gates leading into the Colony. He stopped and honked the truck's horn. Johnny's face lit up as he appeared in the large window of the guardhouse. He waved to Celia in the passenger seat, leaned down and hit a button. The gate opened.

"How about I park and we run the rest of the way? We've been cooped up in this truck all day, and I for one need to stretch."

"And heal."

"You game, then?"

"Sure. It will be nice to run without fear of exposure, or guns, or…anything else." She almost smiled then, and he hated how badly he'd wanted to see it. He drove through the gates, parked the truck and got out.

"Hey, Johnny!" Celia greeted as he ran toward them and enveloped her in a giant hug. "It's good to see you."

"Not half as good as it is to see you, darling. I wasn't sure the man here could come through for us."

"You doubted me?" Malcolm mocked.

Johnny smiled and shrugged.

"We're going to run home," Malcolm said to him as he unbuttoned his shirt. "Would you mind giving us a little time before letting anyone know we're back?"

Johnny's lips pressed together in hesitation as his eyes filled with doubt.

And Malcolm didn't blame him. He'd left the Colony, disappeared before they could bring him in for questioning in Jaya's death. He was certain they had a cell all warmed up and waiting for him to await his Judgment. They would expel him. He knew that. It was the ultimate punishment for causing the death of another. Especially one as needed as Jaya. These last few hours with Celia were all he had left now.

"I'd really appreciate it, Johnny. I need to heal. I'll call Jason in the morning and tell him we're back myself."

"Heal?"

"Yeah, it was nothing. Don't worry about it."

Celia started to say something but thankfully didn't. The last thing he wanted to do right now was explain about the human.

"All right, Malcolm. I'll call him in the morning."

"Thanks. I owe you." More than he knew.

"Good to see you again, Johnny," Celia said as she walked into the woods.

"You, too, darling. Have a great run."

They stepped into the thick trees, undressing as they

moved, transforming and running side by side as they used to long ago and hopefully as they would many more times to come. But Malcolm knew better than to get his hopes up. His time was almost over.

Following the river along the lake, running with Celia at his side, free without worry about demons or humans, he enjoyed the familiar terrain, their hunt and freedom, until finally they arrived at the back gate to his house. Would she stay with him? How he hoped she would. He knew it was selfish, but he wanted to spend this one last night together before Jason and the Council came for him in the morning. There would be a public tribunal where she would hear every sordid detail of his mistakes, the damage he'd caused, the blood that was spilled, while he would await the Council's final Judgment. But what would be worse than being expelled from the Colony was seeing the recrimination and loathing that was sure to be in Celia's eyes.

"How does it feel to be home?" Malcolm asked Celia as they entered through his back gate and walked into the lush backyard he'd designed around a large saltwater pool. This had always been Celia's favorite place and he'd hoped once she was here, she'd want to stay. He locked the gate behind him and they walked toward the pool and the back of the house.

"Better than I expected. I've missed it," Celia admitted. "A part of me wants to run home and talk to my mom. To tell her all about Sedona and the twins."

He winced at her words. No, her mom wouldn't ever be there again. "By twins, you mean your cousins? The ones with the baseball bat?" he asked, diverting the subject.

She nodded. "They're pretty awesome, aren't they?"

He didn't know about *awesome,* but certainly tenacious and a bit intimidating.

She sighed. "I know my mom's not there. I'm just not ready to accept it yet." She blinked back her tears. "I don't even want to think about it."

He longed to pull her into his arms, hold her tight and comfort her, but he knew he couldn't push her or she'd be gone in a flash. "How about a swim?" he asked instead.

Her gaze drifted to the large pool he'd always kept heated just for her even long after she'd left, and her lips lifted in a slight smile. Not much, but he'd take it. He knew how much she loved to swim, especially at night when the stars were bright. She stared at the gleaming water, then bent down and drew her fingers across the glassy surface and nodded. "That would be great."

"Your clothes are still in your room."

She looked up at him, her eyes wide.

"You look surprised."

"I suppose I expected you to box up my stuff and send it back to my mom's. Especially after…everything."

He took a step toward her. "I wasn't ready to let you go."

Their eyes met for a moment and he longed to reach for her, to brush her beautiful hair back behind her ears and pull her into his arms.

"I'll be back in a minute," she said, turned away and hurried into the house.

He watched through the floor-to-ceiling glass windows as she walked through the great room and disappeared down the hallway toward the bedrooms at the back of the house. He collapsed into one of the patio chairs, closed his eyes and waited for her to return. He'd half expected her to leave for her mom's already. He certainly never thought she'd stay here with him and go for a swim. Maybe there was still hope for him yet.

"Jeez, what is this place?" Ruby asked as they pulled in front of a large iron gate flanked on either side by stone pillars. Beyond the gate their headlights outlined a small guardhouse. "I can't believe we followed Celia all this way just to end up in the middle of nowhere. Are you sure they went in there?" she asked, staring up at the large gate in front of them. "It's kind of creepy."

"Well, it is dark and we're on an isolated road. I didn't want to follow too close or they'd have seen us. Besides, where else could they have gone? All roads lead here."

"All right, let's give it a try," Ruby said.

Jade parked the car in front of the gate. They got out and tried to open it. It didn't budge. "I think they're locked up for the night. The guardhouse looks empty."

"What should we do now?" Ruby looked at the bleak forest surrounding them. "I haven't seen anyone or anything for hours. And we're a long way from the nearest hotel." She leaned against the car and stared up at the multitude of stars in the sky. "I sure hate the idea of spending another night in the car."

"Me, too," Jade agreed. "In fact, if I don't have to get back in this car for another five days, I'll be happy."

A long howl split the night air, followed by another. "What was that?" Ruby whispered as the hair on the back of her neck lifted.

"Quick, get back in the car," Jade insisted. They practically threw themselves into the front seat and locked the doors.

"Now what?" Ruby asked, as she searched the darkness around them.

"Wolves."

"Wolves?" Ruby's eyes widened with fear.

"Looks as if we're sleeping in the car again." Jade groaned, and pulled the lever that released the seat and leaned back.

"You're kidding me," Ruby grumbled.

"Do you have any other ideas? In case you didn't notice, that's the truck we were following in front of the guard's house. Unless we ram the gate, there's no way in, and we can't very well sleep outside with the wolves. So the way I see it, there's nothing we can do until morning."

"Fine," Ruby muttered, trying to shake the uneasiness from her mind. "But Celia is going to owe me bigtime for this one."

Slowly, Celia put on her bathing suit while looking around her room. Malcolm was right. Everything was exactly the way she'd left it. A bittersweet ache filled her as her gaze roamed the room, falling across the pictures of their life together, the keepsakes they'd collected, the dreams they'd shared. Dreams she'd left behind when she moved to Sedona searching for a new life.

But now she was back. The problem was she didn't want these dreams anymore. She didn't want to marry Malcolm and live in the Colony and be happy ever after. Truth was, she had no idea what she wanted. Other than to have her mother back. But like so many other things, that was impossible. She sighed and finished slipping into her suit. She needed to stop thinking.

She left the room and before she knew it, she was in the warm water of Malcolm's pool, swimming back and forth, stretching her arms out above her head, feeling the water sluice across her body. She'd missed this pool. As always, the meditative powers of the water restored the unrest in her mind and lightened her mood.

She heard a splash and turned to see Malcolm swimming alongside her, matching her stroke for stroke. Long before she'd left the Colony, he'd stopped joining her in the pool or spending much of any time with her. How could she not have seen how preoccupied he'd become? How they'd both begun living lonely, separate lives?

He pulled ahead of her and she quickened her pace. Clearing her mind, not wanting to think about what had gone wrong between them. She redoubled her efforts, swimming faster, trying to outswim the thoughts circling in her mind. Pumping her legs, she sped through the water until at last she stopped, out of breath, her muscles burning with exertion.

Malcolm swam up alongside her, and with his dark

hair dripping on his shoulders and his green eyes shining in the moonlight, it was easy to forget everything he'd done, all the mistakes they'd both made. "Damn, you're good."

She grinned. "And don't forget it."

"How could I?" He moved closer to her. "I'm an idiot, Celia. You know that. You've always known it, ever since we were kids."

"I sure did tell you enough."

He smiled. "All the time."

He pulled her to him and she slipped easily into his arms. And before she could think about it, or pull away, he pressed his lips against hers. Malcolm's kisses always had the ability to turn her insides to mush, to make her forget all her rules and everything else except the feel of his hands on her arms, his lips on her mouth,

His hard chest pressed tight against hers, and she felt the warmth of his skin, the beat of his heart, his soft breath against her. This was a mistake. She knew that. And yet here she was, once again getting too close. Leaning on him, using him to help her forget.

Reluctantly she pulled back from his touch. From his lips. "We shouldn't," she murmured, even as his mouth once more found hers.

"I know," he mumbled without breaking contact. His tongue swept inside her mouth, filling her with desire. It coiled deep in her belly, spreading out to make her knees weak. "But I want you."

And the sad truth was, she wanted him, too. She wanted him to steal her thoughts away and make her numb. She twined her arms around his neck and played with the wet hair curling at the nape of his neck and lost herself in his kiss, in the way his mouth moved over hers, so familiar and warm and strong. His tongue slipped over hers and her knees weakened. She clung closer, feeling his heat move through her.

He pulled her over to the first step, moving his quick, sure, confident fingers inside her bathing suit top, stroking, caressing, tweaking and never lifting his mouth from hers until she had to pull away just to breathe. Without saying a word, he tugged the strings on her top and then it was off and floating away. His mouth was on hers again, devouring her as if he was desperate for nourishment and she was his sustenance. As if he was a man who'd been alone for far too long. And maybe he had.

She knew she had.

And she'd missed him. Missed his touch. His kiss. His gentle murmuring, the way he was doing now as he used his mouth on her, loving her as no one ever had.

Touch me, she thought. Pleading internally, pushing away the doubts and the little voice that warned her she was making a huge mistake. One she might not come back from.

And then her bottoms were off and he was lifting her, filling her, and her head was dropping backward as a guttural moan exploded from inside her.

Fill me.

"Oh, please, Malcolm," she begged as he lifted her again, almost completely off him, her body contracting, searching, aching. He dropped her back down on him, hard and demanding. She shifted her legs, her feet finding purchase on the next step down, and she moved herself, rocking back and forth, bucking her hips faster and faster as the heat between them reached the boiling point.

Move me.

She was soaring, her cries of pleasure echoing around them, and it was all she could do to hold on to his shoulders as her strength abandoned her. And then Malcolm was lifting her up, carrying her into the house and to his bed. A satisfied smile twisted her lips because she knew he was just beginning, and this night, he'd move her again and again.

Chapter 10

The next morning, Celia woke and rolled over. She was lying next to Malcolm in his bed. Their night together, the things they'd said and done, filled her mind, and brought tears of frustration to her eyes. She would never be able to stay away from him. Somehow, even after all he'd done, he still managed to steal her breath, sweep her off her feet and swoop her right into his bed—like a lamb willingly led to the slaughter.

Careful not to wake him, she crept out of his bed, trying to put as much distance between them as she could. She had to get her thoughts together. Now that she was back at the Colony, for who knew how long, she couldn't fall back into this trap. She loved Malcolm. She always had. And she loved making love to him. When she was with him, she didn't think about anything else.

He was the best escape on the planet and was still the best lover she'd ever had.

But she needed more than that. She sighed as she looked down at him, sleeping peacefully. She needed so much more.

She left his bedroom and slipped into the one she'd always kept in his house for herself with her things and quickly dressed. She would go out for a run, revitalize the crystals and perhaps if she wasn't too tired, go by her mother's house.

Tension tightened her chest at the thought. She didn't want to. Wasn't sure she could handle walking into the home she'd grown up in that had always been bursting with life, only to find it empty. No sounds of her mother singing, no smells of her latest concoction bubbling on the stove, no laughter. In the blink of an eye, Celia had lost everything.

She slipped on her tennies and left the house, jogging down the road, heading toward the center of town. She took a deep breath of the familiar pine-scented air. It did feel good to be home. She broke through the trees and jogged up the steps to Tiffany's Café. A cup of coffee and one of her friend's fabulous blueberry scones would make her feel better. She walked into the room to the twinkling sound of bells.

"Celia, you're back!" Tiffany, her best friend since grade school, screamed. She ran around the counter and threw her arms around Celia, almost knocking her off her feet.

Celia took a few steps back, finding her balance, and couldn't help the wide smile that filled her face. Her friend's much-needed welcome felt so good. "I had to come back," she said. "I couldn't find a blueberry scone in all of Arizona I liked better than yours."

Tiffany beamed, her curly brown hair bouncing around her face. "Then you'd better sit yourself right down and let me bring you one. I just took a fresh tray out of the oven. I'll put them in the case and then you can fill me in on everything!"

While Celia waited, she sat at the table by the window, watching the little town come to life—Mrs. Walker at the garden center with her explosion of hibiscus and azaleas, old man Tom at the hardware shop opening his blinds. Even Sophie from the tavern, who wasn't happy unless she was stirring up a pot full of drama, was writing her specials on the blackboard out front. Yes, Celia had missed it here. More than she'd realized.

Tiffany set a tray on the table in front of her with a steaming mug of coffee and a warm blueberry scone. The rich scent of coffee filled Celia's nose as she breathed it in. Tiffany dropped into the chair across from her and placed her hand on her arm. "I'm so sorry to hear about your mama."

Celia swallowed the lump in her throat. "Thank you." She took a deep drink of her coffee while gathering up the courage to talk about it. "I still really can't believe it's happened. I'm trying not to think about it." But she would have to soon. She knew that.

"I know," Tiffany said, squeezing and then patting her arm. "And I'm sure you don't want to talk about it and I don't blame you. But I'm here for you when you do. I loved your mom, you know that."

Celia did know that. Tiffany had spent many nights at her house when they were small, making batch after batch of chocolate-chip cookies or brownies, sleeping over and having pillow fights. Tears filled her eyes at the thought, and Tiffany leaned forward and gave her a tight hug.

"I love you, Celia."

"I love you, too," Celia said, and was more than a little thankful when the bells above the door chimed and another customer came in.

"I'll talk to you later," Tiffany whispered. "I want to hear all about where you've been and what it's like on the outside." Then she got up to greet a woman Celia had never seen before.

"Good morning, Shay," Tiffany said brightly. "What can I get you?"

Shay. Celia stiffened. Dean's child. The woman with the bloodline meant to lead the Pack. The woman Malcolm had hoped would solidify his position as Pack leader if he'd married her. And yet she'd married his best friend instead. Celia shook her head. Her whole life had been turned upside down by this woman, and before today, she'd never even laid eyes on her. Shay was half human and had grown up on the outside, but once she made the change, she had to return to the home of her father. Whether she'd wanted to or not.

She was one of them now. And she was here to stay.

"Good morning," the woman said, standing before her. Celia took in her long flowing dark hair and incredible blue-violet eyes. "We haven't met. I'm Shay."

"Celia," she said, holding out her hand and standing so the woman wouldn't be looking down at her.

Shay's eyes widened. "So Malcolm was able to find you?"

Celia nodded.

"Well, thank you for coming back."

Surprise filled her. Something about this woman was setting her teeth on edge. She acted as if she knew everything about her. Things she probably shouldn't know. How much had Malcolm told her about them? "Of course I'd come back," she snapped. "I grew up here. I would never let anything happen to the Pack."

Shay took a step back. "I'm sorry. I didn't mean to suggest…"

Celia sucked in a deep breath.

"I'm sorry about your mother," Shay said, her voice soft. "She was a very special woman."

"You knew my mother?" Celia hated the feeling of betrayal that rushed through her. The woman had been in the Colony for what, a second? And she'd known her mother, and about Malcolm? What didn't this woman know about her life?

"Briefly," Shay answered, guessing she'd stepped on a land mine. "She showed me how to use the crystals."

"You can manipulate the energy in the crystals?" Celia looked at her with renewed interest. If this woman could regenerate the stones, then there was no reason for Celia to be here or to have to stay.

"Only the healing energy, not the dark energy that keeps the *Gauliacho* at bay."

"Oh," Celia said, more disappointed than she realized. For a moment, she'd seen her path to freedom, and then she knew, no matter what happened with Malcolm, she couldn't stay here. She didn't want to be here. She belonged in Arizona now. In her new life. On her own.

The bells above the door rang again and Mr. Jenks, her old science teacher, walked in. His eyes narrowed with disapproval as he saw her. Surprised, she stiffened and found herself holding her breath as he approached.

"Where have you been, young lady? You have a responsibility to this Pack, to your gift to protect this Colony. You can't go gallivanting around the world risking yourself when there are people here who need you. Who depend on you to keep them safe."

"It's all right, Mr. Jenks," Tiffany said, and led him over to his standard table. "Celia is home now and she's here to stay."

"And not a moment too soon, if you ask me," he muttered.

Annoyed, Celia turned away from him. She had a life, too. The Pack didn't own her. She didn't ask for this gift, and right now she didn't even want it. She took one last look at her coffee and untouched scone, then headed toward the door. "Thanks, Tiffany," she called to her friend, and then left the room without saying another word to Shay or Mr. Jenks.

"Welcome home, Celia," she muttered to herself as she walked down the street toward the woods. Right now she wished she was anywhere but here.

Malcolm woke to an empty bed and a smile on his face. Last night had been wonderful. Better than wonderful. It had been fantastic and the way it used to be, long ago before things started to go wrong. He got up, quickly showered and dressed, then searched the house and back patio for Celia, but she was gone.

Probably up on the mountain regenerating the stones. He wondered if she'd gone to Tiffany's first for coffee and a scone. If he hurried, perhaps he'd find her. He hadn't yet told her of his impending incarceration for his role in the death of her mother and that he'd soon have to turn himself in. With his truck still at the gate, he pulled his motorcycle out of the garage and hurried into town. Celia wasn't at Tiffany's, but Shay was. *Damn*. Now he'd have to call Jason sooner than he'd hoped.

"Hey, Malcolm, you just missed her," Tiffany said.

He nodded his thanks, then approached Shay's table.

"Have a seat." She gestured toward the chair across from her before he could say anything.

"How are things?" he started, not knowing what to say to her. Sorry would never be enough for what he'd done to her and Jason. The plan had started out so simply. Trap Jason in a pit and force Shay to marry him long enough to get Scott to back the hell off. Only nothing had gone as planned. Jason had got badly hurt and Jaya had got killed. He wasn't sure how he could ever get past it. How any of them could. "Jason?"

"Don't bother," she said firmly.

His eyes met hers as he waited to hear what she wanted from him.

"I know you're sorry," she said dismissively. "I know you never meant for Jason to get hurt or for what happened to Jaya. But that's beside the point. A lot has changed in the time you've been gone."

"In six days?" he said drily, wondering how much things could really have changed in a place that rejected anything new or different.

"Yes. In six days," she mocked. "Jason and I have been brought up to speed and we're running things together."

He leaned back in his chair. "Don't worry. I didn't come back here thinking I would lead the Pack again."

"Good. Because right now the Council still thinks you're gone. They've been interviewing my grandfather and Scott trying to figure out how Jaya got killed. Jason and I sat in front of them for hours telling them everything we knew that had happened that day, and I can tell you it doesn't look good for you or Scott."

"Do you believe the Council will put me beyond the gates?" he asked, knowing that after what he'd just been through, he wouldn't make it a week on the outside.

"I honestly don't know. What you did was horrendous. But what Scott did to try and unseat you was worse. I believe that the two of you fed off each other's ambitions and insecurities, escalating events to the point that Jaya was killed. She's dead, Malcolm, putting us all at risk."

He leaned forward. "I know that! I'm in love with her daughter. How the hell am I supposed to tell her what I did? Do you think she'll ever forgive me? Do you think I'll ever be able to forgive myself?"

Surprise entered her blue eyes. "Celia still doesn't know?"

Malcolm shook his head. "Only that her mother is dead. Not everything that I did to make it happen."

"I don't mean to meddle in your personal business, but you'd better tell her. And soon, before she finds out from someone else." Shay's eyes moved to Tiffany standing behind the counter, trying not to make it obvious that she was listening to every word they said.

Malcolm nodded and lowered his voice. "I know. She just… She means so much to me. I don't know how to say it."

She blew out an annoyed breath. "Suck it up, Malcolm. You made this mess. Now show her you're man enough to own it."

Malcolm bit back the need to snap at her as frustration coiled through him. What did she know about him and Celia?

"Let us know if there is anything Jason and I can do to help," she said at length before he could respond.

"Just don't tell anyone we're back yet. I'll tell Celia everything as soon as she comes down off the mountain."

Shay smirked. "If you'd wanted to keep your presence here a secret, this is the last place you should have come." She rose and left.

"What can I get you?" Tiffany asked as she approached the table.

"Just coffee."

"Thanks for bringing Celia home," she said as she placed a cup in front of him and filled it. "I've missed her."

He smiled. "Me, too."

"I'm rooting for you two, you know that, right?"

He nodded and took a sip of the coffee.

"Hey, Malcolm, while you're here, would you mind taking a look at our computer? It hasn't been working. Joe's system over at the grill isn't either, and it's caused us nothing but headaches."

Inwardly he groaned. Fixing computers was the last thing he wanted to do right now.

"And not just us," she continued. "Gerald over at the General Store says he's been having problems, too. It's as if everything around here has suddenly gone crazy."

An uncomfortable twinge lit through Malcolm.

"You wouldn't believe what a hassle it's become. Apparently we are a lot more dependent on these things than we'd thought."

"Sure, I'll take a quick look," Malcolm said, and hoped it would be an easy fix. Hoped it wasn't anything more serious than a good cleaning of the cache would fix. But somehow he doubted that. He stood. Suddenly he didn't like the idea of leaving Celia up there on that mountain alone.

"Ruby, wake up," Jade said, pushing roughly on her shoulder.

"Wake up? I never got to sleep," Ruby complained. "In fact, I don't think I've slept in days."

"You were snoring."

"Was not."

"Listen, this is almost over," Jade said. "The sooner we get in these gates and to Celia's house, the sooner I can get into a hot shower. Which just might save your life."

"My life? Why is that?" Ruby asked, rolling the tension out of her shoulders.

"Because if I don't get a shower and some coffee soon, I will kill someone. And you're closest."

Ruby grinned. "Yeah. I get how you feel." She pulled her ratted hair back into a ponytail, then got out of the car and walked up to the gate with Jade. "Hello!" she called to the man in the guardhouse.

He didn't answer but pointed to their right.

Jade walked over to the column with an intercom set into the stones and pushed the button.

"What is your business?" a male voice came across the intercom.

"We're here to see our cousin, Celia Lawson."

"Names?"

"Ruby and Jade James." She smiled at the guy standing at the window of the guardhouse watching them. She turned to Ruby and whispered, "Boy, he's cute."

Ruby rolled her eyes. No one was cute when you felt this yucky.

"Sorry, you're not on the guest list," the hot guy said.

"Well, can you call her please?" Jade asked in her sweetest voice.

Boy, she must really think he's cute, Ruby thought.

"Just a moment."

"Jeez, Celia never said she came from such a swanky place," Ruby said as they waited what seemed like forever. "Come to think of it, Celia never told us anything about where she'd come from."

"Sorry, no answer," the man said.

Ruby looked at Jade, annoyance narrowing her eyes. "Okay, now what?" Cute or not, he was being ridiculous.

"You'll need to come back later," the man said as if he'd heard her thoughts.

Ruby walked over to the column and pushed the button. "Come back? Where are we supposed to go? We're way out here in the middle of nowhere." Her voice was seriously reaching the whine zone. She was tired and hungry and grumpy and she had to use the bathroom and she was sick of going in the bushes.

"Sorry, ma'am, but those are the rules."

Jade leaned toward the intercom. "Do you think you can come out here for a second and talk to us?" she asked, still using her sweet tone.

The guard hesitated, then lumbered out of the shack. Obviously he was reluctant to talk with them. But Jade was right about one thing, he was hot. Tall, built and manly.

Jade stepped up to the gate. "Listen, we've come a really long way and we're too tired to turn back now. Isn't there any way you can let us in?"

He looked at her dispassionately and didn't answer.

"Our aunt Jaya has passed," she added. "We've come for the services."

Something flickered in his eyes. *Progress?* Ruby hoped so.

"Cousins of Celia, you say?"

"That's right," Ruby said. "Would you mind trying to call her again and let her know we've made it? I know she'll be very disappointed if she finds out we were here but weren't allowed in."

He unhooked the phone on his belt and punched in a number, let it ring for a moment, then hung up. "No answer. She's not home and hasn't been for a while."

"We know because she's been in Arizona with us. But we know she's back because the truck she came in is right over there."

He turned and looked where she pointed, then turned back to them, stoic-faced.

"Oh, come on," Ruby muttered.

Jade stepped forward. "All right, how about if we wait for her at her mom's—"

"Yes, at *our* aunt's house," Ruby said, emphasizing the fact that they were family.

"I'm sorry, but I can't let you in without an escort," Hot Guy said, taking a step back away from the gate. From *them*.

This was getting ridiculous. Ruby grabbed Jade's arm. "What was the name of that guy Celia was with?"

"Jeez, I don't remember."

"How can you not remember? You're the one who sent him into the canyons."

"Malcolm?" the man asked, a touch of disbelief in his voice.

"Yep, that's him," Ruby responded. "He came by our place a couple days ago and picked her up. He told her about her mom."

"It was so sad," Jade added.

"Yes," Ruby said, nodding. "Very sad. So we all had to get up here right away."

"Could you give him a call?" Jade pleaded. "We've come such a long way."

"And we're not leaving until we see her," Ruby continued. "I'm sure you don't want us standing here blocking your gate until Celia finally gets back home."

Reluctantly the guard unhooked the phone off his belt again. "All right, but don't be surprised if Malcolm doesn't answer, either. He's been unreachable lately."

"That's because he's been with us," Ruby reiterated. Was this guy dense or what?

"Thank you so much," Jade said, smiling again. "We really appreciate it."

"Yes, a lot," Ruby added. "We're finally going to get to use a real bathroom."

"And take a hot shower."

"Malcolm," the man said into his phone, stepping away from them. "We have a situation at the gate."

"What?" Malcolm yelled into the phone. "Are you kidding me?"

"I wish I were," Johnny said. "But they're very persistent and they're not leaving until they see Celia."

"Unbelievable." He paced back and forth, trying to figure out what to do. "She's up on the mountain regenerating the stones."

"That could take all day. I tried to send them away until I could reach her, but they refused to go."

"Did you call Jason?"

"No. Not yet. I'm not sure what to do. This isn't the time to be opening the gates to humans. But they are Jaya's kin."

"I know." Malcolm cursed under his breath. What the hell were those two women doing all the way out there? And what was he supposed to do with them? Obviously they hadn't gone back to Sedona after the incident at the rest stop. But how could they have followed him all the way here without him knowing? "What am I supposed to do with them?"

"You got me," Johnny said, his voice sounding tight. "But they're not going to go away quietly, I can assure you of that."

Malcolm supposed he could take them to Jaya's. He couldn't very well bring them back to his house. He was in enough trouble with the Council as it was without harboring two humans. But then again, he couldn't leave them sitting outside the gate, either. He swiped a hand down his face. "I'll come get them. But, Johnny, do me a favor and don't tell anyone. I'll take them to Jaya's house, find Celia and try to get them back out before anyone is the wiser."

"Malcolm, this doesn't sound like a very good idea to me. What you're asking me to do could get me in a lot of trouble. Get both of us in a lot of trouble," Johnny said, keeping his voice low.

"I know, and I really appreciate that. I'll take full responsibility."

"Yeah, except you're not in charge anymore. Jason is."

Malcolm bristled at his words. Getting things done was going to be a hell of a lot harder than it used to be. "I get that. I'll tell you what, I'll call Jason and have him meet us at the gate. It will be his call whether or not we let them in, okay?"

"Sounds good. Truth is, these women, especially together, look like a lot more than I can handle."

Malcolm laughed as he thought about the blonde brandishing a baseball bat and the brunette with the fire burning in her eyes. "Oh, Johnny, you have no idea."

Chapter 11

Malcolm would have to call Jason. From here on out, he was including Jason in on every decision he made. It was the only way to protect himself from the Council once they discovered what was going on.

"Are you nuts?" Jason bellowed into the phone.

Wincing, Malcolm held the phone out from his ear. "Apparently," he muttered, "but what else do you suggest we do?"

"We absolutely cannot let humans into the Colony right now. Not with the computer problems all over town, the vulnerability of the boundaries, Jaya's death and your upcoming Judgment. Hell, Malcolm, do you really think you can afford to make things any worse for yourself?"

"Hell no! Why do you think I'm calling you?" Annoyance tightened his grip on the phone.

Jason took a deep breath. "How did those girls find us anyway?"

"They must have followed us."

"You let them follow you?" Jason asked, incredulity raising his voice again.

"Yes, that's what I did," Malcolm snapped. "I let them follow me."

Neither man spoke for a long moment.

Finally Malcolm broke the ice. He needed Jason's help. He needed his friend back. "Jason, come on. I was more than a little distracted dealing with Celia."

"How is she?"

"Upset. But she's here. She's up on the mountain rejuvenating the stones now."

"Good."

"I think the only thing we can do now is take Celia's cousins over to Jaya's place until Celia gets back. I don't see how we can send them away, not after following us all the way here. I'll keep them out of sight until Celia gets a chance to talk to them, to explain why they can't stay here."

"What do you think she'll say?" Jason asked.

"I haven't a clue, but we can't leave them standing outside the gates making a fuss. And she's the only one they're going to listen to." Even though he'd only met them for a second, he could see the bond between them was strong.

"This isn't going to end well, I can feel it," Jason said after a long pause.

"Do you have any other suggestions? Because if you do, I'm open." *Very open.*

"I'll call Johnny and tell him you're on your way to get the girls. But make sure no one else see them. And I mean no one."

As if he didn't already know that. "You got it, boss."

"And, Malcolm?"

Malcolm hesitated, not liking the sound of Jason's tone. "Yeah?"

"Once you get them settled, we need to talk about what's happening with the computers."

"You mean the computers no one wanted, but now no one can seem to live without?"

"Yeah. There's a problem with them. With all of them. And I'm beginning to think maybe Scott and Jaya were right, and we never should have brought them in."

Malcolm seethed but swallowed the tension before he spoke. "I'll see what I can do," he pushed through gritted teeth, then hung up the phone before Jason could say any more.

Malcolm rode out to the guardhouse. As he approached he saw his truck parked next to an old maroon Pontiac. Now he remembered seeing this car. Obviously they'd followed him, but Celia had sent them back. How could he not have seen them?

Because the only thing he'd been focused on was Celia.

Stupid.

He got off the bike and smiled a wide, welcoming smile. "Good morning," he said to the long-legged beauties. Celia's cousins. Two of them. Double for his trouble. And he had a feeling they'd be bringing a lot with them. "We haven't been properly introduced. I'm Malcolm," he said, holding out his hand.

"Ruby," the blonde said, stepping forward. He remembered her hair was a shining sunshiny gold that had tumbled in thick wavy curls around her shoulders the day at the rest stop when she'd brandished that baseball bat. Blond hair that highlighted crystal-blue eyes, only now that hair was pulled back in a messy ponytail.

"Jade," her sister said, stepping forward. As light as Ruby's hair was, Jade's was dark—a deep obsidian—cropped short, hovering at her chin, but she had the same incredible crystal-blue eyes as her sister.

"Malcolm," Johnny said, looking very uncomfortable as he stood behind the girls. "Jason just called and told me you are taking them to Jaya's."

"Yep." And the sooner the better.

"Before you go, would you mind taking a look at our computer? It's not working."

Blazes, what was happening around there? Was every computer in town down? He looked at Celia's cousins. "You girls don't mind hanging out a little longer, do you?"

He could tell by the looks on their faces that they did. And he couldn't help the small amount of pleasure he took in that.

"As long as he has coffee," the dark-haired one said.

"And a bathroom," Ruby, who'd been brandishing the baseball bat, added. He should have realized back then at the rest stop that if they'd followed him all that way…

"Thanks, Malcolm," Johnny said. "I wouldn't ask, but these machines link all the perimeter cameras along the fences onto several screens. Right now we're flying blind."

After showing the girls to the kitchen, Malcolm followed Johnny to the back room, where all the monitors were black.

"How long have they been down?" Uneasiness filled him as he took in the dark screens.

"A couple of days now. We've tried everything to fix them, but nothing has worked."

Malcolm didn't like the sound of that. He sat down and tried a few different diagnostics, but nothing seemed to help. He couldn't make heads or tails of what was happening, and the girls were growing antsier by the second. The last thing he needed to do was have to try and explain their security system and why they needed one on top of a mountain out in the middle of nowhere.

"Listen, Johnny. Let me drop the girls off at Jaya's, find Celia and then I'll get back here to work on it. Just to be safe, take the system offline, reboot it and go back to the manual systems until we can get a handle on what's going on with the computers around here. This isn't the only computer acting up."

"All right," Johnny said, but he looked doubtful. "I hope you and Jason know what you're doing."

Me, too, Malcolm thought.

"You should run an antivirus scan, too," Jade said from the doorway. "And a cleaner on your files."

Malcolm turned to her. "You know about computers?"

"A little."

He turned back to the system and checked the records. "The scan is supposed to run every night at midnight. For some reason it's offline." He set the systems and restarted it.

"Okay, when that's finished, reboot the computer and then do me a favor and call Jason. Tell him what's going on with the system and what you're doing about it." He walked with the girls out the doorway and toward the front of the house. Then turned back and said under his breath, "And call the boys and do a manual sweep of the fences. Something about all this is beginning to make me nervous."

"You got it," Johnny said, looking relieved to see the girls getting into Malcolm's truck. "And don't worry, Jason stepped right in and took over while you were gone, nice and easy. There have been no other problems other than the computers. I just thought you'd like to know that."

"I appreciate that, Johnny," Malcolm said, and walked out the door. "That's real good to hear." Too bad his shoes were so easy to fill. Maybe if they hadn't been, things would go easier for him with the Council.

He followed the girls into his truck, then turned around and started back down the road. For an instant, he thought he saw the gleam of chrome bounce off his side-view mirror. He stopped the truck and looked behind him out his window. Was someone else there? Someone else who could have followed him or the twins? A moment of unease wormed through him and he was glad he'd asked Johnny to have them manually check the fences. If someone was out there, they would find them. With everything that was going on right then, upping security might not be such a bad idea.

From the trees, Mark watched the twins get into the truck with the man from the rest stop and drive away. Iron gates soaring at least ten feet high were flanked on either side by stone columns that hooked onto a long line of chain link running for as far as the eye could see. There was no getting past that. With his binoculars he could see cameras at various points and the computer screens in the guardhouse.

What was this place? An exclusive high-end gated community on top of a mountain where there wasn't another living soul for at least fifty miles didn't make sense. Why would anyone want to live way out here? And second, why would they need so much security? What were they hiding? Or maybe the question should be *who* were they hiding?

He drove back down the road and parked his car out of sight, then started walking back toward the fence. He would find a way to breach the border. He didn't know what these people were hiding, but it had to be good. He would find it and discover why the twins were here. Why come all this way? Unless it had something to do with their secret. Maybe there were others like them here. *Other wolves.* Then, were the fences here to keep strangers out or to keep the people in? *To keep the wolves in.*

Anticipation bubbled in his blood. He was onto something here; he could feel it tingling all over him. And he would be the one to prove it. To show everyone there were such things as werewolves. They did exist, and they were living and walking among them.

A couple of hours later, and what had to be several miles of walking along the fence, Mark collapsed onto a rock. All this way and he still hadn't found a way in. He rested as he contemplated his options. The fence was too high to climb, and the barbed wire rolled along the top made it all the more problematic. And from what he'd been able to determine, there were cameras everywhere.

Every time he spotted one, he'd have to go out of his way to make sure he wasn't caught in their sight. Why would they need so many cameras? He had to get a handle on what was going on in there before they spotted him. But so far he'd seen nothing but trees. And certainly nothing that would justify this level of security. There had to be a weakness in their perimeter. There was no way they could properly secure this much land. He just had to find it. He started walking again, certain that sooner or later he would find a way in.

After another two hours, he was thirsty and tired and he started getting sloppy. Sometimes he'd forget to check for the cameras, and at least twice now he had to have been spotted, and yet no one had come. Perhaps this place wasn't as secure as he thought. Perhaps the cameras were all for show. Maybe no one really was watching. He was starting to feel more confident when suddenly he heard something. He stilled, going real quiet. The lilting sound of a voice reached him.

Carefully he stepped forward so as not to step on anything that might crack or break under his feet. He drew closer to the sound until he could make out the low rumble of a chant. He crept forward and then he saw a woman sitting before a boulder, her eyes closed, her hands spread palms up on her crossed legs. A low moan emitted from her throat and echoed through the air.

It was the woman he'd seen in the parking lot of the diner. Ruby's cousin, Celia. The creepy one. What was she doing? Some kind of meditation? And then he saw the crystals before her, large black-and-red ones. The same ugly stones he'd seen in the window of the shop in Sedona. He'd never liked those crystals. Thought there was something inherently evil about a stone the color of blood.

He watched her for a moment, afraid to move lest she hear him. Was this some sort of commune? One of those New Age enlightened places? Maybe you had to pay a fortune to some charlatan in order to find spiritual cleansing or some such. Hell, Sedona was full of crackpots who thought they were in touch with something mystical or "out of this world." And they called *him* crazy.

The woman's eyes popped open and for a heart-stopping second, he thought she'd seen him. Thought she was looking right at him. But then she stood, bowed to the stones, then turned and walked away. He stared at the crystals for a full minute after she left and couldn't help wondering what they were for. Obviously they were important to her. Maybe he could use them to his advantage. All he had to do was get in and take them.

* * *

Celia took her time hiking to the north point of the perimeter. It was a beautiful day, crisp and clear with the scent of pine and cedar thick in the air. The crystals were placed on top of a large outcropping of rocks overlooking a valley of trees as far as the eye could see. She sat before the stones as her mother had shown her how to do, as her mother had done every two weeks all her life for as long as Celia could remember.

Now she sat before the stones, opening herself up to their energy, feeling the earth beneath her palms, the air against her skin. A gentle caress and, for a moment, she almost felt as if her mother were still there. That if she opened her eyes her mother would be sitting across from her smiling, her eyes brimming with pride. But Celia didn't open her eyes, because she knew she was wrong. It was only her heart wishing things could be different. But they weren't.

Her mother was gone.

She forced her thoughts back to the stones and the dark energy rising within them. She chanted the words her mother had taught her, her eyes closed, her hands touching the crystals. She could feel their power emanating outward through her and beyond, stretching along the cliffs, forming the barrier that would protect their energy signatures from the demons that hunted them.

Demons she knew were out there. The *Gauliacho*.

Even now as she sat at the edge of the cliff, her eyes closed, her senses wide-open, she could feel them out there. Could almost hear their insidious whispers reaching into her mind. Calling her name, pulling at her.

Celia.

Her eyes sprang open. For a second the colors around her seemed muted, different somehow. Almost…red. She blinked several times until her vision returned to normal and the only thing she heard was the squawking of a bird being chased by a hawk high above the trees. *Hurry, Celia.* She didn't know why, but suddenly her heart was racing. Sweat dampened her palms and brow. Something was wrong. It was as if the stones weren't enough, as if something was pushing against the perimeter, something stronger than her or her magic.

She had three more stones to regenerate and make sure were working properly. She moved quickly, almost running to the next compass point. She would need to change to make the best time. She had to because the *Gauliacho* were out there, waiting. She knew it. She could feel them. Worse, she could feel the danger growing stronger and pushing at them with each passing moment.

She took off her thin cotton dress, folded it and slipped it into a soft leather pouch hanging around her neck. Then she ran, feeling herself change as she did, happily giving up her human skin for the strong, muscular four legs that would carry her quickly through the thicket.

There isn't much time now.

Chapter 12

"Is this Aunt Jaya's house?" Ruby asked as Malcolm pulled into the driveway of the A-frame cottage nestled in the woods on the outskirts of town.

"Yep," he muttered, staring at the little cabin. It needed some maintenance done, the gutters cleaned, a patch on the roof. He should have done that for her. He would have, if he'd known. She should have said something. He should have noticed.

"Does Celia live here?" Jade asked.

Good question. Did she? She hadn't in a long time. But now… "Sometimes," he murmured, not knowing what else to say.

"Then where is she?" she asked, refusing to give up. She was a pushy one.

"Hiking," he said quickly, and got out of the truck.

"She did like to do that a lot," Ruby said as they walked toward the house.

"So what's going on with you two?" Jade asked.

Malcolm turned to her expectant face, hesitating.

"I can tell you she didn't want to see you back in Sedona. So what did you do?"

"I think that's between us," he said, and started to walk away, but she grabbed his arm, stopping him.

"True. And I realize I'm being nosy, but whatever you did, you better not do it again."

Malcolm's annoyance disappeared and he couldn't help admiring the steely glint in her eyes. She would protect Celia at all costs. Celia deserved to have these girls in her corner, and he had to admit, he was glad they were here for her now. Even if it was the last place they should be.

"Trust me, I know I screwed up and I'm going to do everything I can to make it up to her, if she'll let me."

Ruby smiled wide, and when she did it was hard to see anything else. "That's all we needed to hear."

Malcolm smothered a grin and stepped onto Jaya's front porch. He hesitated before opening the door. He could almost hear her voice calling to him. Almost. Until the image of her collapsing to the ground, the blood spreading across her chest rushed to his mind. He pushed it away, opened the front door and forced himself to walk inside. The small living room was cramped with too many pillows, blankets and an assortment of knickknacks. If Jaya wasn't collecting rocks and driftwood for her craft projects, she was buying other peoples junk, tearing it apart and making something else out of it. She was constantly moving, creating…living.

Damn.

"It's beautiful here," Ruby said, walking toward the large windows that looked out on the thick forest of trees.

"Not to be rude or anything, but I'm in desperate need of a shower. Do you mind?" Jade said abruptly.

"Not at all. Straight down that hall." Malcolm pointed to a doorway leading to a small bathroom they could see from where they stood. Jaya's home was small— a kitchen and living room composed the main area. A large circular fireplace centered the room and soared up to the top of the A-frame high above them. Two bedrooms and a bath occupied the other half of the first floor, and a staircase next to the kitchen led up to a loft where Jaya made her crafts in the wintertime when it was too cold to work out on the deck.

"Do you think Celia would mind if I made some coffee?" Ruby asked.

"No, no problem. Help yourself to anything. Make yourselves at…at home."

She walked into the kitchen. Malcolm watched her, feeling awkward and not sure what to do with himself. He didn't want to be there. And worse, he didn't have time to waste babysitting grown women. He needed to get back to Johnny's and find out what was happening with the computers in town. The fact that they were all acting up at once, at a time when the boundaries were already vulnerable, worried him. But until Celia got back, he didn't know what else he could do. He couldn't chance them not staying put.

He plopped onto one of the bar stools at the long kitchen counter that separated the kitchen from the family room. "Can you tell me why you followed us?" he asked, getting straight to the point.

Ruby looked up from filling the coffeepot with water, surprise widening her eyes. She finished, turned off the tap, put coffee grounds in the filter and then finally switched on the button before turning around to answer him.

"I was worried about Celia."

"Why?"

"She left in the middle of the night. The same night that someone broke into our shop. I was…concerned."

"But you saw us at the rest area. You saw she was with me, and that she was okay." She was hiding something from him; it was written all over her face.

"But she's not okay. Her mother just died. She needs us. We're her family and we're all she has left now."

Dammit, how could he argue with that? "So your mother was Jaya's sister, Sue?"

She gripped the counter with both hands, her eyes drifting to the coffeemaker. "Yep."

"Where is she now?" he asked, though he had a pretty good idea. No one had heard from Sue in a long time.

Ruby looked up at him, her teeth worrying her bottom lip as a shadow crossed her brilliant eyes, darkening them. "She died a long time ago. Or I should say she disappeared. All they found of her was her clothes."

"I'm sorry," he said softly. He remembered Sue. Remembered when she left the Colony. As one of the Keeper's of the crystals, she was certain she would be safe anywhere. Like Celia, he supposed. And just like Celia, Sue had an adventurous spirit and had felt trapped within the gates of the Colony. She'd wanted to go out and explore the world. Though he had a hard time believing Sue had succumbed to the *Gauliacho.*

"You never knew what happened to her?" he pressed.

Ruby shook her head, then turned to pour herself a cup of coffee.

Sue never should have stayed gone so long. Should never have fallen in love with a human. Her husband and even these girls would not have been welcomed here. Hell, they still weren't. But what of them? What were the odds that neither of them had made the change? If one or both would have, chances were good they would have inherited their mother's gift and be a Keeper of the crystals. If even one had, the Colony would be much more secure. And Celia wouldn't feel so trapped.

"Is there a computer here I can use?" Ruby asked. "I haven't been able to check my email in days."

"At Jaya's?" Malcolm laughed. "No. Jaya hated computers and televisions, anything electronic or modern. I think she finally put in a phone once Celia left, begrudgingly."

"You're kidding! Why?"

"I don't know. I guess she thought they were stealing the minds of the youth. She believed in connecting with nature, and said the whine of all our electronic devices was interfering with that."

"Well, I suppose there could be something to be said for that. But take my computer away and I'd have to kill you."

He laughed. "I know how you feel. I have a laptop in my truck. Hold on a sec and I'll get it for you."

Her face lit up with a bright smile.

Glad to finally be doing something, Malcolm went out to his truck and a second later came back with the laptop. He laid it on the counter for her. She opened it up and turned it on and had no sooner connected to the internet than the whole system crashed.

"Oh, no!" Ruby said, her face falling.

"What is it?"

"I think you have a virus. As soon as I connected, it crashed."

"Here, let me see." She pushed the laptop across the counter toward him just as Jade came out of the bath-room.

"All yours," Jade said to her sister. To Malcolm, she said, "Do you think Celia will mind if we borrow some of her clothes? We didn't bring any. We hadn't planned on a cross-the-world road trip."

"What?" he said, distracted. He was still thinking about what could be attacking the Colony's computers. "No, it's fine. Go ahead and take whatever you want. Celia won't mind."

He rebooted the machine and hoped for the best.

"You think it's the same thing that's happening with that guard's computers?" Ruby asked.

"I have no idea." He started running tests and a system-wide analysis as Ruby disappeared into the bathroom. He was still hip-deep in diagnostics when the next thing he knew she was placing a plate in front of him. He'd been working at it for a couple hours and he still didn't have it figured out. And then Jaya's phone rang.

"Malcolm, is Celia back yet? I need you to come over here," Jason said, sounding slightly frustrated and very annoyed.

"No, not yet."

"Can the sisters be left alone there for a little while?"

Malcolm looked up to find Ruby reading a craft magazine. Jade was on the front porch at one of Jaya's tables. A large pile of herbs sat in front of her.

"Yeah, I'm sure they'll be fine."

Ruby looked up at him, her eyebrows raised.

"Good. We've got some major issues going on here."

"I'll see you in ten." He turned to Ruby. "I need to run an errand. Will you two be all right here until Celia arrives?"

"Sure. No problem."

"Help yourself to the food and clothes and whatever else you need. But if you could stay on the property until Celia arrives, I'd really appreciate it."

"O-kay," she said, drawing out the two syllables as she looked at him for an explanation. He didn't give her one. Reasons for why he didn't want them roaming around town, or why no one could see them while they were staying there, would only make matters worse. He'd let Celia explain things to them and hope she'd find a way to get rid of them before they got too nosy.

And from the way Ruby was looking at him now, sooner would be better than later.

"Thanks," he said, grabbed the laptop and hurried out the door. He only made it a few steps toward the truck when Celia stepped out of the woods.

"What are you doing here?" she asked sharply. He hoped that was concern in her voice and not annoyance.

"We have a problem."

Her eyes narrowed. Nope, not concern. "Your cousins are waiting for you inside," he said.

Her eyes grew wide as her gaze flew to the house. "Jade and Ruby?" she asked, amazement raising her voice. "How?"

"They followed us." And yes, it was his fault; he should have been watching. He stiffened, waiting for the recriminations. But they didn't come.

"Did you ask them why?"

"Apparently they were worried about you. You're… family."

She took a deep breath. "Fine, I'll see what I can do," she said at length.

He wanted to say something else. To ask her how she was. To ask her why she had left that morning without waking him. But in the end, he said nothing. "I have to go by Jason's." She stiffened as he drew near. Had someone already told her about what had happened with Jaya? He stopped in front of her. "Listen," he said softly. "We really need to talk about…things. Can you hang here until I get back? Jason has some kind of emergency. I'm running over to his place now. It shouldn't take long."

"Sure," she said, tentatively.

"It's important, Lia."

"I'll be here," she said abruptly, and walked past him toward the house.

"Great. And, Celia?"

"Yeah?"

"Jason said to make sure no one sees them." He gestured toward the house.

She nodded her beautiful red head. "All right. But with those two it's not going to be easy."

"Lately, it seems as if nothing ever is."

Celia stood on her mother's porch and watched Malcolm drive away. Just seeing him here, she could almost close her eyes and forget everything that had happened between them and pretend things were the way they used to be. But they weren't. And they never would be again. She took a deep breath, turned and walked into her mother's house.

Instead of being empty, lonely and sad, there was music playing and the smell of coffee drifted through the house. "Ruby, Jade!" Celia said, and closed the door behind her. The twins were in the kitchen rummaging through the fridge. They looked up and squealed, and then ran toward her.

"What are you doing here? Malcolm said you were here, but I still can't believe it."

"We had to make sure you were okay, so we followed you," Ruby said, rushing forward and enveloping her in a giant hug.

"Followed me?" Celia repeated as anxiety pulsed

through her. "I don't understand. Why would you think something was wrong?"

"Well, as we told you before, when we went to the shop to pick up the keys and the clothes, the place was a total mess."

"Trashed," Jade said, nodding.

"So we waited for you up at the canyon so we could tell you what had happened, but then when we saw you…" She hesitated, her eyes shifting away as a touch of embarrassment lifted her lips.

Celia flinched. They'd seen her naked. With Malcolm! With an expectant breath she waited for Ruby to say the words while hoping she wouldn't.

"We saw you and Malcolm walk out of the ravine stark naked," Jade said for her.

A pink flush spread across Ruby's cheeks, and her head bobbed up and down in agreement.

Celia chewed on her bottom lip.

"You have to admit that is weird. You didn't have a blanket or anything," Jade continued.

"So we got curious," Ruby admitted. "And the next thing we knew, we were following you."

"But I think we would have stopped, even after that weird thing with those men in California, if it hadn't been for Ruby's tingles."

"Tingles?" Celia asked, growing more confused and concerned by the second.

"Something bad is going to happen," Ruby whispered, her face drawn and serious. "I just know it."

"What do you mean?" Ruby's tone was setting Celia's nerves on edge.

"I get tingles," Ruby said. "They're kind of a good-and-bad barometer, and whenever something bad is about to happen, well, I get tingles all over my scalp."

Celia's heart kicked up a notch because wasn't that what she'd been feeling all day? In fact, for more than a few days? "Are you sure it's not too many lattes?" she asked, hoping beyond hope there was a rational explanation.

"I wish, but no. It's not," Ruby said, her eyes and her face dead serious.

Celia sighed. Since when did her cousin have a tingle barometer?

"Ever since we were kids, Ruby has felt things," Jade explained. "It would always start as a tingling, but then it would grow, becoming so insistent that sometimes she actually became sick. But she's never, ever wrong. And if she says something bad is coming, then something bad is coming."

"Why didn't you guys ever tell me this before?"

Ruby shrugged. "I don't know. I guess it never came up."

"Well, how long have you been feeling these tingles now?"

"I've been trying to pin it down, but it started that morning Malcolm showed up. But I'm not sure if they came before he got there or after he arrived. But ever since that day, my scalp has been doing that tingle dance all over the place."

Celia swallowed the panic rising up her throat. What in the world was she was going to do? She knew the rules. No interactions with humans and no humans in the Colony. But she couldn't send them away now. Because they were right—something bad was coming.

"It's how we knew that you were in trouble and that we had to help you," Jade added, her big eyes wide.

Celia stared at them. Was it possible that Ruby could sense the *Abatu?* There were more than a few hanging around the shop that day. And if she could…did that mean that she might be ready to make the change? Could Ruby become one of them? Usually their kind transformed during adolescence, but she did have a human father and had grown up outside the Colony. Maybe that made a difference. And if she was ready to transform, well, then, that changed everything. Celia would not send her back out there on her own. She couldn't.

"So, Celia, what is going on with you? Is everything all right?" Ruby asked, her face scrunched with concern.

"Yes, everything is fine. There is no reason to worry."

"Really?" Jade asked. "Because it doesn't seem like that to us. Why did you leave like that? What happened at the shop? And what is up with the security around here? We're way out in the middle of nowhere and it's buttoned up like Fort Knox."

"People here just don't like contact with the outside world." Celia walked past her into the kitchen, not knowing how to answer their questions and suddenly famished.

"You mean they're all hiding from something," Jade said, following her.

"I didn't say that."

"No reason to get snappish. We were worried. You're family," Ruby said.

Celia took a deep breath. "Sorry. I know and I appreciate that." She pushed her hair back behind her ears. "There's just a lot that's been going on."

"We know," Jade said, and put her arm around Celia's shoulders. "And we want to be here to help you."

"We're so sorry about your mom. We really would have loved to meet her," Ruby added.

"So what can we do to help you?" Jade asked.

"Yes. What do you need us to do?" Ruby added. "What arrangements have you made?"

Celia looked around the house, chock-full of a lifetime of her mother's things. Her mom hadn't been a woman to sit around all day. She had always been working on one project or another. Her arts and crafts were everywhere: half-finished knitting, her recipes and her gardening. Even the tiny pieces of broken tile and glass on a nearby table were going into a large mosaic tabletop for her deck. The magnitude of the job before her weighed her down. She didn't want to touch her mother's things. To dump all her projects as if they didn't matter. As if it was all for nothing.

Tears threatened. She pushed them down. "I honestly don't know," she said at length. "There's just so much to do. And no, I haven't done anything yet. I just don't know what to do. I still can't believe…I can't believe she's gone."

Ruby wrapped her arms around her and gave her a

big hug, holding on tightly. Celia felt the tension seep out of her arms. "We know."

Celia nodded and wiped away an errant tear. They did know what it was like to lose their mother, more than anyone else. "Thanks. Yes, I would like your help."

"So, then, why do I hear a but?" Jade asked.

"Like I said, it's just the people here. They're nervous about outsiders."

Jade's mouth opened in protest. "But we're not outsiders, we're family."

"And besides that, we're not going anywhere," Ruby added. "We're here to help you through this, period. We're not leaving."

Celia looked at her, at the stubborn set of her jaw and the sparkling determination in her eyes, and felt her heart swell. "You're not?"

"Nope. My scalp has been doing the jig ever since we got here. And I've got to tell you, sometimes when it's real quiet I think I hear someone whispering. It's beginning to freak me out."

Chapter 13

Malcolm walked through Jason's open front door and found him sitting at his kitchen table, a computer system set up in front of him.

"Oh, good, you're here," he said. "I can't make heads or tails of this thing. I hate to admit it, but I'm clueless." Jason dragged his hand through his hair as he stared at the frozen monitor.

A surge of annoyance and frustration swept through Malcolm, tightening his fists. Since when did Jason even have a computer, and why was it such an emergency? Malcolm needed to be back with Celia right now, explaining to her what happened and helping her with the girls. "Tell me this isn't why you called me over here." Malcolm walked over to the computer and disconnected the Ethernet cable, and then powered off the system. "No one's computers are working and havoc is spreading through the town. I've spent all morning trying to figure out what's happening and get things back under control, but it's been a futile effort. The best thing to do for now is to unplug and shut them down."

Jason sat back and let out a deep breath, obviously relieved to be done with the thing. "Johnny just called and told me about the problems he's having at the gate. He was hoping you'd be back there hours ago. What's going on around here?"

"Celia just got back and I didn't want to leave the girls alone."

"You are planning on going back over there, right? The guardhouse's systems need to take priority right now."

"I get that. And yes, I'm going back over there. But first…there's something else you need to know."

"I'm almost afraid to ask." Jason leaned back in his chair, a worried pinch around his eyes.

"One of Celia's cousins asked if she could check her email. I brought her my laptop and as soon as she started it up and connected to the internet, it crashed."

"Okay?" Jason said, looking unimpressed. "That seems to be what's been happening everywhere. Even here." He gestured toward the computer in front of him.

"I believe that somehow a virus has gotten past our firewalls. It's infected everyone. I'm going to have to go to each business, unplug them from the internet, run the virus scans, clean up the systems and reestablish their firewalls and virus protection, and only then allow them to be reconnected to the network."

"Fine. If that's what we'll have to do, then we'll do it." He stood.

Malcolm hesitated. "I'm not sure we should reconnect everyone right away. We need to find out what this virus is and how it got past our defenses. In fact, I think everyone should stay offline until we do. My first priority is Johnny. But no one is going to be real happy about no longer having their internet, which is just going to hurt my case when I go before the Council for Judgment."

"I can only imagine," Shay said, walking into the room. "I have to admit to being a little upset myself. I have clients waiting for my work, and I can't get on the system to send it to them."

Malcolm nodded, remembering that Shay had had her own graphic-design business on the outside before she'd made the transformation and had to come here. "I'm sorry," he said. "Until I can get my hands wrapped around this virus, we can't take the chance of connecting people back to the network. This is the most bizarre thing I've ever seen."

"I understand," she muttered, but he could tell from the look on her face that she wasn't happy about it. It was the same look he'd seen from the others that he had tried to help earlier that morning. "Perhaps if Jason and I say the directive came from us, that should insulate you a little when it comes time for your hearing."

"Thanks, I'd appreciate that," Malcolm said, somewhat surprised and a little disconcerted by how easily Shay had been able to step into the leadership of the Pack. It was what he had expected, and why he'd thought marrying her would solidify his position as Pack leader, but it was still a little hard to take.

Shay's dog, Buddy, ran into the room and right toward him. Malcolm held his breath as the large, beautiful husky stopped before him, holding his head quizzically, his large brown eyes staring right at him.

"Hey, Buddy," Malcolm said tentatively, and wondered if the animal realized he was responsible for dropping him into the pit that day with Jason and then leaving him there. He held out his hand for the dog. Buddy sniffed it, looked up at him and took a step back, then growled and turned away.

"It doesn't look as though he's forgiven you yet," Shay said.

"I don't think he's alone," Malcolm muttered, and stood. He needed to get back to Celia. He only hoped she would be more understanding than the dog. He turned back to Shay. "I just want to say again how sorry I am about everything that happened before."

"I appreciate that," Shay said harshly. "But I won't tell you that all is forgiven, because it's not. When I see you, I see Jason lying on the ground bleeding to death, Jaya getting shot and then you forcing me to leave them there. I still relive that horrible day whenever I close my eyes at night."

Her words tore him up inside. But he deserved to hear them. He'd been completely out of control.

"I also know you are trying to make up for what you did in the only way you know how," Shay continued. "But right now what's important is that we protect the Pack at all costs. If we lose the Colony, there is nowhere we can go and be safe. I lived out there, I felt the *Gauliacho,* I heard their whispers. And no matter what some think, I know they are real."

"Of course they're real. What are you saying?" Malcolm asked, not sure where she was going with this.

"I'm saying I'm not sure everyone here believes the *Gauliacho* are real. Why should they? They've never left the gates. They've never heard or felt them."

Malcolm shook his head. "That's plain crazy."

"That's the reality we're facing," Jason said. "And why people are starting to doubt our rules and the way we do things. And for the record, I'm not quite as forgiving as Shay is, but I can't think about how angry I am at you right now. Not until we can get past this current crisis."

Malcolm nodded. "Fair enough." He turned toward the door.

"I met Celia this morning," Shay added, walking with them. "I must admit, she didn't look too happy to see me."

"She needs a little time. She wasn't ready to come back. Finding out about her mother's death has been hard."

"I'm sorry. I can only imagine," Shay muttered.

Jason wrapped an arm around her waist. They looked good together. Comfortable. As if they'd been together years and not weeks. "Is that why it took so long? We expected you back days ago."

"I had to go all the way to Arizona to find her. We tried to get back as fast as we could, but we were attacked at every turn. There were *Abatu* everywhere, not to mention the humans with their guns."

"We know," Shay said. "Trust me."

Jason and Shay had faced very much the same thing when Jason had gone to the California coast to bring her here. "I didn't have to go as far as Arizona to find Shay when she started her transformation, but there were *Abatu* everywhere," Jason admitted. "And considering the fact that I've been going beyond the gates for years now, I can tell you there is a big difference. There are a lot more *Gauliacho* out there than ever before and they're moving ever closer."

"Why do you suppose that is?" Malcolm asked as anxiety twisted through him.

Shay placed a protective hand on Buddy's head. "Not knowing what they were, I lived with the cracks in my walls for a while. I heard their voices and felt their presence. It's as if they are waiting for something."

"Or someone." Malcolm thought of Celia's dreams. She'd been hearing the voices for years now. Even here inside the Colony.

"Whatever it is, it can't be good," Jason said.

"What are we going to do?" Shay asked.

"Hope Celia can keep the borders secure," Malcolm answered, and thought about her insistence on going back to Sedona. But unless they found another Keeper, she'd be stuck, and she'd resent the hell out of them for it.

"How is Celia, really?" Jason asked, his voice low, his tone tentative.

"Angry. Confused. Hurt. She didn't want to come

back. And I haven't had a chance to tell her everything yet."

Jason looked grim. "That's what Shay said. But I wouldn't wait much longer. You don't have a lot of time left. The Council knows you're back. They want to hear your side of what happened that day. And to make matters worse, Jaya's funeral has been scheduled for four o'clock this afternoon. Everyone will be there. Including the Elders."

Malcolm swore under his breath. "I thought I'd have more time. I'll have to take my chances with the Council and hope they'll have mercy with me. In the meantime, I'll try to fix Johnny's computer and figure out what the virus is."

"At this point, I'm beginning to wonder if maybe Scott and Jaya were right all along," Jason said. "Perhaps installing these systems wasn't such a good idea. We are not in the outside world. Maybe it's time we stop pretending we're a part of it, because we're not. We need to focus on putting this Pack back together, on healing—"

"You're right," Malcolm interrupted. "Which is why I want all the systems shut down. There might be a chance that having so many computers connected to the internet has left us vulnerable to attack."

"Attack? By who?"

"By the *Gauliacho*."

Jason's eyes narrowed. Shay looked shocked, her expression moving from fear to thoughtfulness. At least she was listening.

"I can't say why I think this," Malcolm said, trying to explain. "It's just a gut feeling. I have nothing to back it up, which is why I am hesitant to even say it. But if it's true…"

"It's a stretch," Jason countered.

"From where I sit, timing is everything. With Jaya's death, the barriers have been weakened."

"Is that even possible?" Shay asked, looking down at her computer.

"I really don't know. But to be safe, everyone should be powered down and disconnected."

Jason looked doubtful. "Are you sure this isn't just a ploy to buy you more time with the Elders?"

Malcolm stared at him. Annoyance pricked at him, but he tried to keep it off his face and out of his voice. He was on borrowed time here and he knew it. "Actually, I hadn't thought of that, but hey, if you think it will work, I'm all for it."

Jason shook his head. "I'd believe Scott did something to the computers before his incarceration before I'd believe it was the *Gauliacho*. If he brought the network down, it would just be one more way of proving his point that the decisions you made as leader hurt the Pack."

"If it had happened before, but why bother now? After what happened to Jaya, I'm no longer in charge and I never will be again."

"Scott could have started this ball rolling before Jaya's death," Shay said. "He and my grandparents are antitechnology to the extreme, and after everything else he's done, burning his house and attacking us out there in the forest that day, I wouldn't put anything past him. He is a broken man. Especially after he shot Jaya."

"I suppose it's possible," Malcolm said, thinking about Scott and his extreme hatred toward him and his policies. There was always something a little crazy about the man. "He is a lot more probable than the *Gauliacho*. All right, I will definitely consider that Scott could have sabotaged the system as I try to figure out what in the hell is going on around here."

"Sounds good," Jason said. "But right now we need you to focus on Johnny's computers. He called right before you got here and said our entire security system is down." Frustration hardened Jason's voice. "We've let ourselves become too dependent on them and it's made us vulnerable."

Malcolm stilled, feeling the dig straight to his gut. He was the one who'd brought the computers into the Colony, who'd introduced everyone to the wonders of the internet and the world out there beyond their gates. And yes, he knew how dependent people had become, but the trade-off of the higher efficiency plus the pure amazement of the machines was worth it.

Wasn't it?

"I told Johnny to switch over to the manual systems and to call the guys to do a sweep of the fences this morning. At least until I can get everything back up and running. So if we're done here, I'd like to get back there. Trust me, I know the security of the Colony needs to be first and foremost. Just do me a favor and stay close by. I might need your help."

"Why? Is there something else I should know?" Jason asked, worry in his tone.

Malcolm thought of the reflection of sunshine he'd seen beyond the gate this morning. So quickly he hadn't been sure what he'd seen. But what if someone else had followed them there? He thought of the man standing in the middle of the street, the gun in his hand, pointing at Celia.

"Celia and I could have been followed by someone other than the twins," he admitted after taking a deep breath.

"What?" Jason exploded.

"I don't know for sure, but it's a definite possibility. Someone shot me out there. Unprovoked, and from out of nowhere."

"Blazes," Jason said under his breath. His eyes swept over him. "You look okay. Was it serious?"

Malcolm thought of the bullet in his side and knew he would have to go by Manuel's at some point today to have it removed. He just couldn't now. Not yet. Not until he got a handle on what was going on around there and had a chance to speak to Celia.

"I'll heal. Celia went after him, and she was hit, too. Just grazed, though." Before Jason could respond, he asked, "Has someone called Celia about the funeral? She didn't mention it when I saw her earlier."

"Manuel is taking care of it." Jason paced the room. "Are you sure you're both okay?"

"Not really, but the gun wounds are the least of our problems."

"Blazes, Malcolm. What if you'd both been killed

out there? Do you realize the danger we would all be facing?" Jason asked, disbelief thick in his tone.

"More than you know," Malcolm said drily.

"And you think this guy could have followed you, too?"

"Maybe. Johnny's men should be checking the fences now."

"All right," Jason said. "Let me wrap up a few things here, and then I'll meet you at the gates."

"Give me twenty minutes. I need to talk to Celia. As you said, time is running out. I have to tell her about what I did to you and Shay before someone else does."

Jason took a deep breath, then nodded.

Malcolm walked out the door, knowing it wouldn't be long before the Council found him and brought him in for their questioning. And once that happened, chances were good he'd be locked up to await their Judgment and he might never get to tell her how sorry he was. And how he wished more than anything he was the man she always believed he was.

But now they both knew better.

Chapter 14

Celia froze. Horror seeped through her veins, rendering her paralyzed.

"Celia? You're as white as a sheet," Jade said. "What's the matter?"

She was overreacting. She had to be. Ruby was not hearing whispers. *She wasn't!* Because if she was, if she could hear the *Gauliacho,* then that meant— It meant she was about to make the change.

"Celia?" Ruby said, her face full of concern. "Is everything all right?"

Celia shook off the fear, the bone-deep terror. Not only that her cousin could be changing but that she could hear the *Gauliacho.* That they actually were *here.* She forced herself to look straight ahead, to move her arms, to take a step forward and smile. "Yes," she said, trying to sound cheerful, but instead just sounded shrill. "Of course. I know this place seems crazy. All of it. Us. Me. Malcolm. But I sure am glad you're here."

She flung her arms around both of them and hugged them tight, burying her face so they couldn't see the lie so easily through her dismay. What if Ruby really was changing?

"So are we." Jade extricated herself from the group hug and walked toward the counter, where she picked up a floral wreath sitting next to a pile of flowers and a glue gun. "I just wish we could have come earlier and met your mom. I know we would have hit it off."

Celia smiled, even as a piercing ache clutched her heart. "Yes, you would have." Just as quickly as it came, the smile died on her lips as she took in the room around her. "I don't know what I'm going to do with all this stuff. It just seems wrong to move it."

"Are you going to live here?" Ruby asked, a note of hesitation in her voice.

Celia knew what she was really asking. Was Celia going to go back to Sedona, to their shop, or was she going to stay here? How could she tell them the truth? That she wanted to go back, more than anything, but she didn't know how she could. Until they found someone else who could manipulate the crystals, she was stuck in the Colony.

"I'm afraid I don't know what I'm going to do past the next minute," Celia answered honestly.

"What can we do to help you?" Jade asked again. "We could pack up some of your mom's stuff for you.

At least organize it. Should we go to the store and buy some bins?"

If they only knew there wasn't a store with bins for at least a hundred miles. "No, that's all right." Celia dropped into her mother's favorite big comfy chair in front of one of the large windows and looked at the book lying half-open and facedown on the arm of the chair. A book her mom would never get to finish. The familiar ache gripped her again. "I'm sorry," she said over the golf-ball-size lump in her throat. "I'm just not ready."

"There's nothing that says you have to be," Jade said, resting her hand on Celia's shoulder, causing a flood of tears to fill her eyes again. She didn't know how she was going to get through this.

"Well, I know what I can do to help," Ruby said. "That garden out there is in desperate need of watering and weeding." She stared longingly out the large back window.

Celia's heart lightened. This was how she was going to make it. With these two here. And with Malcolm? Perhaps. "Have at it," she said to Ruby. "My mom grows anything and everything. I'm sure there's a lot that needs picking and eating, too."

"Homegrown veggies, yes!" Ruby walked out the door, picked up a pair of gloves, a straw hat and a till off the back porch, then stepped into the yard and into Celia's mother's huge garden. As Celia watched her out there in that big floppy hat, she could almost pretend, if only for a moment, that it was her mother out there bent over her vegetables. Her mom loved life. She never let a day go by sitting around feeling sorry for herself.

Celia only hoped she could live up to her mother's example and contribute as much to this world as she had.

"I just don't know how I'm going to get used to the idea that she is really gone," she said to Jade.

"You never really do," Jade said softly as she plopped onto the small sofa facing her.

"My mom would have loved you guys," Celia said again as she watched Ruby ferociously hacking at the weeds with her till.

Just then the phone rang. Celia rose and walked toward it, hoping it wasn't Malcolm, and yet hoping it was. She was hopeless. And in too vulnerable a place to have to deal with anything. She snapped up the phone and gave a reluctant "Hello."

"Hello, darlin', how you holding up?" Manuel's voice came through the line, bringing an immediate mist to her eyes.

"Hi, Manny."

Manny was the closest to a father she'd ever had. He'd always been there for her, helping her hone her craft with the crystals, trying to help her become a healer, though she'd failed miserably at it until they discovered that unlike with her mother, it was only the dark energy of the crystals she could manipulate, never the good. The light. The healing properties of the stones. After that, the torturous lessons had stopped.

"I have to admit I've been better," she said.

"I know, sweetie. I know."

Of anyone in the Colony, he would know. He had always been there for both her mom and her. Why he hadn't married her mom years ago, she'd never know.

"All the arrangements for your mom's burial have been made. She is waiting for us at the Sanctuary. The ceremony is set for four o'clock."

"You did everything all by yourself?" Celia asked, feeling amazed and a touch guilty.

"I wanted to. You know how much your mom meant to me, and I had help. It gave me some peace and a sense of closure. I couldn't see a good reason to wait any longer than we had to. I knew you'd get here as soon as you could."

"My mom should have married you, Manny."

"I should have forced her hand, but we both always thought there'd be time."

"I'm so sorry," she whispered as tears caught in her throat and stole her voice.

"Me, too. But I've learned not to take anything or anyone for granted. I hope you will learn that, too."

She sighed. "I'm trying, Manny." She knew he meant Malcolm. And maybe it was time to put the past behind them and try to move forward again. Maybe if her mother had done that, had gotten over whatever it was that had happened between her and Celia's father, who'd disappeared when Celia was a baby, maybe she could have found happiness with Manny. Whenever Celia had asked her mom why she wouldn't marry such a great guy who obviously adored her, her mom always scoffed and said she was too set in her ways to change them up now. Just thinking about it broke Celia's heart all over again.

"Do you want me to come by and pick you up?" Manny asked.

Celia looked at her cousins and wondered how she was going to deal with their presence. She couldn't keep them from the ceremony. But how could she explain them to everyone else? Hadn't Jason said to keep them out of sight?

"Yeah, in fact, I think you'd better come by a little early. I have someone, make that two someones, here I want you to meet."

"Oh, yeah? Now you have my interest piqued, little girl."

She laughed at the endearment he'd been using for as long as she could remember. "They're my cousins from Sedona. Aunt Sue's daughters."

There was a brief pause before Manny said, "Oh, boy. I'll be right over."

Before Malcolm could even start the truck, Jason came running out the front door with a phone in his hand.

"Blazes, what now?" Malcolm muttered, and took the phone from Jason.

"It's Johnny," he said, a grave look on his face.

"Hey, man, are you on your way over here?"

"I was going to go by Celia's first. Why? What's up?"

"I couldn't get the computer system back up, so I was doing a manual sweep, checking everything, when I found a car parked not too far down the road hidden in the bushes."

Malcolm cringed and thought again of that flash he'd seen earlier. "Blazes."

"That's what I thought," Johnny said.

"Can you give me half an hour? I haven't had a chance to talk to Celia yet. To tell her...everything that happened."

"Why the hell not?" Johnny demanded. "Didn't you just bring her all the way back here? How many hours did you have alone with her for that?"

"I know. I just—" Malcolm swore under his breath. "I just couldn't find the right time."

"Bullshit. You were being a coward."

"Thanks, Johnny. Anything else you want with that serving of my balls?"

"Hey, I just tell it like it is. And right now I'd love to tell you to go to Celia and try to clean up the mess you made, but frankly it wouldn't help. There's no climbing back out of that hole and I need you here now. There's something going down. I can feel it in my gut."

Malcolm sighed and glanced at Jason. "Fine. I'll be there in ten."

Malcolm stared at the car hidden in the trees, at the damaged front end, and felt his blood run cold. He stiffened as he turned to Johnny and Jason. "This car belongs to the man who shot me and Celia."

"Shot you?" Johnny asked.

"Yeah. The night before last. Celia and I had been cooped up in the truck for hours and we just wanted, no, we *needed* to run."

"And he shot you?"

"Yeah, after he almost ran down Celia in the road."

"Wow. You both okay?" Johnny asked.

"Yeah, Celia was just grazed and I will be fine once

I get over to Manny's. But the question rolling through my mind right now is who is this guy and what in the hell is he doing here?"

"I pulled this out of his glove box." Johnny handed him the car's registration. Mark Goodwin. Sedona, Arizona.

"Shit," Malcolm muttered.

"Looks as though he followed you all the way here from Arizona," Jason said.

It was a statement of truth, not an accusation, though to Malcolm it burned as one.

"There was no one behind me," he stated. Not a defense, just a fact.

"And yet the twins followed you here, too."

Malcolm scraped his hand across his face. "I don't know how that happened."

"You were distracted. You still are. You need to have Manny heal you," Jason insisted.

"I know. And I will, I just haven't had a second to breathe."

"The question we should be asking ourselves is, was he following you or Celia's cousins?" Johnny asked.

"Either way, it's not good," Jason said.

"Nope." Johnny ran his fingers through his thick, unruly hair.

"When you going to get yourself a wife?" Malcolm asked, looking at Johnny's wrinkled shirt and day-old stubble. He walked around the car, peering inside the windows, wondering where the guy could be.

"A wife? Now, why on earth would I want one of those around telling me what to do?"

Jason nodded. "That's a fact, but they do keep your bed warm at night."

"Yeah, well, I'll let you know when I need one of those. Though I must say, those cousins of Celia's sure are pretty."

"They'd kick your ass from one side of this Colony to the other," Malcolm warned.

"They're both way out of my league. I could tell that just by looking at those ridiculously tall shoes they were wearing. And painted nails. Why on earth would anyone put paint on their nails?"

"You got me," Malcolm said as he followed a set of fresh footprints. He peered into the woods around them. "Looks as if he disappeared into the woods."

"Honestly, that's what has me so worried. I've been watching this car for going on an hour and he hasn't come back to it. By now, he could be anywhere. He could be following the fence."

Anxiety pricked the fine hairs on the back of Malcolm's neck. "Just tell me he hasn't found a way into the Colony."

"I wish I could," Johnny admitted. "But the truth is, with the security cameras down we really don't know where this guy is."

"But the fences are secured? All the way around the perimeter?" Somehow Malcolm knew this was going to come back to bite him on the butt. Bad. He should have been watching more carefully. Not only had he led the twins right here, but he'd led a gun-happy idiot right to their doorstep.

"Call the others and post sentry duty. We're going

on high alert," Jason said. "And, Malcolm, any way you can get Johnny's cameras back up and working, do it. We need to have eyes around the boundaries."

"I can try. I have tried. It's much more than your standard infection. It's hit everyone and everywhere at once. Every time I turn around, there is a computer problem. Whether Scott is the culprit, or..." He glanced at Johnny, who was digging through the car. "Or what we talked about earlier, we need everything electronic shut down until we know what we're dealing with."

"Isn't that a little extreme?"

"Maybe. But the way I see it, the computers are a doorway to the outside. An opening that the *Gauliacho* can slip in through. It's an energy source, and could be fairly simple to follow the network from one system to the next and come back out into the walls, into anything electronic." The more Malcolm thought about it, the more certain he was that they were in serious trouble.

"You realize what you're saying?" Jason asked, incredulous.

"Yes. Let's hope I'm wrong. But until we know for sure, it's all going to have to come down. Everything."

"All right, I'll put out the word. In the meantime, stay here until it's done, even if you have to miss Jaya's funeral."

"Jason, I have to be there."

"It's a bad idea, Malcolm. The Council will be there. All of them. They will want you brought in for questioning. I will have no choice and you will be no good to us locked up."

"If that happens, I'll be depending on you to take

care of things and make sure all systems are shut down. And perhaps you could tell the Council about my concerns regarding the computers and try to buy me a little more time." Malcolm hated the sound of pleading in his voice.

Jason shrugged. "I just don't see that making much of a difference. Not to them."

"The threat is real."

"Maybe it is, maybe it isn't. But to them, you should have been arrested a week ago. You've had your reprieve."

Malcolm couldn't help the surge of frustration surging within him. "I brought back Celia. That must count for something."

"My gratitude. But face it, Malcolm. She never would have left in the first place if you hadn't driven her away."

He sucked in a quick breath. "Man, you sure know how to hit a guy in the soft spot."

"I just tell 'em like I see 'em."

Before Malcolm could respond, a line of jeeps drove up the road and parked in front of the guardhouse. Eight of Jason's top guards jumped out and ran toward them.

"We need you at all the sentry points around the perimeter, especially the back gates. Make sure everything is still secure and there is no sign of a perimeter breach," Jason commanded.

"What are we looking for?" Bobby Saunders said before the others fell into line, one after the other, nodding, checking their coms and loading up their gear.

"White male, about five-nine, hundred and eighty pounds. Brown hair," Malcolm said.

"Don't forget," Jason added. "Shay and I got over by propping a dead tree up against the fence less than two weeks ago. Check for that, too."

"We removed all the dead trees right after that," Bobby said. "We checked the entire fence line just last week. We are secure. If he made it over, we'll find out where. And then we'll find him."

"Good. Let's hope he's still wandering around outside the fence searching for a way in. Call in all updates to Johnny. I have to go to Jaya's funeral. I'll be checking in for status every fifteen minutes."

The guards left as quickly as they had arrived, jumping into their jeeps, leaving for the various checkpoints.

"I forgot what a damned good security chief you were," Malcolm muttered.

"I'm going to be passing the torch to Bobby soon."

Malcolm nodded. "Good choice."

"Have you given any thought to what you're going to do…after?" Jason asked.

"You mean if the Council doesn't throw my ass in the brig or kick me out beyond the gates?"

Jason nodded. "Yeah."

"No. Not really." Being Pack leader was all Malcolm had ever wanted to be. And he'd been a damned good one. No matter if some people hadn't liked the changes he'd made, the Pack was thriving. Or at least it had been, until now. But it didn't matter. Not anymore. There was no reason for him to plan a future for himself when chances were good there wasn't going to be one. Not for him. Not here in the Colony.

"I'll be at Celia's if you need me," he said, and walked away, glancing at his watch.

"Make it quick," Jason called after him.

Malcolm didn't respond and he didn't turn back, because without Celia, none of it really mattered. Not anymore. For once he was putting her first. Before the Pack. Before everything. He only hoped it wasn't too late.

Chapter 15

"Holy cow!" Manny said, stepping into Jaya's house and staring at the twins, his head swinging from Ruby in the kitchen, who was washing the vegetables she'd picked, to Jade sitting on the sofa in the family room. "There are two of them. And they both have their mother's eyes."

"Hi," Jade said, standing and then stepping toward him, her hand outstretched. "I'm Jade."

"Nice to meet you, Jade," Manny said, a goofy smile on his face. "Wow, you are the spitting image of your mama."

Jade beamed. Celia's heart went out to her cousin. She was being compared to a mother she'd lost at such an impressionable age. "Her mom disappeared when she was only twelve."

"I'm sorry to hear that," Manny said. He then turned to Ruby and stared at her for a long moment.

"What?" she said at last, an uncomfortable laugh leaving her lips.

"You have your mother's gifts with the crystals," he said, slightly awestruck.

Startled, Celia looked at him, then at Ruby, then back at him again. "Are you sure?"

"No," Ruby said quickly. "Not crystals." She picked up a handful of basil from the counter. "Herbs, yes. Oils and spells, you name it. Rocks? No."

"Really? Pick up that red stone in the window next to you," Manny instructed, walking toward her.

Ruby turned to look at the crystal in the window. "That's like the one Celia put in the windows of our shop."

"Yes," Manny agreed.

Ruby hesitated.

"Problem?" Manny asked.

Celia looked at him. What was he up to?

"No," Ruby said quickly. Too quickly. She reached for the crystal, picked it up, then plopped it right back down on the sill. "Okay, fine," she said. "It bothers my skin."

"An uncomfortable prickling feeling in your palm?"

Her mouth dropped open in surprise. "How did you know?"

"I can read it in your aura."

"You can see my aura?" she asked.

"Yep. Why?"

"Because I can see yours."

Celia dropped onto the sofa next to a confused Jade. "What about you? Can you see auras, too?" she asked her cousin.

An abrupt laugh erupted from Jade's throat. "Uh... no."

"But how is this possible?" Celia asked. Ruby was way beyond the time of transforming. But then hadn't Shay been too old, too?

Manny looked thoughtful. "Perhaps being around you, Celia, and now being here with the rest of us has jump-started what had been lying dormant."

"What are you guys talking about?" Jade demanded.

"Yeah," Ruby echoed. "The way you're looking at me is creeping me out."

Celia didn't know what to say or how to say it. How could she tell Ruby that chances were she was finally beginning her transformation into her true self? *Into a wolf.* Even though Jade wasn't, and might never. She might always be human. And if that happened, if Jade never changed, then she'd have to go back to Sedona. Alone.

Anxiety rushed through Celia, speeding up her heart. Jade would never leave the Colony without Ruby. And Ruby would never let her. *Blazes.* Why did they have to lie and turn away the ones they loved just to keep their sacred covenant?

"Sorry." Manny smiled. "Didn't mean to freak you out. I just wish Sue could see you girls right now. And Jaya."

"Me, too," Celia said, and gave a weak smile. She glanced at the clock. It was almost time to say her final goodbye to her mother. She didn't know how she was going to do it. She looked at the people around her, her family. Rules or no rules, she wasn't going to do it alone.

Twenty minutes later, Celia walked into the Sanctuary with Manny and the twins, her head held high, not bothering to turn and look at the curious stares of those already seated in the large room. They had started toward the front of the room when Jason walked into the Sanctuary with Shay next to him and the Council of five Elders right behind him. She squeezed Ruby's hand and looked up at Manny. "Take the girls up to the front. I'll meet you there," she mumbled, then turned toward the Council, determined to make her stand.

"Celia," Jason greeted, looking past over her shoulder at Manny and the twins.

"This is my mother's funeral," she said, her voice sounding firmer than she'd expected. "My cousins are staying."

Jason had opened his mouth to say something when Shay placed her hand on his arm. "Of course they are," she said, giving the men around her a look that dared them to say anything different.

Celia had to admit, she was impressed. Even if she didn't like the way Shay seemed to have taken over leadership of the Pack. How long had she even been there, five minutes? But still, she was helping Celia stand up to these men, and she had to be appreciative for that. Connors and McGovern, the two most outspoken Council members, stared at Shay with openmouthed shock that was quickly turning to fury. They weren't used to having their rules broken. Well, this time they'd just have to live with it, or try to live without her. Their stunned gazes flitted back and forth from her to the twins, then back to Shay again.

"They are human!" McGovern said, outraged. "Why are there humans in the Colony?"

"They are Sue's daughters," Celia explained. "They wanted to be here to say their final respects to their aunt. And I want them here," she added firmly, almost daring them to stop her.

Shay stepped forward in front of the men. "At a time like this, family is necessary. We can discuss the particulars later, after the ceremony, in private. Don't you agree, Jason?"

"Absolutely."

"We are *all* very sorry for your loss, Celia," Shay added.

"Thank you," Celia muttered, and Jason squeezed her shoulder as they walked past her toward the chairs in the front of the room, Jason and Shay in the lead and the Council members reluctantly following behind her.

Celia stood still for a moment, stunned, as she watched them take their seats. Once they did, she returned to Manny and the twins.

"Everything okay?" Manny asked.

Celia nodded. She gazed around the room at the huge bouquets filled with pine boughs and large cones interspersed with wildflowers sitting in each corner of the room. The Sanctuary itself was built in the middle of a redwood grove. The floor-to-ceiling windows circling three sides of the room made you feel as though you were sitting in the forest. Beautiful white sashes circled several of the trees outside the windows, and candles burning in large iron sconces filled the room with the scent of cinnamon and pine.

Tears misted Celia's eyes. "You've done a wonderful job, Manny. My mother would have loved this."

Manny placed his arm around her shoulders. "I didn't just do it for her, little girl. I did it for you, too." He kissed her forehead, then left to take his seat as tears rolled down her cheeks.

She purposefully looked everywhere but toward the front of the room, where her mother was lying on a redwood altar. She knew she should go forward and take this opportunity to say goodbye before the room filed up even more, but she just wasn't ready.

She glanced up at the redwood arches above her formed to create a stunning apex. At the front of the Sanctuary, panels in the north-facing wall opened up into a beautiful garden, letting in a gentle breeze. A place of honor had been designated for her mother's ashes to be buried beneath a tall redwood surrounded by gardenias, one of her mother's favorite flowers.

Manny had thought of everything. The twins stood on either side of her, offering comfort and warmth. Together they approached her mother. She tried to breathe, but her chest tightened, her throat and stomach clenched with each step forward. Before she could stop them, tears once more filled her eyes and spilled onto her cheeks. And then she was standing over her mother, staring down at her lifeless form, wishing her mom would open her eyes and come back to her. That it had all been a terrible mistake. A lie. But it hadn't been.

She'd never see her mom's warm brown eyes smil... at her again.

"She was beautiful," Ruby said.

Celia gently touched her mother's hand, the coldness of her skin surprising her, and then she saw the eagle feathers artfully arranged in her hair, signifying her mother's freedom. A lot like the feather her mother had placed in her own hair the day before Celia decided to leave the Pack. She looked at those feathers and remembered her mother's fingers in her hair, remembered how impatient she had been for her mother to finish, for her to say goodbye, so she could get on the road, never realizing it would be the last time she'd see her.

The sobs came from nowhere, stealing what control she had left, and overtook her in a flood of emotion. Her knees buckled and the tears washed over her, burning her eyes, choking her as she gulped for breath. She wavered as a sense of surrealism broke over her. This wasn't happening! Denial and protestations forced their way through her mind as she desperately tried to block the torrential downpour of grief breaking over her and stealing her strength. But it was a lost cause.

"I'm so sorry, Mama. Sorry I left you," she sobbed, her voice breaking as she tried to form the words. And then Malcolm was there—her rock, filling her with his strength. She turned to him and buried her face in his chest and let him hold her. She breathed in his warm scent and lost herself in it.

"Come on," he whispered, his voice reaching deep inside her and touching her in a way no one else could. With both arms holding her tight against him, he led her

...er seat in the front row and sat next to her, holding
...r while she trembled and listened to the eulogy with
a mind-dulling numbness.

Through all the excruciatingly long minutes, she
hung on to Malcolm, focusing on him. His strength,
his love. His heart. He was always there for her. She
knew that. She counted on that. And she supposed she
always had. The service finally over, they stood in a line
as people came forward offering her their condolences.
Mechanically, she thanked everyone for coming. She
stood through it all, though honestly she didn't know
how. Leaning against Malcolm, listening and nodding.
Even the twins were smiling and graciously explaining over and over that they were Celia's cousins, there
for her support.

Afterward, when they'd reach her, the townspeople
would look at Celia and Malcolm, their eyes full of concern and confusion, but Celia would just nod and thank
them until they'd move on, and the next person would
come through and repeat the same process again and
again. Until once more, Jason approached. Malcolm
stiffened next to her and she felt her heartbeat acceler-
ate in response. She turned to him. "What is it?"

"I was hoping to have time to explain earlier, before the services, but we had a problem at the gate that
kept me. By the time I got to the house, you were already gone."

Tension and fear filled her, chasing away the numbness. "Explain what?"

Before he could say more, Jason was standing before them.

"Any luck finding him?" Malcolm asked, obviously trying to hold him off.

"Not yet," Jason said stiffly.

"Who?" Celia asked.

Malcolm leaned toward her and whispered so only she could hear. "The man who shot us. His car is parked outside the gate."

Her eyes widened. Here? He followed them here?

"What is it?" Ruby asked, stepping closer.

"We were followed. Do you know a Mark Goodwin from Sedona?" Malcolm asked under his breath.

Ruby's face went white as she grabbed for Jade's hand. "Mark? Why?"

"He's here now," Jason said. "He must have followed you."

"There was no way he followed us all this way. Why would he?" Ruby asked, a tremor to her voice. She visibly shuddered, and Jade put her arm around her.

"He's a cop. They have all kinds of ways," Jade muttered, her voice full of bitterness.

Dread crawled inside Celia. Ruby's stalker cop was the one who'd shot them? He'd seen them in their true forms. He'd shot them, and now he was here. Why? To finish the job? It was too much. "Where is he now?" she whispered, unable to fully process the implications.

"No one knows," Jason said. "His car was found outside the gates."

"What are we going to do?" Ruby asked.

"Don't worry. We can keep you safe," Malcolm said, but even as he said the words Celia wondered how he could. With everything else going on here, how were ney going to deal with yet another human in their midst? A human with a gun.

"Isn't that right, Jason?" Malcolm asked, turning to Jason with the question in his eyes.

Before he could answer, the Council members along with the sheriff, Cal Reynolds, stepped toward them. Jason saw them, hesitated, then turned back to Malcolm. "I'm really sorry to have to do this here, but, Malcolm, you're going to need to come with us. The Elders are insistent."

"Now? But why?" Celia demanded, louder than she'd expected. Several heads turned to look at them. But right then she didn't care. She needed him, especially now that there was some nutcase crazy enough to follow them all the way from Arizona.

"We've been trying to reach you all day, Malcolm, but we kept missing you," McGovern said, stepping forward.

"You must not have tried very hard," Malcolm muttered through gritted teeth. "I've been right here, helping people with their computer problems all day."

"We understand and appreciate that," Connors added as he stepped up next to Jason. "And I'm sorry for this, Celia. But your mother of all people would be the first to understand that questioning Malcolm right now before we lose any more time is a priority."

"Questioning him?" Celia asked again, panic creeping along her insides. "About what?"

"About your mother's death," McGovern said.

Sheriff Cal stepped forward. "Malcolm, we need to

take you in. Either you come with us peacefully or I'll have to use the ropes."

Celia's head was spinning.

Malcolm leaned toward her and pressed his lips against her temple. "It'll be all right. I promise. I'm so sorry, babe." Then he stepped forward, leaving Celia's side. "That won't be necessary, Cal. I'll go willingly."

"Why?" Celia demanded. "Why does he need to go? Why would he know anything about my mother's death? Scott shot my mother. Jason, you'd better tell me what's going on here, and you'd better tell me now."

Before Jason could say a word, Malcolm put his hand on Jason's shoulder, a question in his eyes. Jason nodded and Malcolm stepped in front of him, in front of Cal and the Elders, and faced her. His eyes were brimming with anguish. He took both her hands in his and held them tight, as if not only wanting to give her comfort, but needing to garner strength for what he was about to say.

Celia's heart dropped and her stomach soured. For once she wished she'd kept quiet. Whatever it was he was about to tell her, she didn't want to know. She could tell just by looking at his face. She couldn't handle it. Whatever it was. Not now, not when she was still so raw and still needed him so much.

"It was my fault Jaya died, Lia," he said softly.

"What?" she asked, her voice a mere whisper. "But you said it was Scott." Her world started to crumble beneath her. She could feel the floor shifting under her feet, feel her head swimming.

"I set a trap for Jason," he said. "I didn't expect him to get hurt. No one was supposed to get hurt, but he did.

Lying with Wolves

Your mom was close by in the woods. She was trying to heal him. She never should have been anywhere near there. None of them should have. But they were. Scott arrived with his men, they attacked and she got shot."

She glanced at her mother's body lying so peacefully on the altar. She looked again at Jason, who was nodding with grim acceptance, acknowledging the truth to Malcolm's words. It couldn't be true. She wouldn't believe it. Malcolm and Jason were best friends. How could things have gone that far? "My mother died because of your war with Scott? Because she was trying to heal your best friend, who you'd hurt?"

Her voice was shrill now. She saw through the corner of her eye the confusion on the twins' faces. People around the room had stopped talking. All were turning to stare at her. To watch poor Celia, who had been duped by her love for Malcolm once again.

"Are you sure it was Scott who killed my mother?" She directed the question at Jason; she wanted to know the truth. All of it.

"We don't know yet. That's why we're detaining everyone involved that day and questioning them," Cal said. "Right now it looks as if Scott fired the shot."

"He was there because of me," Malcolm said. "He wanted to stop me from marrying Shay, but he'd been too late."

"The bullet was meant for her," Jason said.

Celia's world shifted as nausea swept through her. "Too late? You married Shay?" she asked Malcolm through gritted teeth as astonishment at his betrayal seeped through her. "These past few nights we've spent together? How could you have not told me?"

"I wanted to," Malcolm said, his voice breaking.

"Then why didn't you?" Celia started to shake. It was too much to hear, too much to bear. Her world crumbled and she stumbled, leaning into Ruby, who was suddenly holding her up, her arm wrapped solidly around her waist.

"It was annulled," he said, his voice sounding weak.

So weak she barely heard him. A bullet meant for Shay. Because he'd married her. Celia's knees weakened as the implication of his words hit home. He'd married her, and because of that ultimate betrayal, and his blind ambition, her mother died.

Chapter 16

As Mark continued to follow the fence that encircled the community, looking for a way in, he was surprised and amazed by the sheer size of the place and the amount of fencing required to enclose so much land. Surely the fence could not cover the entire property? Why would it? What would be the point way out here in the mountains?

The steep trail he was on dipped down significantly. He continued following the path until suddenly it narrowed to a small deer trail that hugged the side of a mountain cliff. He looked down and saw that it led to a river far below. You'd have to be very adventurous to attempt that path. Much more adventurous than he.

His only option was to go back the way he'd come or find a way through the gate that was built into the end of the fence. He climbed up the few rock steps to a gate flanked on one side by the chain link and on the other by barbed wire that was embedded into the granite cliff wall.

He could try to climb it, but if he fell—he looked down. He'd never stop falling. He stepped up the sharp incline to the chain-link gate. It had an industrial lock on it, one that couldn't be broken into or picked. He could walk back to the car and then drive forward past the main entrance, park and walk around the other side of the compound. Maybe there he'd find a break in the fence.

But he'd walked most of the day already just getting to this point. It would be dark by the time he made it back. He'd have to sleep in the car and then start again in the morning, with no food. No change of clothes. No water.

Unless... He stared at the lock for another moment, took out his gun, aimed and shot it. The report boomed through the quiet mountain air.

The gate swung open.

He smiled. Or he could just go get the bitches now.

He stepped through the gate and up the incline into the woods. He was hungry, and tired of messing around with these girls. He'd been waiting and watching for years for the sisters to show their true selves, and now they'd finally done it. He would find them, but more than that, he would find out the truth. Vindication was close. So close he could feel it itching in the palm of his hand. He continued forward, moving deeper into the woods, heading inland away from the fence.

The forest on this side seemed denser somehow, or maybe it was just that the sun had slipped behind one of the tall craggy peaks and the shadows were growing deeper. The smell of rotting, damp earth filled the air. He grimaced, trying to move out of this part of the woods, out of the darkness and up the hill toward the light.

A bird squawked high overhead—a raucous roar that sounded like a warning. Anxiety nipped at the back of his neck. He pulled out his gun, holding it in his hand, liking the feel of the cool metal as it warmed to his touch. A twig broke behind him. He stopped and spun toward the sound, certain by the sensation prickling him that someone or something was watching.

He moved cautiously toward the sound. Whatever it was, he wasn't afraid of it. How could he be? He was armed and he was ready. Before it could get anywhere near him, he'd just blow its head off. He thought of the wolf who'd attacked him the night before, and his fingers rose to the deep gashes on his neck. Ruby or Jade? He couldn't be sure, but she could have killed him and she hadn't. That had to mean something.

He pictured the wolf as he'd seen her in his headlights. Beautiful gray-and-white fur. Large blue eyes. Majestic. Stunning. He'd only meant to wound her so he could capture her and bring her back, but she'd gotten away from him. But not this time.

Another snap. This time to the left. He tried again, moving cautiously through the thick brush as long shadows enveloped him. It was much too early to be losing the light. He would need to find the twins and get out of there soon. He didn't relish the idea of these woods after nightfall.

He glanced at his watch. Four-twenty. Yep, way too early. He moved forward, pushing the overhanging branches thick with pine needles and cones out of his way, only to get smacked with another prickly branch as it tried to tear the flesh from his face.

"Damn," he roared, wiping the sting off his cheek, sidestepping a tall bush and treading right into a depression of slimy muck. His right foot sank to the ankle in gray, stinky slime. He struggled to maintain his balance, pinwheeling his arms. Once he felt steady, he pulled on his foot, trying to free it, but the muck gripped his shoe with a great sucking pull that knocked him once more off-balance. He hit the ground on his backside with a bone-jarring thud that ripped his foot right out of the hole.

"What the hell?" Holstering his gun, he banged his foot on the ground, trying to get most of the muck off his shoe before he got unsteadily back to his feet. Moving more cautiously, he watched each step as he made his way back up the hill, his foot sloshing in his shoe, making a terrible squeaking noise as he walked.

There was something really off about these woods. They stank of death, but more than that, they hid something, some kind of menace he couldn't see but could feel in the dark angular shadows reaching toward him through the thick trees. He much preferred the wide-open spaces and fresh, clean air of the deserts back home, where the sky above was a stunningly bright blue, not a muted gray blotted out by the sea of trees.

He pushed past another huge trunk of a soaring tree, turning with the path and wondering where in the hell he was, when he heard it again. Not only the breaking of a twig, but the thrashing of a bush. He pulled out his gun once more, his nerve endings firing on high alert.

"Who's there?" he demanded, stepping forward, his eyes searching the trees for any movement. "I have a gun. And trust me, I'm not afraid to use it."

He turned, inching forward, ears straining. Out of nowhere, a flock of birds flew into his face, wings flapping against his head, loud squawking rupturing his ears. "Holy shit!" He jumped back, swatting at them, his throat catching on a strangled yell as they rose into the sky and flew away.

He watched them, his heart pounding an uneven staccato in his chest. *Birds.* Just a few birds. Nothing to get bent about. He took several deep breaths, then started forward again. There had to be a town here somewhere. Houses, stores, hotels, people. He just had to find it and get the hell out of these woods.

Then he'd find those girls, and all this would have been worth it.

Malcolm had been sitting in a room at the Town Hall for hours going over every detail of every mistake he'd ever made in the past six months. Hell, in the past three years. But none of them could compare to the disaster he caused Celia. He kept seeing the horror and pain searing her eyes, crippling her. As long as he lived, he would never forget that look and the way it made him feel. Hopeless. Worthless. And he deserved it. She was right; they all were. He'd let the power go to his head, his ambition had become all he could think about and because of that, he'd lost everything. How would he ever make it up to her? Could he?

"I've told you everything," he said finally. "Please, let me get back to work. There's a problem with the systems, and it's critical—"

"Yes, yes," Council member Connors interrupted. "We've heard all the complaints all day. In fact, that's all we've heard about for the past few days. But to us they aren't important. What is important is keeping the law of the Pack. Our rules are put in place for a reason, and you have broken our most sacred law."

"But we have to get out there and disconnect everyone from the network. There is a virus—"

"You and Scott caused the death of another," McGovern said, interrupting him. "And not just any other, but the death of our Keeper, putting us all in jeopardy."

"So, like Scott, we propose your Judgment be our most severe punishment," Connors said gravely. "Therefore, letting the others know that this kind of behavior will not be tolerated. Not in our Colony. Not if any of us are going to survive."

Malcolm felt the blood drain from his face in a cold whoosh. *Their most severe punishment.*

Jason stood. "I would like to state in Malcolm's behalf that he did travel all the way to Arizona at great personal risk to bring Celia back. It has been my belief that while sometimes misguided, Malcolm has always acted in what he thought were the best interests of the Pack."

Malcolm stared at his friend, and his chest tightened. He didn't deserve his support. Not after what he'd done to him and to his wife. Jason had almost died that day, and yet he was standing up for him. If Malcolm got out of this mess, he had so much to make up for, so much to prove.

"We will take that into consideration," Connors said. "With such a severe punishment on the table, we will take twenty-four hours to discuss it further, and will receive input from any Colony member wishing to make a plea on his behalf. Let it be shown that our preliminary Judgment has been rendered at 11:00 p.m. on this twenty-sixth day of September. We will meet again at 11:00 a.m. tomorrow to hear the town's pleas before entering our final Judgment."

Malcolm stood and let Sheriff Cal lead him through a back door and into the holding rooms where he would await his Judgment. Sickness rolled through him. He'd known it was possible, but he'd never believed they would actually send him beyond the gates. Not after everything he'd done, everything he'd sacrificed for the good of the Pack all these years.

Defeat and disillusionment tore at him. What he meant to the Pack, what the Pack meant to him, didn't matter. Nothing mattered anymore, not after watching Celia when she'd learned the truth of what he'd done. He'd broken her. Everything she'd ever believed about him, about them, was destroyed in that one instant.

After that, nothing could cut him deeper. He'd done that to her, to himself. Now every time she thought of her mother, thought of him or of what they had together, she would remember this day and the damage he'd done to them all.

There would be no getting past that.

For any of them.

Shock, numbness and fatigue washed over Celia as the twins took her back to her mother's house. She didn't want to think about Malcolm, about the services, about his lies and all the terrible things he'd done. When she did, the pain slicing through her, physically, mentally, was just too much. Closing herself off to everything and everyone, she let Ruby lead her into her mother's room. At first she didn't think she could go in there, didn't want to see her things, smell her distinctive scent. Thought it would hurt too much, but she didn't have the strength to stop, to reject. She just dropped onto her mother's bed, and once she was lying there, among her things, she felt comforted. She nestled her head into her mother's pillow and cried.

She thought of everything her mother had ever said about Malcolm. All the times she'd warned Celia, but she had never listened. Never believed. She'd loved him too much. And that love had cost them all...*everything*.

How could a love so deep and so strong be so damaging? She'd been such a fool. Obviously she was still a fool. She sobbed into her mother's pillow, letting her grief over the loss of her mother mingle with her shattered heartache until she wasn't sure where one pain started and the other ended. She hurt everywhere, aching as if she were bleeding on the inside.

She'd been completely gutted. Everything she'd ever

had or ever loved was gone. Destroyed. She ran the past few days over and over in her mind, tormenting herself until finally she fell into a blessed sleep. She didn't know how long she was spared her torturous thoughts when she opened her swollen eyes and saw the picture of herself on her mother's nightstand.

It had just been the two of them for so long. How her mom must have missed her when she'd left. Tears filled her eyes once again. She never would have left if it hadn't been for Malcolm. She'd wanted to get him out of her system. But even moving all the way to Sedona hadn't done it. He'd been too deeply ingrained. No matter how hard she'd tried, she hadn't been able to get him out of her heart. Obviously there was something wrong with her. She had to get out of here and go back to Sedona. There was nothing left for her here. Not now.

She sat up in the bed and tried to formulate a plan. First she'd have to go to Manny and then the Council. Everyone in the Colony would need to be tested. There had to be another Keeper. Someone she could train. She couldn't be the only one. She *couldn't*.

She pulled open the drawer in her mother's nightstand and saw a picture of her father, still in its frame, lying there. She pulled it out and stared at it. The man she'd never met. He'd left before she was born and had broken her mother's heart. How many times had her mother held this picture and longed for him to come back? Was that why she'd never married Manny? Sadness filled Celia. So many dreams lost. Maybe her mom was right—maybe living life without love was better. Safer.

Before she could search further, she heard the sound of glass crashing and got out of the bed. She had almost reached the door when she heard the twins scream. She froze, fear slamming into her chest.

Mark watched the twins through the windows of the A-frame house. They looked like normal beautiful young women without a care in the world as they chopped vegetables, throwing them into a big pot on the stove.

But he knew better.

He knew the truth of what they were. The secret they were hiding. Ruby looked up and saw him through the glass, her eyes widening, her face filling with shocked horror. He had to admit, he enjoyed the stunned terror contorting her face as she reached for her sister. In two steps he bounded across the porch and twisted the handle of the front door. Locked.

"Hell."

He picked up a clay pot off a nearby table and threw it through the glass panel on the side of the door. Shattered glass flew inside the house. The girls screamed. He looked inside and saw them clutching each other in the kitchen. A large smile spread across his face, and he had the urge to say, "Here's Johnny" as a flash from a horror movie filtered through his mind. He reached inside the broken panel. A shard of glass still embedded in the frame snagged his shirt, ripping at his skin as he turned the lock on the door. He pulled out his arm, removed the shard of glass from his shirt and pushed the door open wide.

He stepped into an empty room, his gaze sweeping the interior of the small house. "There is nowhere you can hide, girls." He walked farther into the house, glass crunching beneath his boots as he stepped across the tiled entryway. The hearty scent of soup cooking on the stove filled the room and his stomach rumbled. He was starving. He pushed the thought out of his head and turned down the short hall with a bedroom on both sides and a bathroom directly in front of him. He quickly checked both rooms and the bath but found no one. Where were they?

He looked up. Surely they hadn't been foolish enough to trap themselves up in the loft? With those two he wouldn't be surprised about anything they did. He turned back toward the kitchen, stepping out of the hallway and into the main room, turning toward the stairs. "Girls!" he yelled jovially.

Out of the corner of his eye, he saw something coming toward him. He spun around, raising one arm as a cast-iron pan came down on his head. Pain exploded through his skull. "You bitch." He stumbled backward, unprepared for the second blow that hit him on the back of the head and dropped him to the floor.

Chapter 17

Ruby stared at Mark lying on the floor, blood trickling down his forehead, and felt her insides clench into little knots. "He's surrounded by darkness, Jade."

"What do you mean?"

"I mean, he's surrounded by a cloud of darkness. Something's wrong with my eyes." She looked around the room, but everything else looked normal—the kitchen, the living room, even the porch outside. No shadows anywhere.

"What about me? Can you see me fine?" Jade asked, her brow furrowed with concern.

Ruby looked at her. "Yep."

Just then Celia stepped out of her mother's room, a baseball bat in her hand, and stared wide-eyed down

Mark sprawled out on the floor. "Is that your cop friend from Sedona?"

Ruby bristled at her words. "He's no friend. The creep is a stalker."

"Blazes, what did you hit him with?"

"I used your mom's antique cast-iron frying pan," Jade said, hefting the pan up and down. "They sure don't make them like this anymore."

"Apparently," Ruby said, kicking his shoe to see if he was really out. "Though you could have killed him."

"Would that have been so bad?" Jade asked. "What kind of nutcase follows us for days into the wilderness?"

Ruby shrugged, shaking her head. "I don't know. But I don't want him dead. I don't think."

"The man is certifiable," Jade muttered.

Ruby turned to Celia. "You don't look so good, hon. Do you want some frozen peas for your eyes?" She walked toward the freezer.

"Trust me, there are no frozen peas in that freezer," Celia responded, setting down the bat. "I wonder how he got past the gates."

"I guess security around here isn't as tight as you thought." Jade laid the pan on the counter and hopped up onto a bar stool.

"Well, thank goodness my mother finally put in a telephone. I'm calling Bobby." Celia picked up the phone.

Ruby shut the freezer door empty-handed, then walked back toward Mark and stood over him. "I'm telling you, Jade. It's like he's entombed in this black shadow. You don't see that?"

"What did you say?" Celia asked, holding out the phone.

"Nothing," Jade said. "She's fine."

"Obviously I'm not fine," Ruby muttered as Jade brushed passed her and walked into the kitchen.

"What's obvious is that we can't worry about weird shadows now. We've got to find something to tie up his feet." Jade started pulling open drawers.

"Bobby, get over to my mom's quick," Celia said into the phone. "That guy you've been looking for has broken into my mom's house."

"You think this will work?" Jade held up waxy string used for tying up stuffed turkeys.

Celia shrugged as she hung up the phone. "Better than dental floss, I guess."

"Yeah, but not much," Ruby said, looking at all the glass on the floor.

"Check him for his gun," Jade demanded while wrapping the string around his feet.

"Me?" Ruby stared down at Mark, not wanting to go anywhere near him, let alone touch the man. "I don't think so."

"Seriously, Ruby?" Jade said, disgusted. "He's your boyfriend."

"A couple of dates does not a boyfriend make," Ruby snapped.

"Yeah, tell that to this guy."

"Fine. I'll get the gun." Ruby let out a loud sigh, then grabbed a wooden spoon off the counter and used it to lift his jacket. A huge, shiny gun gleamed from its holster and sent a chill rocking through her. "Damn."

"It looks even more deadly considering it's strapped to an insane man," Jade muttered.

Ruby couldn't argue with that. Tentatively, she reached for his gun. Jade was right—what kind of nut-case would follow her all the way here from Sedona? Constant phone calls was one thing, but this was ridiculous. Gingerly, she wrapped her hand around the gun and pulled it out of the holster, holding it in two hands in case somehow it came alive and fired itself. Before she could move, a man walked through the door.

"What on earth are you doing?" he asked, his eyes wide as he rushed toward her across the room. "I'll take that."

"Oh, thank goodness," she said as he reached for the gun dangling from her outstretched hands. Once he had it, she immediately brushed her hands across the back of her pants. "I'm so glad—" She looked up at him, her words frozen on her lips. The man was drop-dead gorgeous. But it wasn't his strong chiseled cheekbones or wide ooey-gooey melting chocolate eyes that had her hand fluttering to her chest as she stared at him.

"What?" he asked, his face riddled with confusion.

Ruby laughed, the sound coming out in an awkward bark. "I'm sorry for staring, but you are surrounded by the most beautiful colors I have ever seen. They're like a blue-green, aqua, purple rainbow. Unbelievable."

"Ruby, are you sure you didn't knock yourself on the head?" Jade asked.

The man's beautiful brown eyes shot to Celia. Their eyes met and a knowing look passed between them.

"What's going on?" Ruby asked. "What is that look about?"

"What look?" Celia asked, feigning innocence.

"First shadows and now colors," Jade muttered. "I don't know what's wrong with her. Ruby, maybe you should sit down."

Maybe she should. Obviously something was going on with her. But from the concerned look on Celia's face, she'd guess Celia knew exactly what it was. "You going to tell me or what?" she asked Celia.

"Let's deal with this guy first," the man said, looking down at Mark turkey-tied on the floor.

"I'll call Jason," Celia muttered, walking to the phone and turning her back on Ruby.

"I'm sorry," the man said, stepping forward. "I'm Bobby." He held out his hand.

Ruby stared at his outstretched hand and was almost afraid to touch it.

"I'm Jade," Jade said, stepping forward to take his hand. "And the weird one here is my sister, Ruby."

"Gee, thanks," Ruby said drily.

"So this is Mark Goodwin. Did he cause this mess?" Bobby asked.

"Yep," Jade answered.

"What did you do to him?"

Jade held up the frying pan and Bobby smiled, shaking his head in wonder. "What do you think he wanted? Do you know why he's here?"

He was looking at Ruby now, obviously expecting an answer. But what could she say? After dinner and a cup of coffee the man was obsessed with her? Even she didn't believe that. "He wanted in?" she said weakly, her words more a question than a statement.

"That's putting it mildly," Jade said. "He's Ruby's stalker from back home. He's a cop."

"Great," Bobby muttered. He pulled his ropes out of his pocket and started tying the man up properly just as a guttural groan escaped Mark's lips.

Ruby took a step away from him. "Thank goodness you're here," she said to Bobby as he tightened the ropes on Mark's wrist, then stood. She tried not to stare at Bobby, but she really couldn't take her eyes off him. He was just…so…beautiful. She knew men weren't supposed to be beautiful, but he definitely was. And it wasn't just the fantastic colors surrounding him either, but his strong shoulders, his thick arms and neck, or maybe it was the wavy brown hair that curled slightly below his ears and was a perfect complement to the deepest, warmest brown eyes she'd ever seen.

"Stop it," Jade whispered.

Ruby smiled and turned to her sister. "I can't help it. I really can't get over—"

"Are you on drugs or what?" Jade demanded. "Celia, did your mom grow psychedelic mushrooms in that garden of hers? I think Ruby must have put some in the soup."

"Of course not!" Celia put her arm around Ruby's shoulders. "I think you need to lie down for a little while."

Ruby turned to her, her gaze automatically going up to the area right above Celia's head. "You have them, too. Colors, colors everywhere." She sighed as she took in Celia's concerned frown. "Maybe you're right."

Obviously something was going on with her. She started to leave the room, but stopped as an uneasy sensation pricked the back of her neck. She looked back and saw a worried look pass between Celia and Bobby once more. There *was* something happening to her. She was sure of it. Annoyed, she snapped at them.

"You can stop all that whispering. I can hear you."

Fear at Ruby's outburst slammed into Celia. Could she hear the *Gauliacho?* Were they here?

"You hear whispering?"

The sound of crunching gravel filled the silence of the room.

"Not anymore," Ruby muttered.

"Thank goodness. Jason's here," Celia blurted, and bolted toward the door. "I'll be back in a sec."

She glanced at Bobby as she ran out of the house. He understood what was happening, even if she was having a hard time accepting it. She slipped out the front door and met Jason at is truck. "Thanks for coming, Jason."

"Is this about Malcolm? The hearing went real long—"

"No," she said quickly, not wanting to think about Malcolm, let alone hear about what happened. "This is about my cousin Ruby."

"Oh?" he asked, surprised.

"I think she's changing."

"What?" he asked, obviously not expecting to hear that news.

"She's seeing auras."

"And she never has before?"

"No. And what's more, she's hearing whispers."

"Whispers?"

"Like I do." She paused, not sure how to say it. Not sure she wanted to, but having to just the same. "When the *Gauliacho* are near."

Concern filled his face and he got real still.

"Whispers, Jason. Right here in my mother's house. How is that possible?"

"I don't know. Are you sure there isn't some mistake?"

"Blazes, I really hope so. But changelings are so much more susceptible, their senses much more heightened than ours are. What if the *Gauliacho* are already here, Jason? What if they've found a way inside and only Ruby can hear them?"

"Why would you even think that?"

"I don't know. It was something I felt today when I was regenerating the crystals. They felt close. Too close."

"Malcolm did say—" He shook his head. "It's crazy. I know that, but he said the computers could be a gateway to the outside. An opening that the *Gauliacho* could slip in through."

Celia's chest tightened. "That sounds crazy."

"I thought so, too. But he swears it's too much of a coincidence that first all the computer systems go down across town, and now we're starting to have problems with other electronics, too. If the *Gauliacho* were able to find a breach or weakness of some kind that allowed

them to get through as an energy source, they c⸣
jump on the network, moving from one system to ⸣
next, and come back out into the walls."

A cold certainty seeped through Celia, weakening her knees. She reached out and braced herself against the truck for support. "What if he's right?" she whispered. "What if they found a way to slip past the crystals and they're already here?"

The front door opened and Bobby stepped out onto the porch. "He's awake."

Jason looked at her, confused.

"Ruby's stalker, the man who followed us here, is inside."

Jason looked stunned. "Why didn't you tell me?"

"I hadn't got to it yet."

"But how did he find you?"

"I have no idea. Except Ruby said he was encased in a black shadow. Obviously he's close to becoming an *Abatu*. If so, as focused on her as he is, he would have been able to sense her here."

Jason raked his hands through his hair. An *Abatu?* Inside the gates? "Blazes, Celia, what is going on around here?"

"I don't know," she admitted. "But it scares the hell out of me."

They walked quickly into the house and saw their intruder awake and propped up against the wall.

Jason strode right toward him. "Why are you here and what do you want with these girls?" he demanded.

"Ruby is my girlfriend. I was worried about her."

"Worried people don't break into other people's ...ses," Celia retorted.

"Nor is Ruby your girlfriend," Jade added as she swept up the broken glass from the front door into a dustpan.

"Damn right," Ruby said, showing up in the doorway.

"You're supposed to be sleeping," Jade said.

"Not tired."

"Let's try this again," Bobby said. "We know you're from Sedona. Why go through so much trouble to drive up here? You walked the perimeter of our fence all day to reach the back gate and then shot out the lock. That's an awful lot of trouble to go through for one girl who doesn't want to have anything to do with you. So I'm asking again, why?"

Surprise crossed Mark's face.

"Yes, we found it hours ago. We've been searching for you. How you found this place, I can't imagine, but it couldn't have been easy."

"Nope. Took me most of the night."

"Again. Why?" Jason pressed.

"No bullshit this time, Mark. You've been stalking me for months and I want to know why," Ruby insisted.

Propped up against the wall, with a trickle of dried blood crusted on the side of his face from the bash in the head Jade had already given him, Mark just looked up at her and laughed. A low, throaty sound that raised the fine hairs on the back of Celia's neck. Jade was right. This man was insane and a perfect candidate for the *Gauliacho* to jump on board and hitch a ride.

"I've been stalking you since you were twelve years old, my dear Ruby. You've just been too completely self-absorbed and oblivious to notice."

"Why?" Ruby asked, her lips trembling, her face pale.

"Watch it, buddy," Jade warned, picking up the frying pan again. "I'd be happy to give you another one."

"Because I know the truth about you two," he stated. "I know what you are. And I'm betting once your friends here know what I know, they won't be so eager to help you."

Celia's stomach clenched.

"What truth? What are you talking about?" Ruby shrieked.

"That you did this to me!" He nudged down the collar of his shirt with his chin, showing the edge of a nasty blood-tinged bite mark on his neck.

"What in the hell are you talking about?" Ruby shook her head in disgust. "That looks like a freaking dog bit you, not me. Like I would bite anybody anyway."

"Like hell you didn't. I shot one of you. I followed the blood trail, and you fucking attacked me."

Celia gasped, her hand rising to cover the wound on her arm.

"You're insane," Jade said, stepping back and putting the pan down on the counter. "Certifiable."

"Yeah. I've heard that for years," he said bitterly. "Ever since I saw what happened to your dear old mom. But I know what I saw. It happened, and I knew if I watched you long enough, I'd see it happen again. And then I'd be able to prove to everyone that I am not crazy.

I know what I saw, and you're coming back with me to prove it."

"What are you talking about?" Ruby demanded, her voice high and shrill.

Celia closed her eyes as dawning horror seeped through her.

"Your mother destroyed my life," he said, his voice low and broken. "Now you are going to come back with me and tell them all the truth. Tell them that what I saw happen to your mother that night in the desert wasn't a lie."

Ruby grabbed the back of a bar stool, wavering on her feet. "What happened to our mother?"

"I know what she was. What you are."

"What are you talking about?" she shrieked.

A cold, hard glint sharpened his eyes. He looked up at Ruby and said, "Woof."

Celia's heart stopped cold. She couldn't let him tell her. She couldn't find out the truth. Not like this.

"Did you just bark at us?" Jade turned to Celia. "Where's the nearest loony bin? Because this guy obviously needs a ride."

"Jason. Bobby. Is there someplace we can take him?" Celia said, stepping forward.

"I've seen you change," Mark said. "I know your secret. And soon everyone else will, too."

"Seen what change?" Ruby asked softly.

"No," Celia blurted.

He ignored her, stared right at Ruby, his eyes narrowing. "You as a wolf."

Celia stopped and watched confusion play across Ruby's face.

"What I want to know is how did you heal so quickly?" Mark asked. "Is that one of your powers? Because I know I got you. And as soon as I get you back home, I will prove to everyone that what I saw back then was the truth. I'm not the crazy one."

"And just how do you plan on making that happen?" Bobby asked, stepping forward, looming over him, his voice tight.

"She's a freak. They both are. Her mother turned into a wolf, right before my eyes. I saw it. And I saw her die."

"What did you do to my mother?" Ruby demanded, her voice trembling.

"Don't even bother, Ruby. Obviously he's crazy. He didn't know our mother. He never saw her." Jade put her arm around her and squeezed.

"Oh, but you're wrong. I saw her in the canyon. She came out to the desert and stripped her clothes off. At first I thought I was just going to get a girlie show and, let me tell you, at fourteen that's a pretty cool thing to happen to a guy. But then she started running, naked, across the desert. I couldn't believe it, especially when she was no longer running but loping, down on all fours. The next thing I knew, she was no longer a naked woman but a wolf—a beautiful white-haired wolf."

Ruby started to laugh. "You're crazy."

"Yep, that's what everyone has called me. Crazy Mark. But I followed her. I kept going even though she was too fast for me. I lost her in the night, but then I heard her howling in pain. When I caught up with her, I saw what was happening and why she was so afraid."

"What the hell kind of drugs were you on?" Jade asked, her voice bitter, her eyes shooting fire.

He smiled up at her. "You should have been there. I almost peed my pants. I've never been so scared."

Celia stared at him. She should stop him. Her fingers gripped the bar stool so tight she felt the wood cracking beneath her grasp. Everyone was waiting for him to finish. But she knew how it would end. *Badly.* Ruby's and Jade's eyes were wide with shock and disbelief. Bobby's and Jason's were tinged with wariness and curiosity. No one in the Colony knew what happened when the *Gauliacho* finally caught up with them. No one ever survived to tell.

Apprehension seeped through her veins, and she realized this was like watching a great tragedy unfold before her eyes. She wanted, she needed to know what had happened to her aunt, but at the same time, she didn't want to hear the excruciating details verbalized. Didn't want the images burned into her mind for her to relive every time she closed her eyes.

Every time she dreamed of the *Gauliacho*.

Chasing her.

Attacking her.

Calling her name.

"As I got closer to the wolf," Mark said, breaking into her thoughts, "I saw something attacking her. At first I thought they were bats, coming at her from all sides. But in the end, after what happened, I realized they weren't bats at all. They weren't anything anyone had ever seen before."

"What were they?" Celia asked, though the second the words were out of her mouth, she wished she hadn't.

"Shadows," he said.

"Shadows?" Jade repeated skeptically.

Yes. Shadows, Celia thought.

"They were flying at her and she was nipping at them, biting them, trying to get away, but there were too many. The next thing I knew, the ground split open into a deep chasm beneath her. She fell in and disappeared. I ran forward to the spot, but it was as if she'd never been there. There wasn't even a mark on the ground. Nothing but this." He struggled with his binds. He looked up at Bobby. "In my shirt pocket."

Bobby reached inside his pocket and pulled out a necklace with a lone red crystal hanging from a pendant.

Celia felt sick. She collapsed onto a bar stool at the counter. How could that have happened? How had the *Gauliacho* found her? She'd been wearing her crystal. She should have been invisible to them. She should have been protected.

Her mother's words the day she'd left for Sedona echoed in her mind. *You are never truly safe outside the borders of the Colony. Remember that, Celia. You can't stay gone for long.*

She promised she wouldn't. But she had. Had the *Gauliacho* been closing in on her, too? Was that why she'd felt them, why she'd seen them in the woods that night? Had they been following her? Had they followed her all the way back here? The thought froze the blood in her veins. But what scared her even more was the idea that they could be here now. That, like this crazy man, they had somehow found a way into the Colony. Maybe Malcolm was right. Maybe they'd got in through the computers and were here now, and that was what Ruby had been hearing. What she heard today.

"You're crazy," Ruby whispered, snatching the necklace from his hand. "You killed my mother out there in the desert and you made up some crazy story to cover it up. What did you do to her? Where is she?"

"I told you what happened," he insisted.

"You're lying," Ruby said, her heartache breaking in her throat. "You killed her, didn't you?"

His face grew hard, his eyes narrowing. "No. I didn't."

"Is that why your family thought you were crazy? Had they known what you'd done and helped you cover it up?" She was screeching now. Screaming at him, looking as though she could easily, in that moment, pounce on him and kill him herself. "They're all cops. They could have done it."

Bobby slipped his arm around her waist. "Come on," he whispered, trying to pull her away.

"How did you know who she was? Who we were?" she demanded. "How? Unless you followed her. Unless you planned the whole thing."

Instead of answering, Mark looked up at Jason. "In my jacket pocket."

Jason leaned down and pulled out a wallet. He opened it and they all saw a picture of Sue on her Arizona driver's license. Ruby stared at it, her eyes widening, and then she threw herself at him, but Bobby caught her with both hands around her middle. Loud sobs erupted from Ruby's chest as he led her out the front door and onto the porch.

Celia felt sick. Crazy or not, this man was telling the truth. She knew that, felt it deep inside, but it didn't matter. He'd still come after them. He'd refused to let it go. He wanted everyone to know their secret, and they couldn't let that happen.

Jade looked at Mark with hatred gleaming in her eyes. "How did you get my mother's wallet and necklace?" she demanded, her voice cold and deadly. She picked up the cast-iron pan once more and stepped toward him. "Tell me."

"Jade," Celia warned.

"Tell me!" she screamed.

Mark didn't even flinch. "I did tell you. It's the truth. She was a wolf. A wolf!"

Jade lifted the pan, readying to bring it down on him again. Jason stepped forward and took the pan out of her hand.

"We got this, Jade." He set the pan down on the counter, then leaned forward, grabbed Mark by his arm and hefted him to his feet.

Celia understood Jade's fury, but this man hadn't killed her mother. The *Gauliacho* had. And somehow she'd have to explain that, and explain what was happening to Ruby.

"What are you going to do with him?" Celia asked Jason as he untied the ropes at Mark's feet so the man could walk. If they let him go, he'd just come after the twins again. He knew too much, had seen too much. But they couldn't keep him there in the Colony, either.

He was human.

He was just as big a threat to them as the *Gauliacho*.

"For now I'm going to take him to Johnny at the guardhouse. Malcolm and Scott are in the holding rooms in the Town Hall, so I don't want him there." He started walking him through the house and toward the door.

"Right," she muttered, following him. *Malcolm*.

"A preliminary Judgment has been made, Celia. Both Scott and Malcolm are to be put *beyond the gates*."

A fierce ache shot through Celia's heart, surprising her with its intensity.

"If you want to say anything in Malcolm's behalf, they're opening the floor up to appeals at 11:00 a.m. After that, their fate is sealed."

She glanced at the clock and couldn't believe it was after one in the morning already. "There is nothing I want to say." She felt like a coward and a traitor, but she couldn't forgive him. She couldn't get past what he'd done.

Jason nodded grimly. "I understand. But do me a favor and think about it. I'd hate for you to have any regrets later."

"You mean once it's too late."

"Yes."

It would be too late after a couple of days. Neither man would last long on the outside without crystals.

They walked out the door, past Ruby and Bobby and toward the truck.

"All right. I'm going to call an emergency Council meeting to try and explain this mess. Can you be there in one hour?"

Celia cringed as he placed Mark in the backseat of the truck and shut the door. "Do I have a choice?"

"No."

"They're not going to be too happy about him or the twins. They're going to blame me and Malcolm."

"Yes, they are. And trust me, Malcolm doesn't need any more trouble."

She couldn't think about him right now. "What are we going to do about Ruby?" she whispered, glancing toward the front porch. "She's beginning her transformation."

He looked grim. "Looks like it."

"So there's always the chance that Jade…"

"They're both older than normal—"

"Not much older than Shay," she countered. "It must have something to do with growing up on the outside, away from all of us. Or maybe from having a human parent."

"Maybe." He looked thoughtful. But she knew it didn't matter whether Jade might make the change or not; she wasn't changing now. That was what he was thinking. She was still human and they couldn't take the chance that she'd discover the truth about them, and the longer she stayed here, the greater the risk that she would.

"I can't send Jade away knowing she could change,

too, Jason. It wouldn't be fair, but more than that, it wouldn't be safe."

"I understand what you're saying, but what if she never changes? What then? Whatever you or I believe, the Council members will never open up the gates to humans. It's one of their sacred rules."

"You're thinking of Dean, aren't you?"

"He'd be alive today if it wasn't for that rule, and Shay wouldn't have had to grow up without a dad."

"And Ruby and Jade without a mom," Celia agreed.

"But it doesn't matter what we believe—the Council governs the law over the Pack. You know that."

Celia bristled. "At this moment, the only thing I know for certain is that Jade will never leave without her sister. And I won't send her away alone. I just won't."

"Luckily for tonight that's not the issue on the table," Jason said, his voice solemn.

"I get that. I broke the rules. I brought humans into the Colony and now we have more problems than we know how to deal with. And for obvious reasons, you're right, what we're going to do about them is not a decision we can make on our own."

"No. Not by a long shot. The consequences of the girls being here are too dire, and I have a feeling they will live on for a very long time. And this man is just one of them."

Chapter 18

An hour later, Celia and Jason entered the Town Hall and sat behind a long wooden table. Celia was mentally exhausted and physically drained, and was in no shape to be confronting the Council of Elders—the oldest members of their Pack who were responsible for keeping the law. They faced a large heavy slab of redwood stretching across the front of the room where the Council would sit.

She tapped her fingers across the table, wondering if she was doing the right thing while she waited for the five Council members who passed Judgment over the Colony to arrive. The Elders' sole function was to make sure everyone lived by the rules set forth by their ancestors years ago. They were not always warm and friendly and definitely not easily approachable.

She glanced around the room at the tenets they lived by carved with intricate script into the wooden walls. Rules she'd had pounded into her since she was a child. Rules that must never be broken. The survival of the Pack depended on them.

And yet she'd broken them. She brought not one, but two humans into the Colony. And now there was a third. *A dangerous third.*

Just then the Elders, Connors, McGovern, Wilson, Young and Taylor, walked in and sat behind the large table facing them, looking just as tired as she.

"Celia," Connors said, and nodded to Jason. "It's good to see you, but if this is about Malcolm, it could have waited until morning." His annoyance was clearly defined in each syllable.

Malcolm? Yes, the Judgment. They wanted to send him beyond the gates. Her stomach flipped over in an upside-down somersault as she stared at the hard faces weathered and lined with age. Could she let them send him to his death and not say anything?

"Actually this isn't about Malcolm," Jason said, much to her relief.

"Oh?" Connors's bushy eyebrows flecked with streaks of gray rose and his dark eyes narrowed.

"This is about my cousins," she said.

"Sue Lawson James's daughters," Jason added quickly.

"The ones at the Sanctuary today?" McGovern, who had a mean streak of impatience, demanded.

"Haven't they been living in Arizona?" Taylor, the quiet, thoughtful Elder, asked.

"Yes," Celia said, answering them both. "That's where I've been. We started a business together."

The five of them stared at her, condemnation in their eyes. She could almost hear them breathing, almost feel their disapproval. Fraternizing with humans, one of their golden rules that must never be broken. But they weren't just humans. Not to her. They were family.

"When I found out about my mother's—" Her mouth dried up and she couldn't finish. "About my mother, I left Sedona very quickly. I was being chased, and to top that off, a few *Abatus* tracked us to our shop. They made a mess of the place, and I'm afraid my cousins were concerned for me. And...well, they followed me here to make sure I wasn't in any trouble." She tried to leave Malcolm out of it. She didn't want to give them any reason to condemn him further. To blame him. Though she knew they would anyway.

"They followed you all the way here from Arizona and neither you nor Malcolm noticed?" McGovern asked, his disbelief echoing off the walls. His accusation sat heavily in the room.

Why hadn't they noticed? Because they'd been too busy thinking about each other rather than paying attention to what was around them. Her thoughts flashed to that night in the hotel room after their run-in with Mark and the *Gauliacho*. Malcolm had tried so hard to tell her something, but she wouldn't let him. She didn't want to hear it. She'd thought it had been about Shay. Now she realized he'd wanted to tell her about her mom and what he'd done.

She pushed the thoughts away. It didn't matter now.

Jason looked at her, concern heavy in his eyes.

"Celia?" Elder Young prompted. If there was ever an Elder who would be on her side, who would help her, it would be him.

"We were being chased by *Abatu,*" Celia said. "They attacked us when we stopped for a break. We...we were lucky to have escaped. Worrying about them and trying to deal with the news of my mother's death, well, it was more than a little distracting. We just... We didn't know they were behind us."

"Where are the girls now?" Connors asked.

"They're at my mother's house. Other than the Sanctuary for the services, they haven't been anywhere else."

"That's a relief," Wilson, who'd been silent until then, said.

"Once Jade and Ruby heard about my mother, they insisted on staying for the funeral. I couldn't exactly send them away. They are family and they'd driven all that way. There was nothing I could say, no reason I could give not to let them come."

"No. You were right, Celia," Young said.

But then Connors turned to Jason. "It's imperative we get them out of here as soon as possible. The longer they stay, the more disastrous the consequences."

"I understand, but that could be a problem, sir."

"And why would that be?" McGovern asked, not bothering to conceal his impatience.

"It appears one of the girls is beginning her transformation."

The room had grown so quiet Celia was certain everyone in it could hear her heart pounding.

"Are you sure?" Connors asked with a heavy note of caution.

"Quite."

Silence thickened between the two tables.

Celia finally spoke. "There is no way we can tell Ruby what is happening to her without also telling her twin sister. They are inseparable. And there is also the chance that with time, Jade will change, too."

McGovern dropped a heavy hand to the thick table, making a loud thud. "We cannot keep her here on the notion that she may someday change. You know that."

"We can't send her away without Ruby, either. She'd never go."

"She is human. We do not tell humans about who we are. Rule number one," Young said diplomatically.

"But she is the twin of one of us. She will not betray us," Celia said, her voice rising.

"We have rules," McGovern insisted.

"True," Jason interjected. "But we've never had a situation like this before, either. Sometimes exceptions need to be made. Sometimes rules need to be changed."

The men started shaking their heads, muttering to each other, growing more and more agitated by the second.

Jason stood. "With all due respect, our Colony's numbers are dwindling. Not all of our youth are surviving their transformations. The outside world is growing closer. The town on our eastern border is exploding. How long can we continue like this? We are going to need to change with the times if we are going to survive."

"We need new blood," Celia added, her temper growing short. It had been too long and too hard a day. "Even if it is human blood."

She was met with stunned gazes that quickly narrowed, becoming glowing amber, slitted and deadly. And from somewhere in the room, she heard a low, thundering growl.

"I'd like it to go on record that I'm adding my support to Celia's proposal. Jade needs to be brought into the fold," Jason said, then sat back down.

"A human cannot live within the gates," Connors spat.

"It's unheard of," Wilson agreed.

"Unprecedented," McGovern insisted.

"I will not send her away alone," Celia stated calmly. She'd had enough.

"Is that a threat, Miss Lawson?" McGovern asked, his face reddening.

"I won't let her go out there alone. If she changes, she will be all by herself, and I won't take that chance. She and Ruby are my family. My only family. And I can tell you right now, Ruby will not stay here without her, and I won't let her go back to Sedona alone."

"Let me get this straight," Connors said, outraged. "You are telling us you will leave here and risk the safety of this entire Colony if we don't do your bidding and let these two humans stay? Just who do you think you are?"

Before she could give him a resounding yes, Jason took her hand in his. "She is our Keeper," he said. "Right now our only Keeper."

Jason held up a hand as the sputtering outrage started up all over again. "Before things get too heated, I just wanted to add that there is a chance Ruby, like her mother before her, could also be a Keeper."

"How so?" Elder Young asked.

"She's reacting strongly to the crystals," Jason replied.

"She has been for days," Celia added, feeling a flicker of hope for the first time since she'd walked into the room.

"That doesn't mean—" McGovern started.

But Young placed his hand on McGovern's arm and silenced him. "Well, you've certainly given us a lot to think about," he said, trying to keep the peace.

"I'm afraid there's more," Jason said reluctantly. And Celia's stomach tightened as dread knotted within her.

Eyebrows shot up along the table and Connors dropped his head, shaking it back and forth.

"While the girls were following Celia, they were being tracked by a man who apparently witnessed the death of their mother, Sue, in her true form by the *Gauliacho*. He has been watching the family ever since."

No one said a word for a full ten seconds. Celia was so tense she thought she might break. She was beginning to regret coming here, beginning to understand why Malcolm made so many decisions without including the rigid guidance of this Council.

"Please continue," Young said without much enthusiasm.

"Earlier today we found a car parked outside the

gates. We placed guards at all the checkpoints, but the intruder still managed to get inside the Colony and find the girls."

"What?" McGovern exploded.

"He broke into Jaya's house and threatened them," Jason continued without stopping. "The girls were amazing. They knocked him unconscious and tied him up and then Celia called Bobby and me. Bobby has him incarcerated at the guardhouse with Johnny."

The silence in the room thickened to dangerous levels.

"So you're telling us there is yet another human within the gates of the Colony?" Connors asked with disbelief.

"Malcolm is to blame for this," McGovern said. "If he'd never left—"

"If he'd never left, then I wouldn't be here now and your precious crystals would not have been regenerated," Celia interrupted.

"We now have three humans residing within our gates. What do you suggest we do about that, young lady?" Connors asked.

"Yes, if you hadn't left here in a juvenile fit—" McGovern added.

"What is it about the youth that you don't know your place in society—" Wilson threw in.

"Your responsibility to the Pack," Connors finished for him.

Celia's head was spinning as accusations flew around the room, growing louder and louder by the second. She stood and leaned over the table, planting both palms on the flat surface. "Apparently it's time for some changes around here. Maybe all your rules—" she flung her arms wide to encompass the words etched on the walls surrounding the room "—are out of touch and out-of-date. Maybe Malcolm was right. The world outside our gates has changed significantly while we've been isolated up here on this mountain. We aren't going to be able to continue living the way we are. The outside world is closing in on us. We need to find a way to deal with that and with situations like these."

"Malcolm brought lots of changes and look what that got us," Connors insisted. "Nothing—"

"Exactly my point," Celia interrupted. "What did it bring you? An improved economy that pulled us up and out of the Dark Ages. Had you kept a better handle on those trying to stir up trouble and sabotage his efforts, then perhaps the situation never would have escalated to such an intolerable level that my mother had to die."

Her emotional outburst echoed around the room, and as she heard her own words coming back at her, she couldn't believe they had come from her mouth. First, that she was standing up to the Elders, blaming and judging them in a way she was certain no one had ever done before, but that she was also standing up for Malcolm. Even after everything he'd done.

Shocked silence, thick and heavy, met her. And in that moment, she knew if they didn't need her so much, if she wasn't the one and only Keeper they had, they would probably send her beyond the gates for treason. Which at this point would be fine with her.

Finally Elder Young spoke, his words soft yet firm,

his hands clenched on the table in front of him. "If we don't have rules, Celia, then we have anarchy. There must always be boundaries for people to live by or we no longer have a community, we just have individuals living in close proximity with no one caring about each other or about the Pack. And survival of the Pack must come before all else."

"Then don't put Malcolm outside the gates. We need him. No one has ever cared about the Pack as much as he has. And you know this," Celia pleaded.

"Right now I believe we are here to discuss the humans, not the wayward choices of our previous leader," Connors stated, and she could tell by the stubborn set of his jaw that with him, Malcolm didn't stand a chance.

"Ruby is going to have to be told what is happening to her," Celia said.

"And what happened to her mother," Jason added. "There is not going to be any getting around that."

"And I can tell you right now, she has no loyalty to this Pack. Her sister is her Pack. And she won't stay here without her and she won't keep something this significant from her. Jade is going to have to be told," Celia reiterated, bringing them back full circle.

"If you tell her," Connors said, his tone severe. "You will be put out *beyond the gates*. Those are our rules. They will not be pushed aside, altered or broken. Not even for you—our Keeper."

Stunned by the finality of his ruling, Celia stared at him openmouthed. "Then you'll all be damned."

Chapter 19

Celia sat in the front seat of Jason's truck shaking, staring out the front windshield, as they pulled away from the Town Hall. "I can't believe I said all that."

"Me, either," he said, although she could see his small smile highlighted by the dashboard lights.

"The Elders are just so frustrating."

"Yep."

"They don't listen," she ranted. "All they care about is their stupid rules, and to hell with everything and everyone else. I think I need to see Malcolm," she said suddenly.

Jason turned to her, surprise filling his face. "Are you sure?"

"No. Not really. But I have to."

"You were a strong advocate for him tonight, whether

you meant to be or not." He turned the truck around and headed back toward the Town Hall, where the jail facility with its two holding cells was located on the backside of the building. "You surprised me."

"Yeah, well, I guess I surprised myself."

"He loves you," Jason said.

"I know." She sighed. "But not enough to keep from ripping our lives apart."

"Power and ambition have made many men lose their way."

She fidgeted in her seat, trying to rid herself of the nervous energy and the doubts circling in her mind. "Excuses won't heal all the damage that's been done."

Jason sucked in a deep breath. "If it helps, I do believe he's learned from his mistakes."

"What choice did he have? He's hit rock bottom here."

"And yet you stood up for him."

Yes, she had, without forethought and without good sense. When it came to Malcolm, she was a lost cause. "I guess I still love him, too," she admitted. "But that doesn't mean I can live with what he's done."

"But can you live with it if they put him beyond the gates?"

No. Yes. "Maybe. I don't know. Why was everything so much easier in Sedona?"

"Because it wasn't your home. You were only visiting."

"Perhaps. But even if they do let Malcolm stay, I can't go back to the way things were before. I can't get past everything that he's done."

"You don't have to." Jason pulled the truck into a parking space and turned off the ignition.

"I don't know what to do," she admitted. "Will I ever be able to forgive him? And if I do, will I regret not fighting for him now?"

"Only you can answer that question."

"Blazes, Jason, I wish my mother were here."

He turned in his seat to face her. "If she were, what would she tell you?"

Celia laughed. "She'd say that Malcolm was nothing but trouble and that I was like a moth to his flame. That I thrive on trouble."

Jason smiled. "That sounds exactly like what she'd say."

"It's not as if I haven't tried to get him out of my system before." She sighed, then at length said, "What are we going to do about the twins?"

Jason raked his fingers through his hair, giving his head a good scratch. "We don't have a lot of choices. We'll have to do what the Council commands."

"Not me," she muttered bitterly.

"Don't you, Celia? Bravado aside, Sue was a Keeper, too. She didn't last out there, either."

"I just feel so stifled here by all their rules. I want to be free. I don't like feeling confined or trapped."

He took her hand and squeezed. "The Colony is not a prison, it's a sanctuary. It is your home."

"Is it?" she asked, pulling her hand back. "Because it doesn't feel that way. And it hasn't for a very long time."

"Personal perception is everything. Be honest, Celia,

when you were in Sedona, were you truly happy? Were you truly free?"

Celia thought back to all the nights she'd longed to run as her true self but couldn't. Fear of discovery and loneliness had been her constant companions. If it hadn't been for the twins, she never would have stayed there. But she hadn't wanted to come back to the same trap she'd built with Malcolm in the Colony, either.

And yet here she was, parked outside the Town Hall ready to go see him, to face their problems instead of just running away. That all sounded good, but the sad, pathetic truth was, she just couldn't seem to stay away from him. Her mom was right—she thrived on trouble. When she'd left for Sedona, she'd wanted Malcolm to come after her to bring her home. Because he'd wanted her. Not because he'd had to. Who was she fooling? She hadn't been any more free in Arizona than she'd been here. Nothing had changed.

Except perhaps Malcolm. As Jason said, perception was everything.

"How'd you get to be such a smart guy?"

"I got it the hard way," he admitted, and Celia knew it was true. She remembered how devastated he'd been when his wife died all those years ago. She never thought he'd fall in love again and yet he had. "I was glad to hear about you and Shay. And not just because that meant Malcolm couldn't have her."

Jason grinned. "Shay's changed my life. She's really…special."

"Well, she must be if she captured you."

"I'm not sure if it's because she made her transformation so much later than the rest of us or because she has human blood in her also, but she kept her gift to see inside people. To see their hearts through their auras."

"Seriously? If that's true, could the same be said for Ruby after she makes the change?"

"It will be interesting to find out. But my point is that when Malcolm came to see us that last day before he left the Colony to find you, Shay saw inside his heart, Celia. She saw the goodness within him, and his determination to put things right. It's because of that that I've been able to forgive him, to move past what he's done and give him the chance he's seeking. To make amends. To find resolution. That's why, even after all he's done, I still believe in him. And I'm still willing to give him a chance to prove that the old Malcolm is still in there. The one who believed the best in everyone and wanted to give them the world."

Celia smiled. Yes, she remembered that Malcolm well. "The idealism of youth."

"He had it stronger than anyone I'd ever met."

"I hope Shay's right," Celia said finally. "I hope you're both right."

Malcolm couldn't believe his eyes when the door opened to the hallway outside his cell. The lights turned on and Celia walked into the hall. He rubbed the sleep out of his eyes and stood up from the narrow cot. "Celia? What are you doing here?"

"I wanted to see you." She moved closer to the bars even though it was obvious from her tentative step and the way her hand was trembling that she wasn't sure she should be there.

"How are you holding up?" he asked, his voice low.

"I've been better."

Yes, he was sure she had. They all had. "I take it you heard about my preliminary Judgment?"

She nodded, her upper teeth worrying her lower lip. "Yes."

"I'm afraid the Council is going to put me out beyond the gates, and there is nothing that can be done about it."

She closed her beautiful chocolate-brown eyes, and when she opened them again, they were shimmering with tears.

He grabbed the bars with both hands. "I'm sorry I did this to you. To us."

She placed her hands over his. "It's not over yet."

"For me it is."

"I won't accept that."

"You have to. It's time to move on. I've been selfish and I took you for granted. I brought all this down on us."

"Maybe," she whispered. "But there is a lot more going on here than just your Judgment." She told him about Ruby and Jade, and Mark the cop from Sedona and what he'd seen. Malcolm couldn't believe what he was hearing.

"And you went to the Council with all this?"

"Yes, Jason and I both. We had to. They told me if I told Ruby and Jade what was happening, they'd put me out beyond the gates."

Malcolm was stunned. "They wouldn't. They need you."

"They are arrogant and unreasonable."

He smiled. "True."

"They can't separate Ruby and Jade. Ruby won't let Jade go back to Sedona without her, and if she goes…" Her lips tightened into a thin line. "I won't let them send Jade away."

"What are you going to do?" She had the stubborn-determination thing going on, and she was mad. A dangerous combination where Celia was concerned.

"I'll leave the Colony with them. You can come with us and we'll all go back to Sedona together. It's the perfect solution."

Malcolm stared at her, a mixed bag of emotions tumbling through his insides. She'd just said she wouldn't leave him out there alone to die, that she'd build a life with him away from here. He wanted that more than he wanted anything, but he couldn't let her do it. "Celia, you can't leave the Colony. You have a responsibility to the Pack. You can't let all these people die."

"Really? Why not? Where are they now, Malcolm? After everything you did for them. They aren't here. All they think about is themselves. That's all they've ever cared about."

"Celia, that's not true. We're a Pack. A family."

"Really? You need to take off your blinders, Malcolm, and see these people as they truly are. Do family turn out members in need?"

"When did you become so jaded?"

"I guess when your world falls apart and you're left

standing on the outside, you get a different perspective.
You see things from a new angle and sometimes what
you see isn't very pretty."

Pain and sorrow ripped through him. "I'm sorry. I
did this to you."

"No, you didn't, Malcolm. I did. I finally woke up
and saw the world for what it truly was. Sometimes no
matter how hard you try to make a difference, people
really just don't get it."

Celia walked into the Town Hall five minutes before
eleven the next morning after very little sleep. She was
tired, but worse than that, she was disillusioned. She
wasn't sure exactly when it had started, but it was before she left for Arizona. The infighting, the backstab-
bing, the out-and-out lies had torn their community
apart, polarizing them until she no longer had faith in
her neighbors or her friends.

It wasn't a good place to be.

And as she sat in this room, watching old friends and
neighbors file in, she couldn't help wondering whether
they were for Malcolm or against him. How many of
the business owners sitting in this room had he given
up hours of his free time to, to set up their computer
systems, to help them with their businesses, working
with them to make sure they were successful? Would
they turn their backs on him now?

At precisely 11:00 a.m., the five Elders filed in, wearing the ceremonial robes of their ancestors that hung
down to the floor. They took their seats behind the long
redwood table polished to a high shine, sitting before

the elaborate carving of a wolf covering the wall. Once they were settled, the sheriff brought Malcolm and Scott into the room to stand before them. Even now, Celia could see the division in the room—the Colonists who supported Scott sitting on one side and those there for Malcolm on the other.

How had things gotten so bad? Would they ever be able to heal and come together as a community? Right now she had no idea, but she knew whatever was decided today, no one would be happy. For the first time, she wondered if the Pack would be able to get past this, if they'd be able to heal and go back to the way things used to be—one big family with neighbor helping and supporting neighbor. Sadly, she didn't think so.

Her eyes met Malcolm's and her heart lurched. Even after everything he'd done, she still cared about him. He was like a drug to her, one that she couldn't seem to be able to live without. She ached with her torment; it pulled at her, twisting her insides into knots. Was Jason right? Had Malcolm changed? Had he learned from his mistakes? She ripped her gaze away from his. The bond between them was too strong to be easily broken.

But if they did sentence him to be put beyond the gates, she'd be forced to move on, to live life without him. Not of her choice, but of theirs. She looked at her fellow Pack members and their leaders and wondered, could she live with that? Was she ready to say goodbye to Malcolm for good? Was she ready for him to die? Because putting a wolf beyond the gates amounted to a death sentence. They all knew that. Every wolf in this room. But if she couldn't live with it, could she really go with him and leave the rest of the Pack here alone to die?

Elder Connors, leader of the Council, rose. "We are here today to reach a final Judgment on the rulings of Scott Craigs and Malcolm Daniels. Both men have grievously broken our sacred covenants and placed the welfare of this Pack in jeopardy, including causing the death of another—our sister and the Keeper of the Pack, Jaya Lawson. Our initial ruling is that they will both be put out *beyond the gates* for all time. Now is your opportunity to state an appeal of Judgment. After our final decision, there will be no more discussion of these two men and the ruling will not be spoken of again."

Nausea soured Celia's stomach.

Scott's teenage daughter, Natalie, started to sob, her shoulders shaking. The proceedings deteriorated from there. Accusations started flying, ugly words slung back and forth across the aisle, turning the hearing into a spectacle that was both embarrassing and enlightening as to the pitiful state they had reached. Connors banged his fists against the table. "One at a time," he yelled. "One at a time," he began again once the room quieted. "You will come up here and state your case individually."

One by one, Pack members started going up, pleading for why Scott or Malcolm should be given a second chance. But in the end, Celia couldn't see where anyone said anything that would make a difference. Especially not for Malcolm. And then finally Jason stepped forward. The room hushed.

"This is a dark day in the history of our Pack," he

started, his face grave. "From where I stand, the reason all of you are here is that both these men have cared deeply about the success of this Pack, and more specifically about all of you. But they let their differing passions get the better of them and people were hurt. It's a tough decision. Do we allow them to stay and hope they find a way to live peacefully in the Pack or take the chance that they will continue on their destructive paths causing even more division? Have these men, not strangers, but friends, family members and neighbors, learned the error of their ways? Do they deserve our forgiveness?"

His eyes fell on Celia as he said the words. She could see where he was going and what he wanted from her. She wanted to give it to him, to save Malcolm, but to do so she'd have to take that last step. She'd have to open herself up to him once again, and walk up there and publicly say, "Yes, even though he hurt my family and me, even though he directly caused the death of my mother, I forgive him. And you should, too." She loved him, yes. She'd always loved him. She didn't want him to die.

"The question we all have to ask ourselves is can we forgive them?" Jason continued, still looking at her. Still making her squirm. "Do we believe they have learned their lessons and that if we let them back into our society, they will have something positive to contribute? Can we trust them?"

"Hell no!" someone yelled from the back.

"Put them both beyond the gates," a familiar voice said to rousing shouts of agreement.

Celia swung around, stunned to see the voice had belonged to Tiffany. Her best friend, the woman who had been bugging her to marry Malcolm for years, who had always preached what a good catch he was. The hypocrisy, the lack of loyalty of so many of the town's people was astounding.

She couldn't take any more. She stood on shaky but determined legs and walked toward Jason, who was nodding at her, his appreciation heavy in his eyes. She locked her gaze on his, not wanting to look at Malcolm. Not sure she could handle it and afraid that if she did, the thin layer of resolve she'd built around herself would crumble.

As she stood beside Jason, the crowd silenced. She looked at their faces filled with hostility and judgment and felt a chill spread through her. "As you know," she started, her voice surprisingly strong, "I've been gone for a while. I've been on the outside."

"Yeah, when you should have been here," someone yelled.

Someone she couldn't see. And she was surprisingly thankful for that. "I know many of you are curious about what it's like out there in the human world. In one sense, it's wonderful—the artistry, the innovation. There are so many people, more people than you can even fathom. They are all busy trying to better their lives, so busy that they forget to enjoy the very short time they have.

"They waste hours sitting in their cars moving from one place to the other, or just waiting, idling, forgetting to look at what is around them, to feel the breeze on their faces or to listen to the music that nature has given them, the precious wonders of life. Instead they focus on noise piped from speakers or images coming from a screen.

"Their communities are so big they don't see each other as individuals but as groups, divided by their belief systems and constantly at odds with each other. A lot like what I see in this room today. When I was gone and I thought back on the Colony, I thought of it the way it used to be, when we acted like a family, like people who cared about one another. That's not the way we're acting today, and it saddens me."

Some people, she noticed, had the decency to look ashamed, to look down when her eyes passed over them, while others glared at her with open hostility. Her gaze moved to Shay. "Sometimes I wish I had a gift that would let me see inside each one of you, so I could tell if you are dangerous or a threat to the Pack, or if somewhere deep inside there is something good, something that still cares about our future. I'd like to believe that in each of you there is the same longing that is within me, for community, for family. And I hope it is still there within these two men. I can only believe that it was that deep need to want to better our Colony that drove each of them to make the mistakes they have made."

She looked at them then. At Scott. At Malcolm. Her heart hurting so much it must surely be bleeding. "I can only hope that you both see that your actions were wrong and destructive. That you aren't making excuses for your behavior." She turned back to the crowd. "And that those of you in this room today who helped them, who helped contribute to the death of my mother realize that nothing is ever gained by fighting with each other. We need to come together, trust one another again and be respectful of each other's dreams and visions.

"Yes, I wish I could see into each of your hearts, but I can't, so I suppose all we can go on is faith. Do we believe these two men can get past their differences and become friends and neighbors once more? I truly hope so, because I believe that if we put them beyond the gates, it will cause a rift in this community so deep and so wide that we will never heal."

Silence met her when she finished and, she hoped, a little shame on the parts of the townspeople. Jason squeezed her hand and nodded his thanks as she turned to go back to her seat.

"Is there anyone else here who would like to say anything in these two men's behalf?" Connors asked, addressing the room.

The crowd grew hushed and no one said a word.

"Then let the voting commence. There is a box for each man at the back of the room. Please put an aye or a nay slip into each one. The votes will be counted and will be taken into consideration in our final Judgment, which will be posted at eleven tonight."

People rose and started moving toward the back of the room, the unnatural silence continuing. Celia saw Shay start toward her. She couldn't talk to her, not yet. She considered turning and walking away before Shay could reach her. But before she could step away, a loud pop ripped through the air. Everyone stilled, looking around the room, not knowing what the sound was or where it had come from. And then it came again. A booming report that shook the building. Electricity crackled through the air. The smell of ozone filled the room.

Celia stiffened as fear shot through her, tightening her muscles and sending adrenaline pumping into fight-or-flight mode. Shay's gaze immediately flew to the walls. She knew what was coming.

"Everyone out, now!" Shay yelled.

No one moved. They all stood frozen. Horrified. Waiting.

And then the floor shook beneath them and a huge crack split the wall in front of them, breaking through the wolf carving, destroying it.

"Now!" Shay yelled. "Move! *They're* coming."

It was as if she'd held a gun up to the ceiling and fired. Everyone started running and screaming, fleeing the room.

Celia ran toward Malcolm as the first whisper seeped through the crack, racing through the room. They were coming for her.

The *Gauliacho* had finally arrived.

Chapter 20

"Wait! Everyone make sure you go home and unplug everything electronic. Especially the computers," Malcolm yelled over the din of screaming voices as panic overtook reason and people bolted out of the room.

Malcolm watched in horror as big men elbowed and pushed smaller, weaker people out of the way, even knocking women to the floor. He was glad to see Jason and the sheriff rush forward to help before someone got hurt, or worse.

"I've regenerated the stones," Celia said, her voice bordering on panic. "They shouldn't be here. This makes no sense."

"I think they're coming in through the computers," Malcolm said. "They've been moving from system to system, moving through the power lines until they spread a net over the whole Colony."

Celia's mouth opened, her hand trembling as she raised it as if the gesture alone could stop him. Terror spread across her face as the true meaning of his words hit her.

"I'm sorry I didn't believe you earlier," Shay said, hurrying toward them. "I just didn't think it was possible."

"I wish it wasn't," Malcolm muttered. "Everything electronic needs to be shut down and unplugged now."

"All right, let's do it." Shay rushed toward the back where the offices were kept.

Malcolm grabbed Celia's hand and squeezed it. "Are you going to be okay?"

She nodded, looking slightly shell-shocked.

"Can you spread the word? Let everyone know to unplug everything."

"I don't understand. It just doesn't make sense," she whispered. "They're already here. How will this work?"

"I don't know, but we have to do something." He bent down and gave her a quick kiss, not adding that if they didn't, if they froze and did nothing, then they'd all die. He watched her leave and wished for her sake that there was some way to contain this situation, but if there was, he just didn't see it.

"I want to help," Scott said, coming toward him.

"I thought you would have run off like everyone else," Malcolm said bitterly.

"I'm not like everyone else. Besides, you and I

caused this mess together. You brought in the computers and I fired the bullet that killed Jaya."

Malcolm didn't know what to say to that. He stared at the man, trying to clamp down on his hatred and anger, knowing it would get them nowhere.

"I know I fucked up," Scott said. "I was determined to stop you even if it meant killing Shay. She moved, and Jaya got hit. I couldn't believe it when I saw her." He looked down at his hands. "Jaya wasn't supposed to be there."

Malcolm stared at him, a shiver coursing like ice water down his spine, making him feel numb. "Are you sorry Jaya's dead? Or that Shay didn't take the bullet instead?"

Scott looked at him, his eyes dull. "At this point, I don't see where it makes any difference."

Malcolm wanted to yell at him that hell yes, it did, and then send him on away. Hell, he wanted to put the man beyond the gates himself. But he needed him. "If you're serious about helping, we need to hit every business in the center of town and disconnect everything electronic. I want nothing plugged into the walls."

Scott nodded, and they hurried toward the door.

"Wait just a minute," Connors yelled, crawling out from under the table. "You two aren't going anywhere but back to your cells."

Malcolm paused. "We don't have time for this, Connors. Unless you want the *Gauliacho* on your doorstep."

"Pah! The *Gauliacho* aren't here. This is another one of your games, Malcolm. I can see that. You think if you save the town from these imaginary demons, then we will vote to save your hide and not put you beyond the gates where you belong."

"Imaginary?" Malcolm couldn't believe his ears. Shay had tried to tell him, but he hadn't believed it. "I think you've been in the Colony too long," he said to the Elder. By definition, they were the Keepers of their history. They should know better than anyone about the *Gauliacho* and the *Abatu*.

Connors's face reddened. "Watch your place, boy."

Malcolm looked around for the other Council members for some reasoning, but they were all gone.

"If you didn't believe in the *Gauliacho,* then why was it so important that Celia be brought back to regenerate the stones?" Malcolm asked, unable to comprehend this madness.

"It wasn't important. Not to me. You did that on your own."

"Yes, and it almost killed us. Just like the *Gauliacho* killed Shay's dad and Celia's aunt Sue."

"So you say," Connors said.

"He's going senile," Scott muttered under his breath.

"Am I? And yet I hold your future in my hands, don't I?"

"Let me get this straight," Malcolm said. "You're going to vote to put us beyond the gates because you really don't believe there is any danger out there?"

"Why would there be? Frankly, I don't care where you two troublemakers go as long as you get out of my town. Now get back in your cells."

"No," Malcolm said, standing up to him. For the first time in his life, he was out-and-out defying an Elder.

But were they all really this out of touch? Or was it just Connors?

"You dare defy me?" Connors spluttered.

"What do we have to lose?" Malcolm turned his back on the man and started walking out of the room. He heard a growl behind him, low and deadly. He turned back and saw Connors staring at him, his eyes narrowed and glowing amber. "You coming, Scott?"

"Yep." Scott hurried toward him and they both ran out the door.

Celia rushed back to Jaya's house and to the twins, who had no idea what was happening. Both were outside in the garden enjoying the morning. She contemplated just leaving them there, but she didn't know how much of a signature Ruby was emitting. Would the *Gaulia-cho* still find her?

Luckily her mother never allowed a computer in her house. Celia used to think her mom was being stubbornly old-fashioned. Now she knew better. Her mother always had been in better touch with nature's flow of energy than Celia had. If only she'd paid more attention. She should have trusted her mom more.

"Hey, Celia," Ruby said, holding up a large purple vegetable. "Fried eggplant for dinner!"

"Great." Celia had no idea what she should do. How much, if anything, she should tell them. She mulled it over and over in her mind, but the truth was, she could get a call any minute and then she'd have to leave. What if something happened to her and she didn't make it back? They'd be left here defenseless and vulnerable.

"Hey, would you guys mind coming into the house? There's something I need to talk to you about."

"Not at all," Ruby said, and started walking toward her. Jade dropped the weeds in her hand, looking more than a little thankful.

They walked into her mother's house and as the twins cleaned up, Celia checked each crystal in the four compass points of the house and made sure they were all energized and working properly. At least here they'd be safe. For now.

"What's up?" Ruby asked.

Before Celia could answer, the phone rang.

Reluctantly she picked up the phone. She stared at the cord plugged into the wall and remembered how much her mother had fought her about the phone. She didn't want one in her house. Celia had insisted.

"Celia, this is Bobby. I have bad news."

Celia's stomach twisted. "More?" She couldn't imagine what could be worse than the *Gauliacho* breaking into the Town Hall.

"Mark has escaped."

Her heart lurched. Yes, worse. "Escaped? How?" She looked at the twins, who were suddenly turning to lock the doors and windows even though it wouldn't matter. The window by the front door was still broken. They didn't have a need for high security here in the Colony.

"Johnny left to help Malcolm and Jason with the computers and somehow this guy got away."

"But we can't have him running loose all over the Colony now!" Celia said, trying to keep her voice low.

But it was no use. Her cousins could hear everything she was saying. "What about the girls?"

"Take them to Malcolm's. This guy doesn't know where it is. I'll meet you there and stay with them."

"All right. Do you know how Malcolm and Jason are doing? Are they having any luck?"

"I don't think so. From what I've been able to see, the whole town is falling apart. People are panicking, trying to barricade themselves in their homes, but walls are cracking everywhere. I honestly don't know what we're going to do."

There were a lot of homes in the Colony like this one that didn't have a computer. Would they be safe? Somehow she didn't think so. Because once the Shadows arrived, seeping out of the cracks, there would be no protection from them.

"Bobby, what if we moved everyone into the Sanctuary? There is nothing electronic in there, not even a telephone. I could set up a crystal perimeter inside to protect everyone and give Malcolm a little more time."

"I like it. I'll start spreading the word."

"The twins and I will meet you there." She only hoped they wouldn't be too late. Celia grabbed her mother's crystals and she and the twins piled into Malcolm's truck.

"I can't believe they let him escape," Jade muttered. She was patting Ruby on the knee. "It's going to be okay. He won't find us."

"But we still don't know how he found us the first time," Ruby said, her gaze furtively checking their surroundings as they drove down the dirt road, as if she expected him to jump out from behind one of the large trees at any second.

"That's true," Celia said, and that was a concern. A big one. "I'm going to take you to Malcolm's and Bobby is going to stay with you. But first, we have to make a quick stop at the Sanctuary."

"Why? What's going on?" Jade asked, always the perceptive one.

Celia took a deep breath while trying to figure out what she should say and how much. "I have to drop off some crystals. Bobby is going to meet us there." But when they pulled up to the Sanctuary, people were running in from the street as if they were being chased by the devil himself. And in one sense, Celia supposed they were.

"Something's wrong," Ruby said, watching a mother run toward the Sanctuary door clutching one child in her arms while pulling another behind her, tears streaming down their small scared faces. "What's happening?"

Celia parked the truck and turned off the ignition, trying to determine whether or not to leave them there or take them inside.

"Celia! What in the hell is going on?" Jade demanded.

"Come on," Celia said, picked up the bag of crystals, then ran toward the Sanctuary, passing the large statue of a wolf carved out of stone.

Jade followed after her, but as soon as Ruby got out of the truck, she bent over, clutching her ears. "Ruby!" Jade called, running back to her.

Celia stopped and turned, anxiety twisting through

her and filling her with fear. What was happening to her? She ran back to Ruby and grabbed her by the waist. "Come on, sweetie. Just a little farther."

"Make it stop," Ruby cried.

"What?" Jade demanded, her eyes widening with fear and helplessness.

"The voices. They're all talking at once in my head. I can't stand it."

"Don't listen to them, Ruby," Celia insisted. "Focus on me. As soon as we get inside, you won't hear them." They ran through the door and into the main room.

"Talk to her," Celia told Jade. "Don't leave her alone. Not for a second."

"But wait—"

Celia couldn't wait. She ran to each compass point in the room, putting the crystals in place, saying the chants as quickly as she could. Trying to focus through the terror that had gripped her insides in a bone-crushing squeeze. Ruby wasn't just hearing whispers; she was hearing their voices. Once she was finished, Celia rushed back to Ruby, who was sitting in a chair in a back corner, tears streaming down her pale face.

"Blazes, I'm sorry, Ruby. Are you all right?"

Ruby looked up at her, her luminous blue eyes wide and scared. "What is happening to me?"

She knelt down in front of her. "You're transforming, baby. I'm so sorry. You shouldn't have had to find out like this. I didn't want—"

"Transforming?" Jade said, her voice too loud.

The room, still only partially full as more and more of the Pack members were making their way to them, was quiet enough that several people turned to stare at them, open curiosity in their eyes.

"What are you talking about?" Jade insisted, lowering her voice.

"Jade. Ruby. Your mom, like my mom, like me, we're a little different." That was putting it mildly. They looked confused, as they should. She was making a mess of everything. She struggled for the best way to say it, to try to explain the unexplainable. "You know the story Mark told you about your mom?"

"Yeah, the guy was a total crackpot," Jade muttered.

"Actually, what he was saying was true."

"No way," Jade said, shaking her head back and forth.

But a strangled sound came from Ruby and her hand flew to her lips. "He said my mother turned into a wolf."

"Yes."

"Are you saying I'm turning into a wolf?" Ruby asked, her voice shaking.

"Yes," Celia said, nodding and squeezing Ruby's hand.

"That's crazy!" Jade exploded, standing up and backing away from them.

"Please, Jade." Celia glanced again at the people in the room, many more than before, all now openly staring at them. "You must keep quiet."

"Why?"

"Because of our rules. You're not even supposed to be here. And you definitely aren't supposed to know about us. It's our sacred covenant, and I'm breaking it."

"Celia, you sound crazy."

"I understand that. I know how it sounds. That's why I was hoping we'd have more time."

"Why? What difference does it make?"

"Because I wanted to see if you would change, too."

Jade stared at her, speechless.

"I'm sorry. But otherwise, you aren't supposed to know about us."

Jade stepped closer to her. "Not that I'm saying I believe you, because I don't. But if something is happening to my sister, then why can't I know about it?"

"Because you're human, Jade."

Jade's eyes widened as she stared at her. "Of course I'm human. We're all human!" Her arms opened wide to encompass the room. But then she turned and looked behind her, at the crowd of people all staring at her. As if she was not wanted there. As if she was intruding.

"Abomination," Ruby whispered. "That's what the voices keep saying. Over and over again."

"This is enough, Celia," Jade said. "No more. Ruby and I are leaving."

"I don't blame you. But Ruby can't leave. Not yet."

"Why not?" Jade demanded.

"I don't want to get into that right now, but the Pack is in crisis. We need to stay here in this room, under the protection of the crystals."

The Pack? Jade shook her head, disbelieving, as she glanced around the room looking at the crystals. "They're the same ones you had in the shop in Sedona."

"Yes."

"And at your mother's house. You said they were for protection."

"Yes." Celia tensed, knowing what was coming, knowing what had to be said.

Jade looked her dead in the eye. "Protection from what?"

"From the demons that want to kill us."

Ruby started rocking back and forth, making small baby sounds. Celia put her arm around her. "It's going to be okay, Ruby. They can't get you in here. I promise."

"Come on, Ruby. We're leaving." Jade held out her hand to her sister. Ruby looked up at her, fear and confusion heavy in her eyes.

"You are free to leave, Jade. But Ruby can't. None of us can."

"What are you saying?" Jade whispered, her voice cracking.

"I'm saying that you're the only one who is safe to leave the Colony, Jade. Ruby and I can't."

Ruby started to swing her head back and forth. "No. No. It's not true."

Celia held her tighter. "It is true, Ruby. The colors you've been seeing, the voices you've been hearing. They are all the beginning stages of your transformation. There must be other signs, too. Are you becoming stronger? In better shape? Hungry all the time? Suddenly craving meat?"

"I'm a vegetarian," she cried, her eyes brimming.

"But?" Celia prompted.

Ruby sniffled, her mouth contorting with disgust. "I want a hamburger so bad."

"She is not changing into a wolf," Jade said. "Just

because she wants a burger doesn't mean she's suddenly a werewolf."

"Not a werewolf," Celia said. "A shape-shifter—we are not bound by the cycles of the moon. We are not made. We are born."

"Do you not hear how ridiculous you sound?" Jade yelled, once again too loud.

Celia cringed. "Yes."

At that moment, Bobby and Shay hurried into the room. Celia had never been more relieved to see anyone.

"We've spread the word," Bobby said, approaching them, his eyes immediately going to Ruby's tearstained face. "Is everything all right?"

"I don't know," Jade said, her voice full of bitterness. "You tell me, Bobby. Are you a werewolf, too?"

Shocked, Bobby turned to Celia.

Celia closed her eyes and took a deep horrified breath.

"Oh, excuse me," Jade said in a mocking tone. "Not a werewolf. A shape-shifter."

"Jade, that's enough," Celia said.

"You're absolutely right. Come on, Ruby." Jade held out her hand and Ruby took it. Together they ran out of the building.

"Are you just going to let them go like that?" Bobby asked.

"What else can I do?" Celia asked. "They won't listen to me. Besides, Ruby is hearing the voices. She won't be able to stay beyond the protection of the crystals for long."

Shay watched them leave, a worried frown on her face. "Let's hope you're right."

Chapter 21

Ruby let Jade lead her out the door of the Sanctuary and into the parking lot.

"It can't be too far to the car," Jade said, and started walking toward the main road.

Ruby tried to follow her but only made it a few steps into the parking lot when she started hearing the whispering again. She tried to block it out, to ignore it, but the insidious sound was reaching inside her skull. Scratching against her nerves. She stopped in front of the statue, staring up at the large wolf perched on a rock, its nose tilted upward as if howling. Was it really possible? Could she actually shift into a wolf? Could Celia and everyone else here in the Colony turn into wolves?

"Ruby, come on," Jade called, her voice full of annoyed impatience as she stormed down the street.

Ruby didn't move. The truth was Ruby could see colors around everyone in that room. Everyone except for Jade. *Because she's human.*

"I knew I'd find you," Mark said, stepping out from the woods adjacent to the parking lot.

Ruby turned to him, no longer afraid, though she didn't have a clue why. Suddenly he just seemed pathetic rather than scary. "Did you really see my mother turn into a wolf?" she asked, staring up at the statue.

"As if you don't know," he said, sneering. "Now come on, you're coming with me. You're going to tell everyone the truth." He grabbed her by the arm and pulled her into the woods.

"Ruby," Jade yelled, but she was too far away to help her stop him.

The whispering grew louder here, filling Ruby's head, disorienting her. "I can't go with you," she said, covering her ears and dropping to the ground.

"Yes, you can. And you will." Mark yanked her back to her feet, his eyes filling with anger and hatred.

"No, I won't!" she yelled, and tried to pull away from him, but he just held her tighter. "What is wrong with you?" she demanded.

"What is wrong is that all my life people have called me crazy. But I'm not crazy. I know the truth, and soon everyone else will, too."

He had forced her farther into the woods when a deep growl filled the air behind them. Ruby stiffened as fear coiled within her. Slowly she turned, glancing behind her, and saw a wolf standing not four feet away, its dark, luminescent and eerily familiar eyes boring into hers.

"Mark! Let go," she cried, and tried again to pull out of his grasp.

The wolf growled again, louder this time. Mark turned, his eyes widening. He fumbled for his gun, but when he realized it wasn't there, he yanked Ruby up against his chest, using her as a shield. The wolf growled again, moving toward them, its lips pulling away from its sharp teeth in a vicious snarl.

"Let me go, please," Ruby cried. Jade ran toward them but skidded to a stop when she saw the animal, her eyes widening with shock and fear.

Mark took a quick step back. The wolf lunged. Ruby screamed. A hard shove against her back sent her reeling forward toward the creature. She hit the ground as the wolf jumped over her and attacked Mark. She looked up just as the wolf's paw scraped across Mark's cheek, drawing blood. He screamed as the wolf ripped into his arm and chest, pulling, thrashing, its growls filling the air and mingling with Mark's cries of horror and pain.

And then Jade was pulling her up off the ground and dragging her away from Mark, from the animal, and back toward the Sanctuary.

"We can't just leave him there," Ruby said. "That wolf will kill him."

"Yes, we can," Jade answered matter-of-factly as they ran through the woods.

They reached the parking lot, and as Ruby ran back toward the Sanctuary, Jade stopped.

"I can't go back in there," she said, holding her ground beneath the statue.

"But, Jade, I have to. Whatever is happening to me, I feel better inside."

Jade stared up at the stone wolf. "I refuse to believe you're a werewolf."

Ruby grinned halfheartedly. "Shape-shifter. I don't quite believe it myself. I don't know what is happening to me. All I do know is that I can't stay out here with the voices."

"Maybe you won't hear them once we get beyond the gates."

"Maybe," Ruby said.

"Please, Ruby. This place is scaring me and I'm afraid if we stay here any longer something bad will happen. I'm afraid they won't let you go."

"All right," Ruby said, and walked away with her sister, but before they got too far, she heard a faint rustling behind her. With a hand reaching for Jade, she turned quickly, ready to sprint away, when she saw Bobby walking out of the woods, not a stitch covering his incredibly fine body. Ruby's mouth dropped open.

"Where are his clothes?" she muttered, and then noticed the blood on his naked chest. Bobby didn't say a word but walked over to a pile of clothes on the ground next to the Sanctuary and stepped into a nice-fitting pair of jeans and a chambray shirt. She took a deep breath as he turned to look at her, his dark brown eyes locking on hers. A shiver skittered along her skin.

"My God," Jade whispered.

"Wolves," Ruby muttered. "They're all wolves."

As more and more people filed into the Sanctuary, the room became unbearably cramped. Emotions were running high as space in the room that was never meant to hold so many people became scarce and the walls closed in on them. Celia only hoped she was doing the right thing.

She rechecked the crystals again. Their energy levels were high, but so were the ones along the Colony's boundaries. There was no reason for the *Gauliacho* to be there. But if Malcolm was right, if they were getting in through the internet, how would Malcolm get them back out of the Colony again? If it could be done, Malcolm was the only one who could do it.

She glanced out the window, looking for the twins, but didn't see them. She was worried about them outside, especially with Mark on the loose, but Bobby had said he would find them. She turned back around and saw Manny standing by the far window, his shoulders slumped, his back turned to her as he looked out on her mother's grave. Her stomach knotted as a fresh wave of grief rolled over her. She started to walk toward him, but a soft touch on her arm stopped her. She turned.

"Hi," Tiffany said, her voice tentative, her eyes searching. For what? Anger? Forgiveness?

Celia stared at her, not sure what to say or how she even felt about the best friend she wasn't sure she knew anymore.

"I'm sorry about before," Tiffany said. "I guess, well, I got carried away. I know Malcolm was just trying to help us. I'm so sorry." Tears glistened in her eyes. "I should have listened to him about the computers. I was just so anxious to get everything back up and running the way it had been before. He should have told me. He should have made it clear what he was doing."

"What do you mean?" Celia asked, not liking the sound of that. "I'm not following you."

"He was at my shop yesterday turning everything off, but he didn't tell me why."

"Let me guess, you turned everything back on once he left?"

She nodded. "I didn't know what would happen."

"No one knew. Malcolm is still trying to shut everything down now, but honestly I don't see what good it's going to do at this point. The *Gauliacho* are already here. All we can do now is try to protect this building."

"But for how long?" Mrs. Walker, who'd been sitting quietly by listening, asked.

"Yeah. How do we know this is going to work?" someone chimed in. Celia thought it was Gerald from the General Store. He had a computer, too. So many of them did.

"We can't stay in here forever."

"There's no room. No food."

"Mommy, I'm scared."

Snippets of people's fears filled the room, breaking into Celia's thoughts. They were all right, but the real question they should be asking was, how did Malcolm plan to get the demons back out of the Colony?

"We have no choice," McGovern said, his hands raised above his head as he tried desperately to settle down the crowd that was growing more agitated by the second.

"If the crystals didn't work on the Colony's perimeter, what makes you think they will work here?" Mr.

Jenks demanded, his voice rising from the other side of the room.

Babies picking up on their parents' anxiety started to cry, and scared children demanded attention.

"Everyone calm down," Bobby said, stepping into the room, followed by Ruby and Jade. Relief surged through Celia and she hurried toward them.

"Are you okay?" she whispered.

Ruby nodded, her eyes wide and slightly shell-shocked. But Jade didn't look so good. Her face was pale and she looked ready to bolt at any second.

"You're not going to have to stay in here forever," Bobby continued.

"Then for how long?" Mr. Jenks demanded.

"From what we've been able to determine, the *Gauliacho* were able to break through our barriers using a virus downloaded from the internet. Malcolm and Jason have disconnected the network and all the computers. All we can do now is reestablish the boundaries, block by block."

"How long is that going to take?" Tiffany asked.

"Yeah, how long are we going to be stuck in here?" Mrs. Walker added.

Bobby sighed. "As long as it takes."

Elder McGovern stepped forward into the center of the room. "If it's true and they are within the walls of almost every building in the Colony, before the boundaries can be reset, they will need to be removed. Just how do you plan to do that?"

People started talking at once. Some voices panicked, some raised in anger.

"I can tell you," McGovern continued. "There is no easy answer, and that is why we never should have had the computers here to begin with. We wouldn't be facing this situation right now if we'd just left things well enough alone."

Celia's throat tightened. What was he doing?

People in the crowd raised their voices in agreement. She heard Malcolm's name being thrown about, how he never should have been allowed to make so many changes, to stay Pack leader for so long. Celia couldn't believe it. Did McGovern ever turn it off? Why incite these people's fears just so he could push his agenda to get rid of technology? To get rid of Malcolm?

"We're hoping to lure the *Gauliacho* out," Shay said, raising her voice above the din. "That's how we're going to get rid of them."

Celia turned to her, surprised by this little tidbit no one had bothered to tell her about. "What do you mean, lure them out?"

"Once Jason and Malcolm are sure every computer has been disconnected and powered down and every one of the shifters is safe in the Sanctuary with our energy signatures hidden by the power of the crystals, they will leave the boundaries of the Colony. They hope that together, they will be able to entice the *Gauliacho* to follow them out of the Colony."

"They're going to use themselves as bait?" Celia asked, horrified. "But that's crazy."

A shadow entered Shay's eyes. "Yes, I agree. But it's the only chance we have. Once the *Gauliacho* are beyond the borders, Celia, you'll be able to broaden the boundaries, moving the crystals outward block by block until our Colony's borders are fully established once more."

Celia stood speechless in front of the crowd that had finally grown quiet. They expected her to play her part, to be the dutiful Keeper of the Crystals, while Malcolm sacrificed his life for them? "I can't do it," she whispered. "I can't let him sacrifice himself. There has to be another way."

"You expect us to put all our faith in Malcolm?" Mr. Jenks yelled, followed by murmurs of agreement. "After all the problems he's caused us?"

Celia could not stay and listen any longer. She had to find Malcolm and she had to stop him. There had to be another way. A different way. And together, they would find it.

"Wait! Celia," Ruby called, following her into the parking lot. "Please don't leave me here."

"I have to," Celia said, turning back to her and Jade. "You'll be fine if you stay here. Promise me you won't leave."

Bobby came running out the door and placed his arm around Ruby's waist. "Don't worry, I'll look after them. Are you sure you know what you're doing?"

"No, but I can't lose him, too. I know he's made a lot of mistakes, and I'm still angry at him, but I can't be mad if he's not here. If he's…" She couldn't finish the words, and it was just as well. She wasn't making any sense. All she knew was that she couldn't lose him.

"Stay safe," Ruby said, hugging her.

Celia gave her a grateful squeeze. "You, too." Then

she turned to Jade and hugged her, too. Jade didn't hug her back but stood there stiff, her back ramrod straight. "It'll be okay," Celia whispered into Jade's ear, and then let her go. She looked at the three of them, knowing it could be for the last time. "I love you guys," she said, then turned to go. But she stopped when Jason came toward them, a bloody gash on his head.

Her insides tensed and she clenched her hands. "Blazes, Jason. What happened? Where's Malcolm?" She searched the street behind him.

"He's gone. He hit me, and when I came to he was gone."

"Hit you? Why?"

"I'm sorry, Celia. He said he had to do this alone, and apparently wouldn't take no for an answer."

"No." Cold terror turned her blood sluggish.

"He's a fool," Bobby said.

"Where is he going? What was his plan?" Celia demanded as adrenaline pumped through her veins.

"He's heading for the caves. He's taking Manny's small crystals with him. He's going to hide out in the caverns until you get the boundaries reestablished."

"He'll never make it that far," Celia insisted. *Why does he always have to be the hero?*

"He might. Except…"

Celia's heart skipped a beat. She was afraid to ask, and almost couldn't get the word past the lump in her throat. "Except?"

"When Shay and I hid out there a couple weeks ago, the *Gauliacho* came after us. They formed a crack in one of the cavern walls."

She tried to swallow the lump and almost choked. "Does Malcolm know?"

Jason scrubbed a hand down his face. "I didn't get the chance to tell him."

"They'll all be after him, Jason. There are too many."

Bobby squeezed her shoulder. "He can do it, Celia. Have faith."

Celia looked back at the Sanctuary, at the townspeople ready to form a lynch mob watching them through the windows. "I lost that a long time ago."

Terror unlike anything she'd ever felt before flooded her veins and drove Celia down the embankment, running toward the cliffs, toward the back gate that would take her to the cave system and to Malcolm. He was trying to make amends, taking full responsibility for this mess by sacrificing himself, and she wasn't going to let him do it. She knew as well as he did that Connors and McGovern were planning to put him beyond the gates no matter how the vote went, so if he was going to die, why not save the Pack on his way out? She knew how he thought, and she wasn't going to let him do it. He figured he was saving her the trouble of having to choose the Pack over him. To live with that decision of having to leave him to die alone.

Well, he wouldn't die. Not if she had anything to do with it.

She ran through the woods, changing swiftly into her true self, following Malcolm's scent. Maybe she was more like her father than she wanted to admit. He couldn't stand being locked up within the Colony's boundaries, couldn't stand the idea that he could be responsible for everyone as one after another of the Keepers died.

Her mother had never talked about him. She'd never admitted how much his leaving had hurt her. She must have believed he'd come back one day. How could he not? Was that why she'd never married Manny? Had she been waiting for a man who never returned? Whether he was dead or just didn't care, Celia would never know. But right now, as she ran through the woods after the man who would leave her for her own good, for the good of the Pack, the effect was the same. He was gone. Well, she for one wouldn't sit back and let him go and then spend the rest of her life hoping he'd find a way back.

Because he wouldn't.

They never did. Not once had anyone who'd ever left the Colony for longer than a month ever come back. Though why, she could only imagine.

She tore through the woods with even more speed and determination, her heart swelling in her chest. She had to find him. He needed to know that she believed in him, that she forgave him, because in the end, that was all that mattered. The damage he caused was already done. There was no fixing it. No making amends. No making sacrifices. All they could do was learn from their mistakes and hopefully not make them again. But they couldn't move on if they didn't make it back.

Malcolm!

She reached for him again, using her senses, using the connection they'd always had, the tenuous line that bound them together. He was near. She could feel him.

But she could also feel it weakening, stretching, pulling so thin it was almost gone. She burst through the trees and saw the cave's opening ahead.

And saw the shadows moving within.

Hang on, Malcolm! I'm coming.

Chapter 22

Malcolm knew this could very well be a death sentence. He wasn't brave and he wasn't heroic. What he was was guilty. He'd caused the death of another, and in all likelihood more would die today because he brought in the computers, brought in the internet, and by doing so left them all vulnerable to the one thing that could kill them all. Jaya had begged him not to do it, but he hadn't listened; he'd been too full of pride. Too sure that what he was doing was best for everyone. He'd been arrogant and narcissistic.

And yet, even after she'd known what he'd done, Celia had said she would leave with him. She'd take him with her and the twins to Sedona. She'd give up her life here for them. He wouldn't let her and he wouldn't let her watch him get locked out, knowing there would be no coming back. For the first time in a long time, he finally felt as if he was doing the right thing—even if he did wish he could spend just one more night with her. He'd wasted so much time. Time they could never get back or replace.

He ran out the back gate and down the hill, heading toward the caves. If he could just reach them in time to get to the room they'd always used in the back, then he could set up the crystals and perhaps be safe for just a little while, just long enough to lure the *Gauliacho* away from the Colony so Celia could reset the boundaries.

He saw something moving fast out of the corner of his eye. *A shadow.* Dammit, they were with him already. He wrapped the pouch of crystals tightly around his neck. He ran faster, stripping out of his shirt, pulling off his shoes as he stumbled and fell, ripping his pants off without breaking his stride. His breathing deepened as he focused, concentrating on the smells of cedar, the singing of the birds in the trees, the feel of his heart pounding in his chest as his blood pulsed through him. Rushing through his ears. *Thump. Thump. Thump.* And then he was changing, his legs lengthening, his bones and joints popping into place as he stretched and transformed into his true self.

He raced through the forest, heading for the granite-and-limestone peaks that housed an extensive array of caves. Caves that had been used many times over through the years to protect them from the demons, but this time he didn't know if he would be protected. He wasn't sure if the crystals were working anymore or if the shifters' time here in this place had finally come to an end.

He could hear *them* now, their whispers echoing with the wind. They were calling his name, trying to draw him to them, to confuse him. He couldn't be swayed. He had to get as far away from the Colony as he could, had to draw them away from its borders. It was the Pack's only chance.

Malcolm. Come to us.

The whispers taunted him, seeping inside his mind, pulling at him. He wanted to stop running. To find the peace their whispers hinted at. To give in to them and follow them home. Their ancestors had once been like them, but then they'd come here to this plane and took the form of the animal, and the shape of the man. And they liked it. They'd never returned, and the *Gauliacho* had never stopped hunting them down and dragging them back to whatever hell they came from. He had to admit, the lure was strong. Part of him wanted to stop fighting and give in, to finally find the peace they promised, even if he knew it was a dirty lie. Was this what Celia had been hearing, had been feeling all these years? How had she stood it? The whispering grew louder and more intense. Fear-spiked adrenaline pushed him onward.

Abomination.

Abomination.

Abomination.

And then he saw them, dark shadows flitting through the trees. So many, coming for him, surrounding him, swooping down and blinding him; he was plunged into darkness. He zigzagged through the trees, rushing even faster as he nipped at them. But it was no use. There were too many of them. The entrance to the caves was up ahead. He could see it, darkness in a sheet of granite beckoning him. He bolted forward, reaching the opening just as they attacked and knocked him to the ground.

Celia!

Celia ran toward the cave's entrance, but before she could reach it a cloud of darkness swarmed over her, swirling around her head, flooding inside her nose, her mouth, probing her mind. Pushing. Squeezing. Scratching. She could hear them, whispering, calling to her, taunting her, louder and louder, until she wanted to scream at the top of her lungs for them to stop. To leave her alone.

But they'd never leave her alone. She knew that.

Blackness filled the edges of her vision and pooled in her eyes until she could barely see. Practically blind, she couldn't hear anything beyond them. She stopped, hesitating as the ground shifted and moved beneath her. They were everywhere, moving too fast for the eye to see, peppering her skin with tiny, sharp, stinging nips as they attacked. She collapsed to the ground, whimpering, trying to shield herself as they came for her, knowing that it was too late, for her, for Malcolm, for them all.

Celia!

Malcolm's voice filled her, and then she felt him, in her mind and heart. He was reaching for her through their connection, their bond that she'd cursed so many times yet could never run away from.

Celia!

His pain and terror pulled her out of her stupor.

Malcolm was in trouble! She had to help him. That need to protect him grew within her, almost bordering on panic.

Celia.

He was growing weaker. Her panic, her need to help him grew stronger than her fear of the *Gauliacho* and what they were doing to her. She forced open her eyes and found herself lying inside one of the caves. Malcolm was nowhere in sight.

Quickly she jumped up and ran through the cave, transforming into her human self and screaming his name. Barely able to see, she hurried deeper down the rock pathways, through one chamber after another. Mineral-rich water dropped on her shoulders and sloshed beneath her feet. The cool, dank air filled her lungs as she gasped it, breathing deeply in her full-out panic.

"Malcolm!" she screamed again. She couldn't lose him. Not like this. The luminous glow of a lantern shone through the darkness up ahead. She ran toward it—the proverbial light at the end of the tunnel. "Malcolm, hang on," she yelled again, turning sideways and sliding through the narrow opening and into the chamber. Malcolm was lying naked on the ground, surrounded by the shadows pouring into the room from a large crack in the wall.

"Malcolm!" She dropped to the ground next to him and pulled him into her lap. "Fight them," she cried. "Focus on me. Me!"

"Celia," he gasped, but when he opened his eyes, she could see the shadows moving within them.

"Blazes, Malcolm!" She pulled the pouch off his neck, obviously useless, and lay on top of him, covering his body with her own, trying to protect him from the shadows. She opened the pouch still attached to her neck and placed a crystal at his head, his feet and each side of them, then lay back down on top of him, chanting the words that would activate the crystals, all the while focusing, concentrating on him. On them. On his kiss. His touch and everything that they'd meant to each other most of her life.

"Malcolm, don't leave me," she whispered, but his eyes didn't open again. He wasn't gone. He couldn't be gone. "Fight!" she yelled, and squeezed him tight, shaking him even as the stinging nips once more started peppering her skin. This might be her last chance to tell him the truth of her heart. The truth that she'd run all the way to Arizona to escape, but could never run long or far enough from—how she truly felt about this man.

"I love you, Malcolm," she cried. "I've always loved you and I always will. I want you, but more than that, I forgive you! Don't give in to them. Stay with me and fight. Fight for us, Malcolm."

She kissed him with frantic desperation, clutching his face, pressing her lips hard against his, sweeping her tongue inside his mouth even as the ground began to move beneath them.

"Kiss me, Malcolm!" she demanded, tears filling her eyes and spilling down on her cheeks. "Come back to me!"

She pressed her mouth against his, refusing to give up. And then he was kissing her back just as fervently, his tears mingling with hers. *Wasn't he?*

Or was she only hoping?

Imagining his lips moving beneath hers.

Imagining the sensation of falling even as his arms tightened around her.

Malcolm?

Celia's eyes sprang open. The cave was gone. The darkness. The cool, damp air gave way to a warm, fragrant breeze. She stood, disoriented and alone. *Malcolm?* She took a step forward, peering through the trees, searching for him. But didn't see him anywhere. She walked through the forest, more lush and tropical than she was used to in the Colony. Large blooming vines fell from the trees. Blossoms with oversize petals of red, orange and fuchsia were vibrant and almost glowing. Water was everywhere, dripping from large leaves, running down vines and bubbling in brooks. She stopped near a stream. The water looked so pure and clear she could see smooth stones glittering beneath the surface. Some red, some black, some the most beautiful color of jade she'd ever seen.

Where was she? Where was Malcolm?

She looked up and gasped. The sky was a swirl of pinks and reds, as if she were encompassed in a brilliant sunset. But there was no sun that she could see. Nor was there any blue. None at all. Her chest tightened and her heart skipped a beat. Where were the animals? The birds? The insects? There were none. *Anywhere.*

She felt something tug on her hand and spun to find Malcolm standing next to her, her hand clutched in his. Where had he come from? She opened her mouth to say something, but no words came out. She had no breath.

Her hand flew to her throat.

She wasn't breathing. *Malcolm!* She looked at him, her eyes wide, her fear filling her throat.

It's all right, Celia. His words were there, in her head. *We're home now.*

No. She looked around her. This wasn't home. This wasn't anything like home. She could be on the moon for all she knew. *Malcolm, I can't breathe.*

You don't need to breathe. We don't need these bodies. You just feel better wearing it, more comfortable. But you don't need it. Not here. Not anymore.

And then she knew what it was he was trying to tell her. The *Gauliacho* had gotten them.

But they weren't dead.

No, Celia. You aren't dead. You've just come home.

Suddenly her mother was standing before her. No, not really standing, more like hovering. And she didn't quite look the same. She wasn't corporal. It was as if she was made out of mist, beautiful and shining, luminous mist.

Mom?

There's nothing to be afraid of, Celia. Open yourself up. Move past the fear. You are connected to everyone here. You always have been. It's part of your gift.

No. It is just Malcolm. Malcolm is the one I feel.

Out of the corner of her eye, she thought she saw

something soaring in the sky. An eagle? She turned quickly, wanting—no—needing desperately to see it.

But it was gone. If it had ever been there at all. *Where are the animals?*

There are no animals here, Celia.

But I saw... What did she see?

Reach for him, Celia. Reach for Malcolm. Pull him to us.

But he's right here. She turned, realizing she no longer felt his touch. Panic shot through her, turning her limbs to ice. He had been here. She had seen him. Where was he?

Reach for him, her mother commanded, her voice echoing through Celia's head.

But there was something wrong. Her mother never commanded. She never sounded like that.

Celia stared at the woman who looked like her mother but didn't feel like her mother.

Malcolm! Celia screamed with her mind, searching, grasping. She couldn't be here alone. She wouldn't be here without him. Not now. Not ever again. She loved him. She always had.

She reached for their connection, searching for his signature, for his heat, for the spirit that was Malcolm, and felt him far away. Too far. *Back in the cave?*

Or had he ever been here? Had that been Malcolm talking to her, holding her hand?

She reached for him again, stretching. *Don't give in, Malcolm! Fight!* She pushed herself harder and harder, until an explosion of energy pulsated through her and the essence of a million entities engulfed her, seeping within her being.

She collapsed to her knees, the impact too much to bear. As the woman who would be her mother said, she wasn't just connected with Malcolm, she was connected with everyone. Instantly her fear dissipated and was replaced by an overwhelming sense of safety, of oneness.

Home. She was finally home where she belonged.

Yes, Celia, we've been waiting for you for a long time. You are part of us and we are part of you. We want you back here with us.

Part of her wanted to stay, to lose herself in the sense of just being, with no fear, no anger...no love. But would that mean she'd live without Malcolm.

Let him go, Celia. He will be here soon, but it won't matter. Here, we aren't encumbered by human emotions. Here, you are truly free.

Free. Wasn't that what she'd always longed for? No, not like this.

I don't want to be free, Celia cried. *Not if it means giving up Malcolm. If it means forgetting everything we meant to each other. I can't live like that. I won't.* She turned and ran back the way she'd come, looking for the cave. Looking for Malcolm.

Malcolm! she cried again. And then she heard him, faintly. Far away. And for just a second, she thought she felt his lips on hers. She looked around her, staring into the trees that suddenly shifted, wavering like a mirage off the Sedona Desert at the hottest point of the day.

Malcolm? She reached for him again with everything she had, and then she felt him. His mouth pressed hard against hers, his tears tickling her cheeks, his hands clutching her back as he pulled her to him. But she couldn't see him. She lifted a hand to her skin, confused, and turned around, searching for him—the trees, the flowers, the rushing river.

Malcolm? She pushed with her mind again, harder and farther than before, and then she felt him, mentally and physically, holding her. Whispering in her ear. His desperation thick in his voice.

"Celia, come back to me!"

And then she saw him above her, holding her tight in the dank and dark cave.

"Malcolm!" she said, and drew in a deep breath. She wrapped her arms tightly around him, afraid to let go. Afraid she'd lose him again. She didn't want to go back to that place. She didn't want to be free of her body, her emotions. She wanted to feel *everything*— love, pain, regret and forgiveness. She wasn't running, not anymore. She wanted to feel alive. To feel connected. With him. Now.

She kissed him again, so thankful he was there, that he had been able to pull her back. "Love me, Malcolm," she whispered. "Keep loving me and don't ever let me go."

"I couldn't let you leave me even if I wanted to," he whispered. "You're under my skin and buried deep in my heart. I can't live—I won't live without you. Ever." And then he kissed her again, over and over until she forgot about the *Gauliacho* and their strange world and lost herself where she wanted to be—in Malcolm's arms.

Chapter 23

Celia didn't know how much time had passed, but when she opened her eyes, she and Malcolm were lying on the floor of the cave. The *Gauliacho* were gone. She could no longer hear them or feel them anywhere.

"Are you all right?" Malcolm asked, running the tip of his finger across her jaw.

She smiled. "I am now. What happened?"

"I'm not sure. I was kissing you, holding you, and then it seemed like you were no longer here. The *Gauliacho* all started flying back into the cracks in the wall. Hundreds of them coming from everywhere, zipping past me toward the crack. I was so afraid they had you somehow, but I refused to let you go. I just kept holding you, calling for you, kissing you."

She smiled and touched his cheek with the palm of her hand. "I heard you. Your voice led me back to you."

"Do you think they're all gone?"

"It appears so, at least for a little while."

They got up and started walking back to the Colony. She used the time it took to tell Malcolm everything she'd learned about the demon dimension that their ancestors had come from so long ago.

"I can see why our ancestors didn't want to go back. Why they wanted to stay once they were in human form," she said.

"And yet they were still connected to the *Gauliacho* on the other side?"

"Yes, it's how the *Gauliacho* can always find us. Apparently the crystals block that connection. For most of us."

"But not for you?"

She shook her head. "That's how they were able to pull me to them, and yet they weren't strong enough to take all of me. You were able to pull me back. My connection to you, to this world and the shifters here, is stronger than my connection to them."

He draped an arm around her shoulder, pulling her closer and kissing her forehead. "It terrifies me how close I came to losing you. I don't ever want to lose you again." He stopped on the trail. "Celia, if the Elders grant me my freedom, will you marry me?"

She looked up at him, tears springing to her eyes. "You don't know how long I've wanted to hear you say those words."

He drew her to him, a fine mist filling his eyes as he

shook his head. "You don't know how long I've wanted to ask."

"Why didn't you?"

"I never believed you'd stay with me. That I was enough for you."

"You, Malcolm, are every kind of fool."

He laughed. "Only for you." Then he kissed her, and stole her breath. Part of her wanted to pull him to the ground right then and there and make wild, passionate love to him, but they couldn't; they had to get back to the others. They'd have lots of time to show each other how much they loved one another once they got home.

"There's something I need to know," Malcolm said.

"Yes?"

"Why didn't you stay with your mom on the other side?" His voice was tentative, almost as if he were afraid to know.

"Because she wasn't my mother. She bore no spiritual resemblance to the woman I used to know. In that place, your emotions are stripped, along with your body."

"I'm not sure that would be so bad."

She smiled and slipped her arm around his waist. "I'd rather love you, with all the problems we've had, than to not feel anything at all."

He grinned, that same charming schoolboy grin that had stolen her heart so many years ago. "Does that mean you're going to stay in the Colony?"

"Yes, and so are you. I don't care what those idiotic Elders say. And Ruby and Jade are staying, too. If they want to. I don't see why we can't open up our shop right here. It's time we made some major changes around here. We're going to have to if we're going to survive."

Malcolm blew out a whistle. "Sounds as if we have a fight ahead. Are you sure you're up for it? The Elders, some of the others, they aren't going to make it easy on you."

She looked up as an eagle soared overhead and watched it for a moment, its beauty and grace. "Malcolm, for the first time in my life I feel free to make my own decisions. I can go anywhere and do anything. The *Gauliacho* had me. I was there, but you brought me back. Our connection, our love is too strong. We have all been operating, making decisions based on fear for too long. It's time we changed that. If the shifters want us to stay and help them understand *Gauliacho*, to help them rebuild, then they are going to have to accept all of us."

"Including Ruby and Jade?"

"Especially Ruby and Jade. My cousins mean the world to me and I'm not going to lose another minute with them. Or you. I'm planning on making a big ruckus around here. You think you can handle that? Handle the new me?"

He smiled and brought her hand up to his lips. "A new challenge? If you're by my side, I can't wait."

"Then let's hurry. I want to get back and see everyone."

They changed to their true forms and ran through the forest toward the Colony, toward home. After stopping by Malcolm's home for fresh clothes, they hurried to the Sanctuary, where everyone was waiting for them. The others looked tired and hungry and worn out. But there were lots of smiles as they saw them arrive.

"Celia," Ruby called when they walked through the door. She ran up and hugged her.

Bobby clapped Malcolm on the back, then pulled him into his embrace. "I didn't think you'd make it back."

"Neither did I," Malcolm admitted.

"Manny's been helping me work with the crystals," Ruby said, beaming. "He said I'm a Keeper and naturally gifted like you. Soon I'll be able to help you with the stones."

"That's wonderful," Celia said, then looked over at Jade, who wasn't smiling, and felt her heart break a little. "Are you okay?" she asked her cousin.

"Sure," Jade said, but she wasn't. Celia could see the hurt and confusion written all over her face.

Celia put an arm around her waist. "It's going to be all right."

"What's happening out there?" Bobby asked.

Celia took a step into the middle of the room, and everyone hushed to hear what she had to say. "The *Gauliacho* are gone. For now. I traveled to their realm, and once I was there, they all seemed to follow me. But I don't know how long they will be gone. My cousins and I will go around the Colony and reset the boundaries. Once that is accomplished, you can all go back to your homes." She reached for Malcolm's hand. "Malcolm, can you drive us to the compass points?"

"Malcolm is going back to his cell in the Town Hall where he belongs," Connors said loudly.

"No, he's not," Celia shot back. "Malcolm just saved

all of us, including me. He pulled me away from the *Gauliacho*. We need him to help us understand how they got into the computer's network in the first place. Was it sabotage or do we need stronger security? He is the best one equipped for the job."

"I agree," Jason said, stepping forward into the center of the room.

"And I." Shay joined them.

"So, what? You think the four of you can just change the way we've been doing things here? Allow criminals to walk our streets and humans to live among us?" Connors's cheeks reddened and his eyes glowed amber with his fury. "I know how we can fix the computer problem, get rid of them all and get rid of Malcolm."

Celia's back stiffened. "Computers are already here. We can't turn back the clocks and go back to living in the Dark Ages. All we can do is be aware of the threat and do our best to make sure what happened today never happens again."

"I agree. And for that we need Malcolm," Jason said.

"Not only that," Celia added. "I think it's about time we opened our gates to family—human or otherwise."

"So do I," Tiffany shot from the back of the room, catching Celia's eyes and smiling.

"Me, too," Shay agreed. "If it wasn't for your rules, my parents would not be dead right now."

"Nor ours." Ruby took Jade's hand and stepped forward.

"We will be able to get a lot more accomplished if Malcolm and Celia were to stay here and help us lead this Pack," Jason said as Shay stood next to him, nodding in agreement.

"Ruby is not just some random human. She and her sister are the daughters of Sue. They are part of us. And Ruby is beginning to make her change," Bobby said proudly. "She, too, will be a Keeper, gifted with the crystals. We need her."

"And her sister, Jade," Shay added. "She hasn't made her transformation yet, and maybe she never will, but she is family. And we don't turn our back on family."

The crowd roared their approval.

With their hands raised above their heads, McGovern and Connors tried to voice their objections, but no one was listening to them.

Not anymore.

A sense of empowerment and happiness burst through Celia. She had choices. She didn't have to give up her home to be with the ones she loved. Together, they could make the changes they wanted. "You ready?" Malcolm asked, squeezing her hand.

"More than I ever have been before." She leaned in to kiss his lips, feeling for the first time in her life that she was exactly where she should be.

She was home. And together, she and Malcolm would finally be a family.

* * * * *

vixen at heart, **Vivi Anna** likes to burn up the pages with her original, unique brand of fantasy fiction. Whether it's in the Amazon jungle, an apocalyptic future or the otherworld city of Necropolis, Vivi always writes fast-paced action-adventure with strong, independent women who can kick some butt and dark, delicious heroes to kill for.

Once shot at while repossessing a car, Vivi decided that maybe her life needed a change. The first time she picked up a pen and put words to paper, she knew she had found her heart's desire. Within two paragraphs, she realized she could write about getting into all sorts of trouble without having to suffer any of the consequences.

When Vivi isn't writing, you can find her causing a ruckus at downtown bistros, flea markets or in her own backyard.

SEDUCING THE HUNTER
Vivi Anna

For Crowley, the cheekiest demon of them all…

Chapter 1

The candlelight illuminating the small chamber flickered when the heavy wooden door opened. Daeva looked up from the backgammon board to see who had entered her private room. She smiled as the little green creature, carrying a bronze tea tray, hobbled in on his spindly and knobby legs.

He set the tray on the small round table next to her, then slid onto the velvet-covered chair on the opposite side of the backgammon board.

She reached over and poured tea into two porcelain cups then handed one to him. "Prompt as usual, Klix."

The creature accepted the offered cup and took a sip, his beady black eyes staring at her over the rim. "I wouldn't miss our daily game, Mistress."

She drank the hot, spiced tea and watched the goblin set up the game. It was her one small pleasure in the day, to play the ordinary game with him in her private chamber away from the others. Away from the reality of her situation.

Here she couldn't smell the rancid odor of brimstone and sulfur or the stench of burning flesh. Here she could block out the woeful screams and pitiful mewls of those being tortured in the fire pits below. She didn't have to make polite conversation with the other demons she wholly despised. As long as she had to stay in hell, she could at least pretend she was elsewhere when she was here in her room playing her games with her friend Klix.

Hell was the place of Daeva's birth, but she'd done everything possible for thousands of years to get out and stay out. And she'd done pretty well. Staying topside most of her life, possessing bodies, living their lives, until some clever exorcist or demon hunter would exorcise her back to hell. Then the process would start all over again. It wasn't perfect but she'd accepted the fact that she'd never be able to walk the mortal realm in her true form, so she'd stolen identities and pretended to be those people. It wasn't quite like being a real mortal. But it was the best she could do in her circumstances.

At least when she took over a body, she kept her host in a dream state. They didn't know they were being possessed. They just thought they were having one heck of an amazing dream. Daeva always gave them good, happy dreams.

Despite what a lot of lore said, not all demons were wicked. In fact, most lived, just as other beings did, somewhere between good and evil. Here, in hell, demons were split into seven types. Daeva was of the second, which consisted of lust demons. She wasn't a full-blooded lust demon though; there had been some mixing of types over millennia, but she had one in the family tree somewhere. She didn't possess people to just suck the sexual energy from them or those that they seduced. She wasn't what some people would call a succubus.

But she did derive some energy from sex. Which was one of the reasons she preferred to possess the bodies of women. She liked sex with men. She supposed her affinity to them was one of her weaknesses. She'd been told as much by every other demon in her family tree. Which was one of the many reasons she hated it so much in hell.

She'd been doing okay as a mortal for years, surviving, forging a pretty good new life with a job, a home, friends, family and a man she loved. The woman whom she'd possessed had been near death in a coma when Daeva had come along. Her brain had little function so it would've been like being in a dream for her when Daeva had taken over. The girl was mercifully unaware of Daeva's presence. But that all had come to a halt about three years ago when she'd been exorcised out of her most favorite body, her most favorite life, and sent back to this…hell. She'd been looking for a way back ever since.

She'd been looking for payback on the man who'd sent her back, who just happened to be the same man she'd loved.

Klix had the game set up—he always played the black—then picked up the dice and rolled. She watched him move the pieces with his crooked fingers and smiled. He was her only comfort in a place that offered nothing but misery and suffering.

"So, my friend, what is the word out in the world?" she asked as she took her turn.

"Loir is going topside," he said as he rolled again.

"Really?" This surprised Daeva. Loir was Klix's twin sister. Goblins usually didn't go to the mortal realm. They weren't very good at assimilating into the human world. Seeing a four-foot, bald, green-skinned creature with bulbous eyes, razor-sharp talons and four sets of teeth would send anyone into a panic or an asylum. "What is her purpose?"

Klix shrugged. "I am not sure. She would not tell me much."

"She must be accompanying someone on a task."

He nodded. "Yes, that would be logical." He moved some of his black pieces into the winning box. "She did say something about a key."

This perked Daeva up. There were only a few important keys up there in the world. "What kind of key, do you know?"

"Not sure. But I did hear it is supposed to open something of great value to demons. Something powerful. Something ancient."

Daeva nearly dropped her teacup. She set it on the table, her hand shaking.

"Are you ill, Mistress?"

She swallowed, then gave him a small smile. "I must

be a bit under the weather, Klix. Could we finish our game later? I believe I need to rest a bit."

"Yes, of course." He rose from his seat. "Shall I take the tea tray?"

"No, that's fine."

He bowed his bald head to her. "I will be back later to check on you, Mistress."

"Oh, Klix, could you deliver a message to your sister for me?" Daeva reached for parchment and a quill. She scrawled three words on it, and folded the paper. She handed it to the goblin.

"I will do this right away."

"Thank you, Klix. Please tell her to burn it after she reads it."

The little goblin left her chamber, shutting the door firmly behind him.

Once he was gone, Daeva rose from her chair and went to the floor-to-ceiling bookcase along one wall. She ran her finger along the book titles until she found the one she needed. She slid it off the shelf and went to sit on the sofa.

She opened the thick tome on her lap and flipped through the pages. She stopped at a picture of a large wooden box with an elaborate lock on it. She read the text that went with it, then her finger circled another picture, that of a key. A skeleton key. The key that fit the lock. The key that opened a box that had been buried.

A plain wooden box she had buried herself, over a hundred years ago.

She sighed and leaned back against the sofa cushions. She prayed that this wasn't the key Loir had gone topside to look for. As far as she knew, she was one of only a few people who knew who had the key. If someone was looking for it, then they were looking for the box.

The box had been entrusted to her more than a century ago by an elderly human scholar. He'd been an intelligent, well-read man who knew about the curse on the box. He knew exactly what had been sealed inside. And he had pleaded with her to bury it where no one, no human, no demon, would be able to find it again. He had been her friend, one of the few she had as a demon, so she did as he asked. With the help of a local man, she'd buried it deep in the earth in northern Canada.

They couldn't allow what lay inside the box to be used again. Daeva feared what would happen if it fell into demon hands. It had been used against demonkind two millennia ago, used to enslave them and do one insane man's bidding. But if it fell into demon hands, it could be used to subjugate the entire human population. It would overthrow humanity.

Recently, she had heard rumors and whispers about who possessed the key. And the last confirmed report had chilled her blood. If only she was still topside, she could've protected him, the key keeper, and he would never have even known.

Because she'd spent years right under his nose, hiding in plain sight. Hiding inside the woman he'd fallen in love with. The woman she'd been possessing for years, before she even met him. So, in Daeva's mind, he had fallen in love with her.

And she had loved him. Damn him for it.

She pushed the book to the side and stood. Pacing

the room she flicked her hand and all the candles in her chamber lit. She tried to warm her body with their flames. It would surprise everyone to know that even in hell she could be cold. She worried about what was to come, fretted about the future.

Daeva knew she would be called upon. There was only one being still alive who knew she'd hidden the box. The man she'd loved, the man who had sent her back to hell.

Soon, Quinn Strom, exorcist extraordinaire, would come a-knocking at her hellish "door."

A knock startled her. It couldn't be Klix; she had told him to come back later. Her heart thudding in her chest, she opened the door.

Two soldiers with swords at their sides stood waiting for her. "Daeva, you must come with us."

"What is this about?" Although, deep down in her churning gut, she knew.

"Please comply, or we will be forced to be unpleasant."

Swallowing the fear that was quickly rising, she nodded and stepped out between them, firmly shutting her door behind her.

Chapter 2

The sound was faint, maybe only a creak of the house, but Quinn Strom heard it. He sat upright in his bed, peering into the darkness of his bedroom and straining to listen.

Trained to sleep lightly, he was always alert at any out-of-place sound. He'd lived in his modest house long enough to have memorized every normal creak, squeak and groan of the place. And the creak he'd heard was from the stairs just outside his room; the fourth step from the top had a soft spot that only a certain amount of weight triggered.

The creak came again, prompting Quinn to bolt off the bed and reach under his bed for the arsenal that he'd stashed there when he first moved in. Fortunately he always slept in sweatpants, so in emergencies like these he didn't have to bother dressing. He grabbed the shotgun, loaded with silver and rock salt, and the beat-up old satchel that contained ampoules of holy water and his blessed silver crucifix.

Quinn had been a demon hunter and exorcist for most of his life, so he was always prepared for any threat, be it human or other. His father had trained him since he was ten to be vigilant, to be wary of the things that went bump in the night.

All the doors and windows had been warded against demon attacks, so the intruder had to be human. But just because they were human didn't make them any less of a threat. He knew that firsthand. He'd had his fair share of run-ins with sorcerers, especially those from the Crimson Hall Cabal, a powerful organization of one hundred members who were always searching for more power.

Quinn took position at the side of his door, his gun raised, the satchel hung over his shoulder. He couldn't cock the gun now because of the sound it would make, but the moment the door opened, he would pump it and point it in a nanosecond. In his other hand he had a glass ampoule of holy water ready to be released, just in case his wards had failed. One splash of the water on unholy skin would incapacitate any demon for a few minutes. Enough time for him to shoot silver into a demon body and kill it.

Breathing deep and even, he counted down the seconds in his head. The attack would come any moment now. He could sense movement on the other side of the door, hear the swish of fabric moving. What the hell were they waiting for?

Could this be a regular, run-of-the-mill home burglar? Looking for expensive things to steal and hock? Quinn didn't live in an affluent neighborhood. There was no indication in either his house decor or the vehicle he drove that he was anything but a blue-collar working man with nothing of worth to take except maybe a plasma TV and a game console. But nothing worth searching the rest of the house for.

No, Quinn didn't harbor any delusions that the intruders were after his valuables. At least, not the type that a person could buy in a department store. He did possess some things of worth. Things that only certain types of humans and demons would know about.

Were they after the key? God, he hoped not. That thing had been nothing but trouble from the second his father had bequeathed it to him. He'd tried to hide it in plain sight by giving it to his sister disguised as a pendant, but it had ended up back in his hands anyway. Back to being his responsibility.

Before he could consider that further, the door burst open. And not in one push. It splintered into a hundred pieces, as if C-4 had been placed on it and lit by a fuse. But he didn't hear an explosion. Something else of great power had rendered his door into kindling.

He cocked the shotgun and, stepping over the wood pieces scattered on his floor, he took a stance in the doorway, pointing his weapon. But he couldn't get a shot off before he was catapulted backward by a ball of green light that hit him full force in the gut. All the air was knocked out of him when he hit the wall.

He slumped to the floor just as a man with long dark hair and glowing green hands stepped into his bedroom. He smiled down at Quinn.

"Quinn Strom, I presume. Where is the key?"

All of Quinn's muscles quivered. It was as if a thousand volts of electricity surged through his body. He could barely blink.

The man stood over him, threatening green sparks dripping like melted metal from his long fingers. "I don't want to kill you. But I will to get what I want."

Quinn licked his lips, trying to get his mouth to work. "I don't know what you're talking about."

"Don't play with me, Strom. I know you have it. Your lovely sister, Ivy, had it and then she gave it to you."

Quinn tried to sit up at the mention of Ivy's name. "If you touched her, I'll kill you."

The man chuckled. "Don't worry, she is quite safe. The cambion of hers is quite formidable. I should know, he killed Reginald, the man I succeeded as leader of the Cabal." He turned his glowing hands this way and that, looking at them affectionately. "Although I probably should thank him for that…"

Quinn now knew who had broken into his house. The Crimson Hall Cabal. They were a ruthless group of powerful sorcerers who ran their organization pretty much like the mob and a gentlemen's club combined. Not long ago, his sister, Ivy, and her lover, Ronan, a cambion, otherwise known as a half demon, had had a run-in with Reginald Watson. He'd initially hired Ronan to find Quinn and steal the key. But Ronan had had a change of heart—everything to do with the fact that he'd fallen in love with Ivy—and had given the key back. Then he ended up killing Reginald to keep Ivy and the key safe.

Obviously, the legend of the key had been passed on to the next in line for the cabal throne. The legend and the desire to possess it.

"You've wasted a trip. I don't have the key," Quinn croaked, his throat dry from the pain that still zipped through his body.

There was movement behind the sorcerer in the doorway. He turned as a small squat creature hobbled into the room.

"I could not find it, Master."

It was a goblin, a female one by the way it was shaped. It regarded Quinn with its big, opaque eyes, and Quinn thought maybe he saw a quick flash of remorse in its wide-eyed stare. He couldn't be sure. He'd only ever seen a goblin once before. It was rare to see one topside. They usually resided in hell, acting as servants to the demons that inhabited the pits.

"Yes, well, I did not suspect that the great Quinn Strom would have it lying around." The sorcerer looked back to him. "You're much too much like your father. Paranoid to a fault. Too bad that didn't help him before he died."

"I'd leave my dad out of this."

"Or what?" the sorcerer sneered. "You're going to kill me?"

Quinn nodded. "Something like that." He pulled his

hand out of his satchel and a dagger glinted in the light cast by the sorcerer's hands. The sorcerer saw the knife too late.

He lifted his hands, just as Quinn sank the lethal blade into the sorcerer's leg, and dodged his magic green rays. The green light slammed into the wall behind him, just missing his head, and burned a hole through the wood and concrete.

Dragging the shotgun with him, Quinn gained his feet, but the sorcerer was already turning toward him, the knife still sticking out of his thigh. Quinn dashed past the little goblin and out of the room. A blast of green fire hit him in the shoulder as he rounded the doorway.

It sent him to the ground, and he rolled dangerously close to the first step on the staircase. Pain shot through him like acid, but he managed to pull himself up using the railing and started down the stairs. Another bolt of green hit the wall next to him, causing him to stumble. Sparks sizzled on his cheek.

He reached the bottom step just as the sorcerer started down. Quinn risked a glance at him. The sorcerer had pulled the knife from his leg and dark droplets splattered the rug with each step he took. It wouldn't be long before the blood loss affected the sorcerer's vision. He'd be seeing black spots soon. Or least, Quinn hoped he would.

Quinn ran into the living room. He had to get to his bookcase. There was one book he needed before he could get out of the house. The room had been trashed by the little goblin. Sofa cushions had been sliced open and spilled out on the floor. All his shelves were tossed. The bookcase was broken apart on the rug, the books scattered everywhere.

He surveyed the damage, desperately seeking a thick black tome. He spied it in the corner, off by itself. As if waiting for him.

He dashed for it even as the sorcerer came around the corner, his hands glowing brighter. Quinn had a feeling that if he was hit by another wave of magic he wasn't going to be getting up so easily. He'd crossed paths with the sorcerers before, but this one's magic seemed much more powerful.

Ducking to grab the book, he barely missed being hit by a large orb of green. It crashed into the wall just above him. Liquid green sparks rained down on him, burning holes in his skin. He sucked in a breath to deal with the pain and shoved the book into his satchel.

If he could just make it to the kitchen, he could escape out the back. He had an escape route planned in advance. One he'd practiced repeatedly. He'd dash across the yard, out the back gate, down the alley and over the fence of his neighbors who had two dogs he'd already made friends with. After going through their yard, out the front and down another block, he'd get to the old junker he had sitting there. The keys were sitting on the right front wheel, under the fender.

But the thoughts were moot. Just as he reached the archway to the kitchen, he felt the impact on his back.

Quinn catapulted forward. Luckily he had the presence of mind to put his hands out, so he didn't land on his face. But he did manage to smash his knee against the kitchen island as he fell. Dark, searing pain surged over his back, up his neck and over his skull. His vision wavered.

He tried to gain his feet, but dizziness seized him and he collapsed to his knees, agony bursting through the one he'd just battered. "Damn it!" he yelled.

He half crawled, half pulled himself on his stomach, toward the back door. But it was pointless. He was down.

"Admirable, Strom. But face it, I have more power than you do."

Quinn rolled onto his back to see the sorcerer limp into the kitchen, the little goblin trailing behind him.

"Loir, grab the bag."

The little green creature shuffled past the sorcerer to where Quinn was sprawled out on the kitchen floor. He clutched the satchel to his chest. "Touch it, goblin, and I'll bite your hand off."

The goblin grinned at him, showing off four rows of pointed, razor-sharp teeth. "Not before I bite yours off, first."

The sorcerer laughed.

The goblin reached for the bag, but Quinn wouldn't relinquish his hold on it. The creature dragged one sharp talon across the back of Quinn's hand. His skin split open, bubbling with infection.

"Jesus!" he dropped the bag and cradled his injured hand. The pain was intense. It made his head swim. Nausea filled his mouth.

The creature took the bag and handed it to the sorcerer, then shuffled in beside its master.

The sorcerer pulled open the leather bag, and withdrew a Holy Bible. He smiled when he saw it. "Cute."

The sorcerer opened it and flipped through the pages until, Quinn imagined, he came across Quinn's hiding spot. He'd hollowed out pages of the book and set the key inside.

The sorcerer tossed the Bible aside, and held up what he'd found between the pages. It was the key. The key that had been entrusted to Quinn to keep hidden. The key that unlocked the Chest of Sorrows, which contained a book that could end the world.

The sorcerer closed his hand around it. "Thank you, Quinn. Give my best to the demon horde when you get to hell." He turned on his boot heel and glanced down at the goblin. "Make it quick. We have places to be."

"Next time we meet, sorcerer, I'm going to bury that blade in your neck and watch you bleed out," Quinn said.

The sorcerer shook his head with a little smile at his lips. "So much drama, exorcist."

He hobbled out of the kitchen and Quinn could hear his steps through the living room and out the front door, leaving Quinn alone with the little assassin.

The goblin tilted its head and looked at Quinn. "I have longed to meet you, Quinn Strom."

"Is that right?" Quinn cradled his hand to his chest. The infectious bubbling hadn't stopped. The wound had widened and blood joined the phlegmy green liquid oozing out of his hand.

"You are most famous in hell."

Quinn imagined he was. He'd exorcised hundreds of

demons back to the fiery pits. He imagined he was hell's Most Wanted. He wondered if there were posters of him nailed to the walls. He hoped they got his good side.

The goblin neared him, regarding him curiously. "Are you afraid to die?"

Quinn boldly met its gaze. "No. Are you?"

"Is there anything you want to say before it happens?"

He nodded. "Yeah, who was that sorcerer bastard?"

"His name is Richter Collins." It smiled, then reached for him.

The goblin squeezed Quinn's head between its mottled green hands. Quinn could feel the scaly skin on his cheeks. It leaned down and looked him straight in the eyes.

"I will not kill you. She would hate it and I will not do that to her, although you have done worse to her, I think."

"Who are you talking about?"

"You know who. The one you wronged. The one you loved, once upon a time. I am one of her loyal servants."

"And she sent you to get her revenge?" he spat.

The goblin shook her head. "No, to save you, stupid man."

Before Quinn could respond, everything went dark.

Chapter 3

"Who has the key?"

"I'm sure I don't know what you are talking about."
Daeva pulled at the brown leather straps binding her to
the iron chair. They were secure and she didn't think
any amount of wriggling was going to get her out of
them. The torture room—there really wasn't any reason not to call it that—was small and stifling, with no
color anywhere except the dark brown stains on the
stone that could be nothing but old blood.

Her torturer loomed over her, a maniacal gleam in
his inky black eyes. "Don't bother. You can't escape.
Where would you go? Topside?"

"Well, you can't blame a girl for trying, now, can
you?"

He circled the chair that was bolted to the stone floor,

leering at her, cleaning under his talons with the tip of the silver blade clasped in his hand. She wondered when he was going to use it on her. Likely after the theatrics. Lord Klaven did enjoy his drama.

"You'd like to go back topside, wouldn't you, Daeva?" he sneered. "To live like a human."

"Better than living like an animal like you, Klaven."

He chuckled, and it chilled her to the bone. "But you are like me, Daeva. I remember the fun we used to have together."

"That was millennia ago."

"True." He leaned into her face, and she could smell the rotten meat on his breath. "But they were so deliciously twisted that I remember them like it was yesterday." He licked his lips. "You were one depraved woman."

"Were is the operative word here. I'm not that person anymore."

"True." He straightened and regarded her with contempt. "Now you are weak and human tainted." He sniffed the air. "You still smell like the exorcist, even after all this time. Did you steal some of his clothing when he sent you back?"

She winced inside at the mention of Quinn. It still hurt to think of him.

"Although he didn't want you, now, did he?"

She glared at him. "Come closer and say that."

He laughed again, then twirled the blade between his fingers. "Oh, poor Daeva. Exorcised by the man you loved. At least, that's what I heard. Is it true?" He leaned down into her face.

She turned away. She didn't want to look into his vacant eyes, didn't want to see the total lack of empathy or emotion there.

"Oh, you're not going to cry are you?" He drew the blade tip across her lips. "I do so hate to see a lady shed tears. Especially over a man who tossed her away like the heathen she is."

Klaven took a step back, and the air shimmered around him until it was Quinn standing in front of her and not the demon lord. The fake Quinn image smiled.

"It must've hurt when he banished you." He took a step toward her.

She didn't look at him, she stared at the stained floor. She couldn't see Quinn looking at her like that, not again. As if she was an animal. As if she wasn't a woman but pure filth.

"Did he torture you first? Did he sprinkle holy water on you? Burning your flesh, burning your soul."

She didn't rise to the bait, although she remembered that night three years ago when Quinn exorcised her as though it had just happened. It was still fresh and raw in her mind. And being reminded of it by the horrid Lord Klaven didn't help matters. Her stomach churned at the memory.

He moved closer to her again, gripping her chin with his long, bony fingers. He lifted her head up, forcing her to look upon him. She wanted to scream at seeing Quinn's face with black eyes and fangs poking out between his full lips. Lips she used to kiss for hours on end.

"Does the exorcist have the key?"

She spat at him.

Klaven wiped the spittle from his cheek, then grinned down at her. "Does he have the chest?"

"You're wasting your time, Klaven. I won't tell you anything. You can't kill me, so you might as well let me go."

He wrapped a hand in her hair and pulled her head back, exposing her neck. Leaning down, he slammed his mouth on hers, kissing her fiercely. She bit his tongue when it invaded her mouth. His sulfur-tainted blood filled her mouth.

He jerked away, his crimson-stained lips pulling back into an evil sneer. "I might not be allowed to kill you, Daeva. But I certainly can have my fun."

He drew his knife down her arm, slicing open her skin. She bit down on her lip to stop from crying out at the pain. She looked down at her damaged flesh, knowing his demon-cursed blade would leave a scar and that she would use that as a reminder of this day. Of Klaven's betrayal—and that of all of the demon horde.

"Do your worst. I do not fear you or anything that you can do to me."

Klaven, still looking like Quinn, clapped his hands, and the heavy metal door opened. The two guards that had brought her here marched in.

"Grab her and tie her to the rack."

When they came to unbind her, she kicked and struggled and lashed out at them, but they were twice her strength. There was nothing she could do when they dragged her across the room to the ancient wooden rack that was once owned by the Marquis de Sade, a close personal friend of Klaven's.

Her torture was going to be savage. She'd seen Klaven's artwork before. But she swore to herself she would hold out as long as she could. No matter what Quinn had done to her all those years ago, she still didn't want to see him harmed. And if the demons knew he possessed the key, he would not be safe. His death would be her fault.

Chapter 4

When Quinn finally woke, the sun was streaming in through the big kitchen and his head was pounding something fierce.

He made his way to his knees, then up to his feet, using the kitchen counter to brace himself against. His hand still throbbed where the goblin had wounded him, but it was no longer oozing with infectious goo or blood. It still needed tending to, though.

Arduously climbing the stairs, he went into the bathroom to retrieve his first aid kit. While he doctored himself, he thought about his next move. The Cabal had taken the key. He could form a small army to get it back by force. But he'd been through so much fighting recently.

It had only been a few months since the slaughter by

demons in Sumner, Washington. It had taken him and Ivy hours to bury their friends and burn the rest of the dead. He didn't want to go through that again. And it would be a bloodbath if he went after the Cabal, he had no doubt in his mind.

He washed the wound, poured antiseptic onto it, biting on his lip the whole time. It stung like a thousand bees. He wrapped it tight, then went back down the stairs to his ruined living room. The goblin had done a thorough job of wrecking everything he had. Which, by some standards, wasn't much. His lifestyle didn't really permit the luxuries of living a normal, comfortable life.

Usually on the move, Quinn had only just set up shop in this small starter home, basically for cover. It wasn't as if he worked nine to five at an office. No, he hunted demons. That was his vocation, his life. He'd been born into it.

As far as the people he bought the home from knew, his name was Quinton Sterling, and he was a divorced small-business owner. They'd been more than happy with his story since he paid cash for the place they couldn't afford anymore.

The money came from the other jobs he did. Jobs he wasn't necessarily proud of. Demon hunting wasn't exactly lucrative. He'd pulled a few cons over the years, something he'd learned from his dad. It was a dishonest way to bankroll a lifesaving job of hunting down and destroying demons. Quinn didn't ponder the ethics of it too much.

Righting the overturned sofa, he shoved the ruined

cushions back on and sat. He had to think. He had to figure out what to do.

Rubbing his good hand over his face, he sighed. Ultimately, he knew what had to be done next, but he just didn't want to do it. It would be way too complicated and messy. Two things he hated.

If the Cabal had the key, that meant they were going after the chest that contained the book that could unleash hell on Earth. There was only one choice here and that was to find the chest first. Find it and protect it.

Sighing, he leaned his head on the back of the sofa. Maybe there was another way. There had to be. To do what he needed—to uncover where the chest was hidden—would almost be too much to bear. He wasn't sure he could see *her* again.

Quinn found his cell phone on the floor. He picked it up and dialed a familiar number. He glanced at the wall clock. It was only six in the morning. It rang only four times before being answered.

"You do know what time it is?"

He smiled. "Yup, I know, Q. I need to talk."

There came a long, drawn-out sigh. "Fine. Meet me at my office in an hour."

Quinn stood and headed upstairs to get dressed. It was going to be one long, hellish day.

One hour later he stood in the office doorway of Quianna Lang, one of the youngest professors on staff at the San Francisco State University and resident mythologist to the university. But he knew her talents and knowledge lay in demonology. She possessed more knowledge about demons and demon lore than anyone he knew.

She barely looked up from whatever she was reading on her old mahogany desk when he entered. "Sit."

He came all the way in and slid onto one of the leather chairs situated in front of her big wooden desk.

She finished reading, slammed the book closed and looked up at him. "Okay, so what's going on? How much trouble are you in?"

"Why does something have to be going on?"

She smirked. "Because you're here. The only time you demon hunters come here is when the shit has hit the fan. First Ronan and your sister, and now you. Something major is happening, I suspect."

He sighed, then met her gaze. "The key is gone. Stolen by the Cabal."

Quianna bolted out of her chair and came around the desk. She was a compact woman, short and petite, but she possessed more fire in her pinkie than most people did in their whole bodies. She pinned him to the seat with her intense, determined gaze.

"How?"

"Richter Collins is how. And he had a goblin with him."

She shook her head. "I thought that once Reginald died, the Cabal would fall. I guess I was wrong."

"I should've been more diligent in hiding the key. I had been planning to move it…"

"Well, what's done is done. Now, what are we going to do about it?"

"That's why I came. I thought if anyone would know what to do, it would be you."

She sat on the edge of her desk. "You have to find the chest. You have to get it before they do."

He groaned. "I was hoping there was another way."

"There isn't. If they have the key, they will be going for the chest. That's just logical."

Quinn leaned forward and put his head in his hands. He had been hoping for another answer. Another way to solve the problem.

"I take it you know where it is?" She eyed him curiously.

He shook his head. "Not where. But I know someone who knows."

"By the look on your face, I'd say this someone is pretty bad."

"You could say that."

She nudged him with her foot. "Well, man up, Quinn. Whatever you have to do, you better do it. This isn't some small problem. We're talking end of days stuff, here. If the Cabal finds that chest and uses that book, it won't matter who this person is, because we'll all be dead."

"When I find the chest and the book, what do I do with them?"

"Bring the book to me. I know a place where even demons fear to tread. I can keep it safe there."

Quinn left Quianna's office with a deep sinking feeling in his gut. It almost made him sick to think about what he had to do to find the chest. But the powerhouse professor had been right, he had to man up and do what needed to be done. No one else was going to do it. He had been entrusted with the key and he had lost it. It had been his responsibility. Now finding the chest was his as well. He was the only one on Earth who could do it. He just had a pit stop to make first.

The new age store located downtown looked like any other crystal and tarot shop. Mary, the proprietor, doled out spiritual wisdom and metaphysical prophecy to every patron that passed through her doors. But when Quinn walked in, she frowned deeply and shook her head.

"I was having a good day," she said.

"Hey, Mary, how's business?"

"On the light side." She moved her hefty frame around the counter to stand in front of him. The beads on her wrists clicked when she moved. The scent of patchouli and lavender wafted to his nose. "But I take it, since you're here, that's going to change."

"I need some supplies."

She sighed heavily, as though she was going to deny him, but she swept her arm toward the back curtain. She never said no; she just liked to put on the drama. She knew he was one of her best customers. He and the Crimson Hall Cabal.

"Come on, then."

Quinn followed her into the back where she kept her stores of "other" types of metaphysical supplies. The type reserved for those who dabbled in the darker side of the magical arts.

"What do you need?"

Quinn examined the shelves of bottles and tins. "Goofer dust, asafoetida, horehound, another blessed chalk stick and some yarrow."

Mary narrowed her eyes at him. "Who are you calling?"

He shrugged. "Don't know what you're talking about."

"The stuff you're asking for, Quinn, is for calling forth a powerful demon and keeping it in line. Who is it?"

"It doesn't matter. Do you have the stuff or not?" He pulled out a wad of cash from his pocket.

She nodded and went to the shelves to start pulling down jars. "I have everything you need." She stacked it all on the table. She sighed. "Between you and the Cabal, I'm surprised demons aren't running amok on this plane."

Quinn opened his leather satchel and shoved the ingredients inside. He peeled off money and handed it to her.

Mary slid it into the pocket of her flowered house-dress but pinned him with a hard glare. "Be careful, Quinn. You're playing with fire."

He nodded. "I know. But it has to be done." Closing his bag, he hefted it onto his shoulder and left the store, his heart as heavy as the bag he carried.

When he got home, he went straight down to the

basement to prepare. Using his new blessed chalk he drew a large pentagram on the cement floor, inscribing it with familiar symbols. Symbols he'd been using his whole life as an exorcist and demon hunter. He left two open triangles in the pentagram. This was where he would put the two sigils that would call the demon he needed. They'd been burned into his memory. But for different reasons.

He chalked them in. Around the pentagram he sifted a thick line of goofer dust. It was a protective circle. The demon couldn't cross it if Quinn didn't want it to. And until he got a binding agreement, he didn't plan on letting the demon go anywhere.

Once that was done, Quinn set everything aside, lit seven white candles and started the ritual.

In Latin, he spoke the words to invoke the spell, then he called the demon using its real name. The one that gave him power over it.

"I call you, Daeva, Seductress of Shadows."

At first nothing happened, and Quinn wondered if he'd mistakenly written the symbols backward or upside down. But then a slight breeze blew through the basement. None of the windows were open. Then came the smell. The delectable scent of cinnamon. He tried not to inhale it. But it was difficult not to. Cinnamon had always been one of his favorite smells. It made his gut clench with the memories it brought.

Three popping sounds echoed in the room. Like fingers snapping.

Then it appeared.

Dressed in tight black pants, black leather knee-high

boots and a sapphire-blue blouse that accentuated full, firm breasts, the demon smiled at him, and he couldn't suppress the shiver that raced down his back.

"Hello, lover."

Chapter 5

"You look surprised to see *me*, Quinn." Tilting her head, she looked him up and down. "Oh, that's right. You never did get to see me in my preferred form. You were so quick to get rid of me. Never gave me a chance to introduce myself properly."

It had been three years since Daeva had seen Quinn Strom. And she had to admit that he looked as dangerous and delicious as ever. His inner darkness called to her like a moth to a flame. But she couldn't let him see that. She couldn't let him have the upper hand here. She'd never give it to him again.

"How's my favorite exorcist?"

"I didn't call you to have a trite and pointless conversation."

"No? Too bad. That's definitely one thing I missed about you."

She saw him bristle and grinned. Score one for Daeva.

Quinn had always prided himself on his ability to speak on all kinds of subjects. On several occasions, he'd bored her to tears. But she'd listened to him attentively. That was what a person did when they were in love.

Love. Ha. Quinn Strom knew nothing about the emotion. If he had, he'd never have done what he did to her.

But, alas, she obviously was not here to discuss the past. Quinn had something dire to talk to her about, or he would never have called her forth. Never. She knew him well enough to know that he held a grudge the way a miser held money.

"So, to what do I owe this utmost pleasure of seeing your handsome face again?" Although she had her suspicions that it had everything to do with her twelve-hour torture session and Klaven's questions.

Thankfully, that had ended without Daeva revealing much of anything—nothing important anyway. He'd poked and prodded at her until he'd gotten bored. And her restorative powers made it look like she'd barely been bruised. Although the truth was it had taken a lot out of her and she was feeling its effects.

"I need information."

"I gathered that. On what?"

"The Chest of Sorrows."

And there it was. She'd known it deep down, the moment she'd heard that the little goblin Loir had gone topside for a key. Loir had confirmed it herself when she snuck into Daeva's chambers as she healed from her torture session to warn her. Sorcerers used goblins for some of their work. She assumed it was one of the cabals that had stolen the key from the great Quinn Strom. She was surprised he was still alive.

"What do you want to know that you don't already?" she asked.

He paced nervously in front of the pentagram. Usually he paced when he wasn't quite confident in what he was doing or the decisions he was making. "Where is it?"

She laughed. "Are you kidding? Do you really think I'm going to tell you that?"

"Yes, I do." He gave her a hard stare.

She'd always loved his gray-green eyes. They were so intense. Always searching for something. At one time, he'd look at her with those eyes and she'd see the desire in them and succumb to it. She'd surrender to him without a second thought.

Now, he looked at her as if she was the worst thing he'd ever seen. She supposed betrayal did that to a person.

"What are you going to do, Quinn, if I don't tell you?" She arched an eyebrow and ran a finger along her lips. "Torture it out of me?"

"I might."

"You're a bastard, true. But I don't think you have it in you to do that to me."

"Maybe I've changed in the last three years."

She met his gaze, looking for something of the old

Quinn. The man she'd loved, who had loved her. After a few seconds, she wasn't sure he was still in there. "Oh, I suspect you have. But you still have those interesting morals. Those you will never let go of, I am sure. I fell victim to them, as I recall, once upon a time."

He sighed and rubbed a hand over his haggard face. It was obvious he hadn't slept in a while. He looked harder, sadder. As though he held the world on his shoulders. She supposed he did, in a way, considering that he'd been the key keeper and now no doubt felt responsible for finding the chest and keeping it safe.

Quinn had always been a crusader. It was one of the things she'd loved about him. And that had also been the thing that had killed their relationship in the end. His single-minded sense of justice.

He could never see the shades of gray in between those morals of his.

Gray had always been her favorite color.

"I called you, Daeva, thinking there was some sort of good person inside you. A person who would do the right thing."

She laughed again. "The right thing? Huh. And what exactly is that, Quinn?"

He stared at her and she stared back. It was the show-down they'd never had when she'd possessed the body of the woman he'd fallen in love with. The woman she'd been, mind, body and soul for ten years. Seven years before she'd even met Quinn and fallen for him.

At first when she'd confessed her secret about being a demon, he hadn't truly believed her. He'd thought she was pulling a really bad prank on him. He'd asked her a lot of questions to prove it. Daeva had told him things only a demon would know, and she'd also told him about burying the Chest of Sorrows over a hundred years ago. It was then that he had truly believed. And it was as if a switch had been flicked on. He'd gone into demon hunter mode.

He'd bound her to a chair, drawn a pentagram around her, sprayed her with holy water and sent her screaming back to hell. How he'd dealt with Rachel's comatose body, she could only imagine. Maybe the real woman had woken up.

Daeva had never gotten a chance to say goodbye to anything that had mattered to her. The friends she'd made, family members who had loved her like their own, coworkers she'd grown accustomed to. She hadn't had a chance to say goodbye to the life she'd made. She hadn't been able to say goodbye to Quinn the way she wanted to.

When he had her tied in that chair, he'd acted as if they hadn't spent three wonderful years together. That they hadn't just spent the entire day before in bed, making love and talking about their future. He'd pretended that he hadn't just told her that he loved her more than anything in the world. She remembered the tears, though, and the way he'd looked at her through them.

He dropped his gaze. "Are you going to tell me or not?"

She tapped a finger against her lips. "Hmm, since you asked so nicely, I think not."

"I guess I was kidding myself, thinking a demon would even consider doing the right thing."

"Yeah, maybe you were. You seem to do that a lot."

He glared at her, then went to the wall, grabbed a folding chair and dragged it out to the middle of the room, in front of the pentagram. He unfolded it and sat. "I can sit here all night."

She smirked at him, then settled onto the hard cement floor, crossing her legs. "So can I."

For the next hour, they sat and stared at each other. Daeva broke her gaze once in a while to examine her nails. It seemed to piss Quinn off and that's why she did it. She really didn't think that her nails were more important than the situation. She just liked to revel in the way the vein at his right temple would throb.

"What happened to your arm?" she asked.

"What do you care?"

"I don't. I'm just being polite."

He held his forearm up and looked at it. "Courtesy of your little goblin friend."

"Loir did that to you?"

He nodded.

"Well, then, you must've deserved it. I'm surprised that she didn't kill you. She's usually very bloodthirsty." Daeva spoke with her tongue in cheek, because Loir was anything but. She was one of the kindest creatures Daeva knew. Unless, of course, she was forced to do something. Then she could be lethal.

"I'm surprised she didn't, as well. She said you would hate it if she killed me."

Daeva examined her nails again. "Hmm, she must have been mistaken. I'm pretty sure I wouldn't have alluded to such a thing."

She had though. In her note. She'd simply written, "Don't kill him."

Another half hour went by. He was as stubborn as she remembered him to be. Maybe more so. She didn't remember the stern wrinkles in his brow, the way it was now. That was new. But she had a feeling it had something to do with her. She'd put those lines of pain there.

She sighed. "Are we seriously going to sit here all night?"

"Until you help me, yes."

"I never said I wouldn't help you, Quinn, I just can't tell you where the chest is."

"Can't or won't?"

She shrugged. "Whatever makes you feel better."

"Well, that's the only help I need. The location. So if you won't give it to me, then there's nothing to talk about."

She stood and brushed the dirt off her black pants. "Fine. Send me back, then. I have laundry to do."

He looked at her, and she could see the hesitation on his face. He obviously hadn't expected her to call his bluff. He should've known she would. She possessed all the same personality traits she had when she'd been wearing a human birthday suit. She was basically the same, except for a few physical changes.

Sighing, he shook his head. "What's it going to take?"

"I'll help you find the chest, but I want something in return."

"Of course you do," he sneered.

"Play nice or you can forget it. And when the Cabal

opens the chest and uses the book, and your world goes to shit, don't complain to me about it." She pointed a finger at him. "Besides, you know as well as I do that it's the nature of my…condition to make a bargain."

"What are your terms?"

"I guide you to where the chest is, you get it, and in return I get to stay topside in a new body forever."

Quinn stood, his chair overturning from the suddenness of his movement. The banging of metal on cement echoed through the basement. "Absolutely not."

"Then send me back, because those are my terms and I won't change them."

He shook his head. "Nope. That's too easy." He turned toward the stairs. "We'll see how cooperative you are after a few more hours in that pentagram." He mounted the stairs.

She watched him leave. When he was at the top of the stairs he flicked off the light. The room plunged into darkness. Not a big deal for Daeva, though—she could see in the dark. But it was starting to get drafty. Right now she was almost missing the hot stifling air in hell.

"You're a jerk, Quinn Strom."

He slammed the door shut on her words.

Chapter 6

Quinn tried to keep himself busy. Tried to keep his mind occupied. But it was difficult with a demon in his basement. Especially one that smelled like cinnamon and looked like sex on a stick.

She'd been right, her appearance did startle him. When he'd known her, she'd been a lithe blond with an athletic build and a pert little nose. Her name had been Rachel. The demon who had popped into the pentagram was a curvy redhead with stormy gray eyes. She looked very different from the woman he'd loved, but something about her was still the same. The fluid way she moved, the tilt of her head as she regarded him. If he had passed her on the street, he suspected he would've recognized her.

The thought was completely unnerving. He didn't

want to recognize the woman from three years ago in the demon he'd just called. He wanted them to be two distinct entities, but deep down he knew that they weren't. They were like two sides of one complicated coin. He supposed Daeva had always been a part of Rachel, however much he wanted to deny it.

By the third hour, after straightening up everything the goblin had ruined, Quinn ended up in the kitchen to make dinner. He flung open the refrigerator and started pulling out various ingredients. He grabbed a pot and a pan, and tossed in this and that, frying and boiling, anything to occupy his thoughts. In the end, he had made spaghetti Bolognese. It had been one of Rachel's favorite meals. And he'd made enough for two.

"Damn it," he mumbled under his breath.

He stared at the food, unsure of exactly what to do. He could make himself a plate and put the rest in containers for leftovers. Or he could fix another plate and take it down to his captive. Demons didn't derive any nutrition from food, but he knew they reveled in all mortal pleasures. Like food, and drink, and sex.

Resigned, Quinn grabbed two plates from the cupboard and put spaghetti onto both. Picking up one plate, he got a fork and took it down to the basement.

He flicked on the lights. As if weighted down with leaden feet, he descended the stairs. When he reached the bottom, he saw Daeva sitting cross-legged in the middle of the pentagram with her eyes closed. It looked as if she was meditating.

"Oh, my, is that spaghetti Bolognese I smell?" Her eyelids slowly fluttered open.

He gestured with the plate. "I wasn't sure if you were hungry or not."

She studied him for a moment, then nodded. "I am."

Nearing the pentagram, he reached across the lines and handed her the food. She took it from him and set it in her lap. She picked up the fork, spun it in the noodles, then put it in her mouth. She grinned around the mouthful. When she was done chewing, she looked up at him.

"Good Lord, that is so good." She twirled her fork in it again. "I've instructed the goblins on how to prepare it properly, but they never get it right. It always tastes so sour. Must be the water in hell. Can't seem to get that sulfur flavor out, no matter how long you boil it."

He watched her eat, a sense of pride and satisfaction filling his gut. He'd always loved that Rachel had enjoyed his cooking. There had been many nights when they'd spent hours in the kitchen together preparing a meal, talking, laughing, eating. The thought now made him sad. And angry. Angry that those memories were tarnished by her true existence. By Daeva's existence.

"Where's yours?" she asked.

"Upstairs."

"Didn't want to eat with the demon?"

"Something like that."

She shrugged. "Suit yourself." She shoveled more of the spaghetti into her mouth.

"I don't want to play this game anymore."

She set her fork down and regarded him. "Then don't."

"I can't in good conscience give you what you're asking for."

"Why not?"

"I can't let you possess someone, Daeva. Take over her life like that. You have no idea what I had to deal with after you left Rachel's body."

"Did she die?" Something about asking that made her face pale. She actually looked extremely concerned.

"No, she woke up and was hysterical. She had no idea what she was doing there or who I was."

"What did you do with her?"

"I took her to her parents' house and told them she fell and hit her head and didn't remember me." He rubbed at his face, hating to have to relive it. "They took her to the hospital and ran tests on her. I slowly removed myself from her life. Her parents hated me for it."

She eyed him intensely for a moment. He thought maybe she was going to apologize to him, but then she sighed, and leaned back onto her hands. "You can have the veto over the body I possess."

"In what way?"

"When the time comes, after you have the chest in your hands, I will pick a body and if you disagree, you can veto me."

Quinn looked at her, mulling over her words, trying to find the catch, the loophole. There were always loopholes in demon deals. But in every scenario he conjured in his mind, he couldn't find a way she could deceive him. Ultimately, in the end, he could stop her from possessing anyone. He just had to continually say no.

"Agreed."

"Excellent." She picked up her plate. "Just let me

finish this, then we can hammer out the details." She started to eat again.

Slightly off balance, Quinn mounted the stairs to head back to the kitchen to eat his dinner. All the way there, he was sure that she'd gotten the upper hand on him. She was much too calm and reserved about the whole thing. But, as he ate his spaghetti, he couldn't figure out why.

Once he was finished eating, he returned to the basement with his book of Latin rites. Daeva was standing, her empty plate right on the edge of the pentagram. She must've pushed it as far as she could without crossing the lines.

"Okay. You ready?" she asked.

"No, but I guess at this juncture I don't have a choice."

She smiled. "You always have a choice Quinn. You're human. You've got free will."

He didn't say anything else on the subject. He didn't feel like having an ethical or theological discussion with a demon right now. "Once I release you from the pentagram, will you have powers?"

She nodded. "Although I'll be losing some because of the bargain we've made. I won't be able to zip through the ether with a snap of my fingers. For all intents and purposes I will be human. Well, a human with super strength and other goodies. Not sure what, though. Need to test them out."

Quinn was nervous. He'd never released a demon from a bound pentagram before. That was how his father had died. On the job, after releasing a demon he thought he could trust. *Demon* and *trust* were two words that didn't go together.

He'd dealt with demons when they'd been bound inside a pentagram and when they'd been possessing someone. But he couldn't think of another way to find the chest. He knew that Daeva, alone, had hidden it a hundred years ago. If he didn't bind her with an agreement, he was certain someone else would. Like Richter Collins of the Crimson Hall Cabal. Once the sorcerer found out that the demon was the only one with that knowledge, he'd be looking to make a deal with her. And he wouldn't bother with ethics.

Quinn opened the book to the right page and, holding his hand out toward the pentagram, began speaking the Latin words of the ritual.

When he was done, he took his ceremonial dagger and cupped it in his hand, slicing his palm open. Blood dripping onto the cement floor, he held his hand out to Daeva.

"Now yours."

Palm up, she offered her hand to him. He quickly drew the blade across her skin. Instantly, blood welled to the top.

"Until the bargain is complete, Daeva, Seductress of Shadows, you are bound to the Earth and to me."

They shook hands, their blood mixing, the power of the bargain sealing them together. He could feel the potency of it sizzling the hair on his arms.

Quinn pulled his hand away first and quickly wrapped it with gauze. Daeva squeezed her hand tight, but blood dripped from the corners.

"You aren't going to heal as fast," he offered. "Give me your hand."

Daeva stepped out of the pentagram to stand beside him. She looked around, seemingly surprised to find herself unbound by the blessed lines. She smiled and took in a deep breath. "Finally."

He saw the extreme relief on her face and he wondered if this was her first time being free. Well, not completely free—she was bound to him, which meant no matter where she went he could find her or compel her to return to his side. She was also free from exorcism. Which meant no one could send her back to hell. Except for him, that was.

"You're bleeding all over the place. Give me your damn hand."

She held her hand out to him. As quick as he could, he cleaned her up and wrapped her wound.

She tested it by clenching and unclenching her fist, then nodded. "Thanks."

As he'd doctored her hand, he'd noticed a few scars on her arm. They'd looked fresh and sore. He wondered what they were from but didn't want to ask. He didn't want to seem as if he cared.

"Okay, before we go on this little adventure, we need to set some rules."

Smirking, she shook her head. "You and your rules."

"I just want to make sure I don't end up with a knife in my back and you on the run."

She pinned him with her gaze. He had to suppress a shiver. "Despite everything, I can't believe you'd even think I would do that to you."

Her words gave him a slight pause. He had to keep chanting in his mind, *she's a demon, she's a demon, and not the woman I fell in love with*. But her gaze was fierce and hard and serious. As if he'd actually hurt her feelings by even suggesting she would betray him like that.

"Wouldn't you?" He met her gaze right on. He wasn't about to back down, to cower before her.

She took a step away from him, then licking her lips, she glanced up the stairs. "I'm earthbound to you, Quinn. I couldn't run even if I wanted to. And for the other part, quit being a dick and maybe I won't consider it."

He laughed at that. He couldn't help it. In the past, the insult had been one of Rachel's favorite things to call him when he was being difficult. It had always made him laugh when she said it.

Surprised, she looked at him and smiled. "Oh, so there is a human being in there somewhere."

"Yeah, deeply buried."

"I knew it."

His laughter died down and he set his shoulders straight. They had to get to work. He suspected the Cabal would be on his ass soon. Once they found out that Daeva had been called out of hell, and by whom, they would have little time.

"So, where are we going?"

"Well, we'll need a car, lots of gas and supplies."

"Where are we going, Daeva?"

She sighed. "Look, I can't tell you that. It's for your own safety. If you're captured and questioned, you can't give them the location."

"And I won't be able to ditch you, either."

She ran her tongue over her top lip. "There is that, too."

He nodded, resigned to having to do it her way for a while. He just wanted to find the chest. If he had to follow her directions he'd do it. "Fine."

"Great. Now that that's solved. I need to clean up." She pushed past him to go up the stairs. "Do you have any bubble bath?"

Chapter 7

"No, I don't have any damn bubble bath," Quinn growled at her as he mounted the stairs behind her.

From the stairs she came out into the kitchen. It was small and cozy with a compact island in the middle. The scent of the sauce he'd made for the spaghetti still clung to the air.

She looked left then right. "Where's your bathroom?"

"Upstairs."

She moved through the kitchen and into the living room. She took in the destruction. "Maid's day off?"

"Courtesy of your goblin friend, again, and the Cabal."

She didn't comment as she strode across the room and up the staircase, Quinn right on her heels.

"We don't have time for your frivolous needs, Daeva. We should be on the move."

She found the bathroom, but turned toward him before entering. "Look, I've spent the last few years in a stinking cesspool of misery and mayhem, thanks to you no less. I'm taking time to wash off the smell."

"Well, since I'm the one that called you forth and released you, I think that makes me in charge."

She smiled at him, putting a hand on one hip. "I may be bound to you, honey, but you don't command me. There's a huge difference, you know?"

He frowned. "I know the difference."

"No, I don't think you do." She took a step back into the bathroom, then slammed the door shut on Quinn's next protestation. With a satisfied sigh, she locked the door.

"Daeva, we don't have time for this crap."

"Sure we do, lover. While I bathe this beautiful body of mine why don't you get what you need ready. Make sure you pack an extra pair of shorts, it's going to be a long trip."

She heard his exasperated sigh, and it tickled her inside. Let him suffer for a while. Fair was fair. Besides, she really did want to wash off the stench of sulfur she was sure still clung to her skin and clothes.

Plus, it would give her a bit of a reprieve from the sensations surging through her at seeing Quinn again. She didn't think it would be this hard to be near him, with his masculine scent tantalizing her senses. The urge to touch him warred with the desire to slug him in his pointy nose.

Maybe she was being silly by demanding a bath when obviously there was a level of danger hovering over everything. But she found she couldn't just jump in as Quinn's traveling partner, however forced it was. It was a bit too much too soon. She'd just returned from three years in hell, sent there by the man beyond the door. She needed a little time to decompress her anger. Anger that she was surprised she still harbored. Seeing him face-to-face manifested that bitterness.

Daeva turned on the sink tap and splashed cold water on her face. She looked up into the mirror at herself. It was strange to be topside in her true form, well, almost true form. She was minus the fangs and glowy-type skin. She'd gotten so used to seeing Rachel's face in the mirror that her real appearance sometimes startled her. She could just imagine what it was doing to Quinn. Maybe she should give him a break. This was probably just as difficult for him as it was for her. She gave him credit though, for swallowing his enormous pride and calling her. Asking a demon for help must've really pricked him in the ass.

Straightening, she patted her face dry with the hand towel. She opened the door. She supposed she'd give him that break. Although his suffering was sweet, she did possess a heart and conscience somewhere deep inside.

He was there leaning against the wall when she stepped out.

"I thought you needed a bath?"

She shrugged. "Nah, I just needed a minute to adjust to topside. It's a bit unstable up here. The Earth's always moving."

He stared at her as though he didn't know whether to believe her or not. He opened his mouth to respond but she grabbed his arm and yanked him to her.

His eyes widened when she leaned into his ear. "We have company."

"Are you sure?" Quinn whispered.

She nodded. "Sounds like three or four men. Two at the front, one or two at the back."

"Damn it." He cursed a few more times. "Must be the Cabal. They're earlier than I thought."

"I could go blast them."

He shook his head. "No. No blasting until we absolutely need to." He moved to the stairs. "We have to get back to the basement."

She followed him, close behind. "Won't we be trapping ourselves?"

He shook his head. "Trust me. I'm always prepared."

They made it back downstairs without incident. He rushed to one wall, slid his hands along the wallboard until he found a groove. He dug his fingers into it and pulled a piece off. Behind it were two duffel bags.

He grabbed them both, tossing one to her, then he pointed to the small window. "We'll go out that way. I have a car parked about five blocks away for emergencies."

She watched him pull the metal bars from the opening. Obviously they were there only for show. He tossed his bag through then dragged a chair over and set it underneath.

"You first."

Although she was better equipped to stay behind and deal with the Cabal if they rushed down the stairs, she didn't argue with him. Stepping up onto the chair, she pushed her bag out then reached through the window, grabbed hold of a tree root that was pushing through the grass and pulled herself up. Kicking her legs, she managed to wriggle her way out the small opening.

Once on her feet, she reached down and helped pull Quinn through. It proved a little harder for him to squeeze out the window opening. He was much thicker than she was.

They peered around for any sign of sorcerers lurking. She couldn't see anything, even with her night vision. "We're clear," she told him.

"Okay. We run east about five blocks. There is a dark blue sedan parked on the right side. Keys are hidden on the right front wheel under the fender."

"Got it."

Quinn draped a bag handle around each shoulder, then took off. Daeva did the same and was right behind him. She'd run barely a block before she felt the first zing of magic behind her. She glanced over her shoulder just as a green bolt of energy slammed into the azalea bush she'd just passed.

"They're on us!" she shouted to Quinn who was maybe three feet in front of her. "You get to the car. I'll slow them down."

She didn't wait for him to respond. She stopped running and turned, already conjuring a ball of dark fire in her right palm. As a demon on this plane, she should have possessed many powers. Telekinesis, manipulation of elements—especially fire—moving through shadows. But she wasn't sure which ones would work now that she was Quinn bound.

Her hands heated quickly, so she assumed her fire-power was still intact. Once she had a good-sized fiery globe in her hand, she launched it at the two sorcerers running down the street toward her. The ball hit the pavement in front of them, sending up sparks, and a wall of flame.

It wouldn't last long, so she hoped Quinn had made it to the vehicle. Before the flames could go out, she made another ball in her left hand. It wasn't nearly as big or powerful, but it would have to do. She had always been right-handed.

But before she could release it, a bolt of magic clipped her in the shoulder, and she dropped the sphere of fire. The moment it hit the sidewalk, it exploded in an array of sparks and flames leaped at her. She dived to the right and fell onto her side on the grass before her pants started to burn.

She looked up just as two other sorcerers advanced on her, their hands glowing green with power. Rolling, she gained her feet and started to run, but they were right on her ass. Sudden jolts of searing pain rushed up her back. The impact of their magic pushed her forward and she stumbled again, falling to her knees.

She couldn't believe the pain surging over her body. She'd never felt anything like that before. Obviously she was more fragile topside than she was in hell. The binding must've made her human-like.

A kick in the back of her head sent her facedown to the cement. She tried to push up, but one of the men pressed her down with his boot on her back.

"We got the demon bitch," one of the men called.

"There's no need for name-calling." Daeva pushed up with all her strength, sweeping her leg at the man. She knocked over the sorcerer standing on her.

Once he was down, she stumbled to her feet. But the other one was there, grabbing her by the back of the head.

"Where do you think you're going?"

In the distance, she could see a vehicle bearing down on them. Twisting around, she punched the goon in the sternum and sent him sprawling backward. Fortunately he let go of her hair.

She bolted to the right just as Quinn barreled the car right into the sorcerer. He rolled over the hood, then off the car to land in a heap on the road.

Daeva opened the back door and dived into the car. Quinn backed it up, tires squealing, did a four-point turn and raced away from the magical goon squad.

A couple of bursts of green magic hit the back of the car. One busted a taillight, but it was nothing that would stop the vehicle. Tires squealed as Quinn turned the car around a corner to the main road, then finally out of the neighborhood and onto a major highway.

Daeva lay on her stomach in the backseat, gaining her breath and trying to gauge her injuries. Which was something new. She remembered being hurt when she had possessed a body. She'd felt pain before, but it had been buffered in a way. This was excruciatingly different. She felt the burn all the way to her bones.

"Are you okay?" Quinn asked.

"I'll live." She sat up, careful of her shoulder and her head. She had a headache that thumped all over her skull and neck.

He looked at her in the rearview mirror. "Are you injured?"

"A little. Nothing that won't heal."

He nodded, and it looked as if he wanted to say more, but he didn't, just glanced down at the car controls and turned up the heat. "So, now that we're out, where are we going?"

"North."

"To?"

"Just drive north for now."

"I need to know, Daeva."

She sighed. "Get us to the Canadian border, then I'll let you know."

"Got a passport? You're going to need it to get over."

She smiled, then rested her head on the seat. "I'll figure something out."

"Which border crossing?"

"Through Washington. Easier to cross." She shut her eyes, blocking out the pain, the streetlights and Quinn. For now, she needed to think about how she was going to get out of their arrangement and be able to stay topside. Because she knew deep down that he would look for some way to screw her over.

Chapter 8

Quinn watched Daeva in the rearview mirror as he drove out of the city. She had her eyes closed, and she looked as though she was asleep. He'd be surprised if she was. As far as he knew, demons didn't need sleep. They recharged in other ways.

Wrath demons gained strength from anger, sloth demons from being lazy asses, and lust demons, of which he was sure she was one, got it from sex or sexual energy. She was certainly built like a lust demon. Curvy, sexy, intoxicating, really. He found it difficult to look at her and not think of sex.

He reached over to the controls and turned down the heat. He was already sweating; he didn't need to make it worse. He flipped the vent toward his face and blasted it with cool fresh air. This was going to be one long journey.

"I'm not one, you know."

He glanced in the mirror and saw that Daeva's eyes were open. "Excuse me?

"A lust demon. I'm not one. Not really." She shrugged. "Well, I definitely have ancestors in that realm, but I'm not full-blooded."

"I don't know why you're telling me this." He licked his lips feeling uncomfortable.

"Yes, you do. Don't be coy."

He met her piercing gaze in the mirror. "It's not polite to read people's minds."

She smiled then, and it lit up her face. "I wasn't reading your mind. It was your…ah, other parts I was getting information from."

Quinn grunted, then pulled the car off the road and into a busy roadside gas station and diner. "We should dump this car and get a new one. The Cabal saw this one. They might be tracking us."

There were roughly twenty vehicles in the parking lot. He pulled along the side of the station, where there were another five. These likely belonged to the staff. They'd take one of these because it would likely be a longer delay until the vehicle was noticed as missing. Hopefully they'd be long gone and have switched vehicles again farther along the road in one of the small towns.

Quinn parked the car, then turned in the seat to look at Daeva. He took in her black leggings, noticing the small burn holes and the frays in her blouse. "You need to change clothes. You look too conspicuous."

She smirked. "I didn't really pack an extra set of clothes."

"I have a pair of jeans and a T-shirt in one of the bags."

She tilted her head to look at him. Something sad filled her eyes. "Just like old times, hey?"

He stared at her, anger, sorrow and regret filling him to the brim. He had to fight two urges, one to punch his fist into the seat and the other to breach the distance between them and take her mouth with his. He hated her for making him feel both.

"It's not old times. The woman who wore my T-shirt to bed is not here anymore. You killed her."

"No. You did when you exorcised me back to hell."

He'd had enough. He jumped out of the car, grabbing the bag off the front seat. Angrily, he pulled open the back door. "Get out."

She did.

He shoved the bag into her arms. "The clothes are in here. I suggest you get changed quickly. I'm leaving in ten minutes."

For a minute, it looked as if she might cry. He could see the liquid in her steely eyes. Quinn tensed up, guilt churning in his gut. But when he looked again, her face was hard and icy again, like a granite statue.

"Oh, I doubt that, Quinn. You don't even know where you're going." Hooking the bag over her shoulder, she sashayed into the gas station as if she hadn't a care in the world.

Once she was gone, he surveyed the choice of vehicles. There were three trucks and two sedans. Making sure no one was around, he discreetly tried the doors on the first sedan. All locked. The second sedan wasn't as secure. The right back door was unlocked.

He slid in, jumped into the front and busted the ignition panel. There were several wires peeking out, but he knew which ones to cut and tie together. He'd hot-wired many vehicles in the past. It was part of the transient demon-hunting lifestyle. The trick was something his dad had taught him years ago.

He tapped two stripped wires together and the engine jumped to life. Quinn tied them off, then opened the door and slid out. He had to retrieve the other bag from his car. Then they'd be ready to go.

After he got his other bag, he walked back to the sedan. That's when he saw Daeva coming toward him. She'd changed clothes as he requested. He'd been sure it would make her less sexy, less of a standout, more like the average girl next door. But seeing her with his T-shirt on, pulled tight across her breasts, his jeans tight around her hips and with her long hair pulled back from her face into a high ponytail made his heart skip a few beats and his gut tighten.

She looked like the woman he remembered loving years ago. She'd often wear her hair pulled back, especially on the weekends. It was something he'd always found attractive about her, because her face was striking, electric, and it had always lit up when she'd seen him.

Like now.

He rubbed a hand over his stomach. Damn, she was potent. It was like getting hit in the gut by a battering ram. But it had to be her demon powers working their mojo on him. It had to be. Because the alternative made every part of him hum with nervous energy.

"What?" she asked as she neared him. "You look like you've seen a ghost."

He scanned her, spotting a rather long scar on her forearm. He gestured to it. "How did you get that? I thought demons can regenerate."

She lifted her arm and regarded at it. "Yeah, well, let's just say it's a reminder of why I'm here and what I need to do."

"That's pretty vague."

"Yes, it is."

He shook his head. "Fine. Forget I cared." He pulled open the car door. "Let's just go."

She rounded the car, opened the back door and dumped the bag, then opened the passenger door and slid in. After buckling up, she tossed him a granola bar. "Thought you might be hungry."

He picked it up and looked at it. "You didn't steal it, did you?"

She unwrapped the one she had in her hand and took a bite. "Nah. I found a ten-dollar bill in your jeans pocket."

He laughed then. He couldn't help himself. He tore off the wrapper and took a healthy bite. "Thanks."

"You're most welcome." She smiled around the next bite in her mouth.

He put the car into Drive, backed up out of the parking stall and drove it out onto the road.

After about ten minutes of Quinn fiddling with the heat controls, seat adjustments and the radio, Daeva turned it off. "Are we going to talk about it?"

"Talk about what?"

"You know what."

He sighed, and ran a hand over his face. He was tired. There was nothing more that he wanted right now than to lie down and sleep for a few hours. To turn the world off for just a little while. But Daeva wasn't giving him that time.

"Why? What difference does it make?"

"If we have to work together for the next few days, I think we should clear the air."

"I'd rather not, okay?" He flipped on the radio again.

She shut it off. "Why? It's been years, let's just talk about it."

"Because it still hurts, damn it!" He slammed his fist against the steering wheel.

She was silent, but he could feel her gaze on him. He didn't want her to look at him, to see the hurt on his face. He'd been sure he'd gotten over it, gotten over her. The way his heart throbbed and his gut churned told him he wasn't over anything.

"I'm sorry, Quinn."

He glanced at her. There was a liquid shimmer in her eyes. A shimmer he wanted to convince himself couldn't possibly exist. That she was incapable of such emotion.

"You never gave me a chance to explain. To tell you

how it happened. How I came to be inside Rachel and how I fell for you."

He shook his head. "I don't want to hear it."

She reached across the seat and settled her hand on top of his on the steering wheel. "You need to hear it. And I need to say it."

He was about to respond when bright lights flashed on behind the car. Headlights bore down on them. Quinn could hear the roar of an engine.

"Shit! They found us."

Daeva swirled in the seat to look out the rear window. "How did they track us?"

He shook his head. "I don't know, but hang on to something."

Daeva gripped the door handle and the dash as he stepped on the gas and veered around a truck on the road in front of them. The vehicle behind them followed closely. It was going to take more than going faster to shake them.

"I can blast them."

Quinn glanced over at Daeva. Her right hand was starting to glow red. "Wait. Wait until we're off the main road. I'm going to take the next turnoff."

Racing at seventy, it was hard to see the exit. But the second Quinn spied it he yanked the wheel to the right and they were skidding sideways to take the road. The car felt as if it was going to tip, but he had control. He'd done his fair share of fancy driving in the past. He knew how to handle a car.

Once they were righted, he pressed on the gas. They needed to find a way to hide. He wasn't going to be able to outrun the other vehicle. Not out here in the middle of nowhere without anything to hide behind.

"Look for a place to turn off. Lots of trees would be good," he instructed.

He checked in the rearview mirror for the other vehicle. He saw headlights not far behind them. "Damn it! If we turn they'll see it."

"Turn off the lights."

He gaped at her. "How is that going to help? I'll crash if I can't see."

"I can see in the dark." She unbuckled her seatbelt and started to slide across the seat. "Trust me. Let me drive."

"We can't do this at this speed."

"Slow down a bit, then." She glanced back. "We have some space."

Quinn thought it was crazy, but he couldn't think of another way. Being in the dark would give them the advantage. He braked a little, slowing to fifty. He undid his seatbelt, then lifted up so Daeva could slide in under him.

He felt her foot next to his, and he took it off the gas pedal and pushed himself to the right over top of her. The car veered a bit, but Daeva was down in the seat, hands on the wheel and foot on the pedal before they could go into the ditch.

He settled in the passenger seat and buckled up. "Okay. We're good to go."

She fiddled on the left side of the steering wheel and then the headlights flicked off. She fiddled some more with the wires hanging out and the brake lights blinked off, as well. It was nearly pitch-black in front of them. It scared the hell out of him, driving blind, but it looked as though Daeva had it under control. She was focused on the road without any problem.

"Get ready. There's a turnoff ahead on the left. Lots of trees and bushes."

Quinn braced himself against the dash and floor.

Without another warning, Daeva yanked the wheel to the left. He could hear the gravel spitting up behind the tires as they took the corner. Once around, she slowed down a little.

He turned and watched out the back window. After another five seconds, he saw the vehicle speed past. "It worked."

"We should still get off the road." She made another left turn onto a heavily treed gravel road, then slowed even more.

"Pull it into the ditch."

She did, in a space behind some bushes. She put the car in Park but left it running just in case. "How could they track us? We ditched the car."

He rubbed at his forehead, a headache threatened to come. "Not sure. They do have magical tracking abilities. As far as I know they can't pinpoint an exact position, just an area."

"Yeah, but don't they have to physically touch you or something?"

"Just their magic," he said.

Her eyes went wide as she looked at him. "I think I'm bugged."

"What? How?"

"I got clipped in the shoulder when we were getting out of your place." She hooked her fingers in the hem of the T-shirt and pulled it over her head.

"What are you doing?"

She pointed to the burn on the back of her right shoulder blade. "Look."

He did. At first he saw nothing but the raw and bloody skin, but when he peered at the wound closer, he spied the telltale green glow of magic still pulsating. It was a tracer and it was deep inside Daeva's flesh.

Chapter 9

"It's there, isn't it?"

Quinn nodded grimly. "I'm going to have to dig it out."

"It's going to hurt like hell, isn't it?" The thought of more pain made her stomach roil. She hadn't quite gotten used to the agony of being almost human yet.

He licked his lips, then nodded. "Yeah."

"Then do it quickly."

"Daeva…"

"Look, we are only safe for a little bit, then they will be following this tracker. You know it's the only way. So just do it."

Quinn unbuckled the knife on his belt. "Turn a bit, so I can get at it."

She did, then one of his hands was on her shoulder

and the other had the blade tip braced against her skin. She sucked in a breath, preparing for the pain that was sure to come. But Quinn was hesitating.

"What's the holdup? You need to do it."

She looked over her shoulder at him, but he wasn't focused on her wound. He was looking farther down her back. And she knew what he saw there. Long raised welts. Ones a person could only get from a whip.

"Jesus, Daeva. What happened?"

"It doesn't matter. Just do what you need to do."

"Who hurt you?"

She sighed, not wanting to talk about it. She wanted to forget the whole thing ever happened. But she knew she couldn't, not with the evidence on her skin. "Before you summoned me, I was…interrogated about you."

"What? Why?"

"Because the demons are looking for the same thing the Cabal is, or are working with the Cabal. Don't know which. Everyone is looking for the key and the chest."

"You told them where I lived?"

"No." She licked her lips, not wanting to remember the torture. "But after twelve hours of…well, I sure wanted to."

She laughed it off, but she felt no humor in it. This was just one of many reasons she never wanted to go back to hell. She couldn't and stay sane.

"No one should have to go through something like that."

She shrugged. "It's just another day in hell." She saw him cringe at that, maybe feeling a little guilt at having sent her back there. "It's done, so let's move on and get this over with. We don't have much time."

Quinn nodded. Then, gripping her shoulder hard to keep her from flinching, he pressed the tip of the knife to her skin. Without any more hesitation, he slid the blade in, slicing skin and flesh.

The pain ripped through her, but she kept still, knowing he had to dig the tracker out. If she moved, he might cut her unnecessarily. She bit down on her lip as Quinn scraped at her flesh. Sweat popped out on her forehead. It took all she had not to cry out.

Then it was done, and he was wiping his blade clean of her blood.

"It's gone. It dissipated." He set the knife down, then grabbed one of the bags and took out a first aid kit to doctor her up quickly and efficiently.

Once she was bandaged, Daeva pulled his T-shirt back on. The ache in her shoulder was deep, but she'd push through the pain. It could've been worse, she supposed.

"Let's get out of here. They could still be around." She put the car in gear and pulled back out onto the road. The one back wheel spit back gravel, but they got out.

As she drove, making several turns and loops in case they were still being followed, Quinn busied himself by cleaning his knife and re-sorting his medical supplies. She caught him glancing at her every so often. She could tell he had something to say to her.

"Just spit it out," she said.

"What?"

"I can tell you have something on your mind. You're looking at me when you think I won't notice."

"Do they hurt?"

She glanced over at him, saw the remorse on his face. She didn't have to ask what "they" he was talking about. "A little. It's manageable, though."

"I'm sorry they used you to get to me."

"That helps a little." She returned his smile.

They were silent for another half hour as Daeva got them back onto the main road. So far, they hadn't been followed by the Cabal.

A yawn escaped her lips as she put the car on cruise control. She was tired, which was a new sensation. Normally she could go for days without having to rest, but obviously being out and being human-ish made her body desire rest and recuperation time.

Yawning again, she tried to hide it behind a hand, but Quinn noticed.

"You need to rest."

She shook her head. "No, I'm sure it's just a strange reaction to being topside."

"Daeva, you need to sleep. It'll help you heal."

"Yeah, but aren't you tired?"

"I can go another five hours." He pointed to a rest stop. "Pull over there, and we can switch."

She did, and she moved into the passenger seat as Quinn took up as the driver. When they were back on the road, she rested her head against the glass of the window. Her eyes were heavy, and eventually they drooped. Then, for the first time in years, she drifted off to sleep and dreamed.

The sunlight streamed in through the kitchen window and played across Quinn's face as he grated parmesan cheese. He was smiling and there was a little dimple in his right cheek.

She couldn't resist. Daeva reached up and smoothed her finger over it. "So damn cute."

That had him smiling harder, and he took her hand in his and pressed his lips to her fingertips. "I can't finish this if you keep touching me."

She got up from the stool she'd been sitting on at the kitchen island and came up behind him, wrapping her arms around his chest. She splayed her fingers over the hard muscular plane.

"Then don't finish."

He chuckled. "I thought you were hungry."

"Just for you." She nibbled on his shoulder, her favorite spot.

He dropped the grater, spun and grabbed her around the buttocks. He lifted her and set her down right next to the cheese he'd been grating.

"Spaghetti Bolognese is so overrated anyway," he said as he nibbled on her chin.

"I totally agree."

She wrapped her hands in his hair as he took her mouth. It didn't matter how many times he'd kissed her before, it still sent jolts of pleasure zinging through her. He was skilled with his tongue and teeth and lips, making her head spin.

He ran his hands through her hair, then down her back, pressing her close. He nuzzled into her ear and spoke the words she'd been longing to hear.

"I love you."

She pulled his head back and looked into his face. "I love you, too," she answered back with the same words, words she'd never spoken to another in her entire life. She kissed him hard, her love for him overwhelming her completely.

With clever fingers, he had her skirt pushed up and her panties off before she took another breath. Laughing, she wrapped her legs around his waist.

"You're a naughty boy, Quinn Strom," she panted as she nuzzled into him.

"You don't know the half of it."

Then he was buried deep inside her.

Daeva jolted awake, hitting her head on the passenger side window. She sat up and wiped at her chin. Drool had dribbled there.

She stretched out her neck, then glanced over at Quinn. He was looking at her funny.

"What?"

"Were you dreaming?"

She frowned. "Why?"

"No reason." He put his attention back on the road.

Had she talked in her sleep? The dream had felt so real, she wouldn't have been surprised if she had said something out loud. Anyway, it wasn't so much a dream as it was a memory. That had been when Quinn had asked her to move in with him—after they'd had sex in the kitchen, eaten dinner, then made love later in bed with wine and candlelight.

It had been one of the happiest moments of her life.

When she'd come topside to live a life, she'd never,

ever expected to fall in love. All she'd wanted to do was live a normal life as a human. She'd been lucky to have found Rachel near death in a coma. Daeva had been able to give her body another chance to live. Rachel's mind had been damaged, enough that she never regained consciousness, so Daeva didn't have to quiet her when she moved in. Falling for Quinn had been an unexpected but pleasant surprise.

Daeva stretched her legs and looked out at the dark road. "Where are we?"

"Somewhere in Oregon. I got off the interstate just in case we're still being followed."

She watched his profile, searching for the dimple she knew was there. He yawned and rubbed at his eyes.

"Why don't I drive for a while? You look tired."

"How's your shoulder?"

She tested it by rotating her arm. There was still a deep ache but it was nothing compared to the pain before. "It's good."

"Good." He yawned again. "There's a rest stop just ahead. We can switch there."

At the turnoff, he pulled over. They switched duties, Quinn opting for the back seat to stretch out in.

Daeva pulled out onto the road and set the cruise control. She turned on the radio, quickly finding a station. The first beats of "Viva Las Vegas" came out of the speakers.

She chuckled.

"What?" Quinn asked from the backseat.

"I was just thinking about that time we did a road

trip to Vegas and you kept playing this song over and over again."

He was silent for a moment and she thought maybe he didn't hear her, or maybe he didn't want to answer, but then he said, "I remember."

"I got so sick of that song that…"

"You threw the CD out the window while we were on the interstate."

"Yeah." She laughed. "I thought you were going to get mad but instead you slid in another annoying CD."

"Johnny Cash."

She shook her head, still laughing. "I never could understand your love of fifties music."

He was silent after that. She glanced in the rearview mirror and saw that his eyes were closed. She watched him off and on for a few minutes as his chest rose and fell steadily. He was asleep.

Smiling to herself, she turned up the volume a little and started to sing along to the song.

Chapter 10

As he slept, Quinn dreamed about the first time he'd seen Daeva. She'd been Rachel at the time but that didn't make her any less potent. He'd been on a job and she'd been the right girl at the wrong time.

Friday night the Shark Club was bursting at the seams with people. Quinn sat at the bar nursing a soda water and lime as he surveyed the crowd for his quarry. Not a demon this time, but a sorcerer named Todd who liked to call demons to do his dirty work. The sorcerer was part of the Crimson Hall Cabal and a badass. Or so he thought. Quinn had dealt with the guy before, so he knew who to watch for and what to watch for. The sorcerer liked to pick up drunk women; blondes were his favorite flavor. And there was a smorgasbord available in this club.

Quinn didn't have to wait too long before he spied the sorcerer cozying up to a table of ladies, two of them blonde, the others a brunette and a redhead. The sorcerer pulled up a chair and sat down. Luckily his back was to the room, so Quinn would have the advantage of stealth. He could sneak up on his quarry and take the sorcerer by surprise, hopefully avoiding anyone getting in the way or getting hurt.

Leaving his soda at the bar, Quinn pushed through the crowd toward the table. When he reached it, Todd was leaning toward one blonde, whispering something into her ear. She didn't look all that impressed.

Quinn put his hand on Todd's shoulder and bent down to speak quietly. "Let's go outside for a little talk."

Todd flinched and quickly glanced back at Quinn. In an instant, recognition filled his eyes. And he reacted.

Pushing to his feet, he swung an arm and backhanded Quinn across the face. It was a hard hit, intensified by the telltale glow of magic. A jolt sang down Quinn's body, making his knees ineffectual. He dropped to the floor, the back of his head making a resonating smack on the hardwood.

Black dots clouded his vision. He blinked them back. When he could finally see clearly, a slim hand came into view. He looked past it to the owner and lost his breath all over again.

She smiled down at him. "Need a hand up?"

She was radiant, with long blond hair that flowed around her pale face like sunshine. Her eyes were a piercing blue that speared him to the core. Her smile was genuine and full of good humor.

He let her pull him up. When they were face-to-face, her tantalizing scent filled his nose. Every part of his body responded to it. He had yet to relinquish his hold on her hand.

"You might have a bruise in the morning." She lightly brushed his cheek with her fingertips. An electrifying jolt sizzled down his spine.

All thoughts of Todd drained from his mind. This woman had taken up the space.

"Can I buy you a drink?" he asked her.

"No, but you can buy me breakfast in the morning. I'm already starving." She tugged on his hand and together they left the club.

That had been the beginning of a three-year love affair that Quinn still ached for.

"Quinn?" A hand touched his leg and he jolted awake.

Blinking back sleep, he looked at that slim hand then up at those devastating eyes. So much the same. But different.

"What?" Sitting up, he rubbed at his face, trying to brush off the remnants of his vivid dream. So vivid that her scent was still caught in his nostrils. "Are we close to the border?"

"No, not really."

He looked out the window and saw the pancake house that was connected to a motel. "Why are we stopped here?"

"Because I need me some pancakes with strawberries and whipped cream. And I thought we could both use the rest. We could get a room with one of those Magic Fingers beds."

She turned off the car.

He sighed, exasperation filling him. "We don't have time for this, Daeva."

"We're off the grid. The Cabal doesn't know where we are." She opened the door. "And I'm pretty sure you'd just about kill for some stuffed French toast." She got out of the car, slamming the door shut on any argument he could give.

His stomach grumbled. He could eat. And stuffed French toast was, indeed, his favorite. It figured that she would remember that and then throw it in his face.

He opened the door and followed her into the restaurant.

Once they were seated and had ordered, Quinn relaxed a little. The smell of coffee, butter and grease always filled him with a sense of the familiar. He and his dad, and sometimes Ivy, often used a place like this as a meeting place during a hunt. Or as the place they went to celebrate after a successful one.

He'd taken Daeva, when she'd been Rachel, to one of these for their first breakfast date. She'd had pancakes with strawberries and whipped cream.

Quinn played with the salt and pepper shakers as they waited for their food.

"So, how's Ronan?"

His fingers stilled. "You know Ronan?"

"Yeah, he used to call me all the time."

"Did he?"

"Yup." She leaned on the table. "You're not jealous, are you?"

"Of course not," he sputtered. "Besides, Ronan is with Ivy now."

Her eyes widened. "Really? Well, I guess I should have seen that coming. They seemed pretty cozy last time I saw them."

"When did you see them?"

"During all that trouble in Sumner that went on."

"You knew about that?"

"Honey, everyone knew about that little war. It was the talk of the town for weeks down under." She picked at her napkin. "Ronan summoned me to help him find a demon that needed killing."

"That was nice of you."

"Yeah, I thought so."

Quinn had tried to put Sumner behind him. He still blamed himself for what happened. If he hadn't been hiding out in that small town, demons wouldn't have come looking for him, and they wouldn't have possessed a lot of the townfolk and pitted neighbor against neighbor in a bloody war for his head. He'd seen a lot of people die in that town. Strangers and friends.

The waitress arrived with their food. Before she even left the table, Daeva was chowing down.

"I'm so hungry. Who knew being bound to the Earth made a demon so darn hungry all the time?"

A spot of strawberry juice dotted the side of her full mouth as she chewed. He had to fight the urge to reach across the table and wipe it away with the pad of his thumb. Instead, he put his attention onto consuming his delicious French toast without seeming like a glutton.

He tried to avoid looking at her while she ate. Her face was all lit up with delight as she devoured her pancakes. She licked her fork after each bite, gathering every bit of syrup and strawberry sauce she could get. It reminded him a bit of a child discovering candy or chocolate for the first time. A look of pure joy.

When his lips threatened to twitch upward into a smile, he grabbed his coffee and drank.

She set her fork down and, leaning back in the booth, sighed contentedly. "That was better than I remembered."

"Can't get pancakes in hell?"

"Nope. The goblins have no concept of light and fluffy. Or sweet, for that matter." She wiped her face with the napkin. "Now I need a nap."

"We should really press on."

She shook her head. "I can't. I need to heal, Quinn." She moved her shoulder and he could see the pain on her face. "I'm no good to you if I'm not one hundred percent. If we get attacked again, I can't guarantee I can save your life."

He sighed and pushed his plate away.

"Besides, you could use the sleep, as well. It doesn't look like you've slept in days."

After paying the bill, they made their way over to the motel office to rent a room. The moment Quinn unlocked the door to their ground-floor abode, Daeva stumbled in, shuffled to the bed and collapsed on top of it. She reached behind her, grabbed the blanket and flipped it over her body. Tucking one hand under her chin, she closed her eyes.

"Got any change for the Magic Fingers?" she mumbled sleepily.

After setting the bags on the table, he dug into his pants pocket and came away with a few coins. He flipped them to her.

She snatched them out of the air without even opening her eyes.

"Cool trick."

She smiled, then opened her eyes to slide the money into the metal box on the side table. "I have my moments."

The massager kicked in and jiggled the bed violently. Daeva groaned. "Now, that's what I'm talking about."

Quinn pulled a chair up to the table, sat and rummaged through his bag for his knives and whetstone. He thought he might as well make use of the wasted time to prepare for the next leg of their journey. He needed to keep his wits and hone his weapons. Who knew what they would come up against? More sorcerers, certainly, but he wouldn't be surprised if they also came up against demons.

Unfortunately he didn't know anyone he could call to help them. A lot of hunters he knew were dead, some killed in the war in Sumner, and others were entangled with their own demons, literally and figuratively. Alcoholism was an epidemic in his line of work.

He glanced at Daeva and wondered if she would fight against her own. Did she harbor any loyalty for her own kind? Did she have family? Friends?

"What's it like in hell?" he asked, before he could think better of it.

She opened her eyes and stared at him. "Are you asking to bother me so I can't sleep, or do you really want to know?"

"I want to know."

Tucking the blanket tighter over her shoulder, she closed her eyes again. At first, Quinn thought she wasn't going to answer him, but then she started to talk.

"The stories of fire and brimstone are true. Everything stinks to high heaven of sulfur. It's always hot in the honeycomb."

"The honeycomb?"

"Yeah, it's shaped like that. Many levels that open up to the center, which is the fiery pit. The place where souls are tortured for an eternity. Doesn't matter where you go, that's always there. It's a daily reminder that hell exists. You can smell the burned flesh and hear the strangled cries of tortured souls 24/7." She shuddered under the blanket.

"I can't imagine."

"No. You can't."

"Do you have your own…ah, place?"

"Yes, it's like a small apartment. I have a few luxuries, like books, and my goblin friends Loir and her brother Klix. They take care of me. I'm luckier than most because of my level two status. Most demons, those in the lower levels, live in squalor, in dormitories, I guess you'd call them. All scrambling for scraps of food and comfort.

"It's what I see and hear every day that torments me,

though. The stench of burning flesh and the screams of the damned can really get to a girl, you know? Thankfully I'm not forced to participate anymore. I did my time in the pits."

He stared at her, unsure of what to say. He had no idea what it was truly like in hell. There had always been stories, he'd even heard some accounts from other hunters, but obviously those had been lies. He wasn't sure exactly what he thought demons did in hell, but he certainly never thought of it like a prison for them. The souls that were condemned there certainly, but not its residents.

She opened her eyes and he witnessed the horror in them. "Now you know why I would do anything not to be in that…hell." She rolled over on the bed, wrapping herself tightly in the blanket like a cocoon. "If you'll excuse me, I need to sleep."

He watched her for a few minutes more before setting his blade and whetstone on the table, then standing. He had to get some air. The room had gotten progressively stifling and uncomfortable as she talked. He was having trouble breathing.

Sliding a knife into his belt sheath, he grabbed the key and left, shutting the door quietly behind him. Just outside, he took in some deep breaths of the fresh, untainted air.

He walked around the motel trying to shake the images Daeva's words had planted in his mind. In his lifetime, he'd seen a lot of death and destruction and horror but nothing compared to what she'd experienced every day of her life. For more years than he could even comprehend. To be forced to live with that, in that, and have no escape.

He stopped walking and took in another deep breath. Would he do whatever he could to escape that situation? Lie? Cheat? Steal? Possess? Hell, yeah. He had no doubt.

And the only escape afforded a demon was possession. He understood that now. He understood why Daeva had chosen to possess Rachel for so long. Like a woman in hiding from an abusive husband, she had escaped and hidden from her tormentor. Which was her origin. Hell.

By the time he made it back around to the motel room, he was tired. The last few days were catching up with him. Daeva had been right that he needed rest, as well. But he couldn't go back into the room. There was this needling sensation in his gut. And he was pretty sure it was guilt. A feeling he didn't really want to deal with right now.

So, instead of facing it, he opened the car's back door and crawled in. He settled his head on the armrest and shut his eyes. He'd deal with it all later, but right now he just wanted some peace.

Chapter 11

A knock on the car window jolted him awake. Stretching, Quinn sat up and looked at Daeva, who was smiling at him through the backseat window. He bounced across the seat and, opening the door, slid out of the car.

She handed him a coffee she'd obviously gotten from the restaurant. "Morning, sunshine."

He just grunted at her and took a needful sip of hot coffee. It chased away some of the haunting images he still had in his head.

"You don't look so good. Did you get any sleep?"

"Some."

"Why didn't you sleep in the room?"

He gave her a look. "You hogged the whole bed."

"Oh." She shrugged. "Sorry about that."

"Yeah, I'm pretty sure you're not too sorry."

She gave him a saucy grin. "You'd be right." She went around to the trunk, popped it and tossed their bags inside. "I already checked us out. So we're ready to go." She opened the passenger door and slid in.

After three hours on the road they'd edged closer to the border crossing. Quinn looked at Daeva casually flipping through a fashion magazine she'd gotten earlier at the motel shop.

"You never did explain to me how you plan to get across the border without a passport or any type of ID."

"Drop me off before the border crossing. I'll get across."

He was silent for a moment, considering that. Was she trying to ditch him? Trying to wiggle her way out of their deal?

As if reading his thoughts, she said, "I can't leave you, remember? I'm bound to you."

"How are you going to get across?"

"I think I can still be invisible. No one will see me. I'll meet you on the other side. Just pull off the road about half a mile from the crossing."

Quinn wasn't so sure about the plan but he couldn't think of an alternative. He had to trust that she would do as she said. He did bind her to him during the ritual, but that didn't mean she couldn't take her sweet time in showing back up.

"Okay. I need to eat and use the bathroom, anyway."

"We should probably fill up, too."

After another ten minutes, Quinn pulled the car off the road and into a gas station. As he went inside, she pumped the gas.

He used the facilities, thankful for a reprieve from Daeva. He had a lot of conflicting emotions racing around inside. It proved difficult to consolidate the woman he'd loved for years with the demon-ness he'd vowed to hate. That hate was quickly fading away.

So used to everything being black and white, Quinn only saw human good, demon bad. There was no middle ground. But that had started to change when his sister, Ivy, had fallen in love with a cambion. Ronan was half-human, half-demon and completely in love with Ivy. He'd sacrificed everything he'd ever wanted in life for her.

Quinn had even grown to like the guy, for that sacrifice alone. He'd never admit it to Ronan or Ivy, but he wouldn't put up a fight at all if they decided to get married.

He was starting to realize that just because someone was a demon didn't automatically make them evil or bad or wrong. And that thinking messed up everything he'd worked out about Daeva over the past few years. Seeing her, being with her, respecting her, messed it up even more.

As he stood in line to pay for the gas and two sub sandwiches, he watched Daeva as she finished filling the tank and set the nozzle back in the cradle. The light played across her hair, making it shine like newly minted copper pennies. She lifted her face to the sun and a smile spread her lips. Not for the first time, Quinn thought about capturing those lips with his own. He wondered if she would taste the same, feel the same in his arms.

She turned her head and their gazes met through the window. Her smile widened. His gut churned and he returned his focus to the cashier ringing up his purchases.

He had to force himself to remember that this was not a road trip to Vegas. Daeva was not the woman he fell in love with six years ago. This was strictly a business arrangement. He needed the chest and she knew where it was. It was that simple. He had to stop his emotions from complicating the situation.

Just because he sympathized with her desire to be out of hell didn't absolve her from past mistakes. He supposed it wasn't her actual possession that had angered him, it was that she never trusted him enough to tell him.

Resolved to keep his emotions about the past and present in check, he grabbed the subs and headed back to the car.

They ate and drove in silence the rest of the way. About a half mile from the border crossing, Quinn pulled over to the side of the road.

"I'm not keen on this plan," he said.

"Neither am I. I'm not a big fan of hiking through the wilderness. But it's not like I have Jedi mind tricks. I lost my mind mojo when you bound me to this plane and to you."

"But you still have your invisibility cloak?"

Friday nights had been their movie night. Daeva had a penchant for sci-fi films and Harry Potter.

She smiled. "Sort of. Enough that I can get by unnoticed. If someone was specifically looking for me, a demon named Daeva, well, then I'd stick out like a sore thumb."

"Okay. Once I'm through, I'll pull over to the side of the road. I'll pretend I'm having a picnic in the great Canadian outdoors."

She went to open the door, then looked at him. "You know, I'm more worried about how you're getting across. Last time I remember, Quinn Strom had a warrant or two out for his arrest."

He held up a passport. "That's why I'm Todd Sheppard today."

She laughed. "You stole that sorcerer's identity?"

"Yup. Years ago. Believe it or not he's squeaky clean and even pays his taxes ahead of time."

She shook her head, but he could tell she was extremely amused by the turn of events.

"Stay safe," she said.

"You, too."

She slid out and shut the door. Before any of the people in the other vehicles coming up the highway could spot her, she dashed into the thicket of trees. He saw one flash of red through the greenery, and then she was gone.

The line of vehicles at the border stop wasn't long. Twenty minutes and Quinn was pulling up to the guard post. He rolled down his window and handed his passport to the uniformed woman inside.

She took it, scanned the number, looked at the computer screen, then at him. "Where are you headed, Mr. Sheppard?"

"Kelowna."

"What is the purpose of your visit?"

"Pleasure. Taking a little vacation. Going to do some camping."

She glanced into the back of the vehicle, likely spying the backpack and gear. She looked back at him for a long moment before turning back to the screen. She typed for a minute, then with his passport in hand, she stood.

"Please pull up into one of those stalls, sir."

"Is there some problem?"

"Just do it, sir."

Heart thudding, Quinn drove the car forward and parked in front of a long glass-and-brick building. Something was definitely wrong. He could've been pulled out randomly from the long line of cars, certainly, but he didn't think so. There was something in the way the officer had looked at him. And he'd swear he saw a slight smirk on her lips and a flash of inky black in her eyes.

Chapter 12

Daeva was wearing the wrong footwear for hiking through the woods. Already her feet hurt and she'd only been walking for forty minutes. Through the trees, she could see the immigration building and the lineup of vehicles leading to it.

She looked for Quinn but couldn't see the car. He'd probably already gone through. She just hoped his passport held up. Using another person's identity was risky, to say the least. Maybe that person had just gotten arrested for assault or murder. Using their ID then would be a huge mistake.

But it wouldn't have surprised Daeva if Quinn had kept records on the sorcerer. The exorcist was usually thorough when it came to his job, which really was his life.

Because of that, it had always surprised her that Quinn had never realized she'd been possessing Rachel's body. It had taken her moment of truth to reveal her secret to him. Maybe love had blinded him to the truth.

She supposed, in retrospect, she shouldn't have been surprised when he reacted the way he did. She'd been foolish to think that he'd loved her enough to overlook the fact that she was a demon living in a human vessel. Obviously, love had made *her* delusional.

Daeva kicked a rock out of her way as she tramped through the trees. She stepped onto a rotted log and got stuck, her boot heel wedged inside. Frustrated, she wrenched her leg, trying to pull her foot out. It didn't come at first, then let go with an audible snap. She looked down and saw she'd broken the heel right off her boot.

"Perfect," she grunted.

She continued the trek through the trees, limping on the broken heel, which made it that much more difficult to walk through the brush. As she passed, the tip of a gnarled branch snagged a strand of her hair and pulled it from her ponytail. She stopped to put it back in place.

As she pulled the elastic from her hair, a sense of dread washed over her. Swinging around, she stared into the woods. Was an animal stalking her? She felt as though something was deathly wrong. Her gut clenched into a tight ball.

Her gaze moved over the trees, stopping briefly on a chipmunk chattering and a robin feeding her young in the nest she'd built high in the trees. Then she looked at the building separating the two countries. A cold fist wrapped around her heart and squeezed until she couldn't breathe. Something was wrong. Quinn was in trouble. Like the cold, she could sense it all the way to her bones.

She smoothed her hair back into a tight ponytail and stepped out of the trees. After mumbling a quick incantation, Daeva moved out onto the road. The quick spell made her unseen. Not quite invisible. She could be seen if someone was looking for her. But to those who weren't, she was like a shadow that moves in the corner of a person's eye. There, but not quite.

Before she made her way across the tarmac, she took off her boots. It would be easier to go barefoot. She moved around the vehicles slowly creeping forward to the crossing gate. A young child in a baby seat reached for her through the open window as she passed. Children could see more than most adults.

"Hi." The little boy waved as she went past his window.

Daeva turned to him and put her finger to her lips. "Shhh."

His smile faded and he tucked his arm back into the car.

As she neared the gate, she spotted their car in the lot. So Quinn had obviously been stopped. But why? She knew he would've been extremely careful when talking to the immigration officer. So that meant either Mr. Todd Sheppard had done something wrong and his passport had been flagged, or worse, someone knew where they were headed and why.

When she reached the car, she opened the back door and grabbed both of Quinn's bags. They instantly became as invisible as she was. She was surprised they hadn't been confiscated. If this had been a normal inspection, the officers would've taken them inside to be searched. Obviously, this wasn't a normal inspection.

Bags in hand, she went around to the side of the building. She unzipped one. There had to be something inside that could help her. There were clothes, two knives, some holy water ampoules and what looked like two smoke bombs. Perfect.

She snagged the holy water and the canisters, settling them into her jacket pockets. She had a feeling they would come in handy. Setting her shoulders, she took a deep breath, opened the door to the customs building, determined to find Quinn and bust him out.

Chapter 13

There were only two pieces of furniture in the small, dreary room: the folding metal chair Quinn sat in and the cold metal table in front of him. The chair was uncomfortable, but he figured that was its purpose.

Without any explanation, he'd been led to the room, told to sit and wait. He'd asked a million questions, like why was he being detained, and what this was all about. But the officer remained stoic and tight-lipped.

Basically he knew he was up shit creek without a paddle. He didn't even have his bags. The only thing on him was a small silver knife strapped to his ankle and a small ampoule of holy water in his front pants pocket. He sensed he'd need both of those things soon enough. Because he was pretty certain the officer in charge was possessed.

The door opened and said officer walked in. She still had that little smirk on her ruddy, pinched face. It was the kind of look that said she knew everything and that he'd better be afraid.

She stood on the other side of the table and leaned forward, leering at him. "So, Mr. Strom, where exactly are you going?"

"I'm sorry. I think you have me confused with someone else. My name's Todd Sheppard."

Smiling, the officer shook her head. "I don't think so." She leaned even farther. "You see, I know the sniveling little sorcerer. And you ain't him." Inky black bled into her brown eyes and her wide grin grew maniacal and grotesque.

Yup, she was definitely possessed.

He had to play it cool if he wanted to get out of here unscathed. As if interested in what she had to say, Quinn also leaned forward. The movement gave him a better chance to get the holy water ampoule out of his pocket unnoticed.

"I told you, I'm just going camping."

She sniffed. "You don't really seem like the outdoorsy type."

"Oh, I am. I love it. Clean air, surrounded by nature. It's awesome."

"We know you recently summoned Daeva, the Seductress of Shadows, and temporarily released her from hell. For what purpose?"

Quinn smiled. "We're in a relationship. Didn't you know? Have been for years. I missed her, is all."

This had the guard straightening. She almost looked nervous. "Then where is Daeva?"

His fingers gripped the ampoule in his pocket. He slowly drew it out, careful not to give his intentions away. "Oh, she's probably around here somewhere." He hoped.

He didn't want to entertain the thought that Daeva may have tried to bail on him. But it was there at the back of his mind, regardless. She'd have reason to. He hadn't been the kindest person toward her. He wouldn't blame her if she wanted to leave him here to the torturous hands of these demons. She couldn't, of course, because of the binding. She would be compelled to stay close by. Whether she did anything to get him out would be another thing altogether.

"If you don't tell me why you are crossing into Canada, I'm going to hurt you."

He grinned. "Do your worst."

But when the officer produced a taser from her belt, his smile faded. That was the last thing he'd expected. A few well-placed punches to the face and body he could handle; even a few deep cuts were tolerable. But electricity running through his body was a whole different matter. He'd been tasered before and it was awful.

"Last chance, Strom, to be reasonable."

He palmed the holy water then spread his arms out wide to the sides. "Hey, I've never been a reasonable guy. You should know that by now."

She picked up the taser and aimed but Quinn was faster.

He threw the glass vial hard at the officer's face. It

broke on impact, splashing holy water into her eyes and across her cheek. Tendrils of black smoke instantly rose from her burning flesh.

Shrieking, she raised her hands to her eyes. This afforded Quinn time to bolt from the chair and get to the door. But when he cranked on the handle it was locked.

"Shit!"

He looked back at the possessed officer as she continued to screech and wipe at her burning eyes. She had to have a key.

Heart thudding, he raced back to her and pulled at her belt, trying to get it off. She slapped and clawed at him as he unbuckled the strap.

Nails raked across his cheek and forearm, leaving deep divots. He worked past the pain and continued to struggle with the clasp until he had it undone and was pulling the belt out from the loops. The keys hung from a ring latched to one metal ring.

"You're dead, Quinn Strom," she shrieked, her voice guttural and deep. The demon inside was pissed off and trying to get out of its host.

Instead of staying to debate that statement, Quinn found the right key and unlocked the door. He bolted out into the corridor just as a smoking metal canister came sailing through the air toward his head.

"Duck!"

Quinn dropped to his knees. The canister skimmed the top of his head. It landed just outside the interrogation room door, billowing thick white smoke into the air. Hand over his nose and mouth, he jumped back to his feet and ran down the corridor toward Daeva, who waited for him, the second smoke bomb in her hand ready to go.

When he reached her side, she tossed him one of his bags. "Let's get the hell out of here. There are two more possessed coming down the hall."

He wrapped the bag strap around his shoulders, then he noticed she was barefoot. "Ah, what happened to your boots?"

"Long story. Tell you later." She turned to move down the hall toward the main doors. Shaking his head, he followed her out.

Their escape went mostly unhindered. They didn't run into anyone until they reached the front doors. A young female officer was the only thing between them and freedom.

"Stop right here." She held up her taser, her hand noticeably shaking.

"Look," Daeva said, "just let us go. If you don't, you're going to get hurt. I really don't want to hurt you. I'm trying to turn over a new leaf."

Quinn put his hand out toward the girl, who really couldn't be any older than twenty. "This isn't your fight. Just turn away and let us go."

She looked from Daeva to Quinn then back again. "This is my first day of work." Her voice shook.

Quinn could tell she was scared out of her mind. "Don't make it your last. We're not worth it. Trust me. We're not terrorists."

Tears brimming in her eyes, she lowered the taser.

"Thank you," Daeva said, as she brushed past the guard to reach the door.

Quinn followed, but paused with his hand on the door. He glanced back at the young officer. "What size are your shoes?"

"What?" she stammered.

"Your shoes. What size?"

"Ah, seven."

"Give them to me, please."

Daeva came to his side. "What are you doing? We need to get the hell out of here."

"Getting you some shoes."

She gave him a small smile as the officer toed off her shoes. "Wow, Quinn, who knew you were such a romantic."

He grabbed up the shoes and handed them to her. "Don't ever say I never got you anything."

Daeva laughed, then, clutching the shoes to her chest, burst out the door with Quinn right on her bare heels.

Chapter 14

As soon as they were clear of the building, Daeva stopped to put the shoes on. She hated it that her heart thumped just a little bit harder because Quinn had stopped to get her a pair. He probably had no idea how endearing that was. He'd likely been thinking about practicality, about how it would slow them up if she had to tiptoe her way through the woods.

Despite all that, she still found it cute, and it reminded her of the old Quinn. The one she'd been in love with. The tender, compassionate man who used to bring her flowers just because he was thinking of her.

Once she had the shoes on, they sprinted into the trees separating the two countries. They'd have to make a run for it. Stay in the trees as long as possible and then reach the town of Osoyoos, where they could steal transportation and get the hell out of there.

Quinn had his compass out. "The town is northeast of here. We should be able to make it in an hour." He chucked the compass back into his pack. "All right. Let's move."

He ran at a quick, directed pace. Daeva was able to keep stride. Fortunately the shoes were sturdy and comfortable, even without socks, and didn't give her blisters the way her boots had. It was funny to think of a demon with blisters on her feet. She did live in a fiery pit of despair. The word out there was that demons were indestructible. But that was so untrue. Especially for one bound to the Earth and to an exorcist. Daeva could suffer just as much as everyone else. In some ways, even more. She tired more quickly and had been healing more slowly. But she couldn't tell Quinn.

After about twenty minutes of solid running, Quinn stopped to drink from his canteen. He offered it to her and she took it, drinking gratefully. He had to pry it from her hand to stop her from emptying it.

"Don't drink too much or you'll get sick."

"Damn, I hate this thirst and hunger all the time. I'd totally forgotten how much sustenance a human body needs to survive."

"Yeah, it sucks sometimes." He took another swig, then capped the canteen.

"So, what happened in there?"

"The officer at the gate was possessed. It was as if she'd been waiting for me."

"Could have been. Although I'd imagine there are possessed guards at every border stop."

"They knew I'd summoned and released you."

"Of course. We are tagged, to an extent. No one leaves hell without someone noticing."

"But they don't know where we're going or why."

"Well, that's something at least."

He looked at her, searching her face. "You never told anyone about the chest?"

"No. Not in one hundred years."

"Why did you tell me?"

She met his gaze straight on, hoping he saw the feelings she still had for him. She couldn't deny that they continued to exist. "Because I trusted you." She shrugged, lightening the mood. "It was a momentary lack of judgment. I'm sure it won't happen again."

He smiled. "Oh, it probably will."

"Yeah." She nodded, her lips twitching up. "Probably."

He stared at her in the eyes for a long moment. "Thanks for coming for me."

"It looked like you were doing fine all on your own."

He lifted his chin. "Yeah, I was, but it was nice to have backup just in case."

She returned his smile. "You're welcome."

Decidedly uncomfortable, Quinn shifted his weight from foot to foot as she surveyed the trees behind him. "I don't hear dogs or anything. Maybe we're in the clear."

"I wouldn't count on that. They'll use demon magic

to track us. Use the animals around us to keep eyes on the prize."

He rubbed a hand over the stubble on his chin.

"So what's the plan when we reach town?" she asked.

"Steal a vehicle and get back on the road."

"I think we should stay off the main highway and out of hotels. Either we sleep in the car or in a tent."

He nodded. "I agree." He checked the compass direction again. "Okay, let's keep moving. Town should just be over that rise."

Quinn had almost been right about the location of the community. It was over the rise, then down into a valley near a lake. It took them close to another hour before they reached the town limits.

Osoyoos was a small town and definitely a tourist destination, which totally worked for them as neither looked like they were locals. They made their way downtown to scout out vehicles.

As they strolled the main street searching for the greatest concentration of cars, Daeva was conscious of Quinn looking at her. Shifting the duffel bag to her other shoulder, she turned to him.

"What? You keep looking at me."

"You kind of stand out."

"What? Why?" She stopped to look at her reflection in a store window. "Is there something on my face?" Despite a dirt smudge on her cheek she couldn't see anything out of the ordinary. She rubbed at it as she turned to face Quinn again.

"Everyone's staring at you."

She frowned but did start to notice that almost every

guy who walked by did a double take. A few women did, as well.

"Well, I'm sorry. This is my face. This is what I look like. I can't help it."

He chuckled. "You almost sound sad for being so pretty."

She stopped rubbing at her cheek. "You think I'm pretty?"

Quinn dropped his gaze and started walking again. She had to rush to keep up. "Let's just find a car and get out of here."

"Hey, you're the one that made a point of it."

"Yeah, because we can hardly blend in when you look like…"

She put her hand on her hip. "Look like what?"

He stopped and glared at her, as if it was all her fault. "Like sex on a stick, okay?"

"Oh." She was a bit taken aback by his anger. He sounded so miserable that he found her attractive. It was almost comical.

She pulled the elastic from her hair. "Well, does this help?" She put her hands in her hair and mussed it all up.

He watched her with interest, then frowned more deeply, his eyes going dark. "No. That's worse."

Desperate, she looked around and spied a tourist shop with a few racks standing just outside their open door. She went to it, grabbed a baseball cap with a Canadian flag on it and put it on.

"There. Does that make a difference?"

"No, now you just look like a hot girl in a bad hat." He shook his head and grabbed the hat off her head to put it back. "Let's just get off the main drag and find a parking lot where we can jack a vehicle."

"Fine," she huffed, following him down the sidewalk.

Leave it to Quinn to make her looks a detriment to their mission. As if she had any control over them. Didn't he realize that his sexy darkness made it difficult for her to concentrate as well? He should be apologizing to her for having the perfect ass and beautiful shoulders that she always wanted to sink her teeth into. And lips that made her melt with every thought of them being on her skin, kissing her, nibbling on her. It was totally unfair that he made her quiver with possibilities. How could she focus on the mission when all she wanted to do was sink into him, to lose herself completely in everything about him?

When he noticed she wasn't right beside him, Quinn stopped walking and turned around. "Are you coming or what?"

"Yeah, I'm coming. Quit being so damned bossy."

They found a parking lot behind the strip of mom-and-pop businesses. There were about fifteen vehicles parked in the small, cramped space. Some of them were for customers and others for employees. Their best bet was an employee vehicle that wouldn't be discovered missing as quickly. Hopefully not until the end of the day. By then, they would be long gone.

Daeva didn't think the choices looked all that promising: two trucks, both having seen better days, one Smart Car, one Toyota with anti-theft on it and a motorcycle. If their circumstances were different, she would've voted for the bike, but they still needed to get some camping gear and there was no way it would fit on the back with the two of them. Same went for the Smart Car, however adorable it was. That basically left the two pickups.

"I vote for the blue one. It doesn't look as grungy as the other one."

"Stealers can't be choosers," Quinn said with a grin.

She knew he totally loved this part of the job. She suspected if he hadn't been an exorcist and demon hunter, doing the good work, he would have ended up some sort of criminal, likely a car thief. She remembered how he was when he was out doing a job. He'd always return home amped up and wanting to bury himself in her for hours.

After being together for a few months, he'd told her about what he did. She of course had already known. All demons, topside and downside, knew who Quinn Strom was. But she'd put on a good act about being surprised. She'd just been so happy that he'd trusted her enough to tell her. It was around then when she'd fallen in love with him.

"Keep a lookout," he told her as he slid a metal jimmy out of his duffel bag.

She watched the area for any sign of trouble as Quinn slid the metal bar between the window and the doorjamb. After a few seconds, she heard the telltale clicking sound of a lock being disengaged. She turned around to see Quinn sliding into the cab on his back so he could break the ignition panel and hotwire the vehicle. It didn't take him long to get it started. He was certainly skilled in the criminal arts.

Sitting up he glanced at her and mouthed, *Let's go.*

With one last cursory glance down the alley, Daeva went around to the passenger side, opened the door and jumped in.

"I saw a sporting goods store at the edge of town when we first came in. We can get the gear we need there."

"Do you have enough money?" she asked.

"There should be about three grand in that bag. I also have four credit cards, in case of emergencies."

She smiled, he was like a Boy Scout—always prepared.

They reached the store without incident. Once inside, Quinn looked to her. "This is your excursion, what do we need?"

"A tent, sleeping bags, flashlight, food, water, proper hiking boots, warm jackets, gloves and probably a pickax."

He lifted an eyebrow. "A pickax?"

She nodded. "Trust me, we'll need it."

"So, how far north are we going?"

"Far enough that, although it's summer, we're going to need those jackets."

Without another word, Quinn grabbed a cart and started tossing things in.

By the time they were done, they had a truckload of gear, including a couple of backpacks to carry it all in. Quinn's duffel bags wouldn't do for where they needed to go.

When they were back in the truck and on the road, Quinn tossed her a map of British Columbia. "Okay, navigator, where to?"

She unfolded it on her lap and stared at all the lines and dots. She didn't need a map to know where they were going, but she knew it would help Quinn in a way, to ease his mind and give him back some control. She traced a finger over the paper, up and up, and stopped it on the northernmost city dot.

"Fort Nelson. Head there. It'll be the last populated spot before we head even farther north."

She folded the map so their path could be easily read. Then she handed it back to Quinn.

He looked at it, then nodded. "Okay, now I can see where we need to go."

"You're welcome."

"I didn't say thank you."

"Yeah, but I know you wanted to and you were just being shy about it."

He laughed. "Oh, and you're so sure of what I want?"

It was an old argument and she wondered if he realized he'd settled comfortably into it. As she met his gaze, she toed off her shoes and put her feet up on the dash. "For some things, yup."

His eyes darkened as he took in her bare feet, then his gaze traveled the length of her leg up to her shoulders, then to her face. His longing for her was plain. She just wondered if he planned to do anything about it.

He shifted on the seat, clearly uncomfortable, then put his focus back on the road. The moment ended. "Settle in, because it's going to be a long haul. Twelve hours, at least, especially since we have to stay off the main roads."

Daeva cracked the window, letting in a warm breeze. She lifted her face to it as it fluttered over her skin. "Hey, I've been to hell, remember? I can endure anything."

Chapter 15

As Quinn drove he couldn't help but sneak looks at Daeva every once in a while. She was an easy woman to look at but his interest went beyond her physical appearance. He was starting to see the true person inside. And for the first time in years he questioned whether he had made a mistake when he'd exorcised her to hell without getting the whole story first. Would he have listened, though?

After two hours of his occasional glances, she turned and met his gaze directly. "Is there something you want to say?"

"No." He put his eyes back on the road.

"Quinn, I know you'll hate hearing it, but I know you pretty well and you definitely have something on your mind."

He sighed. "I don't hate it, exactly. It's just…"

"That I'm a demon and you're an exorcist, and like oil and water we don't mix?"

"No, I was going to say, that it's embarrassing to have someone know you so…"

"Intimately?"

He nodded. "Yeah."

"Well, technically we were together for three years."

"I know."

That had her gaping and it made him smile.

"So you admit it? You're not denying that I was the woman you were with?"

He shook his head. He was tired of denying it. It was exhausting fighting with the inevitable. "No, I'm not denying it."

She smirked. "Well, that's at least some progress. Maybe there is hope that you'll actually apologize to me for sending me back to hell."

He'd opened his mouth to do just that when he caught something in the rearview mirror. The local law.

"Shit. We've got company."

Daeva whipped around to look out the back window. "Do you think they made us?"

Before he could answer, the blue-and-red lights flashed on.

"Looks like we have our answer."

"What are you going to do?"

"Well, I'm definitely not going to pull over."

Daeva's fingers glowed. "I could blast him."

"Yeah and your little trick will be recorded on his dash cam for the whole world to see."

"We don't have many options, Quinn. Maybe humanity should know about demons."

"No blasting. Not unless absolutely necessary."

"I wasn't going to hurt him, just slow him down."

He sped up a little. The RCMP car following close behind, its light flashing incessantly.

"Can you aim for the tires? Melt them or something?"

"I can certainly try."

She rolled down the window and shimmied her body outside, so she was hanging half in and half out. "Keep the truck straight. I don't want to miss."

A booming voice came from the police car's speaker. "Please get back in the vehicle."

Canadians were so polite, Quinn thought.

Keeping the wheels straight, Quinn watched in the rearview mirror as Daeva launched a glowing ball of fire at the car behind them. The burning sphere hit the front right tire. It was a perfect shot.

Even from the distance, Quinn could see the surprise on the officer's face as the vehicle careened to the right, no longer supported by a tire. That tire was now a puddle of rubber stuck to the road. Before the vehicle flipped, the officer managed to get it stopped in the ditch.

"Nice shot," Quinn said, then put his attention back onto the road in front of them.

As they came over the rise, it was obvious they were far from safe.

Three more RCMP cars, lights on, blocked the road

ahead. Three officers stood behind the hoods, weapons raised.

"I'm going to take a giant leap here and say this is about more than a stolen truck," Daeva said, even as her fingertips sparked with newly developed fire.

"You think?" Quinn slowed the truck, different scenarios racing through his head. None of them ended well.

"What do you want to do?"

He scanned the surroundings. Fortunately they were the only civilians on the long, straight stretch of road. Last thing he wanted was to get a bunch of innocent bystanders involved in this mess. Trees and farmland stretched out from the road like a green-and-yellow blanket.

"Hang on." Cranking the wheel to the left, Quinn took the truck off the road, bouncing across the ditch and into a patch of mustard plants. He gunned it and ploughed through a barbed-wire fence. As he drove across the field, he glanced in the rearview mirror to see two of the three cars giving chase. Although they weren't four-by-fours, they were catching up.

"We won't outrun them." Daeva pointed to a line of trees to the right. "Go there. We can get away from them on foot. Plus, it's getting dark and I'm the only one who can see in the dark. We'll have the advantage."

Quinn did as she suggested and jerked the wheel to the right so they were barreling toward a copse of pine trees. He stepped on the gas, pushing the truck past its limits. He could hear the engine whine, struggling to keep them at this speed. Then the right tire hit a buried tree stump hard, sending the truck tilting to the left.

To keep them upright, he turned the wheel and stepped on the brake. The tail end of the truck swung to the left and smashed into a tree trunk just outside the forest.

Knocked astray, Quinn hit his head against the side window. It was hard enough to crack the glass and send a jolt through his head. Pain exploded behind his left eye.

But he didn't have time to coddle himself before Daeva was yanking him out of the cab. "Come on!"

At first he was dizzy, a bit disoriented, but Daeva's constant pushing and prodding snapped him out of it.

"We need to get the gear."

She led him to the truck bed, then jumped in and tossed a full backpack at him. He caught it, and hooked it over his shoulder just as she jumped out with the other strapped to her shoulders. Together, they dashed into the trees as the two police cars stopped nearby.

Without looking back, Quinn ran, dodging broken tree stumps and jumping over fallen logs. Dusk had settled in, casting an eerie glow through the trees. Soon it would be difficult for him to see well. He glanced at Daeva who was in step with him, leaping and avoiding obstacles easily.

"You lead," he called to her.

With a quick nod, she moved in front of him, setting a pace that was quick and sprightly. He hoped he could keep up. It would do them no good if he lagged behind or, God forbid, fell on his face.

As Daeva led them deeper into the forest, he risked a glance over his shoulder to see if they were being followed by the RCMP officers. He sighed with relief when he couldn't see any movement behind them. But that didn't necessarily mean they had gotten away or were safe. They had to push it hard and long before they could take a breather. He had no doubt that it wasn't just the police chasing them. The pursuit was Cabal or demon motivated, just as it had been back at the border. They were being tracked by unnatural means.

He didn't know how long they'd been running before the light completely disappeared, but it wasn't too long. His head still throbbed, which didn't help his eyesight any. It was more instinct than anything else that saved him from plowing into a rotting tree leaning sideways. He dodged it, his shoulder brushing the bark, and kept going.

Daeva was a good five feet in front of him. But he was having trouble focusing on her. Fortunately she slowed a little when she came out into a clearing. Maybe they could stop a moment so he could have a quick drink of water. His lungs burned with exertion.

Just as he rushed into the clearing, Daeva was turning toward him, her hand thrust out. He knew she meant for him to stop, but it was too late. Momentum took him forward and he tripped and rolled down the incline to the stream below them.

"Quinn!"

Her voice followed him down into the icy water. It was as if a lightning bolt zapped his system when he landed face-first. Instinctually he pushed up with his hands and knees to get his face out. The stream wasn't very deep so he was able to get to his feet easily. But he was soaked right through and already starting to shiver from the chill in the air.

Daeva was beside him in a minute, boots in the water, helping him out. "Are you hurt?" Her gaze searched his face, then his body, looking for injuries.

"I'm okay. Just wet and cold."

"We have to keep going. I don't think we are far enough yet."

He nodded, knowing she was right. "Go. I'll follow."

"Are you sure?"

"Yeah. What else can we do? It's not like you can carry me." He meant it as a joke, but the way she was eyeing him made him nervous. "Hell, no."

"Don't be a baby. I won't tell anyone. It'll be our little secret." Her voice was even, but he caught the little smirk on her lips.

"Daeva, I swear I'll…"

She put her hand up. "Okay. Okay." She smiled. "You can't say I didn't care enough to suggest it." She wiped a hand over his face, brushing the wet hair from his eyes. "Just a little farther and we'll be able to rest."

She turned on her boot heel and crossed the stream to the other side. After adjusting his pack, Quinn followed her back into the trees, cold, wet but a little lighter inside. Her touch still tingled on his skin.

Chapter 16

They ran for another two hours but Daeva could see that Quinn couldn't keep up much longer. Even as he ran, she could see his body shaking with the cold that had probably crept into his bones. They needed to stop, make camp, and get him warm or he'd become hypothermic.

Over the next rise, she stopped in a small clearing. Bending over, she took in some deep breaths, curious that her body seemed to need them all of a sudden. Quinn stopped beside her, trying to do the same, but his chattering teeth impeded him.

"Why are we stopping?" he stammered.

She dumped her pack and dug through it for the small tent. "Because you're going to catch pneumonia or worse if we don't."

He didn't argue with her as she quickly put the tent together, which was a testament to how serious the situation was. And the fact that he knew not to disagree.

Once the tent was up, she pulled out a down-filled sleeping bag. "Strip."

"What?"

"Take off your clothes. They're wet and you need to get dry."

She unzipped the tent and shoved the sleeping bag inside. When she stood back up, he was pulling off his shirt, his hands shaking violently.

"Get in the tent and take the rest off. I'll start a fire and dry your clothes out."

Without a word, he crawled into the tent. Two minutes later, his wet jeans, socks and shorts came flying out. She found a branch to hang them on and proceeded to build a small fire beneath.

As she broke twigs apart and gathered moss and dry leaves together in a pile, she tried not to think about Quinn naked in the tent. Picturing his body, especially with no clothes on, never failed to ignite a fire deep inside her belly. Quinn was exquisitely crafted, with long, lean limbs, washboard abs, a strong, smooth chest and powerful shoulders. She loved big shoulders on a man. They were something substantial to sink her teeth into.

She shook the thought from her mind and concentrated on lighting the fire. She struck a match and held it to the dry moss and leaves. It smoldered and smoked but didn't ignite. She tried again, still no flames. Putting the matches aside she rubbed her right thumb and finger together. Soon, an orange glow emitted from her skin. She built a tiny sphere of red fire and rolled it into the kindling she'd gathered. In an instant, the leaves caught fire. A few seconds later, the twigs glowed, then flames licked upward. She sat bigger pieces of wood on the flames until she had a good fire going that wasn't going to go out anytime soon.

With that task completed, she turned toward the tent and wondered how Quinn was faring. Crouching, she unzipped the tent and stuck her head in.

"How are you doing?"

He didn't need to answer; she could see he couldn't talk because he was shaking so badly.

"Jesus, Quinn."

She crawled all the way in, took off her boots, then zipped up the tent flap. Quinn stared at her wide-eyed as she opened his sleeping bag.

"What the hell are you doing?"

"Getting you warm. Now shove over."

He did and she slid in next to him, zipping the bag so they were pressed right up against each other. Daeva wrapped her arms around his cold, shivering body and pressed herself into his back. She knew he wanted to protest, but she sensed her warmth was already seeping into him and he couldn't deny what his body needed.

"Relax," she said into his ear. "I'm not going to take advantage of you or anything." She nearly chuckled when she felt him relax.

Daeva spread her hands over his bare chest and pulled him tighter to her. His body should've been warming more quickly, but she feared her normal body heat wasn't enough. He was still shivering, his teeth chattering together loud enough to be heard outside the tent. She needed to do something extreme, something that Quinn wasn't going to like at all.

Lowering one of her hands to his stomach, she clamped her eyes shut and concentrated. She focused on the demon fire inside, and instead of making fire on her fingertips she focused on the heat she could create. Within seconds her skin flushed, heat rising to the surface in fiery waves.

Quinn squirmed against her. "Daeva," he whined. "What are you doing?"

"What needs to be done. Don't think about it and just accept it for once."

The heat increased in the sleeping bag and in the tent. It swelled quickly, causing Daeva to sweat. She wondered how upset he'd be if she stripped off her own clothes. Another five minutes of concentrating her fire, and Quinn's body stopped shaking.

"Better?" she asked.

He nodded.

She started to move her hands but he captured them with his own.

"Thank you, Daeva."

She smiled at the sincerity in his voice. Maybe they could finally overcome their past and become friends. To hope for more than that was beyond foolish. Quinn held on to his black-and-white morality too tightly.

"You're welcome," she murmured, then pressed a quick kiss to the back of his shoulder. She pulled her hands out from under his.

To do anything else would be wrong. Although

she wanted to keep touching him, to feel all of him, she knew it was the wrong time, wrong place. Quinn would never forgive her if she pressed him further. Even though she was sure he would gladly welcome her advances, she knew he would berate himself afterward. If they ever gave in to their desires, desire she knew Quinn felt as well, she didn't want any regrets on either side.

She knew he wanted her, but wasn't sure if he even liked her.

Before she could change her mind, she quickly unzipped the bag, slid out and did it up again. Besides, Quinn needed sleep if he was to fully heal. They still had a long journey ahead of them.

She brushed a hand over his hair. "Go to sleep, Quinn. I'll set up wards and keep watch." Before she could see the answering longing in his eyes, she crawled out of the tent.

Chapter 17

Quinn rolled over to watch her zip up the flap on the tent. Earlier he'd nearly turned and asked her to stay with him. Her touch had done more than just warm his body—it had ignited something deep inside him. Something hot and primal.

There was no doubt that physically she turned him on in all kinds of ways. Her eyes, her body, her voice even sent ripples of desire through him constantly. It was his mind and possibly his heart that stopped him from acting on those impulses. His reservations definitely stemmed from their past history, but no longer did he deny that Daeva had been the woman he'd fallen in love with. He understood now that she'd just been in a different shell. A different package. But he could see that she was definitely the same person, although three years would definitely change a person, even a demon.

And that was what gave him pause. Knowingly falling for a demon was not something he wanted to deal with. He had enough on his plate as it was.

Yawning, Quinn pulled the sleeping bag tighter around his body and shut his eyes. He was going to need all his strength to deal with what was to come. Nothing was going to be safe. Certainly not with Daeva involved.

Quinn didn't know what time it was when he climbed out of the tent, but by the pinkening of the sky he could see through the tree canopy, it was early in the morning. He'd brought the sleeping bag out with him since he was still naked.

He didn't see Daeva when he looked around. He peered into the surrounding trees but didn't spy her red hair anywhere. The fire was still going, so she was likely somewhere close.

His clothes hung on a branch above the smoking coals. He hopped over to them. Fortunately, they were dry. Grabbing the shorts he quickly shucked the sleeping bag and stepped into them. He pulled on his pants, socks and shirt.

The snap of a branch made him turn just in time to see Daeva standing nearby, a container of something in her hand. She gave him a wide, cheesy grin. Obviously, she'd been there to witness him put his clothes on.

He shook his head. "Did you just watch me get dressed?"

"Yup. I thought about disturbing you, but you looked

really cold, so I thought it better to wait until you were completely dressed."

That made him laugh as he plopped down on the sleeping bag and pulled on his boots. "Where did you go?" he asked as he tied his laces.

She showed him what was in the container. Plump, red raspberries. "Went to go pick some. Thought it would be a nice complement to the freeze-dried crap we have."

He took a handful and popped them into his mouth. They were sweet and juicy. "Did you stay out here the whole time I slept?"

She nodded, eating some berries herself.

"Did you get any sleep?"

"Nah. I walked around, did some pull-ups on that branch there." She pointed to a thick tree branch about seven feet up. "I sang campfire songs to myself, then made some stick people."

He glanced down at the fire and spied a bunch of odd looking stick figures made from acorns and twigs and leaves. Surprised, he looked back at Daeva.

She shrugged. "What? I had to keep my hands and mind busy."

Not commenting, he crouched and rolled up the sleeping bag tightly. "We need to move on. Do you think the road is safe to travel?"

She offered him the last of the fruit, then said, "To be honest, no. I think every cop will be on the look-out for us."

"We can't hike the rest of the way. It'll take us more days than I'd like to think about."

"Hitchhike?"

He shook his head. "No one's going to pick us up. Maybe you on your own, but definitely not me. And we still have to watch out for cops."

"Then what?"

"I don't know." He kicked at the bedroll, frustrated. They seemed to be at a dead end. He could really see only one option and that was to keep to the trees as much as possible and hike it up north. Maybe they'd find a ride in the next town and maybe they wouldn't. Right now it didn't look too promising, not with the RCMP looking for them.

"I might have a solution," Daeva offered.

Quinn looked at her. "What?"

"You're not going to like it."

"I don't like the thought of hiking for days so you might as well hit me with it."

"Teleportation."

"Come again? I don't think I heard you right."

"I know a spell that could teleport us from here to Fort Nelson."

"Demon magic?"

She nodded. "I imagine you hate demon magic, but it's an option."

He sighed, rubbing a hand over his face, scrubbing away the fatigue. "How far would it take us?"

"I could get us close to where we need to be."

"Why didn't you mention this before now?"

She dropped her gaze to the ground and kicked at the debris on the forest floor. "Because it's not a spell

I like doing. And it has its price." She glanced up and he saw a fierceness in her eyes.

He watched her for a long moment, taking her in, considering her. Trusting her. Then he said, "What do you need to get it done?"

"Your chalk, something purple, and blood."

"How much blood?"

She hesitated then said, "Enough to make a mess."

A half hour later, Daeva had finished chalking a series of symbols on a nearby tree trunk in a pentagram pattern. He recognized a couple, one for travel, the other for door, but the others he didn't know. And probably didn't want to know.

He studied them a minute longer, then studied her. She was nervous. He could see it in the way her hand trembled while she drew the symbols. She also tugged at her hair. It was a gesture he recognized from when they'd been together.

"Are you okay?" he asked, worried about her, worried about the spell she was going to cast.

He was concerned about what teleportation would do to him, traveling through a portal not made for human physiology. How would he come out on the other end? With his arm attached to his head?

She glanced at him, pulled at the strand of her hair again. Those few strands came out with her frequent tugging. Surprised, she looked at them then let them drift down to the forest floor.

"I'm good."

But he could plainly see she wasn't. She really looked afraid.

"Do you have the something purple?"

He handed her a small, square piece of cloth. He'd used it to clean his knives over the years. It had been his father's. She took it, nodding to him, likely knowing its significance and folded it to slip into her pocket.

"Now we need blood. Know how to make a snare?"

After several failed attempts, they managed to snare a young rabbit. It looked pretty scrawny but it didn't matter—it wasn't the meat they needed.

Daeva was quick and deft with the blade. Most women would be squeamish about gutting an animal but he supposed Daeva wasn't like most women. Or any woman for that matter.

She used what she needed, painting the blood onto the tree with her fingers. Once that was done, she reached into her pocket, took out the purple fabric and stuck it to the tree with the knife. When she was finished, she took a step back and reached with her hand for Quinn.

"Take my hand and hold on tight. Do not let go of me for any reason. Understand?"

He nodded, swallowing the lump of fear lodged in his throat. "What about our gear?"

"I can't bring it through. Just you and me." She squeezed his hand. "Are you ready for this?"

"No."

"Shut your eyes and don't open them." She gave him a smile. "Trust me. I won't let anything happen to you."

With that she spread out the fingers of her other

hand and pressed them to the tree trunk, each fingertip touching a symbol.

"Eo ire itum."

The air around him vibrated, then everything went dark.

It was as if he was being sucked through a straw by some huge, cosmic mouth. Quinn felt pulled on and yanked and pushed and manipulated through a series of narrow twisty passages. He tried not to think about it and just concentrated on the feel of Daeva's hand in his own.

The air they whizzed through was ice-cold, then sweltering, then ice-cold again, with each corner they twisted around. It took all Quinn had not to open his eyes. He suspected he didn't want to know exactly what they were moving through. His skin itched and burned from whatever tainted air touched him. Once they were through, he would find a way to have a shower.

As they continued being towed through the ether by some unseen force, Quinn couldn't keep his eyes closed any longer. His curiosity won out over his fear and he risked a look.

What he saw filled him with awe, not fear.

It was almost as if they were standing still with time and space whizzing by them on either side at lightning speed. He only got fleeting glimpses of things but he sensed he and Daeva weren't just moving through this reality but several of them at once. Realities he couldn't even begin to comprehend. It was amazing. He wondered if demons appreciated having this kind of knowledge and access to other worlds. What power that was to possess. His stomach churned watching it all go by.

Curious as to Daeva's comment on keeping his eyes closed, he turned her way and was dumbstruck by her appearance. He realized now why she'd told him to close his eyes. It wasn't the worlds they were spinning through that she thought would frighten him, but her.

She turned and met his gaze, her eyes as black and liquid as ink. "I told you not to look." Her voice was deep and guttural, but not entirely unpleasant.

Her hair swept around as if it were licks of fire, alive and aware. Her already pale skin glowed like blue flame. It was both alien and beautiful, and it made him want to reach out and run his fingertips along her arms and shoulders to feel the heat he was sure she was generating.

"Close your eyes, Quinn, don't look at me like this."

When she spoke he spied the tiny points of fangs in her mouth. For some that might have instilled fear but not for Quinn.

He thought she was exquisite in all her foreignness.

"You're beautiful, Daeva."

Her eyes widened in disbelief at that. It made him sad to see it. That she thought her true form so ugly she'd hidden it from him all along. Although he'd given her every reason to do so. He'd only shown her his prejudice against demons.

Then everything went black again, as if a shutter had snapped shut on his eyes.

And they appeared suddenly on a gravel road in the middle of a thick grouping of evergreen trees.

Quinn stumbled a little from the jarring vertigo caused by their sudden arrival but he succeeded in keeping on his feet. He looked over at Daeva just as she let go of his hand. She buckled like a rag doll. He caught her before she could hit the ground and laid her gently down on the grass beside the road. Her hair stuck to her sweat-slicked face. He brushed it off her forehead. She was burning up with a fever.

He now understood when she said there'd be a price to pay. This was it. Her. She was the price.

"Daeva, what can I do? What do you need?"

She blinked up at him, her pupils dilated. He wasn't even sure she was focusing on him. Smiling, she reached up with her hand and stroked it down his cheek.

"Blackbird," she murmured. Then her hand fell limp to her side and she passed out.

Quinn tried to revive her but it was no use. She was out. He stroked her face, unsure what to do for her. He knew he couldn't leave her out here; he had to get her somewhere safe and warm. A place he could nurse her back to health.

Tucking his hand under her legs, he lifted her into his arms and started down the road. Hopefully he'd come across a house, or a vehicle would come across him.

He'd walked for about an hour before his legs and arms started to feel the strain of carrying her. It wouldn't be long before he had to set her down for a rest. To make matters even worse, the gray clouds that had been swirling overhead opened up and hard, cold rain pounded down on them.

Nearing his breaking point, Quinn jostled Daeva in

his arms to get a better grip on her and that's when he spotted a small sign in the tall grass near the branching of a dirt driveway. It read Blackbird Lodge. Quinn nearly wept with joy.

The lodge was a small log cabin that had seen better days. But there was a light in the window, so someone had to be home. Quinn carried Daeva up the steps to the front deck and knocked on the door.

Slowly the door opened and a woman, maybe a little older than he, with long, silky, black hair peered out. "Yes?"

"I think you can help me."

She glanced at Daeva, wet and limp in his arms. She pressed her fingers to Daeva's cheek and studied her face. "She is one of the fire people."

She dropped her hand and took a step to the side, clearing the doorway. "Bring her in."

Chapter 18

The dream was about one of her favorite days, and one of her last with Quinn.

Sunbeams pierced the fluttering curtains and played over Quinn's bare back as he lay on his stomach, face planted sideways into the mattress.

Daeva had always loved to trace the light's pattern on his skin with her fingertips as they lounged in bed on Sunday mornings. It had been her favorite day of the week. Neither of them had work to do or any other commitments. They would spend most of the day in and out of bed, being lazy, just enjoying the heck out of each other.

On one particular day, Daeva had decided to sneak out of the bed, go down to the market and pick up something special for lunch. They'd feasted earlier on a hearty meal of French toast and bacon, then made love until they both " fell asleep" again. Except Daeva rarely slept. So she would often just lie beside Quinn and watch him sleep.

She slowly swung her legs out of the bed and stood. Padding across the bedroom floor, she grabbed a tank top and shorts and left the room. After quickly dressing in the bathroom, she grabbed her wallet from the table and slid on a pair of sandals.

The market near their condo wasn't too busy, but she took her time browsing and bartering regardless. She loved the process and wondered how anyone could shop any other way. This was much more rewarding, for the buyer and the seller.

Carrying her paper bag of peppers, cilantro and freshly fried beignets, Daeva made her way back to the condo. She was going to make a taco salad with her Hot Pepper Salsa from Hell recipe. It was her special recipe, something she'd literally picked up in hell. Klix had made it for her whenever she'd asked.

As she rounded the corner to their street, she paused. Someone was following her. Not just anyone but someone from the old homestead down below.

She turned in a circle, searching the street, especially the dark and secluded places, for her interested party. She spied the telltale flash of pointy green ears in an alleyway across the street. Squaring her shoulders she marched across the road and into the secluded alley.

She saw him crouched beside a green garbage can. He was camouflaged against it. If a person hadn't been specially looking for a four-foot goblin, they would certainly miss him.

"What are you doing here, Klix?" she asked him.

"I am worried about you, Mistress." His big opaque eyes regarded her openly.

"There is nothing to worry about. You can see I am perfectly well."

He tilted his shiny, bald, oblong head. "Your human puppet clothing suits you."

"Thank you." She glanced down the alley to make sure they were still alone. "Now, what is the real reason for this unexpected visit?"

"There have been questions, Mistress."

"About what?"

"You. Your business topside."

"I'm on holiday. That's all they need to know."

"The exorcist, Mistress."

"What about him?"

His gaze shifted side to side nervously. "They ask about him. His importance to you."

"And what do you say?"

"Nothing. I say I don't know this exorcist. Don't know what they are talking about."

She nodded. "That's good, Klix. You are a trustworthy friend."

He brightened at that, his gnarled lips twitching into a kind of grin. Other demons treated Klix and his ilk like slaves, like servants, but Daeva had always considered him so much more. They were not dumb insignificant creatures. Most of the goblins Daeva knew were clever, fierce and loyal. And Klix was smarter than all of them put together. That's why she'd befriended him over a millennium ago. It was always wise to have a loyal friend in hell.

"But I fear they will not listen to me for long," he said. "I am not equal to them."

She nodded. "Yes, I fear that, as well."

She needed to be prepared for that inevitable day. The lords of hell would come for her eventually, but worst of all, they would come for Quinn. Because she loved him, they would take him from her to punish her for abandoning hell and the demon way. For trying to bury her demon roots and become something else. Something she'd always wanted to be—human. They would consider her a traitor and punish her as much as they could. Destroying the only man she'd ever love would be the perfect way.

She had to protect Quinn. But how? Maybe it was time for her to go back. Maybe only that way could she keep Quinn safe.

Daeva nodded to her little goblin friend. "You've done well, Klix. Thank you for your warning."

He bowed to her. "I will continue to keep the horde at bay but don't know for how much longer."

She gave him a small smile. "I know, and it is not your responsibility, Klix, to do so. It is mine. I will do what I must here."

"Be well, Mistress."

"Be well, Klix."

Then he took a step backward and vanished into the brick wall.

Daeva left the alley to return to the condo. She and

Quinn needed to have a talk. Maybe today was the day to tell him the truth. She had to risk it, risk everything she'd worked for, to save his life.

When she arrived home, Quinn met her in the kitchen. He took the bags from her, putting them on the counter. "I was wondering where you went off to." He peeked in the bag. "What are you making?"

"Salsa for taco salad."

"Sounds scrumptious." He grabbed her around the waist, pulled her close and kissed her quickly on the mouth.

"Ah, Quinn, we need to talk about something."

He kissed her again, this time nibbling on her bottom lip. "Can it wait? Because we have a..."

Surprised, Daeva looked up just as another woman stepped into the kitchen.

"Ivy came for a visit," Quinn finished quickly.

Daeva smiled at Quinn's younger sister. "Hi, Ivy. Good to see you."

"Hey. I hope I'm not intruding."

Daeva could see the sadness in the girl's face. They had lost their father not that long ago, before she met Quinn, and she knew Ivy had been close to him.

"No problem. I can make more than enough for everyone."

Ivy smiled as Quinn kissed Daeva again. "And this is just one of the many reasons I love you."

He let her go, then opened the fridge to take out a couple of beers. He twisted the cap off one and handed it to Ivy. Daeva didn't drink beer.

"Come on, let's leave the culinary genius to go to work."

He guided Ivy out of the kitchen, winking at Daeva on the way out.

She leaned on the counter trying to steady herself. Tears threatened to well in her eyes. She would miss these kinds of days. These normal human days. But she knew without a doubt that she had to do something. Quinn was in danger. And, by default, so was Ivy. Just having her in their lives meant their days were numbered. Daeva didn't want that on her conscience. She'd leave as soon as she could.

"Daeva?"

Slowly, she blinked open her eyes. The room was gloomy. There were no sunbeams playing across the bed. She licked her lips. They were dry and cracked. Blinking again, she turned her head to see Quinn sitting beside the bed on a wooden chair. He was holding her hand, stroking his thumb over her knuckles.

"What…what happened?"

"You passed out after we teleported. You've been out for fourteen hours."

She looked around, taking in the small wooden room. They were definitely in a log cabin; she could see the round logs of the wall.

"Where are we?"

"I didn't know what to do. You said 'Blackbird' before you passed out. So I brought you here."

"Where's here?"

"Blackbird Lodge."

She licked her lips again. Quinn brought a cup of water to her mouth and helped her drink.

"I was dreaming of before."

He gave her a little smile. "I know. You were talking in your sleep again."

"Oh." She was a little embarrassed, wondering exactly what she said out loud.

The bedroom door opened and a lean woman with long, black, braided hair came in. "Good. You're awake."

Daeva stared at her. "You are a Blackbird."

The woman nodded. "I am Leanne Blackbird."

"I knew your great-grandfather, William. I believe he left a map for me."

Chapter 19

An hour later, they were sitting in Leanne Blackbird's kitchen. Quinn had helped Daeva out of the bed and to the table. She'd managed to eat some soup and fresh bread, and he thought her coloring was coming back. She'd been as pale as death when she'd been unconscious, gray almost, her lips a tinge of blue. The thought of her not waking had tied his guts in knots. They were a little less knotted now, but he was still worried about her. More than he'd first realized.

He'd always thought demons were indestructible, unbreakable, but just looking at Daeva told him that was far from the truth.

Leanne had insisted that Daeva eat before she would bring her the map. Quinn had been surprised there had even been a map, but realized he shouldn't have been surprised by anything, especially when it came to Daeva. She had told him that she'd had help hiding the chest over one hundred years ago. He guessed he knew who that help had been—William Blackbird, Leanne's great-grandfather.

What surprised him the most was Leanne's lack of surprise. She'd known Daeva was a demon or fire person, and that Daeva had been well-enough acquainted with Leanne's great-grandfather to entrust him with something very important.

It had been obvious Leanne knew something about demons, because she'd known exactly what to do to make Daeva well.

For those fourteen hours, she'd helped Quinn break Daeva's fever with a combination of liquids and some concoction she brewed that she'd spread over Daeva's forehead, chest and back. It had smelled strongly of pine and eucalyptus. She'd also done some kind of ceremony around Daeva's bed. It was in the Cree language, so Quinn couldn't understand it. All he knew was that it had worked.

Daeva's fever had broken and her skin had started taking on color again. Relief had surged through him at the sight of her cheeks flushing when he'd touched them.

Thoughts of her death had filled his mind. And when they had, the agony he felt was surprising. For a few days now, Quinn had been coming to terms with his feelings for Daeva. They weren't residual emotions for a woman long gone, but new feelings for this demon before him.

After clearing away the dishes, Leanne disappeared into what he assumed was her bedroom, then returned with a rolled-up paper, yellow with age.

She handed it to Daeva. "He must've known you would return one day."

"Have you looked at it?" Daeva asked.

Leanne shook her head. "My grandfather told me many stories when he passed it on to me, but I never wanted to know."

Daeva untied the leather binding around the map and unrolled it, spreading it across the table. Quinn held the edges down for her.

It was obviously a map of the area, but it was old. The date scrawled on the frayed bottom edge was 1913. Over a hundred years ago. He looked at Daeva. She had been here then.

She met his gaze and gave him one of her trademark sassy smiles, knowing exactly what he was thinking. "I look good for being so old, hey?"

"You look barely twenty-five," he said, returning her smile.

"Oh, Quinn, you're such a charmer."

Leanne looked from him to her, then back, probably trying to figure them out. Hell, he couldn't even do that.

Daeva pointed to a small circle on the map and asked Leanne, "Do you know this place?"

Leanne leaned on the table and looked the map over. She nodded. "Yes, I think so. It's an old iron mine."

"Could you take us there?" Daeva asked.

"It's closed now, has been for decades. The roads are overgrown. There's nothing there."

"There *is* something there and I need to find it. Please, can you take us?"

Leanne didn't look at Daeva. Quinn could see the hesitation on her face. He didn't blame her. She had no idea what she could be getting into. Although they seemed safe right now, he knew the Cabal and quite possibly other demons wouldn't stop pursuing them. The chest was the key to more power than any of them could comprehend.

"We understand if you can't, Leanne. You've already done so much."

She looked at him and he saw more than hesitation in her dark brown eyes. He saw regret, maybe even resentment.

"I will take you."

"Are you sure?" Quinn asked. "We won't lie to you, it could be dangerous. There are others after the same thing we are."

"It is my duty as a Blackbird to do so." Leanne sighed, her hands fidgeting at her sides.

"What do you mean?"

Daeva answered, "There was a curse put on her family line a few hundred years ago."

He frowned. "What?"

Leanne gave him a sad half smile. "I never believed the stories. I'd always thought it was one of the old myths about the fire people." She looked at Daeva. "I didn't believe until I saw you on my porch. Then I knew it was my turn to fulfill the conditions of the family curse."

She turned to look out the kitchen window. "I will

get our gear ready to go at first light." She turned and left the kitchen, opening the front door and exiting.

Quinn paced the room. "We shouldn't be asking her to do this. It's too dangerous. With the map we can find it ourselves."

"She's bound to this task, Quinn. She has to do it." Daeva stood, wobbled a little and had to brace herself against the tabletop.

"Can't you find the damn demon that cast the curse and have him remove it? Evil sonofabitch, doing something like that."

She pushed away from the table and moved toward the bathroom. "I'm going to have a shower. I feel like I've been living in these clothes for weeks."

He followed her, not content to let the conversation go. "Did you hear me, Daeva?"

"Yes," she hissed, "I heard you just fine. But there's nothing I can do about it."

He took her arm to stop her from entering the bathroom. "You know the bastard that cast the curse, don't you?"

She braced a hand against the door frame and glared at him. "Yes, I know."

"Who was it?"

"Me." She put her hand on the door. "Now, if you'll excuse me, I stink, so I'd like to shower please."

Quinn slapped his hand on the door before she could close it. "What do you mean you put the curse on the family?"

"I'm a demon, aren't I? That's part of being a demon, enslaving a family to do your bidding."

"I can't believe it. It's so…"

"Evil?" She raised an eyebrow sardonically, but he saw the hurt in her eyes. "I am a demon, Quinn, or have you forgotten? I'd be surprised if you have."

"It's just, I thought…"

"What? You keep reminding me that I'm not human. I'm not sure why this is so surprising to you."

He looked at her, trying to figure her out. She sounded angry, but not necessarily at him. Just in general. Angry at the situation, maybe, or at herself.

"I know you're not the same person you were three years ago, Daeva. I think I know who you are."

"Well, if you're not going to volunteer to wash my back, then I really think this conversation is over."

After a long moment, Quinn removed his hand from the door and she shut it firmly in his face. He'd let her have her privacy for now, but she was gravely mistaken if she thought the conversation was over.

Chapter 20

Daeva stripped off her clothes and stepped thankfully into the shower stall. She cranked the tap all the way to Hot. It hurt when the scalding spray hit her, but only for a moment. Then it just melted gloriously into her skin and bones. Her muscles started to unknot under the blistering jet.

After being in the cold, on the run, and sleeping in uncomfortable positions for a couple of days, the hot, cleansing shower was like a little piece of utopia. She wished she could just stay in here and let the world move on without her, but she had to face her situation sooner or later. Just when she thought Quinn had stopped thinking of her as an evil demon and was regarding her and treating her as the woman he'd fallen in love with six years ago, he'd been reminded of her true nature.

She was born a demon and would always remain so. No matter what she did, he would now forever remember that she'd cursed someone. Well, enslaved a whole family line, really. It didn't matter that she'd only taken advantage of that curse once before, the time she'd buried the Chest of Sorrows inside an iron mine. A place no demon could see through or human could ever get to, to obtain it, especially if they didn't know where to look. She should've gotten extra brownie points for that. She'd saved the human race by burying it deep in the Earth.

Once she was thoroughly warmed through to the bone, she found shampoo in the corner caddy. It smelled of oranges. She glopped some in her palms and massaged it deeply into her scalp. The odor sent an invigorating shiver through her. She wished Quinn had volunteered to help her wash. His strong hands massaging her head, running through her hair, made her body quiver with need. It had been a long time since she'd had sex or any intimate contact with a man; the last time had been with Quinn. She wondered what he would say if he knew that. Would it make a difference to him?

Thinking about Quinn was making her dizzy, or it could've been the steam in the shower that made her light-headed. She took in some deep breaths, but it didn't help, so she reached up for the showerhead to keep her balance, but it was too late. She dropped to her knees, hitting her head on the shower stall.

There was a rush of cold air as the bathroom door opened. "Daeva? Are you all right?"

She didn't answer. Her tongue felt thick in her mouth. All she could manage was an undignified squeak. Quinn slid open the stall door and she fell forward into his arms before she could hit the hard tiled floor.

Not caring that he was getting wet, he reached up and turned off the water. Then he grabbed a large bath towel and wrapped her in it.

"Can you walk?"

She nodded, although she wasn't positive she could, really.

He helped her to her feet. Leaning heavily on him, Daeva let Quinn guide her back to the guest bedroom. She'd never been this weak before, this vulnerable. And she hated it.

He lowered her onto the bed. "You obviously need more rest."

"Obviously," she mumbled.

He ran a hand over her wet hair. "You're not made of steel, Daeva. You can't go two hundred percent one hundred percent of the time. It's apt to take its toll. You said yourself that being bound to the Earth and to me diminished your powers."

"I know. It just sucks."

He chuckled at that. "Yeah, it does." His hand was still on her head. "Wait here. I'll be right back."

"Where else am I going to go?"

He left the room, then came back a few seconds later with another towel. He sat beside her on the bed, nudging her sideways with his leg. He picked up her wet wall of hair and settled it on the other towel.

"What are you doing?"

"Drying your hair. I don't have a comb but my fingers should do."

Touched, Daeva let Quinn comb his fingers through her hair while squeezing the excess water from the strands. It was a tender thing to do. She'd never had anyone care for her like that. Even when they'd been together before, when she was masquerading as a human, he'd never offered to do that. Unexpectedly, tears formed in the corners of her eyes. But she didn't want him to see her so emotional, so weak.

"I want you to know," she started, her voice quavering a little, "that I did that curse a long time ago. I was different then."

"I realize that, Daeva."

"You do?"

"I mean, I've changed in the past five years, so it's easy to think that someone has changed in over two hundred years."

He continued to run his fingers through the wet strands of her hair. She let her head fall back a little, pure pleasure cascading over her like a warm blanket. She sighed happily.

"Feel good?"

"Oh, hell, yeah." She was hyperaware of his presence behind her and the fact that she was still only wearing a towel, was naked and wet underneath.

His hands paused; she sensed that he dropped them to his sides. She glanced over her shoulder and saw the hesitation in his face, the uncertainty. The fear.

"Maybe you should get under the covers and get some more sleep."

"I'm not tired anymore."

She couldn't hide the fact that she wanted him. It was too tiring to constantly check her libido. She wanted Quinn in every way possible. Even when she was furious with him for being judge, jury and exorcist, she'd never stopped wanting.

He'd changed, too. He wasn't as trusting or easygoing, his heart had toughened a little, but she still saw the compassionate and caring man underneath his hardened exterior.

He stood with his hands fisted at his sides. "We both need rest. We still have a long journey ahead."

"Yeah, we do, which is why we should address this thing between us."

"What thing is that, exactly?"

She twisted around, her towel gaping up the length of her thigh. Quinn's eyes tracked the movement.

"The sexual tension."

His eyes darkened. "I think it's best we ignore it."

She reached for his hand. "Quinn, I want you. And I know you want me."

"Do you really think this is the best time or place?"

"It's the perfect time. We might not get another chance." She tugged him closer. "I don't want to lose this one chance, Quinn. I don't want to lose…" She couldn't finish her thought; it was too painful to speak out loud.

By the look in his eyes, she wasn't sure he could handle hearing that she still loved him.

He raised his other hand to her face. With just his

fingertips he traced the line of her chin to her mouth. Cupped her cheek in his palm.

"You won't lose me."

"But don't you see? I will, one way or another, after we find the chest."

He didn't say anything, then, because he knew she spoke the truth. Instead, he ran a hand over her hair.

"Come on. Get under the covers. You need the rest."

She did as he asked and slid under the covers, the towel still wrapped around her. "Will you stay with me until I fall asleep?"

He nodded and crawled onto the bed behind her. He wrapped an arm over her on top of the covers and pulled her close.

Sighing, Daeva closed her eyes. Exhaustion was taking its toll on her and she was finding it difficult to stay lucid. The warmth of Quinn's body and the way he stroked her hair was comforting, lulling her to sleep. When she finally succumbed to it, it was with his scent in her nose and the press of his lips on her shoulder.

Chapter 21

It wasn't quite dawn when Daeva slid quietly from the bed and dressed in the clothes Leanne had given her. After putting her hair up in a high ponytail, she silently padded out of the room, shutting the door behind her. She didn't want to wake Quinn. He needed the rest, both his body and mind.

He'd held her until she fell asleep. But she wasn't out for long. Daeva tried to go back under but she had too much on her mind. Although her body was exhausted from the teleportation, she still couldn't sleep. There was too much to do.

Quinn had been in a deep sleep, by the looks of him. So she'd covered him with the blanket then slid out from under his arm.

The cabin was dark but she knew that Leanne was

already awake and waiting because there was a fresh pot of coffee brewed. Daeva poured a cup, and as she sipped it, she glanced out the kitchen window to the predawn glow. That was when she spotted Leanne outside, sitting cross-legged on a blanket spread out on the deck. Her eyes were closed.

As if sensing Daeva's gaze, her eyes opened and she looked right at her. Daeva could see the latent power in the Cree woman. She possessed more strength than she probably even knew.

A couple of minutes later, the front door opened and Leanne came back in, the colorful blanket draped over her arm.

"You are up early," Leanne said as she put the blanket into an old painted wooden trunk.

"I don't need much sleep."

"Neither do I." Leanne came over to the coffeemaker and poured a cup, liberally adding sugar. She took her coffee and sat at the table. Daeva joined her.

They drank in silence. Daeva watched the woman over the rim of her cup. She knew Leanne wanted to ask her something and was gathering the nerve to do it.

"You are the demon that cursed my line, aren't you?"

"Yes."

"Why?"

"Out of arrogance, I suppose." Daeva ran her finger over the rim of the cup. "Your ancestor was a great warrior but he wanted more power. He called upon the dark forces to help him in his quest. He was lucky that it was me that answered the call and not another more vicious demon." She watched Leanne flinch at that. "He demanded my allegiance to help him become chief. I gave it to him, but told him his entire lineage would forever be enslaved to me. He readily agreed. He didn't even think about it." She picked up the coffee and drank to wet her suddenly dry throat. "I only used the curse once, with your great-grandfather, to help me hide something, a most important and dangerous artifact. And now, of course you, to help me find it."

The Cree woman nodded. "The stories I have heard over the years have changed somewhat."

Daeva smiled. "Of course they did. No one wants to believe that their ancestor was a greedy, selfish, power-hungry jerk."

Leanne sighed. "I will help you find what you seek."

"When we are done, I promise you I will lift the curse so that the rest of your family is free from it."

Leanne nodded. "Thank you."

There was a long pause, then a voice came from the corner. "Good morning."

Both women turned as Quinn stepped into the kitchen. Daeva suspected he'd heard their entire conversation.

As he passed her to get some coffee, he ran his hand over her head. He poured a cup and leaned against the counter with it.

"How long will it take us to get where we need to go?"

"It is an hour drive, then we have to hike the rest of the way in."

"How far?" he asked.

"About sixteen miles."

"That's a long haul."

Leanne nodded. "We won't make it today. We'll have to make camp and not wander the area at night. There are bears and cougars around."

"We might run into other trouble," he said.

"There's no 'might' about it." Daeva lifted her cup. "The Cabal will show."

Leanne nodded. "I have protection."

The door opened and a tall young man with the same long black hair and dark eyes as Leanne came in. He carried a rifle in his big hands.

He glanced at Quinn, then at Daeva, his distrust and distaste evident in the way he frowned.

Leanne stood and greeted him with a hug and kiss on his cheek. "This is my son, Billy."

Quinn nodded to him, but Billy ignored the gesture. It was obvious his only concern was for his mother. He took her arm and guided her into the living room. They also spoke in Cree, but Daeva understood them, anyway.

"Let me come with you," Billy pleaded. "You can't trust these people."

"No, Billy, you must stay here. I can take care of myself. I am not useless."

"I didn't say that, but it is dangerous, especially with that fire hag."

Daeva snorted. "Hey, I resent that. I'm not even close to being a hag."

Leanne looked surprised. "You understand Cree?"

Daeva smiled, but without humor. "I understand all

languages. The beauty of being from hell, I suppose. It's multicultural."

Billy came into the kitchen, his hands fisted. He looked ready to pummel her. She could feel the fury rising off him.

"Leave this house, demon. You are not welcome."

Daeva stood, not liking being threatened while she sat. "Your mother welcomed me. This is her home, is it not?"

He went to speak again, but his mother was there beside him, calming him with her hand on his shoulder. "It is okay, Billy. I will be safe. You don't have to worry."

He turned to her, still angry. Daeva could tell he wanted to say so much more, but he had respect for his mother so he bit his tongue.

"Take the GPS tracker, so I know where you are."

"If it will ease your mind, son."

He nodded, then bent to kiss Leanne on the cheek. He spoke in Cree again. "I love you, Mother."

"And I you. I will see you soon."

With that, he was gone, leaving the rifle in his mother's capable hands.

"My son worries too much."

Daeva smiled at her. "He loves his mother. There is nothing wrong with that."

"No, there isn't." Leanne returned the smile. "I will meet you out back and we will grab the gear we'll need." She left them in the kitchen to prepare for their trip.

Daeva set her empty cup in the sink. Quinn reached for her hand.

"He said those things because he doesn't know you. The real you."

"He has the right to be upset. We're putting his mother at great risk. Because of something I did centuries ago."

"Yeah, but we'll keep her safe. She'll be all right."

Daeva nodded but with no real conviction. Ever since she'd woken, a sense of impending doom had filled her gut. She knew that feeling, had had it before. It meant someone was going to die.

Chapter 22

As they packed Leanne's Range Rover with their gear and supplies, Daeva glanced up at the sky and shivered. The gray clouds of earlier had now turned an ominous, swirling slate black.

Quinn came to stand beside her at the back of the vehicle. "I definitely don't like the looks of that sky."

"Me either."

A bolt of lightning pierced the black clouds, making them both flinch. It was followed by a clap of thunder that shook the Range Rover.

Leanne shut the hatch on the vehicle. "This is not good weather for our journey. We're going to have to postpone."

As if to punctuate her statement, the heavens opened

up and spewed rain and hailstones the size of golf balls onto their heads.

"I'm putting the Rover back into the garage." Leanne jumped into the front seat.

As she pulled it forward into the safety of the car port, Daeva and Quinn ran to the safety of the cabin's covered porch.

They watched in horror as the ground, the trees and surrounding buildings were assaulted by the substantially sized balls of ice. It was so loud that Daeva couldn't hear anything above it. Leanne was pelted hard as she ran from the garage to the cabin. Pieces of ice hung off the tips of her braided hair.

"I haven't seen a storm like this in decades," she confessed.

"Maybe it's a sign," Quinn said.

Although Daeva suspected he was joking, she heard the uncertainty in his voice. Maybe it *was* a sign. But she had no delusions that it was sent by heaven.

She searched the neighboring forest. Were they alone? Or did they have company of the sorcerer kind?

"We should get inside," Leanne said, as hailstones slammed onto the porch right next to her boot. She opened the door and went in. Daeva and Quinn followed her lead.

It was almost deafening inside as the hail pounded against the cabin's wooden and tin exterior. Then the wind picked up, battering the ice against the walls and windows. A sharp crack came from Leanne's bedroom.

"Sounds like a window," Daeva said, pointing to the room.

All three of them rushed in to see an orange-sized hailstone on the floor. Splinters of glass were spread across the floor.

Cursing, Leanne gestured to Quinn. "There's wood, a hammer and some nails just outside on the porch."

He turned and rushed out of the room to retrieve them.

"What can I do?" Daeva asked.

"There's a broom in the kitchen."

Daeva ran out to get it, easily finding it hanging on a peg near the garbage. She brought the broom and dustpan back to the bedroom. She helped Leanne sweep up the glass as Quinn returned with two planks of wood and the hammer and nails.

The wind whipped more rain and ice into the room before Quinn could board it up. Just as he finished pounding in the last nail, the lights flickered then went out.

"Is this normal?" Quinn asked, obviously feeling the same unease Daeva felt.

"We've had storms like this before during the summer." Leanne stared at Daeva. "Is there something I should know?"

"We have sorcerers after us. So it's possible this could be one of their spells."

"This is pretty powerful magic, if it is."

"I agree," Daeva said. "I'm not sure if it's them at all. Could be just Mother Nature doing her damnedest to destroy stuff."

"What do you want to do?" Quinn asked.

He looked nervous. Daeva could see his hands fidgeting at his sides. One of the benefits of night vision was seeing all the things people generally want to keep hidden, especially in the dark.

"Well, we're no good just standing here." Leanne walked out of the bedroom. Daeva and Quinn followed her into the living room. "We'll need light and heat."

She settled some kindling in the fireplace and lit a match, holding it down to the wood. The flame went out without taking. Frustrated, she lit another match.

"Here, let me." Daeva nudged her aside, crouching next to the hearth. She rubbed two fingers together. At first, nothing happened. A ball of fear rolled in her stomach. Was she losing her powers?

Trying not to appear worried, she kept rubbing her fingers together. Harder. Faster. Until finally a spark formed, then more, and she had a small orb of fire that she dropped into the middle of the kindling. The wood sparked and smoked until it flickered with flames.

She let out the breath she'd been holding, then set a few larger logs onto the popping fire. When she stood and turned, Quinn was watching her intently, his brow furrowed.

She gave him a small smile. "No sweat."

But she didn't think he believed her by the way he kept watching her.

"Well, all we can do now is hunker down and wait it out." Leanne picked up the gun her son had left her and carried it into the kitchen. "Anyone want a drink? I'm having a drink." She opened the cupboard and took out a bottle of Scotch.

"Sounds like a helluva idea." Daeva joined her in

the kitchen and took three short glasses down from the shelf.

Leanne filled each glass, then set the bottle down on the table in front of the fire. She plucked one glass up and lifted it in salute.

They all drank. Then Leanne filled up their glasses again.

"If there was any time to get drunk, I think it's now." Leanne chugged back the second drink.

Daeva cheered her with her own glass. "Hear, hear. I've been wanting to get drunk from the moment I arrived topside."

"Come, sit, and tell me what it's like to be a demon."

Leanne took a seat in the overstuffed chair near the fireplace. Daeva slid onto the sofa. Quinn sat next to her. He had yet to say anything and just watched her. She wondered if he, too, wanted to know what it was like to be a demon. Was he looking for some insight?

She gave him a small smile, and he set his hand on her leg and squeezed it reassuringly. She liked that he was near. It made her feel safe. Something she didn't normally feel on a daily basis.

"It's not as fun as you'd think." She laughed, but without any real humor.

Leanne frowned at her. "I didn't think it would be fun at all."

"It isn't. But you can't choose how you are born or what you are born into."

"No, you can't." Leanne poured more whiskey into her glass. "But you must learn to accept the things you can't change."

They were all silent for a few minutes, then Daeva started to tell her tale. Leanne had asked the question, but it was for Quinn and for herself that she told the story.

"For millennia or more, I reveled in my demon-ness, in my powers. I did a lot of bad things. One of them was cursing your family." She paused to drink. "But after a long while, after being with and dealing with humans, I realized I could be different. That I didn't have to accept my fate, didn't have to be like all the rest of my kin. So, I started to find ways to go topside." She watched Quinn as she spoke. She really needed him to understand this.

"I started to possess people and live their lives for as long as I could. I picked people who were looking for a way out. For those who were sick or dying. While I possessed them, they would heal. I tried to give them a second chance at life, even if it was with my soul invading their bodies." She swallowed, hoping Quinn would understand what she was trying to tell him.

His eyes widened. "Rachel? Rachel was dying? That's why you possessed her?"

She set her drink down on the table. "She had ovarian cancer. She would've died in a couple of years. I gave her more than ten."

He jumped to his feet. "Jesus, Daeva. I didn't know."

"I know you didn't."

He rubbed at his face. "I didn't even give you a chance to tell me."

"It's okay, Quinn. It's in the past."

"It's not. I'm such an ass." He fled the living room and went into the guest room.

Leanne tipped her glass. "Looks like the two of you got a lot of stuff to resolve before the end."

Daeva looked at the Cree woman for a long moment, her throat constricting. "You see much, Leanne Blackbird."

"Yeah, it's another curse I have. Seeing the truth in all things."

Daeva stood, intending to go to Quinn. "And what do you see for Quinn and me?"

Leanne drained her glass and wiped at her mouth. "I think you already know that answer."

Daeva nodded, then walked across the room to the back bedroom. When she went in, Quinn was sitting on the bed, his head in his hands. He looked up at her and she could see the guilt, remorse and pain in his eyes.

A week ago she would've given anything for Quinn to feel this badly for what he'd done to her, but now, now she just wanted to be with him. Time was too short to waste with the past. It was today that mattered.

She sat beside him.

"I'm so sorry, Daeva. I've misjudged you for so long."

"It doesn't matter anymore." She ran her hand through his hair, loving the feel of it against her palm. "The only thing that matters is right now. And us together."

He brought his hand up to her face and cupped her cheek. He rubbed his thumb over her lips.

"I've missed you," he murmured.

Tugging him down to the mattress with her, she wrapped her hand in his hair and covered his mouth with hers, claiming him. At least for now. The kiss was fierce and full of unrequited love and passion. She broke away and looked up at him, wondering if he felt the same way.

As an answer, he fisted her hair, dragging her up to his mouth. He crushed himself to her. She opened her mouth, letting him savage it with his tongue, groaning as he teasingly bit at her bottom lip. This was a different Quinn. An aggressive Quinn. And she liked it.

With one hand still wrapped in her hair, he used the other to grab the front of her T-shirt, ripping it away, leaving her bare-breasted. Her nipples hardened in the cool air of the room. He pulled her head back, exposing her neck to his hot, hungry mouth. His hand dipped down to mold her breast with his palm, squeezing her just a little.

Daeva hung on to his shoulders, his arms, anywhere she could gain purchase as he ravished her. She had been taken before, but not with such force, with such need.

Usually reserved and diplomatic, Quinn couldn't be pushed. But in the bedroom, he was the one who liked to push and prod. This was where he took over, where he had always commanded her.

Something animal in her broke, and she clawed at his clothes, desperate to find his flesh, to taste, to feed on every inch of him. She'd been hungry for too long. She ripped open his shirt, her hands finding his smooth skin and hard muscles. Her hands streaked everywhere at once, needing to feel him close, to feel secure.

* * *

Dragging his mouth from her lips down her neck to the fullness of her breasts, Quinn flicked one hard nipple with the tip of his tongue. Her skin was soft and smelled of oranges. Saliva pooled in his mouth just at the thought of her. He wanted to feast on her body for a whole night. And even then he wasn't sure he'd be sated.

Restraint broken, he grabbed her around the waist and tossed her backward on the bed. She gasped in shock but her eyes clouded over with desire. He tore off the remainder of his shirt, shucked his jeans and shorts, then crawled onto the bed.

She let him come, a coy little smile on her lips. His cock hardened at the sight. She was the sexiest woman he'd ever seen. Everything about her pulled at his most primal needs.

He undid her pants, tugged them down her legs, pulled them off and tossed them to the floor. He gripped a leg in each hand, and spreading them, he pulled her forward, sliding her across the mattress until he was nestled tight between her thighs. Her hot, wet center nuzzled his cock and he had to bite down on his lip to stop from burying himself in her. He wanted to take her slowly, to watch every inch of his hard length sink into her silky, warm core.

He looked down at her, so open, so vulnerable, and drank every part of her in. "God, woman, you drive me mad."

"Then do something about it," she teased, as she ran her hands over her breasts.

Gripping his cock in one hand, he guided himself

into her. She was so silky wet that he slid in unhindered. He settled a hand on each of her legs and slowly pulled himself out then thrust back in, taking his time, although it killed him to go slow.

Daeva moaned with every thrust. He teased her with his rhythm, moving with slow deliberation at first, then picking up the pace until he was pounding into her mercilessly. With every movement, he could feel her core tightening around him. Squeezing him.

"Harder," she panted.

He fulfilled her wish and buried himself deep inside her. He let go of her legs and fell over her, settling his face into the crook of her neck. She wrapped her legs around his waist and tilted her pelvis up to meet him.

He thrust into her again and again until they both had sweat pouring off their bodies. He gripped her shoulders and pulled her down as he pushed up. He groaned as his body started to quiver with need and desire. One more powerful thrust and he drove hard, emptying himself into her. Raking her nails down his back, she cried out and followed him down the orgasmic spiral into pure bliss.

Chapter 23

The sun was just starting to rise by the time they got on the road the next day. They drove for a couple of hours to the turnoff marked on the map.

Leanne parked the vehicle on a graveled pad. There was a sign that read *Beware of Bears* posted, big and bold, before the metal barrier separating the road from the forest. Nothing like an omen to start a journey, Quinn thought.

Daeva stood beside him as he looked at the sign. "Well, if bears are the only thing we have to deal with, this trip is going to be a piece of cake." She hefted her pack over her shoulder and followed Leanne into the woods.

At first, the trail was easy. It was well-trod and marked, through flat, wooded land. Then they broke out into a clearing and it was evident it was going to get a helluva lot more difficult from there on. There was no clearly marked path, and it was all mountains and valleys for the next ten miles.

Quinn was in shape and healthy, but this was going to kill him, he was sure. He glanced at Daeva and saw the same look on her face.

Leanne on the other hand, looked as if she could hike for another ten hours and not even be winded. She squinted into the high sky. "We'll hike for five hours more, then make camp."

Quinn wasn't going to argue. He was sure in five hours he'd be ready to collapse.

Leanne started the climb up the rise to the next copse of trees. Daeva followed, Quinn beside her.

"How are you faring?" he asked her.

"I'm good," she said, but he could see the sweat dotting her forehead and upper lip.

"Are you sure? You could transfer some of your gear to my pack."

She shook her head. "I can carry my load. I'm fine, Quinn, really."

But he could see she wasn't fine. Ever since the teleportation she'd been weakened. Far more than she was letting on. But he wouldn't press her on the issue. She was stubborn and she would take his concern for her as being vulnerable. He knew she hated feeling that way. So, he would keep his worries to himself, at least for now.

After another two hours of walking, they stopped for water and some sustenance. Daeva dropped her pack and found a fallen tree to sit on. He watched her drink from the canteen and noticed that her T-shirt was soaked with sweat.

He set his pack down next to hers and proceeded to rifle through it, taking out the heavy stuff and setting it down on his pack.

She jumped to her feet. "What are you doing?"

"Helping you."

"I don't need any help." She grabbed at the bedroll he'd taken.

"Yes, you do, Daeva. Don't be..."

"If you call me stupid or dumb I'm going to smack you upside the head."

"I was going to say foolish. I can see how much you are suffering. You're still too weak to be carrying all this."

She stopped making grabs for stuff and just stood by and watched as he loaded his pack with the extra weight. When he was finished, he helped her with her lessened burden.

He kissed her on the forehead, running a hand over her hair. "You're welcome." He caught her half smile before she turned to get back on the trail behind their guide.

They hiked for another three hours, stopping intermittently for water and rest. Daeva was definitely doing better without the extra weight on her back, but she still looked exhausted. As if time itself was taking its toll on her.

Leanne found a small clearing in the trees and declared it the best spot to make camp. There was plenty of tree cover and a narrow stream nearby to provide them with fresh drinking water.

They were all pretty quiet as they pitched tents, one for Leanne and the other for Daeva and Quinn. Once that was done, Leanne went about constructing a fire pit. Daeva announced she was going to fill their canteens at the stream. Quinn watched her go, a feeling of helplessness filling him. He didn't know how to help her, because he didn't know exactly what was wrong.

"She's dying, you know."

Quinn swirled around to gape at Leanne. "Excuse me?"

"She's been losing her life force since you brought her to me. Every hour a little more disappears."

"Did she tell you that?"

She shook her head. "She didn't have to. I can see it."

"You're wrong. She can't die. She's a demon. They're immortal."

"She is less demon than you think." Leanne stood wiping her hands on her pants. "I know you can see it too, Quinn."

He shook his head, his gut clenching. "I thought she was healing. I was sure of it."

"Ask her. You will know if she's telling you the truth."

After tossing his bedroll into the tent, Quinn went to find Daeva. He found her crouched by the water's edge, splashing her face. She stood when he approached.

"Checking up on me?"

He searched her face, looking for some sign of Leanne's truth. She was pale, definitely, skin slicked with sweat, and her eyes did have a distant look to them. But did that necessarily mean she was dying?

"You're more than drained from the teleportation, aren't you?"

She frowned. "What are you talking about?"

"You said there was a price to pay for the spell. It was your life, wasn't it?"

Her gaze flitted away from him.

"Are you dying, Daeva?"

"What makes you ask that?"

"Can't you just answer the question?"

She was quiet, her eyes settling on everything but him.

He took hold of her arm forcing her to look at him. "Is it because you are bound to me, to the Earth?"

Her gaze lifted to his. She didn't need to answer because he saw the truth in the stormy, gray pools of her eyes. "It doesn't matter, Quinn. All that matters is keeping the chest safe."

He didn't want to believe it. He didn't want to face that truth. There had to be a mistake.

"What if I release you? Would you get your life back?"

Her eyes widened at that. "Why would you even suggest that? It's against everything you stand for. Everything an exorcist is. Your dad was killed by a freed demon."

He gripped her arms tight, pulled her to him. "I would do it for you."

Tears welled in her eyes. And it broke him inside to

see them. As they rolled down her cheeks, he wiped them away. "Say something. Please."

"You would risk all that you are for me?"

"Yes."

She fisted her hands in his shirt and leaned into him, pressing her lips to his. She kissed him hard and he responded in kind, burying one hand in the long silky fall of her hair.

They stood on the stream's edge feasting on each other, desperate for each other. Then, spent, Quinn pulled back, resting his forehead against hers. The taste of her was strong on his lips. Forever, he would remember her flavor, strong but sweet like honey.

"I can perform the ceremony right away. I just need my chalk."

She shook her head. "I don't want you to."

He pulled back to search her face. "Why? You'll die if I don't."

"Because once I am released, I will end up back in hell. I won't go back, Quinn, no matter what."

"But if I don't…you'll die."

She shrugged. "I always said I wanted to be fully human. And this is what it is to be human. To face mortality."

He shook his head, angry and frustrated with her attitude. "It's stupid if I can save you."

She gave him a half smile that was infinitely sad. "You have already saved me, Quinn. You did the moment I met you. You made me realize what being human was really about."

He felt weak inside. And guilty. He'd tossed away

the best thing that had ever happened to him because of his fear and ignorance.

"I'm sorry."

"For what?"

"For being so stupid three years ago. For not listening to you, for not believing in our love enough."

She kissed him softly, lingering on his lips. "I forgive you."

He sighed. "How long do you think you have?"

She shrugged. "I don't know. I hope it's enough to do what I need to do."

"We'll make it enough. Even if I have to carry you the rest of the way."

More tears ran down her cheeks, and he kissed them away.

Chapter 24

Daeva snuggled into Quinn's warmth inside the sleeping bag. After their moment at the stream, they had returned to camp, eaten, talked with Leanne about the next leg of their trip, then sat and watched the fire, listening to the sounds of the forest. They had sat side by side in comfortable silence. There had been nothing to say, not yet anyway. They'd saved their communication until they were alone in their tent.

And now they were.

Bringing his hand up, he cupped her cheek, bringing her down to his mouth and kissing her. It was a beautiful, beguiling kiss that plucked at her heart.

Moaning into his mouth, she trailed her hand down his body. She needed to feel him in her hand. He was hot and heavy against her palm, like silk and steel meshed together. She stroked him once, then twice, until he broke the kiss and gasped.

"I want you, Daeva," he groaned. "I have to be inside you now."

"And you will have me," she breathed. "You'll always have me."

Insane with need, she rolled him onto his back and lay on top of him. Purring low in her throat, she pressed kisses to his chin and neck. She trailed her tongue over his pulse points and up to the lobe of his ear to suck it into her mouth. All the while, she continued to stroke him with a fevered pace.

Still gripping his hard length, Daeva pushed aside the cover and moved down his body until she was straddling his thighs. Leaning forward, she flicked her tongue over the tip of his cock. Quinn clamped his eyes shut and moaned as she took him into her mouth. She licked and sucked on him until she could feel his legs quivering. She wanted him like this, vulnerable to her.

"I can't hold on," he panted.

She held him still until he softened a little and retained his control. Then she licked down the length of him, wanting him to lose it all over again. "Yes, you can."

His eyes were dark and hooded. The muscles ticked along the rugged line of his jaw. She loved that look about him. Dark, fierce, barely holding on. She'd remembered that look from their past and would carry it with her for the hours she had left.

After one final stroke of her tongue, she moved up his body to straddle his hips. The delay was destroying her. She'd waited long enough to find bliss. She held him firmly in her hand as she lowered herself. Inch by exquisite inch, he filled her. He was a big man, but still the perfect size for her. When she was fully seated, she held herself still and looked at him. The man she loved. The man who had given her the only thing she'd ever thought she couldn't possess from humanity.

She rubbed her hands up and down his chest, enjoying the way his hard muscles felt under her palms. Watching his face, she contracted the muscles of her sex, squeezing him tight inside her. Every flicker and grimace of emotion that flashed over his handsome face gave her fierce pleasure.

As she started to rock her hips, Quinn reached up and molded her breasts in his hands. He squeezed and flicked his thumbs over her nipples. Waves of pleasure swept over her and she arched her back to catch them cresting. Up and down, back and forth, she moved on him, finding a rhythm, squeezing her muscles with every stroke.

She watched his beautiful face contort with strain as she quickened her pace. She knew he struggled for control and that he was quickly losing it as she took him up and over. There was a sense of power in that, and she reveled in it.

"You're so beautiful, my Daeva," he panted while he moved one hand down to where they joined. He circled his fingers into her slick core, finding her clit with expert ease.

He stroked her as she stroked him. Firmly, pushing her toward climax. Biting down on her lip she tried to stop from screaming out his name. She didn't want to alert Leanne. Although the Cree woman surely knew the sounds of pleasure.

Grabbing hold of his shoulders, she picked up her pace, moving faster, harder, taking them to the edge. As the first crest of orgasm mounted inside, she dug her nails into his flesh. With a loud drawn-out moan, she pushed down on him, filling herself completely with his hot male flesh.

He pressed down on her sensitive bundle of nerves one more time and flipped her over the edge. She collapsed forward onto his chest as she spiraled toward her climax. He wrapped his arms around her, burying himself deep, soaring over into ecstasy with her.

He found her mouth and kissed her hard as the depths of passion drowned them. Everything went white behind her eyes and she thought she'd pass out. But everything was clearer, everything brighter in her mind's eye. And she knew deep down inside that she'd found the true meaning of humanity in this man's arms.

Chapter 25

Daeva heard Leanne outside the tent packing up her gear and getting ready to press on. Careful not to wake Quinn, she slipped out of the sleeping bag and got dressed.

As she crawled out of the tent she saw the sky was just starting to pinken. Her breath came out in plumes as she zipped up her jacket, and she shivered despite the jacket's warmth. She'd been feeling the cold more and more. It was as if a sliver of ice had been imbedded in each of her bones. She couldn't shake it. The warmest she'd been was next to Quinn, basking in his body heat inside the sleeping bag. But she couldn't go back there now.

She found Leanne at the fire, drinking a cup of instant coffee. She offered some to Daeva. "It's not great but it'll warm you."

Daeva took the offered cup and drank the hot liquid. It scalded her tongue and throat on the way down but she didn't care. Anything was better than the blistering cold inside.

Leanne watched her. "It leaves you quickly."

Daeva nodded, knowing exactly what Leanne was talking about. "I don't know how long I have. Twenty-four hours maybe."

"We will be at the mine in four hours. I hope you know where to look once we are there, because the mine has many tunnels, some of them sure to have collapsed. It will be very easy to get lost."

"Once I'm inside, I should be able to feel where the chest is."

They drank in silence for a while, listening to the breeze rustle the leaves. Daeva found it so peaceful, right here, right now. Peace that she'd never thought she'd ever have in her life.

"Does he know?" Leanne asked her.

"He knows enough for it to hurt him."

Leanne nodded, then dumped the last dregs of coffee out of her cup. "We should get going. Time's more important than ever, now."

As Leanne finished packing, Daeva stared at the tent where Quinn still slept. She knew she had to wake him, knew that they needed to move on if they wanted to get to the mine in time, but it was that time she feared. The closer she got to the mine, to the chest, the closer she came to losing everything that mattered to her.

Less than an hour later, they were all packed up and making their way through the trees and past the stream. Quinn hadn't said much since she'd woken him. She wasn't surprised. She didn't have much to say, either. They had expressed themselves last night in the most intimate way. She knew he loved her. There wasn't anything else she really needed to hear.

The final walk wasn't as arduous as before. She had less weight on her back and but also in her heart. Her steps weren't nearly as heavy.

Daeva wondered if this was what it was like to accept one's mortality. She'd always been curious about death and loss. Now she was getting intimately acquainted. It wasn't so bad. Not really. She'd lived a very long life. Seen more, done more than any mortal could even comprehend. But when she glanced at Quinn behind her on the path, she realized that he'd given her more than any and all of her experiences combined. Love had always been the ultimate prize she'd longed for. And he'd given it to her.

Maybe she could die peacefully, knowing she'd experienced the greatest thing worth living for.

They stopped less frequently during the last leg of their journey. They were all anxious to finish. All for different reasons, she suspected. Especially Leanne. Once at the mine, she'd have fulfilled her part of the curse. Daeva just hoped she could lift it as promised. Just because she'd put it on didn't necessarily mean she could easily erase it. Demon magic wasn't so straightforward, even for a demon. There were a lot of hoops to jump through.

As they neared the entrance to the mine, Daeva sensed they were not alone. And it wasn't the bird and critters that had always been there, surrounding them. No, this was something else. Something unnatural. Sorcerer magic had that unnatural tinge to it.

Leanne must've sensed it, as well, because she had the rifle poised and ready to shoot.

Daeva dropped back to Quinn and whispered, "We aren't alone."

His gaze darted to the left then to the right. "The Cabal?"

She nodded. "I think so."

"How did they find us?"

"I didn't set up wards last night. I wasn't thinking straight."

He gripped her shoulder and squeezed. "It's not your fault."

"Regardless, it's too late to worry about it. I say we make a run for it."

"Do you have the energy?"

"I have enough."

"Okay." He broke stride and caught up to Leanne to tell her the plan.

The guide slung her gun around her shoulder then looked to Daeva. Without a word, she sprinted up the rise. Quinn and Daeva were right behind her.

They tore up a small hill. Once on top, Daeva could see the boarded-up entrance to the mine in the valley below. They'd have to cross open land to reach it. There was no other choice.

She dumped her pack—she wouldn't need the meager supplies now—and raced down the hill. This was a one-way trip for her now. As she ran behind Quinn, she glanced quickly to the left side. She saw two sorcerers emerge from the trees about twenty feet away. Two fiery, green balls of magic splattered the ground near her feet. But she kept running.

Quinn looked over his shoulder at her.

"Go!" She waved at him to keep going.

More green fire landed near her, a few sparks landing on her pants. Instantly they burned through the fabric and seared her skin. She patted the fire out with her hand but didn't slow her pace.

The sorcerers were closing in, running just as quickly as she was, maybe more so. It wouldn't be long before they hit her, or worse, hit Quinn or Leanne. As Daeva sprinted the last of the way, her lungs burning, her muscles screaming in agony, she fisted her hands together and concentrated on the fire inside her. Two perfect spheres of red flames formed in her palms.

Turning, she flung them toward their pursuers. One ball hit its mark. Searing fire engulfed the sorcerer's head as he dropped to the ground. The other dodged the assault and kept on coming.

In the meantime, Leanne had reached the mine's entrance and she was kicking at the boards that crisscrossed over it. She wasn't making any headway. When Quinn arrived, he took out the pickax and started to hack at the wood. It wouldn't be fast enough.

Daeva dodged another assault from the remaining sorcerer just as she formed two more balls in her hands. She was barely seven feet from the mine now.

"Out of the way!" she shouted.

Leanne and Quinn both dived for cover as Daeva flung her magic at the mine's entrance. The wood disintegrated into charbroiled splinters that rained down over both of them and the ground.

Nearing the now-open entrance, Daeva grabbed at Quinn to get him up and going. Leanne was already sprinting through the opening. Daeva and Quinn came in, breathing hard, after her. A spray of green followed them in, kicking up dirt and debris.

She looked at Quinn and Leanne. "Are you both okay?"

Leanne nodded.

Quinn took her arm. "You're hurt." He was looking down at the holes in her pants where she could see the red and raw skin of her leg.

"It's nothing." She nudged him away. "We have to get deep inside the mine but we can't have them follow."

"What do you suggest?"

She glanced up at the tunnel roof, held precariously by an old wooden frame. "Cave-in."

"That'll trap us, as well," Leanne said.

Daeva looked at Leanne. "I know."

Another blast of green fire hit the dirt wall beside Quinn. Rocks and wooden slivers pelted him in the side of the face. Blood spotted his cheek where a piece had nicked him.

"I think we're screwed either way." He wiped the blood from his skin.

Daeva nodded. "Move back into the mine. I don't want to crush you."

After flicking on her flashlight, Leanne obeyed. Quinn hung back with Daeva.

"You're expending a lot of energy."

"I know, but it has to be done."

He leaned in and stole a kiss. "Don't kill yourself in the process."

"I won't."

With that, he followed the faint light trail Leanne left with her bouncing flashlight.

Once he was safely away, Daeva concentrated on all the fire inside her. She built it into her hands, creating a huge scarlet wave of power oscillating between her palms. Closing her eyes, she directed everything she had into that moving stream until it was huge and barely containable.

After taking a deep breath, she directed that pulse at the ceiling near the mine's entrance. It had the desired effect. The wooden frame burst apart, and rock and dirt and slate fell to the ground, completely blocking all access to the mine.

There was no way the sorcerers could get in quickly. And no way Daeva, Quinn and Leanne were getting out. At least, not this way.

Once Daeva was certain the entry was sealed tight, she jogged down the dark tunnel in search of the others.

Chapter 26

"Everything go okay?" Quinn asked Daeva as she came alongside him at the Y of two tunnels.

She nodded. "As well as it could. They won't get through."

"Which way?" he asked her.

Leanne shone the light down one, then the other tunnel. Both were cramped and narrow offering no hint as to what lay beyond them. Already the stagnant air was pressing down on his lungs. He couldn't imagine being down here for long, but he suspected that was exactly what was going to happen unless they suddenly stumbled upon the chest then miraculously found another way out.

Daeva pressed her hand to the rock wall on the left. She closed her eyes, and frowned. Then she moved to the other side and did the same. Her frown was a little less this time.

"This way." She pointed toward the right-hand tunnel, then stepped into it, wobbling a bit on her feet. Quinn grabbed her arm to stop her.

"Just wait for a second. Make sure you're okay."

"I'm fine, Quinn."

"You're not. You can barely walk." He pulled her to him, stroking a hand over her hair.

She sighed, leaning into him a little. "I'll be okay. Let's just keep going. When we reach the chest, I'll rest, I promise."

He kept her gaze, gauging whether she was being truthful or not, then pressed a quick kiss to her forehead. "Okay."

Leanne led the way with the only flashlight they'd been able to hold on to. Quinn went next with Daeva behind him, since she was the only one of them able to see in the dark.

They walked for no more than fifteen minutes before the tunnel seemed to get smaller. Nearer the entrance, the ceiling barely brushed the top of his head, but now he found he had to tilt his head sideways to avoid knocking it against the wooden beams holding up the tons of rock and dirt overhead.

"Is this getting smaller or am I hallucinating?"

"No, it's getting smaller," Leanne said. "Gets even worse up ahead. I think we might have to crawl through."

Leanne was correct in her assumption. Another three feet and the ceiling dropped considerably. It looked as though there had been a partial cave-in a long time ago. Just what Quinn needed to think about while he was feeling claustrophobic.

"I guess we crawl," Daeva said, as she dropped to her hands and knees. "I'll go first, just in case."

"In case of what?" Quinn asked.

"In case it falls again." Without waiting for his response, she started on.

He knew arguing with her was pointless, so he followed her instead. Leanne brought up the rear.

They crawled over stone and dirt for the next twenty minutes. Every once in a while, Quinn would look up, envisioning the ceiling collapsing on him. He had to stop once and remember how to breathe because he was having difficulty doing just that.

"Not much farther," Daeva said, but he was sure she'd said it only to reassure him.

But, true to her word, after another five minutes of crawling and scraping through rock and wood debris, the tunnel opened up into a cavern. Daeva formed a glowing ball of demon light and set it loose. It drifted up in the cavern casting an eerie glimmering over the rock.

Quinn pushed to his feet and, lifting his head, took in several deep breaths. The air was hot and heavy in the cavern, but at least it was plentiful.

Happy to be in one piece, Quinn swung around to share it with Daeva. His joy dissipated. He found Daeva still on her hands and knees, rocking back and forth, her eyes closed.

He rushed to her side and helped her to sit up against one of the rock walls. Her skin was so cold, he thought she was dead. He touched her cheek, then ran his fingers down to her neck to check her pulse. He found it, but it was faint. Her breath came in short shallow pants.

Leanne crouched beside them, taking up Daeva's wrist and holding her fingers over the pulse point. "Her heart pumps, but it is slow."

"What can we do?" he asked, but he knew there was nothing. Nothing that Daeva would allow him to do.

Leanne patted his shoulder. "Pray."

"Please, don't," Daeva groaned.

Relief surged through him. "I thought maybe you decided to leave me." He brushed her damp hair from her brow.

"Nah, you can't get rid of me that easily."

"I don't want to ever get rid of you."

Her eyes opened, and she reached up and touched his cheek. "I know."

"I'm going to get you out of here."

She shook her head. "Have to find the chest first."

"Screw the chest, let the world handle its own shit."

She gave him a small smile. "You don't really mean that."

"Yeah, I do."

"Well, you don't have to go far, because the chest is here." She lifted her hand and pointed high on the rock wall.

"In the wall?"

She nodded. "Going to need to dig it out."

Leanne stood, went over to her pack, and unstrapped a pickax. She walked to the wall, hefted it, and swung at the rock with a thunk. Little pieces of rock scattered on the stone ground.

Quinn watched her swing again. It was going to take more than that to find the chest. It would take both of them digging at the rock. But he didn't have an ax. They'd only brought the one.

"How deep is it?" he asked Daeva.

"Deep enough."

After he made sure Daeva wasn't going to collapse sideways, Quinn went over to Leanne and took the pickax from her. He hefted it over his head and started to dig.

Working at the rock wall took its toll on Quinn. Sweat slicked his face and back. His T-shirt stuck to him like glue. The muscles in his arms quivered with strain with every swing of the ax. And he hadn't gotten all that far. There was maybe a three-foot-deep hole at best. But no chest.

He took a break and sat beside Daeva as Leanne took up the chore of hacking at the rock wall. He drank from the canteen, then offered some to Daeva. She shook her head, refusing the water.

"You need it."

"You need it more. Don't waste it on me."

Quinn's heart squeezed. He hated to hear the defeat in her voice. It was like a spear to his soul.

"Don't give up, Daeva. I won't let you give up."

She blinked up at him, the whites of her eyes blood-shot, a sheen of sweat on her forehead. "You're going to have to let me go, Quinn."

"No, I don't." He cupped her cheek. "I did that once before, and I won't do it again."

"It's okay, you know. I understand why you did what you did. I should've told you from the beginning. I should never have kept such a secret from you."

"If you had we might not have had the years we had together."

She nodded, then smiled. "True."

"I wouldn't give up those years for anything, I'm glad we had them. I'm glad we had this time together."

"Me, too."

He leaned over and brushed his lips against hers. "I love you."

"I love you, too."

Then there came an audible bang, followed by Leanne's awe-filled voice.

"I found it."

Chapter 27

"Help me up," Daeva demanded, her lungs burning with the effort of breathing.

Quinn hauled her to her feet. Leaning heavily on him, she moved toward the hole in the rock wall where Leanne stood staring. Daeva looked into the stone and saw the corner of a wooden box.

"That's the chest."

"It looks lodged in there pretty good," Quinn said. "How the hell are we going to get it out without breaking it? We don't want to damage the book."

Daeva shuffled closer to the wall. "I can melt it out."

Quinn held her back. "You'll waste your energy. You need it to…"

"To what? This is a one-way trip for me, Quinn.

You're the one that will need to get it out of here and protect it."

She saw in his eyes that he wanted to argue with her. But he remained silent. Maybe because he knew she'd do what she willed. And the fact that she was right. She was near her end. There was no getting out of here for her.

Nodding, he let her go.

She stepped up to the wall, and set her hands on the rock surrounding the edge of the chest. Closing her eyes, she searched for the last dregs of demon fire inside. There wasn't much there. Enough, she hoped, to melt the stone and not set the wood on fire.

She gathered it in and forced it through her arms to her hands. Her palms began to warm. The energy grew gradually until there was a heat that burned her skin. Normally, that wouldn't have happened, but she was mortal now. Things were different for her.

It took longer than usual to heat the rock. She pushed the fire through her hands with all her strength. Soon, she could feel the stone give. It grew pliable and liquid. Opening her eyes, she watched as it dripped, bit by bit, down the wall, unearthing even more of the chest until the entire three-cubic-foot box was visible.

Bone weary, she took a step back so Quinn and Leanne could get in there and pry the chest loose using what tools they had. She stumbled, then managed to settle herself down to the floor as they wrangled it out of its century-long stone imprisonment. They set it down beside her.

Daeva set her hand on top of the elaborately inscribed wooden chest, feeling the power inside vibrating against her palm. "It's bigger than I remember."

"It's heavy," Leanne commented. "I'm not sure how we're going to carry it out."

"You won't have to." Daeva grabbed the chest to turn it around. Quinn was there to help. Once it was turned, she ran her fingers over the elaborate lock.

"The Cabal have the key," Quinn said.

"No, they don't." She lifted her arm. "Someone give me a knife."

Leanne unsheathed the small blade on her hip and handed it to Daeva.

She took it and slid it along her arm where a three-inch scar marked her skin. Pain shot up her arm but she kept at it until rivulets of blood rolled off the tips of her fingers to dot the rocky ground beside her.

"What the hell are you doing?"

"Remember Loir? The little goblin that beat you up at your house?"

Quinn nodded. "Very well."

Daeva smiled. "She's very loyal to me." She set the knife down next to her. "She switched the key with a fake and gave me the real one."

"Okay, so why are you slicing up your arm?"

"Because I needed a place to hide it." Biting down on her lip, she split her skin with her fingers and dug into her flesh. More agony made her head swim but she persevered until finally she pulled out the key.

Quinn looked queasy as he plucked the gore-covered key from her hand. "Unbelievable. Why didn't you tell me?"

"A girl likes to keep a little mystery once in a while."

He shook his head, trying hard not to look at the blood still running down her arm. "You have more than a little mystery, Daeva, trust me."

"Well, are you going to use it or not?" She gestured to the chest.

After wiping the key on his shirt, Quinn crouched next to her and slid the key into the lock. She could see his hands shaking. He turned it, and there was an audible click and then a puff of air as the lid released. Slowly, he opened it.

Inside was a book. It was the grimoire that King Solomon used to summon the demons to do his work. It should've looked ominous or important, but it didn't. It looked like a plain black leather-bound book with yellowing pages.

Quinn lifted it out, turned it over and looked at her. "This is it?"

She nodded. "Looks normal, doesn't it?"

"Yes. It's strange."

"Here, let's put it in your pack."

She reached over and grabbed Quinn's backpack, dragging it toward her. She unzipped it and took out one of Quinn's T-shirts, then took the book and wrapped it in the innocuous material. She shoved it into his pack.

"There. Done." She handed the pack to Quinn, avoiding his gaze.

"Daeva, I'm not leaving without you."

She looked at the ground, the threat of tears stinging her eyes. "Don't be an idiot, Quinn. You have to go."

"I'll carry you out of here."

She shook her head. "Don't waste your time. I'm already dead."

He gripped her chin in his fingers and forced her to look at him. "I will not leave you. Ever."

She stared into his eyes and saw the truth there. The realization that he wouldn't leave her, even when she asked him to. And wasn't that one of the reasons she loved his stubborn ass so much?

"Fine. Get me up, then."

He helped her to her feet. Her head swam and her vision wavered but she kept on her feet. She leaned on him, but felt maybe she could walk.

She gestured to the tunnel to the left. "If we follow that one, we should find another way out."

Quinn nodded, but Leanne didn't look convinced. "Are you sure?"

"No, but it's better than sitting here and waiting for the air supply to run out."

Without another word, Leanne held up the flashlight and walked toward the tunnel.

Quinn put an arm around Daeva. "I'll carry you if you can't walk."

"I can walk." And to prove her point she took a baby step forward, then another. "See?"

Unsatisfied, he started toward the tunnel, helping her with every step.

Fortunately, this tunnel was wider than the last one. Crawling through that had been hard. Daeva had been in a lot of tight spaces before—being in hell prepares a demon for a life of small, cramped spaces with no breathable air—but that one had filled her with terror. This mortality thing was surprising in so many awful ways.

They'd traveled for maybe a half hour when Daeva heard something that made her stomach roil and her heart leap into her throat.

"Do you hear that?" she whispered.

Leanne stopped in front of them and turned around. "I don't hear anything."

"What do you hear?" Quinn asked.

"Water."

As soon as she said the word, a trickle of water washed forward from behind them. She looked down at her feet as the swell covered her boots.

Quinn's eyes widened. "They're flooding us."

"We need to go right now."

"I'm going to carry you." He reached down to hook her legs. But Daeva nudged him back.

"I can run."

"Daeva..."

"Go. I will follow. I promise."

Leanne led the charge. After a lingering look, Quinn turned and followed her, his boots slapping in the slowly rising water.

Daeva watched his retreating back and wondered where she was going to find the reserves to follow. Leaning against the tunnel wall, she watched as the water level reached her ankles. It wouldn't be long before it reached her knees, then her waist. If she couldn't walk now, she'd never be able to move through the weight of the water.

Closing her eyes, she took in a deep breath then let it out slowly. It was now or never.

She opened her eyes and took a step forward, then another, then another, until she was running through the pools, water splashing up onto her pants legs. Soon, she was right behind Quinn. He glanced over his shoulder and she saw the relief in his eyes.

The sound of rushing water echoed through the shaft as they ran. Daeva could see the trickles down the rock faces on either side. Water sloshed around her knees. It was getting harder to run. She was already using the last of her energy reserves. It wouldn't be long before her legs gave out. And when she fell, she knew she'd never get up again.

"I see a light up ahead," Leanne called back to them.

"Run toward it," Daeva responded, even as she slowed. The water was up to her thighs now.

Quinn stopped and grabbed her hand, tugging her forward. "Hang on to me."

She shook her head. "I'll hold you back."

"Don't let go, Daeva."

She nodded to him as he pulled her forward. As they ran together, she concentrated on the feel of Quinn's hand in her own. The warmth of his skin against hers gave her the momentum to power on.

The light up ahead that Leanne had spotted grew larger. Daeva could see it now. She hoped it was an opening, a way out. If it wasn't, they would all die down in the mine. Definitely not the way she thought she'd die. Well, she never thought she'd die to begin with so she supposed it didn't matter.

Water rose to their waists, and it was becoming harder to move forward. There was a current coming from somewhere pushing them backward. Daeva suspected the current was sorcerer generated.

"There's a hole," Leanne said. "I can see it." There was hope in Leanne's voice.

Daeva nearly shared it. Until she saw the wooden beams on the right side of the tunnel start to give. The cracking sound was deafening.

"Leanne!" she screamed.

Just as Leanne turned to Daeva's voice, the beams broke. An overhead rafter fell, a ton of rock and dirt giving it deadly momentum. The edge hit Leanne across her shoulders and back. She went down, face-first into the water.

Quinn let Daeva's hand go as he reached down to aid Leanne. He lifted her out of the water so she wouldn't drown, but the way her body twisted unnaturally made Daeva's gut roll over. The woman's back had to be broken. She cried out as Quinn tried to get a better grip on her.

"Oh, Jesus, Leanne." He looked at Daeva. "Her back…"

She nodded. "We have to get her out of here." She moved past him as he cradled Leanne to his chest, pushing against the water level to survey the light source.

There was a hole in the rock about eight feet up. She wasn't sure if it was big enough for them to squeeze through, but she'd make it big enough even if it took the last of her life force.

She pointed up toward the opening. "I'm not sure if I can make it bigger."

Carefully floating Leanne on her back, Quinn moved to stand beside Daeva. "Can you reach it?"

She shook her head. "We'll have to wait until the water level rises." It was now at their chests. They'd have to wait until they couldn't touch the ground any longer and it would lift them up.

It didn't take long for the water to reach their necks, it hovered just at Daeva's chin. It was cold and her body started to shiver, taking up valuable vitality. Slowly, the level crept up her face, over her lips to her nose. She pushed up with her toes to tread water.

"Here we go," Quinn said as he, too, started to kick with his legs to keep buoyant.

As they trod water, rising closer to the hole, Leanne floating next to them, Daeva moved closer to Quinn. Not wanting to lose him. Ever.

But she would, no matter what happened.

"Kiss me," she murmured.

He ran a hand over her head, anchoring her there so he could press his lips to hers. The kiss was soft and gentle and full of all the things they wanted to say to each other but didn't have the strength or time to utter.

"We're going to make it out."

"When did you become an optimist?"

He smiled. "The moment I met you."

The tears came then. As they rolled down her cheeks they mingled with the icy water that was still rising.

Looking upward, Daeva lifted her hands and touched the hole. It wasn't even a foot wide. Not big enough for a full body to squeeze through. She gripped the sides and started to dig and pull at the dirt and rock while Quinn held Leanne. Bits and pieces fell into the water around her, but it still wasn't enough. Soon the water level would rise higher than the hole and they would lose room to breathe. They might be able to stick their faces out the hole for air, but how long would that last?

She settled her hands along the sides and forced the tiny sparks inside her to rise to the surface. They came quickly but they were not strong. She fed the fire into the rock. Gritting her teeth, she pushed it harder and harder. A tooth cracked in her mouth and blood started to pool in her throat. She swallowed it and continued to manipulate the demon magic inside her.

She gave it one final push and, finally, the hole gave. Substantial pieces fell on top of her head and rolled into the frigid waters.

"Get her out," she said to Quinn.

He floated to the wide hole and pulled himself up, wiggling his body until he was completely out. He reached down to Leanne. Daeva lifted her up to him, trying to be careful of Leanne's injuries but knowing that if they didn't force her through she would die.

With one final tug, he was able to pull her body out. Then he reached down for Daeva.

"Your turn, baby."

She let him grip her arms and she kicked when he pulled. She managed to squirm through with Quinn's help. When she was out, she rolled onto her back and took in deep cleansing breaths of the fresh cool air.

Water bubbled out of the hole next to her. A few more minutes under and they would've all drowned.

But now they were safe.

"Well, look what the mine puked out."

Or not.

Daeva blinked up into the sun, and into the shadow of a sorcerer.

Chapter 28

Quinn tried to get to his feet but the boot in his gut forced him down again. He rolled onto his side and looked up into the face of Richter Collins.

"We meet again, Quinn. How fortuitous. For me."

"How's the leg? Still limping?"

Richter smiled but there was no humor or warmth there. His expression was cold and calculating. "Where's the chest?"

"Back in the hole you just filled up."

A muscle in his jaw ticked. Quinn could easily tell that the sorcerer was pissed off that his plan had backfired.

"Well, I guess one of you is going back in to retrieve it."

Richter nudged Leanne with the toe of his shoe. Her head lolled back and forth.

"Don't touch her. She's badly injured."

"I noticed." Then his gaze narrowed on Daeva, who was also lying on her back, arms splayed out, her face pale, her chest barely rising and falling. "Then the demon bitch. She can do it." He reached down to grab her by the hair.

Quinn was up and on him in seconds. "Get off her!"

But he was still so winded and exhausted from the journey that Richter easily backhanded him, sending him sprawling back to the ground. It helped that the sorcerer had magic to back him. Quinn could feel the telltale burn of it across his face.

"Do yourself a favor, exorcist, and stay down."

Another sorcerer stood over Quinn, his hands glowing green, ready to launch an attack at Richter's command.

Richter finished reaching for Daeva and yanked on her hair to pull her up. She was like a rag doll in his hand.

Fury rolled through Quinn but he couldn't see a way to get to the sorcerer without being fried by the fiery magic balls of doom. Then he saw the miraculous glint of steel at Leanne's hip. He just had to get over there.

Richter dragged Daeva across the dirt by her hair. "What's the matter with your demon, Quinn? Is she broken?"

"She's injured, you dick."

Richter frowned down at her, then waggled her head

back and forth. "How can she be injured? Demons can regenerate."

Quinn didn't want to tell the sorcerer that he'd made her mortal by binding her to him and the Earth. It was best that Richter still thought she was a demon. But what if he did something to her that couldn't be taken back?

Richter dropped her by the hole in the ground that they'd just come out of. Water had stopped gushing from it. The ground around it was muddy and slick.

"The water level is going down. So she can go back and get me that chest." He nudged her toward the hole.

It took everything Quinn had not to bolt across the ground, wrap his hands around Richter's throat and squeeze the life out of him. But he had to time it right—he was going to get one chance to kill this guy and he wasn't going to blow it.

As if privy to his thoughts, Daeva opened her eyes and looked at him. Her lips twitched up into a sad smile. Was she telling him something? He kept watching her, then she mouthed the word...*now.*

She reached up and grabbed Richter's wrists with her hands. Her dark magic absorbed his hands and diminished his own green, glowing sparks.

His eyes widened and he cried out.

Quinn kicked the sorcerer looming over him between the legs and knocked him unconscious with a right hook to the jaw. He then rolled twice to Leanne, and unsheathed her knife. He was on his feet in seconds and moving towards Richter.

The sorcerer pulled Daeva up and slammed her back

down to the ground. She relinquished her hold on him, but it was too little too late. Quinn was already on him.

With all the power he could muster, Quinn jammed the knife into the sorcerer's throat. Surprise widened his eyes and his hands came up to his neck. But it was pointless. There was no way he could stem the flow of blood.

"Told you, asshole, that I'd ram it into your throat next time I saw you."

Gurgling nonsensically, Richter dropped to the ground, blood gushing from his wound and soaking the dirt beneath him. Ignoring him, Quinn rushed to Daeva's side, cradling her to his chest.

"You're okay. Everything's going to be okay." He rocked her back and forth.

She blinked up at him. "Liar." She coughed, her whole body convulsing with the sheer power of it.

He smoothed a hand over her hair, trying hard not to let tears flow. He vowed he wouldn't cry. But the emotion inside him was bubbling up too hard and too fast.

"Stay still, now."

She lifted her hand and touched his cheek. "You're sweet." Then her hand fell to the side. She turned her head to look at Leanne. "How is she?"

Quinn glanced at the Cree woman. "Not good. I don't think she's going to make it. I don't know how to get her out of here without killing her."

"Move me closer to her."

He frowned. "Why?"

"Because maybe I can do one last thing in this life that's good."

He didn't argue with her. Lifting Daeva gently, he pulled her over to Leanne and settled her down again. Daeva reached over and grabbed Leanne's hand.

"If she wakes, will you tell her I'm sorry about everything?"

He nodded. "Yes, I'll tell her."

"Good." She smiled at him. "Will you always remember me?"

The tears came then. He let them fall, too distraught to wipe them away. "Always and forever."

"I wish we could've had more time together. We had some good times didn't we?"

"The best."

"Liar," she murmured. "Kiss me one last time, Quinn Strom. Let me go into the abyss with the taste of you on my lips."

He leaned down to her mouth and gently brushed his lips against hers. They kissed, and it was slow and gentle and full of everything they'd yet to experience together. Full of regret for a life they'd never have.

He broke away and looked down at her, brushing his hand over her clammy face. Her skin was like ice now. Her lips were turning blue. It was difficult to watch but he couldn't turn away. He wouldn't let her go without some comfort.

"Thank you."

"You're welcome." He kissed her forehead one last time.

She closed her eyes and gripped Leanne's hand tight. He watched as her chest rose and fell with shallow breaths. He watched and waited, until the last deep breath she took didn't come out. Her face went slack and her fingers uncurled from Leanne's.

Trying hard not to sob, he lifted her body and cradled her against his chest. He nuzzled his face into her hair and breathed in deep. Her smell was still the same. The feel of her in his arms, so right, so perfect.

But gone. Forever.

As he held her tight, rocking back and forth, he sensed movement beside him. He looked over at Leanne as she opened her eyes.

"Quinn?"

"Are you all right?" he asked, unbelieving.

"I think so." She moved her arms. "What happened?"

"Daeva gave you the last of her life to save you."

Slowly, Leanne sat up and looked at Daeva in his arms. She reached over and touched her cheek. "I saw her in my dream. She kissed me, then I felt warm."

He nodded, more tears rolling down his cheeks. The love of his life was dead. He didn't know how to go on without her.

Leanne put a hand on his shoulder. "You will see her again, Quinn."

"When?" he blubbered. "When I die?"

She shook her head. "I don't know when, but do not give up on her."

He pressed his lips to Daeva's cheek, inhaling her in, needing her to *be*. But knowing she'd never *be* again.

Chapter 29

The darkness was heavy and cloying. It clung to her like too-thick cobwebs. She tried to shake the feeling loose, but it failed. In fact, she wasn't certain she could even move. She tried to shrug her shoulders, but didn't get a sense of any movement. Maybe she didn't have a body anymore.

Am I dead?

Daeva pondered that. Is this what death was? A vast stretch of nothingness?

She really hoped not, as it was going to get pretty boring in the afterlife if all she had to look forward to was absolute darkness. It's not that she expected pearly gates and harps, considering her species, but this nothingness was really quite the disappointment.

To her relief, the darkness eventually faded and she

was floating in a sea of twinkly lights. She looked down and saw her form, weightless. She lifted her arm, inspecting her skin. The scar was gone. Her skin was flawless. But she still couldn't *feel* her arm moving.

She grabbed one of the twinkly lights with her hand. She held it there until it warmed her skin. She opened her hand and watched as the light danced on her palm, changing color from white to green to black. Then it exploded and a thousand shards of black glass shot through the colorless sky around her.

She tracked one of the shards through the air as it zoomed away. It seemed to be following someone. She swore she could see a dark form shimmering on the horizon.

Flapping her arms, she tried to move through the emptiness. It seemed to be working because the dark form in the distance was getting larger and more defined.

The closer she got, the clearer the form became. Daeva could see the long, silky, black hair of the Cree woman whose family she'd cursed.

Leanne? Are you dead, too?

She turned and smiled at Daeva. She shook her head, then held out her hand. Daeva took it, feeling the woman's skin vividly against her own.

Come with me.

Where are we going?

You will see.

Smiling, Daeva let Leanne guide her away from the twinkly lights and down to a bridge. Her feet touched down and she could almost feel the structure under her soles.

Holding hands, the two women strolled down the bridge toward a bright white light.

Will I see Quinn again?

Leanne smiled and nodded. *Yes. In time. But not yet. He has to learn to release you first.*

Although Daeva was sad she wouldn't see Quinn soon, she still felt a lightness inside she'd never experienced before. It was nice and unexpected.

Leanne led her forward, pulling on her hand. At first they were in stride, but eventually Leanne pulled ahead. She yanked on Daeva's hand. Finally, they were going so fast, everything became a blur. It was as if they were traveling through the ether. Like teleportation. But that wasn't possible, was it?

It went faster and faster, until Daeva couldn't even see herself. Everything was one big white blur. She opened her mouth to scream, to tell Leanne to stop.

And then it did.

Daeva blinked open her eyes.

Chapter 30

The house hadn't been nearly as bad as Quinn thought it was going to be when he returned. Ivy'd had something to do with that, he was sure. He'd called her when they'd been on the road and she promised to take of it. And she had.

There was no police tape, and the living room had been tidied a bit, as had been his bedroom. Minus the hole in the wall. He'd have to take care of that himself. When he got around to it. Right now he didn't feel like doing much of anything.

He stood in the basement and stared at the pentagram still chalked in white on the floor. He'd been staring at it for the past twenty minutes. But he couldn't leave, he couldn't move. Maybe if he looked at it hard enough or long enough, she would magically appear.

He twisted the chalk in his fingers and considered doing another summons. Maybe she was just waiting for him to call her home. Maybe she'd been wrong about dying. Surely a demon could never die. Not even one that was bound to the Earth.

He nudged the open book on the cement floor. It was one of his summoning books. He'd poured over it for the past hour looking for something, anything, that would tell him that she didn't really die. Even a grain of hope would have been enough. But he couldn't find anything.

His last bit of hope had faded when he'd turned the last page.

He shoved the chalk back into his pocket and took out his cell phone. He scrolled through his contacts and dialed a number. Quianna answered on the fourth ring.

"Hey, Quinn."

"I have it, Q."

An hour later he parked in the university visitor's lot and made his way to the faculty building. The backpack weighed heavy on his shoulders. All that was inside was the book, but it was heavier than anything he'd ever carried before. It had cost him so much.

He knocked on her door, waiting for her to tell him to come in. When she did, he went inside and stood by the leather visitor chair. She sat behind her desk, glasses perched on her perky nose.

"So, do you have it?"

Quinn nodded and reached into his backpack, pulling out the fabric-wrapped package. He handed it to her.

She took it gingerly and set it on the desk. Hands shaking, Quianna unfolded the shirt. Inside was the book. "The grimoire that King Solomon used to summon his demons."

She traced a finger over the old black leather. "Amazing. I can feel the power radiating from it." She looked up at him. "I can't believe you found it."

"It wasn't me who found it." He kept his shoulders straight although he wanted to sag forward. The weight of losing Daeva pressed heavily on his mind, body and soul. He wasn't sure he'd ever recover from her loss.

Quianna sat back in her chair, taking off her glasses. "Who was it then?"

"A friend."

"By the look in your face, I'd say more than a friend."

He nodded. "Yeah, she was."

"I'm sorry, Quinn."

"So am I." He got to his feet, swinging the pack over his shoulder. "Well, I'll see you."

"Where are you going?"

"Home."

She nodded. "Thank you for bringing it to me. I'll take care of it now. You go rest. You deserve a break."

He turned and walked out of her office, shutting the door firmly behind him.

With that behind him, maybe now he could move on with his life. The pain in his chest told him it would be an uphill battle all the way. He was one for challenges, but just getting out of bed this morning had been a struggle.

His cell phone thumped from his pants pocket. He fished it out. "Strom."

It was an old friend and hunting partner, Jake. "I have a job for you."

"I'm taking a break from that for a while."

"I think you'll want this one."

Quinn paused, rubbing at the stubble on his chin. Did he really want another job? Is this what he really needed to forget Daeva? "I'm listening."

"I got a lead on Todd Sheppard. Haven't you been looking for him for a few years?"

"What's the address?"

"I'll text it to you."

"Great."

"Do you want some extra help on this? Gi and I could be backup."

"No, thanks, Jake, but I got this. I need this."

"I understand. Take care, buddy."

"You, too." Quinn ended the call, then waited for the text with the address.

This was closure, in a way. Going full circle to the beginning of it all. It would be good for him to end it. Maybe that would help him move on. Or maybe it would just help him deal with the anger still churning inside him.

It didn't surprise Quinn that Todd was hanging out in a nightclub. It was the sorcerer's usual MO. The guy had no imagination—he was as predictable as they came.

Because of that, it didn't take Quinn long to track him down inside the club. The sorcerer was sitting with a group of women. Quinn searched the table for red hair. For one second his heart thudded expectantly, then it faded when he saw only blondes sitting in the group. Instead of coming at the sorcerer from behind, Quinn decided to approach the subject head on.

He walked up to the table, grabbed an empty chair and sat in it, facing Todd. The sorcerer was about to jump to his feet, but Quinn grabbed his arm and held him in place.

"I'm had the worst week of my life, Todd, you really don't want to piss me off."

The sorcerer must've seen something in Quinn's eyes, because he stayed in his chair. "What do you want?"

"I want you to stop summoning demons to do your dirty work."

At the word demon, the entire group of ladies at the table got up and left.

"I don't know what you're talking about," the sorcerer sniveled.

Quinn slapped him across the face, hard. "Don't be an idiot, Todd. Confession is good for the soul. You do worry about your soul, don't you?"

Todd swallowed. "I'm leaving the Cabal. I'm not practicing anymore."

"Somehow, I don't believe you."

"It's true. Ever since Richter…you know?" Todd eyed Quinn warily. Obviously he'd heard of the Cabal leader's demise and at whose hand. "I don't want to be involved anymore. It's getting too dangerous."

"You've hurt a lot of people, Todd. You can't walk away from that."

He hung his head. "I know. I'm willing to pay for that."

"Okay."

His head came up, surprise furrowing his brow. "Okay? You're going to let me go?"

"No, I'm going to drop you off at the police station and you're going to confess to hurting those women. And you're going to go to jail and do your time."

"And if I don't?"

"Then I'm going to kill you, Todd. Right here, right now."

Todd looked around, maybe questioning whether he could get away or not, then he looked back at Quinn. He rubbed a hand over his mouth and leaned back in the chair, sighing. "Fine."

Quinn stood, and pulled Todd to his feet. He escorted the sorcerer out to his car, opened the door and shoved him into the passenger side.

On the way to the police station, Quinn watched Todd out of the corner of eye. "Let me ask you something."

"Okay."

"You've done a lot of demon summoning. Have you ever bound one to the Earth and to yourself?"

Todd nodded. "Once."

"What happened to the demon? Did you send it back?"

Todd looked at him. "No. I was in love. I wanted to be with her forever."

Quinn nodded for him to continue.

"She passed through to the other side, then I released her."

Quinn nearly swerved the car. "What do you mean she passed? She died, right?"

"In a way. They don't die and go back to hell, but sort of stay in a limbo."

"She came back to you? You saw her again?"

The sorcerer nodded, a small smile on his face. "Oh, yeah, after I did the releasing ceremony she came back, all right."

Quinn's heart was racing. He could still find Daeva. There was the hope he was searching for. She wasn't lost to him forever.

Todd turned his head to show Quinn the scar along his neck. "Yup, she came back, nearly ripped my throat out and took off. I haven't seen her since. Some demons are just not meant to be released, I guess."

Quinn pulled up to the curb in front of the station. "We're here. Go do the right thing."

Todd nodded. "Thanks for the reprieve, I guess." He opened the door and slid out. He hesitated on the sidewalk for a moment, then trudged up the steps to the front doors.

Quinn pulled away from the station; Todd was on his own. Quinn had more important things to do. He had the woman he loved to save.

Chapter 31

The second he reached his house, Quinn bolted through the front door and ran down the steps to the basement, nearly tripping on the way.

He grabbed the book on the floor and flipped through it. There had to be a release ceremony in there somewhere. After several minutes of flipping pages and checking the index, he found the ritual he was looking for. It had been there the whole time and he hadn't seen it. Or maybe he hadn't been looking for it.

But he found it, and that was all that mattered right now.

After reading the ritual repeatedly, he set the book down. Grabbing his broom he swept away the initial pentagram. He had to construct a new one, with different symbols in the corners.

On his hands and knees, he drew a pentagram with his blessed chalk. He put the appropriate symbols in the corners. The usual two for a regular summoning, then one for portal, one for travel, and the last for freedom. When he was finished, he stood, took out his blessed blade and slid it across his palm. He squeezed his hand into a fist. Blood dribbled down his wrist. He held his fist over each of the symbols and spoke the words.

"I call you, Daeva, Seductress of the Shadows. I call you to me. I call you to this realm. I call you forth." He waited a few seconds, then closing his eyes, he breathed a sigh. "I call you so I can release you. I call you because I love you."

He waited and watched the pentagram, expecting any moment for the wild red-haired woman to burst into existence. He listened for the telltale popping noise, lifted his nose for the hint of cinnamon that she always carried with her on her skin.

Seconds went by, then minutes. After thirty minutes, Quinn sat down on the cement floor, crossing his legs for comfort. He sat like that, head in hand, staring at the pentagram for another hour.

It didn't work. She wasn't coming back.

He stood, went up the stairs, flicked off the light and slammed the door shut. He walked into the kitchen, opened the cupboard and took out the three-quarters-full bottle of Scotch. Hooking the bottle between his fingers, he went into the living room and sat on the sofa.

Unscrewing the top, he took a long pull. He forewent a glass because the fact of the matter was he didn't plan on regulating his drinking. He planned on getting drunk. So drunk that he would be numb.

His heart and soul throbbed in agony. He never wanted to feel this much pain again. And if he could anesthetize himself, even for a little while, it would be enough. He just couldn't handle it right now. It was too much. Too real. Too intense.

He took another long drink. Soon, though, he wouldn't be feeling a thing.

Something woke Quinn. A noise. From downstairs.

He rolled over on his bed and put his feet on the floor. He rubbed at his eyes and mouth. He smacked his lips. He had the worst taste in his mouth. After drinking the entire bottle of Scotch, he'd crawled up the stairs, puked in the bathroom and then crawled into the bedroom.

He didn't even know what time it was. It was still dark. He glanced at his watch. Three in the morning. The witching hour.

Thud.

There it was again. Quinn reached under his pillow and slid out his knife. If it was the Cabal again, he wasn't going to be nice this time.

He stood, wobbled once, nearly fell, but righted himself. It was possible he was still a bit drunk.

Gripping his blade defensively, he made it to the door and opened it. He paused in the door frame listening for any more sounds and heard a clinking. Sounded like glass.

He padded to the stairwell, stared down it, looking for any movement. Nothing came. He started down the stairs as silently as possible. At the bottom, he looked toward the living room. There was no movement or sound from there. He turned toward the kitchen. A shadow moved on the floor.

He slid against the wall, keeping his back tight to the kitchen. Quickly, he peered around the corner. Someone was definitely in there. The refrigerator was hanging open.

Keeping low, he crept into the kitchen, his knife hand out. There was someone there, in front of him, doing something on one of the counters. In the dark, he could see the outline of a person. A person his height, with a very curvy figure…

"Daeva?"

The shape turned, and in the beam of moonlight that cascaded through the kitchen window he could see her face. Her beautiful pale face.

He dropped his knife. "Daeva?"

She smiled around the chicken leg she'd been tearing into. "Hey, baby. I'm sorry I was just so hungry."

He crossed the room in two strides and had her in his arms. The chicken leg dropped as she wrapped her hands in his hair, and held on for dear life while he claimed her mouth with his.

He kissed her hard, like a drowning man in desperate need of oxygen. She tasted of everything he remembered, everything he ever wanted or needed in life.

He broke away from her lips and, cupping her cheeks with his hands, just looked at her. Making sure she was real and not a figment of his inebriated imagination.

"Are you real?" he asked, his voice strained with emotion.

She nodded and smiled. "You bet I am. I'm as real as I'm ever going to get. And that's saying something."

"My summoning worked?"

"Yeah. It did. Sorry I'm late, though. I had a little something I needed to take care of first."

"You saw Leanne?" he guessed. It made sense. Daeva had a bond with the Cree woman.

She nodded. "I made sure the curse was gone. I figure I owed her that."

"You saved her life."

"I know. But she saved mine, as well. She was there in the abyss, she guided me home. To you."

He kissed her forehead, drinking her in, inhaling her scent, imprinting it into his psyche. "I thought you died."

"So did I." She shrugged. "Turns out it was just a pit stop before this." She gestured with her hands to the kitchen. "I'm here now. For good. For as long as you want me."

"Is forever long enough?"

She nodded. "It's a start."

He wrapped his hands around her rear end, and picked her up to set her down on the counter. He settled himself in between her legs, his hands running through the long fall of her red hair. It was like silk on his skin.

"I've missed you," he murmured into the side of her neck.

She let her head fall back, exposing more of her throat to him. "Prove it," she teased.

He nibbled at her skin. "I'm going to spend the rest of my life proving it."

"Sounds good to me." She wrapped her legs around his waist and tugged him closer. "Now get busy. I'm still hungry."

Quinn claimed her mouth once more, eager to show her just how much he missed her. And just how much he was willing to do to prove to her that she was his everything and more.

* * * * *

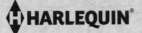

To bring down a serial killer, two detectives must pose as husband and wife. They infiltrate a community, never expecting love to intrude on their deadly mission!

Read on for a sneak peek of

UNDERCOVER HUNTER

by *New York Times* bestselling author
Rachel Lee, coming January 2015!

Calvin Sweet knew he was taking some big chances, but taking risks always invigorated him. Coming back to his home in Conard County was the first of the new risks. Five years ago he'd left for the big city because the law was closing in on him.

Returning to the site where he had hung his trophies was a huge risk, too, although he could claim he was out for a hike in the spring mountains. There was nothing left, anyway. The law had taken it all, and the sight filled him with both sorrow and bitterness. Anger, too. They had no right to take away his hard work, his triumphs, his mementos.

But they had. After five years all that was left were some remnants of cargo netting rotting in the tree limbs and the remains of a few sawed-off nooses.

He could close his eyes and remember, and remembering filled him with joy and a sense of his own huge power, the power of life and death. The power to take it all away. The power to enlighten those whose existence was so shallow.

They took it for granted. Calvin never did.

From earliest childhood he had been fascinated by spiders and their webs. He had spent hours watching as insect after insect fell victim to those silken strands, struggling mightily until they were stung and then wrapped up helplessly to await their fate. Each corpse on the web had been a trophy marking the spider's victory. No one ever escaped.

No one had escaped him, either.

He was chosen, just like a spider, to be exactly what he was.

Chosen. He liked that word. It fit both him and his victims. They were all chosen to perform the dance of death together, to plumb the reaches of human endurance. To sacrifice the ordinary for the extraordinary. So he quashed his growing need to act and focused his attention on another part of his life. He had a job now, one he needed to report to every evening. He was whistling now as he walked back down to his small ranch.

A spiderweb was beginning to take shape in his mind, one for his barn loft that no one would see, ever. It was enough that he could admire it and savor the gifts there. The impulse to hunt eased, and soon he was in control again. He liked control. He liked controlling himself and others, even as he fulfilled his purpose.

Like the spider, he was not hasty to act. It would have to be the right person at the right time, and the time was not yet right. First he had to build his web.

**Don't miss UNDERCOVER HUNTER
by *New York Times* bestselling author
Rachel Lee, available January 2015 wherever
Harlequin® Romantic Suspense books and
ebooks are sold.**

HRSEXP121

HARLEQUIN®

™

A *Romance* FOR EVERY MOOD™

Stay up-to-date on all your
romance-reading news with the
Harlequin Shopping Guide,
featuring bestselling authors, exciting new
miniseries, books to watch and more!

The newest issue will be delivered right to you
with our compliments! There are 4 each year.

Signing up is easy.

EMAIL

ShoppingGuide@Harlequin.ca

WRITE TO US

HARLEQUIN BOOKS
Attention: Customer Service Department
P.O. Box 9057, Buffalo, NY 14269-9057

OR PHONE

1-800-873-8635 in the United States
1-888-343-9777 in Canada

Please allow 4-6 weeks for delivery of the first issue by mail.

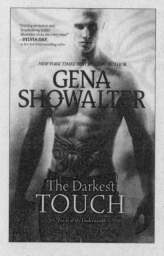